To those who have suffered
every trial and tribulation,
and never lost heart, nor
the hope for a better tomorrow.

AUTHOR NOTE

Dear reader,

First of all, thank you so much for purchasing The Winter Kissed Kings.

I'm so excited that you've decided to continue on with this spectacular journey with me.

I can't wait for you to return to Aikyam and finally meet the rebel king of the west— Atlas.

How I adore his tortured soul.

As always, expect loads of hot, smutty scenes to occur between Katrina and her men. And yes, before you ask, I do mean all of her men. *wink wink*

Also, expect the heavy plotline to continue since this is the final book in The Winter Queen duet, which means all the baddies must get their due.

Oh, and it wouldn't be an Ivy Fox romance if I didn't bring on the angst.

What can I say? I'm a sucker for it!

I'd like to also point out that I do not consider this book to fall in the dark romance genre, but there are some subject matters and scenes that may be triggering for more sensitive readers. Especially since this book is supposed to take place in a medieval setting, so expect some blood and gore. Now for me, there were some scenes that even I wasn't very comfortable in writing, but what can be gruesome for one person, might be tame for someone else.

That's why I always ask if you are on the fence, to please read reviews or join my readers group on Facebook – Ivy's Sassy Foxes and ask for feedback.

Having said that, I would like to also ask the small favor of leaving a review when you finish, so that other readers can decide if they should take the plunge in reading these types of books that have a trigger warning to them.

If you're okay with all that I've mentioned above, please proceed, and get ready to fall in love with the wonderous Kingdom of Aikyam.

Much love,

Ivy

Aikyam Kingdom

North
Current Ruler: Queen Katrina of Bratsk
Parents: King Orville of Bratsk and Queen Alisa of Bratsk
Capital: Tarnow
Season: Winter
Royal Seal: Blue Rose

East
Current Ruler: King Levi of Thezmaer
Parents: King Krystiyan of Thezmaer and Queen Daryna of Thezmaer
Capital: Arkøya
Season: Spring
Royal Seal: Green Hydrangea

South
Current Ruler: King Teodoro of Derfir
Parents: King Yusuf of Derfir and Queen Nahla of Derfir
Capital: Nas Laed
Season: Summer
Royal Seal: Golden Sunflower

West
Current Ruler: King Atlas of Narberth
Parents: King Faustus of Narberth and Queen Rhea of Narberth
Capital: Huwen
Season: Autumn
Royal Seal: Orange Marigolds

Four Seasons fill the measure of the year;
There are four seasons in the mind of man:
He has his lusty Spring, when fancy clear
Takes in all beauty with an easy span:
He has his Summer, when luxuriously
Spring's honied cud of youthful thought he loves
To ruminate, and by such dreaming high
Is nearest unto heaven: quiet coves
His soul has in its Autumn, when his wings
He furleth close; contented so to look
On mists in idleness—to let fair things
Pass by unheeded as a threshold brook.
He has his Winter too of pale misfeature,
Or else he would forego his mortal nature.

The Human Seasons by John Keats

Nothing should survive winter land.
Yet somehow, the warm breaths of southern winds have traveled far enough to thaw the peaks of northern mountaintops with a kiss.

Rivers that were once just blocks of ice run violently free, reminiscing a wild western seashore, boastful in their conquest.

And the long-awaited sparrow's song has finally taken flight from the green meadows of the east, its loud melody of freedom heard across the land as he beats his feathered wings along the north.

All that was, is, or could be, no longer trapped under a winter curse.

Life blossoms, unafraid of ice and snow.

But none have felt the changes of these foreign elements more than its rightful ruler.

Once caged in an icicle prison, the winter queen's heart melted with just one touch.

For what can winter do, compared to the passionate warmth that true love provides?

Chapter 1

Atlas

It's the waiting that's unnerving.

So much so that I find myself furiously pacing my castle's great hall in the early hours of the morning instead of enjoying the comfort of my warm bed.

It's become such a common occurrence that my men have started to joke that their lord and liege has become a creature of the night, taking ghosts as paramours and fucking their spirits to the high heavens where the gods can finally welcome their souls home.

But while my men have kept themselves busy as they wait, even if only by being entertained by my sudden case of insomnia, I'm not as fortunate in finding such amusement to occupy my time.

Unfortunately, not being able to have a full night's rest for the past month hasn't been the only thing that has been plaguing me of late.

Anytime I sit down for a meal, food has a way of tasting sourly bitter on my lips. Even the usual quick fix of drinking myself blind with imported rum does nothing to tame my thoughts—not even the soothing melodic sound of crashing waves slamming against the cliffs beneath my fortress of a castle is able to brighten my tempest disposition.

There is no satisfaction to be had with such mundane things.

Not when true satisfaction is almost within my grasp—even if it does feel like it's coming at a snail's leisurely pace.

Argh.

Like I said… it's the waiting that sets my teeth on edge.

With each passing day, I feel my blood slowly boil to a fevered pitch, threatening to spill over if it has to wait another hour—nay— another second, before its ardent craving is finally satiated.

This unnerving impatience of mine comes as a pesky surprise, though.

I should be accustomed to this tiresome waiting game by now.

After all, I've waited *years* for this.

Years biding my time in this wretched purgatory limbo, just waiting for the blessed day when the reckoning scales of justice would finally tip in my favor and grant me the one thing I've been obsessing over for most of my young adult life—retribution.

Nothing will taste sweeter to me than getting revenge on those who had a hand in destroying my kingdom and ripping the very heart and soul out of it, ensuring its ruin.

Hmm.

Maybe it was my youth that had kept me patient back then.

Time had been my friend, so the tedious affair of waiting hadn't been so painstakingly aggravating to me as it is now, but rather a welcomed gift.

Even then, I knew I needed all the time I could get to prepare myself for the days ahead—but most importantly, I needed time to become the king the west truly deserved.

Gods know my predecessor was anything but.

However, now that I finally find myself at destiny's gates, so close to avenging the innocent blood spilled and sold in the name of power and greed, my usual controlled demeanor is starting to show its first cracks.

And it's all because of *her*—the winter queen.

Damn her to hell.

The memories of our misspent youth have somehow managed to creep into my thoughts lately. Every day I can feel them sink their claws into my subconscious without my consent and take purchase at the very center of my mind instead of staying in the shadows to where I had banished them a long time ago. Every time I swat one of these nettlesome thoughts away, more assault me, like flies to shit. It's not like I will them into being either. No matter what measures I take to prevent them from crossing my mind, the smallest things trigger them into existence.

A cool breeze brings a faint melody of children's joyful laughter into my ear.

The sound of crushing leaves at my feet feels reminiscent of boots treading over pale, white snow.

Even now, the flickering flames in the fireplace that dance in my sight, remind me of four stupid-ass kids who would howl at the moon and dance around a firepit, with a dark blue sky and twinkling stars above them as their only accomplices to such childish shenanigans.

Innocence at its finest… and its cruelest.

Someone like Levi might look back at these memories with a hue of fondness.

Teo would probably smirk with pride at his mischievous ways, even at such a young age.

But me?

All that these memories do is serve to remind me how naïve I was.

How fucking frail and powerless.

And how foolish I had been in believing *her* traitorous lies by calling them the gods' holy truth.

Argh.

No matter.

Those memories can haunt me all they want, for they hold no power over me now.

They can no longer touch me, much less hurt me.

Instead, I can take comfort in knowing that the young lovesick prince that once lived to follow and worship *her* very shadow is long dead.

All that is left of him is me—a king. The very one that will bring fire and brimstone to the north and turn pure white snow into ash and soot.

The north will no longer rule over Aikyam, for there will be no north to speak of—only a wasteland where that vile kingdom once stood.

And as the years cleanse the memories of all the horrors that the north brought to the west, so shall the memory of its very existence be wiped clean.

It's with this thought that I find peace. Envisioning the destruction of the northern reign of terror feels like a soothing balm that eases my black soul and breathes life into my lungs.

My mother always said that the gods have a purpose for us all.

I found mine the day she left her mortal coil.

I shall be judge, jury, and executioner of the north.

They will all pay for their crimes.

Starting with their soulless queen.

A trace of a smile starts to tug at my lips, but before it has a chance to fully form, I hear hurried footsteps running in my direction.

I turn away from the fireplace mantle and see one of my young squires dash toward me.

"Your Grace! Your Grace!" he shouts, still halfway from where I'm standing.

I keep rooted to my spot, impatiently waiting for him to reach me and eager to learn the news he brings.

"Your... High... ness," he belts breathlessly when he's finally within arm's reach. "She's... here! She's... here!"

"Who? Breathe, boy, and tell me who?" I urge, sounding just as frantic as he is. I grab his shoulders, give them a little shake, and ask again, "Who's here?"

Still incapable of speaking coherently, he points to the windows of my hall.

I release my grip on him, leaving him where he stands to regain his breath, and rush to the closest window.

My heart instantly stops at the scenery before me.

Beyond the horizon, black smoke rises to the high heavens, tainting the soft tones of an early dawn sky. On a faraway hill, a burning pyre signals that the day of reckoning has come at last.

Suddenly, all the tension brought on by waiting so long for this day to arrive dissipates, sliding off my shoulders and back like water. As if baptized anew, my body is now rejuvenated, and my mind is clear with razor-sharp focus.

The time for reminiscing on the past is over.

All memories of the dead prince and his so-called friends cease to exist.

There is only one image that persists.

A premonition of the future—the winter queen's slender neck broken at the end of my noose.

The smile that had eluded me is now stretched wide on my face, unable to contain the excitement.

"And so it begins."

The past four weeks have passed by in a muddled daze. All the days blurred into one as we traveled out of the sandy dunes of the south and made our way into the dark foreboding shores of the west.

Even though the scenery couldn't be more opposite of the other, I haven't had the disposition or even the curiosity to appreciate and list their differences. Not when my mind is stuck between southern rays of sunlight beating on my face and eastern hot springs glistening on my skin.

When I left Tarnow all those months ago, I knew I had a battle to face. I never expected that my mind and heart would be in a tug-of-war with each other.

Teo.

Levi.

Teo.

I'm consumed with intense feelings for both kings, not knowing which I will crown when this mission of mine finally comes to a close.

Some things are crystal clear to me, though.

I have no doubt that Levi owns my heart. It beats his name and weeps his absence.

Levi is the best man I know. There is none in all of Aikyam that can be called his equal.

He is a king worthy of his title.

The only one that even comes close is Teo.

He might not have the blind loyalty of his people like Levi does, but that doesn't mean they love him any less. His sacrifices are just as noble, even if less known throughout the kingdom.

And like Levi, Teo has managed to carve his name under my skin and into my bones. I feel him in the air around me, in the very breath I take into my lungs. He's unburdened me from my restrictive chains and taught me how to truly be a free woman.

Teo lives inside me just as much as Levi does. Hence why my heart is torn, and my mind feels like a battlefield.

How am I to choose a king for my kingdom when I can't even decide who I love more?

Even with a dagger to my neck, I couldn't come up with a name if I tried.

Both.

I want both.

That's my true answer.

My only answer.

I want them both.

They belong to me.

And I belong to them.

No other decision makes sense to me other than claiming them both as my kings. But even as I consider that option, I know that keeping both my loves is not only unfathomable, sending my court into a gossiping frenzy, but it's also extremely selfish on my part. Even if hell froze over and Teo and Levi were somehow able to bury their painful past with each other for my sake, they would still have to share me.

Share my kingdom, my body, and my heart.

A tall order to make of any red-blooded man, let alone two prideful kings that have been sworn enemies for longer than the existence of our requited love.

No matter how I play the scenario in my head, in the end, one of us will eventually be on the losing side.

And I fear it will be me.

It's only when my carriage comes to a sudden halt in the middle of nowhere that I'm pulled away from my turbulent thoughts. I slide the pale blue curtain away from the small carriage window and see one of my men on horseback already standing there waiting for an audience with me.

"Your Highness," he salutes before bowing his head.

"Yes? Why have we stopped?"

"I just wanted to inform Your Majesty that we should reach Huwen castle by nightfall. Do you wish to set up camp here for the night, or should we proceed on?"

"I don't see why we should camp now that we are so close, do you?" I arch a defiant brow.

"No, Your Majesty," he replies, somewhat hesitantly.

"Is there something else that troubles you, soldier?" I ask, curious about his hesitation.

He nods in reply and then points to a faraway hill behind us, black smoke tainting the blue sky above it.

"There was no way to see their signals through the thick forest we have been traveling through for the past day and a half, Your Majesty," he tries to defend. "But it's clear the west is already aware of your arrival."

"And? If I'm not mistaken, I did invite myself here. Is there a reason why they shouldn't expect me?" I retort, not caring if Atlas knows I'm close to his doorstep.

It's not like he's shown any enthusiasm for hosting my stay. As far as I'm concerned, this is only a formality. Once I'm able to convince the young rebel king to reinstate our contracts and continue to trade our gems and coal to other kingdoms, then my job here will be done. I'll gently make it known to Atlas that I've already chosen my groom to be—even if it's a lie—and bid my farewell.

I see no need for him to travel all the way north with me either, just for me to reject him later.

I may not know who this new king of the west is, but for the sake of the best friend I used to have in him when we were younger, I'll spare him the public embarrassment of my rejection.

Not that he's shown me the same grace or courtesy since his return to the west.

As a matter of fact, I doubt he'll even care that he's no longer in the running for my hand in marriage. His silence to my letters and decree is an indication of that. Atlas has made it perfectly clear that he has no interest in me whatsoever.

Whereas before my pride might have been antagonized by his blatant disrespect and apathy, I couldn't care less now. All I care about is keeping Aikyam whole, and if I'm going to ensure that, then I'm going to need the proceeds of every trade done with the other kingdoms. Which means I need Atlas' fleets and manpower. As long as he can promise me those, then I'm more than willing to turn a blind eye to his bold contempt. I have more problems on my plate to focus on than an arrogant king needing to have his ego stroked, but I'll do whatever needs to be done for the people of Aikyam. They've suffered too much for too long as it is.

While I may be my father's daughter, I refuse to make the same mistakes he made. I will be the queen my people need me to be. And that all starts by repairing the strife my father caused.

I'm sure Atlas will see reason once I've explained my intentions. Then after the new contracts are signed and sealed, I can go on my merry way back north. And if we never see each other again, so be it. I doubt either one of us will care much either way.

"Tell the train to continue to Huwen," I order the reluctant soldier. "The faster we get this over with, the faster we get to go home."

He nods in contrite agreement and quickly rides away to give out the orders to the rest of my entourage.

I let out an exhausted sigh and slump back into my cushioned seat, looking over at Inessa from my peripheral as I do so. When I realize that she's holding a similar somber frown on her lips, distracted with her own troublesome thoughts, I chastise myself for being such a self-centered friend and being so oblivious to her own burdens during this voyage.

"You've been oddly quiet lately," I say, hoping that tending to my friend's sullen mood will improve my own.

"I don't recall small talk ever being my forte," she grumbles under her breath, still staring out of her window.

"No." I smile. "No one could ever accuse you of that. But you've never been one to keep your counsel or your opinions to yourself either," I say with a taunting grin, nudging my shoulder to hers.

She turns to face me, the dark rings under her eyes proof of her mental and physical exhaustion.

"I'm sorry, Your Highness," she replies apologetically. "I guess I have been a poor companion on this trip."

"It's quite alright, Inessa. It's not like I've been a good one, either. My thoughts have kept me trapped since we left Nas Laed, too."

"Aye. I've been the same." She shrugs solemnly before facing her window again. My intuition tells me that, like me, it's not the scenery outside that has her attention but the memories of these past few months.

"Is your mind as divided as mine?" I ask inquisitively, trying to gauge some kind of clearer understanding of her own melancholy. "Divided between the east and south?"

She snaps her neck my way, her eyes going wide for a split second before taming them into submission.

"I'm unsure what you're insinuating since I have no cares for the east, Your Grace," she explains coldly.

"None whatsoever? Not even a red-haired general that spends his time writing you love letters?" I cock a teasing brow.

I may not have been as attentive as I wished, but there have been a few things that have grabbed my attention. Anytime I ventured into Inessa's tent late at night, I always walked in on her reading Brick's letters. This happened more times than I can count, but I never acknowledged the repeated occurrence, especially with how quickly she would hide the letters under her pillow whenever I did catch her in such an act.

Like me, Inessa is struggling with her feelings, and it would bring me little pleasure in making her feel more uncomfortable with them than she already is. Inessa has always been a true woman of the north, where feelings of the heart take a second seat to duty to the crown. I was much the same way when I left my home.

Now… not so much.

Levi.

Teo.

"There is only one person that occupies my mind, and that is Anya," Inessa replies sternly, coaxing me back to the conversation at hand. "She's the one that worries me. The only one."

My teasing grin falls flat at the mention of our dearest friend.

"I miss her, too." I sigh, grabbing Inessa's hand and giving it a soft, comforting squeeze. "But your worries are unfounded, sweet sister. She is well. She is in love. Take comfort in that."

"Love." Inessa scoffs. "She's barely known the woman for more than a month. How can someone fall in love that quickly?"

My cheeks heat in both embarrassment and shame.

I've fallen in love in such a short amount of time.

Not once, but twice.

What does that say about me?

Seeing that her words have struck a nerve, Inessa is quick to backpedal.

"It's not the same," she defends assuredly. "You were basically raised with King Levi and King Teodoro. No matter how many years you've lived apart, the foundation was already there. Anya's case is different. She's just met Cloe and knows little to nothing about her. And we both know how easily Anya gives her heart away. Not everyone that's crossed her path has been deserving of it."

I try to overcome my own insecurities to focus on my friend's sincere concerns.

"As true as those words are, I saw the way Anya blossomed in Cloe's care. How alive and happy she was when we left her. Even a skeptic like you can't deny that."

"All I know is that decisions made in haste are instruments for disaster," she rebukes coolly.

"Even decisions made from the heart?" I counter.

"Especially those," she deadpans. "The heart is a foolish thing that blinds a person to logic."

"Ah, my dear Inessa, one day you'll be blinded by love too, and when that happens, let's see how well logic will play a part in your decision-making. Or has that day already arrived, and it's only your stubbornness that refuses to give it sway?" This time, it's Inessa who blushes profusely, revealing that my words have hit their mark. "That's what I thought." I offer her a soft grin. "Contrary to your belief, Inessa, falling in love isn't for the weak-hearted but for the brave. It takes courage to be vulnerable. To let down your walls and let someone in. To let someone see you for who you really are instead of the mask you wear to hide your true self from the world. Do not be worried about Anya, sweet sister. She is the bravest of us all."

Inessa's brown eyes soften at my heartfelt description of our absent sister.

"I miss her," she finally confesses, showing her true underbelly.

"I know you do. As do I. So much," I say before dropping my head on her shoulder. "We just need to remember that Anya is loved and cared for. That she is living her truth in her own way. She is free, Inessa. Could we ever want anything less for her?" I feel Inessa shake her head and discreetly wipe away a stubborn tear. "Truth be told, I'd trade places with her if I could right now."

"If I were in your shoes, I'd probably wish that too," Inessa whispers under her breath.

I stand back up straight and stare at my friend, uneasy with her observance. I don't want her to think that I long to be back to Nas Lead because I've chosen Teo over Levi. Especially since that wouldn't be the truth. In all honesty, I'm not sure what the truth is yet.

I open my mouth to explain when Inessa holds up her palm, halting the nonsense that I'm about to spew out.

"What I meant to say is that it's normal to be cautious about meeting King Atlas after all these years. I'm not eager to set foot in Huwen either, and I'm only a handmaiden."

"We both know that you're more than that," I interject before I take in her full insinuation. "But why do you say that? What do you think is about to happen?"

"Nothing good," she all but whispers, looking just as concerned as my soldier had been a few minutes ago.

"It's true that Atlas hasn't exactly been the depiction of an amicable vassal, but I'm sure that all will change when I arrive. He has no choice but to show me his due respect and obedience, no matter how distasteful it may be to him," I assure her.

"Aye, but have you ever wondered why that is? Why has he been the only king to not reply to your decree or even acknowledge you as his sovereign?" Inessa counters, troubled. My brows pinch together at the center of my forehead, taking her words in as she continues to explain her reasoning. "Let's summarize what we have learned on this trip throughout the kingdom, shall we? Your father has kept many secrets from you. Secrets that have put your reign in jeopardy without you even knowing about it. He sent mere boys to die in battle in the east and starved most of the south for years on end. Have you ever considered that he might have done worse in the west?"

"What could possibly be worse than innocent lives dying from war or starvation?"

Her dark eyes turn a somber shade of black as she stares at me.

"Man is a vicious beast, Your Highness. There are no limits to his cruel imagination. Nor how far the lengths an evil man would go just to feed his ruthless ambitions."

I swallow dryly, still unsettled in hearing such words being spoken about my father, a man I loved and worshiped for most of my life.

"As much as it pains me, Inessa, he was still my father. I must believe that some goodness still lived in him. Otherwise, I'll have to admit that most of my life was a lie."

Her expression morphs to one of fear—something I've never seen plaguing her beautiful features before.

"I'm not sure if it's the sins of a dead man that worry me or the one we are about to meet," she says, sending an unwelcome shiver down my spine.

She's right. Atlas has been elusive to me—an evasive puzzle I have yet to decipher—so who knows what we are about to walk into.

Be it friend or foe, it's too late to turn back now. Nor would it bode well for the negotiations ahead showing any signs of weakness on my part.

I am his queen. And, like it or not, Atlas will bend the knee and treat me as such.

Whatever the gods have in store, I know I had a hand in wheeling it into existence when I put this plan of mine in motion.

Whatever it is, I'm ready for it.

Or so I hope.

North meets West

Chapter 3
Katrina

By the time we reach its walls, a dark, eerie night has fallen over the city of Huwen. No moon or stars to speak of, only a fabric of pitch-black sky above us.

The shroud of darkness isn't the only ominous element that's unnerving, though. The violent wind that shakes the carriage, threatening to push it off its hinges, is just as unsettling.

Deadly silence falls over my train as we use whatever candlelight that's been set on the window frames of a few homes as our only beacon to show us the way forward to Atlas's fortress.

It's the smallest of mercies.

Because even though we can't see it, we can hear loud crashing waves under us as we slowly exit the ghost-like bailey to trail over the one-mile-long, narrow bridge, announcing that Atlas's castle is entirely secured and guarded by water.

I've never seen the ocean before, and inwardly, I scold myself for not relenting to my soldier's advice earlier and making camp when he suggested we should. If I had done that, at least I could appreciate the oceanic scenery instead of being cocooned in this space completely absent of light, left to wonder if it isn't some kind of bad omen.

When we finally cross over the bridge safely, I hear Inessa let out a small exhale of relief. Even though I want to share her sentiment, there is this peculiar twist in my gut that warns me the worst is still to come. Unable to shake off this spine-curling feeling, I lean into it and take full stock of my surroundings, needing to be alert to any danger hiding in the shadows.

As I do so, I realize that not only is Atlas's castle safely tucked away in the middle of the ocean, but there's also a large portcullis preventing any unwanted guests from passing through its high stone walls.

Ten minutes pass by as we linger in the dark, waiting for an invitation to be doled out to me. As each second passes, I begin to believe that Atlas will force me and my entourage to camp and spend the night outside his gate as a further provocation to me.

The idea is quickly squashed, though, when a few minutes later, someone draws the metal lattice grille door open for us without so much of a word. Usually, a watchman would at least ask who wished to be granted entrance to such a fortress, but I'm not surprised that doesn't occur.

As my soldier pointed out, their fire signal gave Atlas ample time to prepare for my arrival, alerting him of my impending presence at the gate.

What does surprise me is what I find once we pass it.

The courtyard is ablaze with jubilant activity. Men eat and drink their fill as if in celebration, while troubadours sing cheerful ballads coaxing the more inebriated to dance and sing along.

No wonder we didn't see a soul when we passed the bailey. It seems Atlas invited the whole city of Huwen here to celebrate their queen's arrival to the west.

"Well, this is unexpected," I say, pleasantly astounded by the scene before me.

"Hmm," Inessa mumbles suspiciously. "Quite."

I can't chastise her for being distrustful of this turn of events. I, myself, had been weary of what this night would bring not a few minutes ago. But this changes things.

If this is Atlas's way of offering me an olive branch to start anew and put past offenses behind us, then so be it. I will take this gesture of goodwill as an opportunity to facilitate our negotiations. I refuse to look a gift horse in the mouth and prefer to take this feast as a good sign that the west and north can repair whatever rift has divided us.

Maybe, just maybe, it will enable me to shorten this visit and return home sooner than predicted.

Elijah's chubby face flashes before my very eyes, causing a fist to strangle my heart and pull at its strings.

Although my journey throughout Aikyam has been short of being uneventful, I miss my little brother desperately, especially with Salome's letters being few and far between. Understandably so, since all correspondence with me would need to be vetted by my uncle. And since he is still sore with the latest laws I've passed in the east and south alike without his input or counsel, I doubt his disposition has improved much to allow the mother of my father's bastard to write to me more frequently than polite society would allow.

No matter.

If all goes well here, then I'll be able to wrap my arms around my baby brother sooner than expected.

It will also mean that I will finally have to decide who to crown as my king consort and future husband. That stark realization brings with it the memory of the last night spent with Teo and his last words to me.

"Will you come up north once my visit with Atlas is over?" I ask, already dreading his response.

"I don't know," he answers truthfully. *"I really don't know."*

"What will happen to us then?"

He leans in and places a tender kiss on my temple.

"That, my queen, is a question only you can answer."

In other words, Teo will only make the voyage north if he feels secure in my love for him. Secure that there is no other choice for a husband than him.

But that would be a lie.

It will always be a lie.

Because no matter how much I yearn for Teo's touch and love, Levi has my heart.

Just thinking of my warrior king hurts.

In his last letter to me, he swore to lay down his sword and forget all notions of vengeance just to ensure my happiness, even if that meant it lay with his enemy.

I don't resent you, my heart.

Never will you hear that of me.

You and Teodoro share a history, one that neither I nor Atlas were ever included in.

You loved him first, and while I wanted to be the one you loved last, I fear it's not to be.

If he is the one that you choose to keep, then I won't stand in your way, nor will I demand reparations for my broken heart.

I love you enough to only want your happiness, my queen.

I love you solely and completely, and if he is the man for you, then I won't keep my vow of killing him and taking him away from you."

His trespasses against me, I will never forgive or forget.

But for you, I will show leniency.

For you, my dearest Kat, I will show mercy when none was offered to me.

For you, my love, I will ensure your happiness, even if it means that his is also guaranteed.

Oh, how the gods have blessed me and cursed me with one single blow.

They have shown me what true love feels like yet made it impossible for me to keep it.

"Your Highness? Your Highness? Kat?" Inessa calls out, pulling me out of my pensive reverie.

I face her only for her to point at my carriage's open door as one of Atlas's men holds it for me.

It's muscle memory that has me straightening my back and squaring my shoulders as I take his hand and pull myself out of the carriage. I wait for the man wearing the orange marigold seal to his chest to introduce himself, but I am confused when he turns his back to me and starts heading toward the stairs that lead up to the castle's entrance.

"I guess manners in the west is something only read in books instead of practiced," I mutter to Inessa beside me before pointing to two of my most trusted guards to follow us.

"And that's presuming the west even knows how to read," Inessa snaps back with a distasteful expression plastered to her face as the four of us weave through the crowd of unruly drunken men. "I wouldn't be as gracious to insinuate such a thing."

"Keep such thoughts to yourself, dear friend. Remember our purpose here," I mumble under my breath in warning as we trail behind Atlas's man.

"Trust me, Your Highness. I know how to hold my tongue. I've had years of practice."

I stifled a giggle since Inessa is as blunt as they come, and given free rein, I'm sure her piercing tongue would cut half these men to size. Thankfully her mind is just as sharp. I have no doubt she'll act the part required of her, even if she finds this court to her disliking. She knows how important our stay here in the west is and will do anything to aid my attempts at reconciliation.

Although I'm saddened that Anya isn't here with us, I'm relieved I can still count on Inessa for support. She's become my rock in all things, and I couldn't ask for a better friend and ally.

Once we reach the last step, Atlas's man ushers us in through two grand doors, locking them behind us once we're inside, successfully separating us from my train of highly capable soldiers.

"I don't like this," Inessa whispers. "Something feels off."

I wish I could blame her pessimistic nature for such a feeling, but that uneasy crawling sensation I had earlier comes back tenfold to me too.

"There's only one way to find out if you're right," I reply, with borrowed steel in my voice, taking the first step into the grand hall.

Much like the courtyard outside, this hall is filled with the same festive merriment. Three large wooden tables stretch from the back of the room to the front, men of every age and size seated on both sides while they eat, drink, and laugh the night away. They are so consumed with their celebration that none of them have even seen me walk in.

"That's odd. Where are all the women?" Inessa asks, puzzled.

"I haven't the faintest idea," I reply in a hushed tone once I've scanned the room and only find a handful of women tending to the boisterous mob of men.

But before I'm able to do a recount, my attention is pulled to the front of the great hall, where a large throne made of white bone is stationed at its very center. And on it, rests a terrifying king, worthy of such a macabre seat.

It's only when his soulless, light eyes lock with mine and a faint sinister smirk crosses his lips that I realize the extent of the danger I'm in.

This is not a welcoming celebration but a rehearsal victory feast.

And I didn't come to negotiate a treaty with the west.

I came here to die.

Chapter 4
Atlas

The instant she walks into the room, my immediate gaze lands on her.

Like a moth to a flame, she returns the stare with utter trepidation, causing a thrill of excitement to slither up my spine as I watch the realization of her deadly error start to sink in—the ice queen has just willingly stepped into the lion's den, ensuring no hope of her ever escaping with her life intact.

Gods be good.

I must have fantasized about this moment so many times that now that it's here, I can't help but take my sweet time just to enjoy its splendor. My instant gratification doesn't hold a candle to her prolonged discomfort. Even far away, I can practically smell her fear from my throne. I can taste the cold sweat on her brow without so much as a lick. I can even hear the way her heartbeat drums panicked in her chest over the loud chatter of my men.

If I could freeze time, this is the precise moment I'd wish to stay in.

Watching her, watching me.

The perfect wide-eyed prey has finally come face to face with the ravenous beast that was always destined to feast on her flesh.

Forgoing my chance to pounce on my freshly delivered meal, I continue to stay seated for a few seconds longer, curious to see what her next move will be.

Will she try to run? Use the two poor excuses of bodyguards she's brought with her to fight her way out? Will she kneel before me in humbled submission? Cry and beg for mercy, in the hopes that some form of humanity still lives inside me? One that might show her some kind of leniency? Or will she put on her political hat and try to lie and bargain her way out of the shitstorm she's in?

My smile fades when she does neither, preferring to walk the metaphorical plank directly at me as if uncaring of the fate that awaits her.

Be it either arrogance or foolish bravery that coaxes each one of her steps forward, I'm unamused with her choice. I would rather see her squirm and cower than witness this empty show of bravado.

It's only when she's finally a few feet within reach, stopping before the three steps leading up to my throne, that I rise from my seat. That's all I need to do for my men to cease their chatter, creating a deafening silence in the room. She doesn't look at them, preferring to keep her fixed stare on me as if there were no one else in this great hall but the two of us.

"Atlas," she greets with a coldness that can only be found in the freezing depths of winter.

I don't return the greeting and instead pull my sights away from her devious perfect face to address the men that have suffered under the north's rule.

"You all know that I'm not one for colorful prose," I start calmly, making eye contact with as many of them as I can. "In fact, most of you that have traveled the seas with me these past seven years can attest that I can go for weeks on end without uttering a single word. I've always lived under the assumption that words, once said, cannot be taken back. Words hold power. Therefore, we should choose them wisely, for they can be used to define our character—our whole ethos. Hence why I will not say the next words lightly."

The tension and anticipation in the room are electric as my most loyal of men wait for me to finally give them retribution for the suffering they have had to endure. To give them the vengeance that is theirs by right.

"Here before me stands King Orville of Bratsk's rightful heir. The legitimate daughter that took it upon herself to wear his crown and ensure the north rules over the west," I say, keeping my monotone voice intact, as loud, disgruntled curses fill the silence as I pause.

Once the noise dies down, I turn my attention back to the girl who, at one point in time, had been my whole world but managed to destroy it all in the same breath.

"Here she stands, looking so proud in her efforts to conquer this kingdom once again," I add, gaining another slew of loud protests, this time with my men banging their closed fists on the tabletops to show their righteous contempt.

"Tell me," I interject, "will we bow in foolish obedience to a foreign ruler that has only ever had their best interests at heart, forgoing every other kingdom in the process, or will we get justice for every life stolen from us? Every drop of blood shed in her name? Every soul sold for her greed?"

"Justice!"

"Justice!"

"Justice!" my men call out, their strong voices creating the most beautiful song my ears have ever heard.

"Then justice we shall have! We've been denied it for too long! The west will get its pound of flesh! As your king, I order it so!" I shout, gaining wild celebratory cheers across the room.

My menacing smile returns to tug at the corners of my lips as I step down from the stage and make my way toward the bane of my very existence.

The winter queen doesn't make eye contact with me, preferring to look straight ahead, her head still held high as if her sentence weren't just doled out to her.

"What will you do with me?" she asks through gritted teeth.

"Isn't it obvious?" I lean in and whisper in her ear, "First, I will strip you of your arrogance and higher-than-thou attitude. Then I will steal your dignity and break your spirit. And once you are nothing but a shell of your former self, then, and only then, will any mercy be given… at the end of a noose."

Her silver eyes blaze with both fury and fear.

"You won't kill me. You can't."

"Ah, but I will, princess," I coo, running the back of my knuckles on her cheek. "Just watch me."

Chapter 5
Katrina

"Take her down to the dungeon," Atlas orders, and before I have time to blink, I feel two pairs of hands on me, restraining my arms behind my back.

"KAT!" Inessa screams, making me turn my head over my shoulder long enough to watch the tips of swords being driven into my soldiers' chests, their dead bodies thumping loudly to the ground.

"INESSA!" I call out when two of Atlas's goons pull her away from me.

"If you harm one hair on my handmaiden's head, I'll kill you myself, Atlas!" I yell, but the maniacal king only laughs at my threat.

"If I were you, I'd be more worried about your own pretty little head, princess." He cackles, his men following suit in stomach-churning laughter. "That's the one that will be on a spike soon enough."

I open my mouth to curse him, but to no avail, since I'm quickly being forced away from the unhinged king's presence and out of the great hall. My knee-jerk reaction is to order his men to let me go, to shout obscenities and curse their very existence, but in the end, I opt to do the very opposite. No pleading or threat will sway them into letting me go. All it would do is give them even more satisfaction than the one they are already taking in manhandling me.

I bite into my inner cheek, forcing myself to keep quiet as we walk through the cold corridors of Huwen castle that will undoubtedly lead to the dungeons. When we come to a large wooden door and begin to walk down the steep, narrow stairs, I make a note of memorizing every twist and turn, hopeful that I'm able to use this knowledge to my advantage later on. If I have any hopes of escaping, I'm going to need to know my way around this place without alerting any of Atlas's men that may be standing guard.

However, when we finally arrive at my destination, a foreboding feeling of helplessness begins to take route in my heart when I come face to face with my prison cell. Like most dungeons, it's cold, dank, and bears the foulest of smells. However, it's the absence of prisoners in it that really kicks in my fear.

Dungeon cells like this one are usually filled to the brim with inmates. It's common practice for most royal courts—depending on the crime—to keep their criminals captive for a period of time. Just long enough for them to see the error of their ways. I'm of the same belief—deprive a man of sunlight for a month, and his rehabilitation is more than guaranteed.

But it seems the west doesn't abide by the same rules.

If this dungeon is empty, then it can only mean but two things; either Atlas is a merciful king, shelling out pardons left and right for the offenses done under his rule, or there is only one sentence given for any crime committed in Huwen—death.

Having just been reacquainted with Atlas, it isn't hard to conclude which option he favors.

I try to keep a brave face as one of my captors opens the cell door, and the other one pushes me inside. There is a rotten flea-infested cot on the far left side of the jail cell and a dirty rank bucket to the right. At its center, there is a small rectangular cement block on the floor, with chains hanging loose from the ceiling right above it.

I push down the bile that rises up my throat as the two guards joke about how their king's accommodation for me is more than I deserve.

"Move," one of them orders, pushing me forward so roughly that I lose my step and fall to my knees.

The guards laugh in disgust, ordering me to stand up before they make me. After gathering my bearings, I do as commanded, and on shaky knees, I walk further inside, anxious for the two men to leave me alone in this pit of despair.

"Get on," the same guard commands, pointing to the cement block.

Again, I submit to his order, not wanting to antagonize my captors more than I already have with my mere presence. I've heard plenty of horror stories about how women are despicably treated by male guards in such circumstances. If I have to bite down my tongue to ensure they won't violate or molest me in any way, then it's a small price to pay for my obedient silence.

Death would be preferable to that type of inhumane punishment.

When I place my feet on the cinder block, they immediately raise my arms above my head and restrain my wrists in shackles, the clanking metal sound making my skin crawl.

Just a month ago, I would have been excited to be subdued in such a fashion.

But now?

Now it takes everything inside me not to throw up.

Once both men have ensured that I'm tightly bound and caged, they begin to retreat from the cell, satisfied with the accomplishment of their mission. But my heart stops when the main guard—the same one that has been issuing commands left, right, and center—turns around to take stock of their handiwork.

"What?" his comrade asks. But instead of giving a reply, he walks directly to me, his calloused hands gripping the neckline of my dress and ripping it to shreds. My eyelids shut forcibly down, keeping my hot tears at bay as he tears the fabric in an uncontrollable rage. It takes me a minute to realize when he's stopped, leaving me to fear that the worst of his intentions is yet to unfold.

"There," he scoffs. "Let the bitch freeze."

It's only when I hear the clank of the metal door of the cell close, followed by the sound of footsteps drawing away from the dungeon, that I dare open my eyes. I say a small prayer of gratitude to the gods when I realize that though my dress is now in ribbons lying on the cell's floor, my undergarments remain intact on my body. But after a few hours, any gratitude I had to offer the gods for the predicament I am in flies out the window.

The gods have abandoned me.

Even though I was born and raised in the north, nothing could have prepared me for the freezing temperatures of this dungeon. I can hear the cold ocean's waves beat at the rock a few feet above my head, informing me that this cell is partially below sea level, making it that much colder to withstand. Comfort of any kind is a wishful illusion while my wrists are bound up tight in the air, and my feet have to stay perched on top of such a small piece of cement.

Torture.

That is what this is.

Atlas has found the simplest way to break someone's spirit.

Unable to sleep or gain heat back into my bones, the remainder of the night is spent in utter agony. However, the torment being inflicted on my body pales in comparison to my hellish imagination.

My mind is as much an enemy to me as the west is.

If this is how they treat their rightful queen, then how must they be treating Inessa?

Are they going to kill my best friend? Have they done so already?

Or will they submit the worst kind of punishment to her just by being my loyal friend?

And what of my entourage?

What of those fifty brave souls that have traveled with me through Aikyam these past few months? The same souls that had put their trust and faith in me, believing that this voyage would unite our kingdom once and for all and that I was the queen to do it.

What has befallen onto them?

Atlas's sinister grin creeps into the forefront of my mind, relaying the truth that I have yet to accept.

My people…

My best friend…

Me…

We were as good as dead the minute we set foot on western soil.

All the tears I've held back suddenly rush out of me at the thought. In one miscalculated move, I have sentenced all of us to death.

Never will I lay eyes on my sweet brother's face and watch him grow into the great man I envision he'll become.

I'll never be able to help Salome pick blue roses out of our garden, nor will I be able to seek guidance from her like a daughter would from her mother.

I won't ever joke with Anya or hear her melodic laughter again, or live vicariously through her sweet tender heart, so in contrast to my own.

Never again will I be able to confide all my thoughts and worries to Inessa. Her silent strength and unwavering belief, always giving me the fortitude I need to continue on my path.

And never will I be able to feel Levi's strong arms envelop me in his embrace as I gaze into his eyes and lose myself in them.

Nor will I ever be able to bask in Teo's loving light and be free again.

For my freedom can only be obtained after Atlas has done his worst. And even then, it will be at the end of a noose, like he promised. My head is the price I must pay for the sins the north has committed. Whatever they are, leniency is not in the cards for me.

But if Atlas believes it will be easy to kill me, he is as delusional as he is maniacal.

I will not give up everything I love and hold dear without a fight.

He wants to break me?

Let him have at it.

I'll show him why they call me the winter queen.

For diamonds born in the north do not break under pressure.

We endure.

Chapter 6

Atlas

I t takes great patience on my part not to visit the dungeon in the middle of the night like every fiber of my being demands. Instead, I pace my bedchamber floor, from one corner of the room to the next, just picturing my prize in chains.

Hmm.

I honestly thought that once I had caged my pretty little prey, I'd finally be able to enjoy a good night's sleep.

Unfortunately, that isn't the case.

I'm more alert and tightly wound than ever before, needing to witness every minute of the wretched ice queen's despair for myself. Only after I've had my fill of her agony will I be able to gain a moment of peace.

And yet, I prolong my own agony and force myself to wait.

Even if every excruciating second that passes without me laying eyes on her feels like someone is driving a hot rod through my chest, leaving a gaping hole where my black heart should be.

No matter.

I've known pain and suffering long before she ever stepped foot on my western shores.

Therefore, I go against all my better instincts and wait.

I wait for the sun to rise, bringing with it a new hopeful day filled with new opportunities for my people. I delay my own gratification by taking a stroll through the city, watching my men celebrate our achievement, knowing full well that this triumph is only the first step in my vengeful plan. We may have won this small battle, but our war with the north is far from over.

In fact, imprisoning their queen should be the catalyst for its start, not its end.

So while my men may rejoice in her capture, that doesn't mean they should lose sight of our end goal.

As the gods are my witness, I sure won't.

But even I must admit that her presence in Huwen has lifted my black spirits somewhat.

At this precise moment, the ice queen finds herself completely helpless, with no one to come to her aid, most likely having to resort to prayer as her only recourse for hope.

Just the thought gets adrenaline pumping in my veins and blood rushing to my cock. It gives me a sick kind of thrill knowing she's suffering a similar fate that half of the western population had to endure over the last seven years under her father's rule. A pleasure so all-consuming that I have to force myself to keep still instead of making a run for it to the dungeon and witness for myself how the mighty have fallen.

It's only after the sun has said its final farewell, offering up the night sky to the pale ashen moon, ensuring that a full twenty-four hours have passed since her capture that I allow myself to have a small taste of satisfaction.

"Come with me," I order the two guards standing post outside the dungeon's doors.

As they follow me down the stairwell, the foul stench of decay becomes more intense with each step we take. So much so that by the time my feet are planted firmly on solid ground, a sardonic grin crests my lips. No northerner has ever had to endure such a stomach-churning odor, not when they insist on surrounding themselves with their sweet-smelling, perfumed roses.

The west, though?

We have lived most of our lives out at sea. For months on end, we have called the lower deck of a ship home, accustomed to the stink and disease that infiltrates the cramped space. This spacious dungeon is a welcomed holiday to any man born and bred in the west. At least here, you have enough space to cohabit with the rats, whereas, on a ship, they would be your bedfellows.

"Take me to her," I order, letting my guards lead the way to her jail cell.

Most of the dungeon is pitch black. The only residue of light in the whole place is the flickering flames from the torches carried by the guards. It's only when they shine the torch on the last cell that I finally cast my eyes on her. My dead, black heart stammers for the briefest seconds when her silver eyes lock with mine.

After one of the guards lights the sconce hanging on a nearby wall, I offer my men a silent command to unlock the cell's gate, stepping into it the minute it's open.

"Leave us," I command, needing this one-on-one with my nemesis to be unsupervised.

The guards do as ordered, throwing ugly sneers at my prisoner as they walk away.

"If this is the way you entertain your guests, then it's no wonder you get so few of them to visit," she spews with her head held high, still holding onto her fiery disposition.

"I haven't had many complaints," I smirk.

"Not surprising. I doubt dead men can talk much." She scoffs.

"Is that all that concerns you? That I'm not being very hospitable?" I taunt, leaning against a wall, arms crossed over my chest. "I would have assumed you'd have more important things to occupy your mind with."

"Is that why you're here? To discuss how I spend my time while locked in this cell?" she asks with a faint hint of boredom to her tone.

I shake my head, my evil grin stretching wide on my lips at her pathetic act of nonchalance.

"Aye. I didn't think so. You're here to see your handiwork. Well, here I am, Atlas. Take a good, long look."

Although she's being sarcastic, I take her up on the offer anyway.

It only takes me a fraction of a second to understand how even the most loyal of men could lose their way.

How my own brother was pushed off his vengeful path.

Yes, Levi, I do see how someone could be tempted.

The winter queen is extraordinary.

Even without her elaborate decorations, her natural beauty is enough to make grown men weep at the very sight of her.

But tears are for the weak.

And I am *not* weak.

"Satisfied?" she asks scornfully after my gaze has lingered on her half-covered frame for longer than she's comfortable with.

"Is my satisfaction that important to you?" I goad while my gaze scans the floor to find her torn-up gown in shreds.

She opens her cupid lips in defiance but then quickly seals them shut when I pull away from the wall to pick up the discarded garment. I then proceed to pluck the small aqua-marine diamonds and royal-blue sapphires from its bodice.

"Figures. Not only are you mad but a thief too. The pirate king of the west. Your people must be very proud."

"Pride is overrated when there are hungry mouths to feed. And *this,* princess," I say, holding the jewels in the palm of my hand, "will feed all of Huwen for a month."

"From what I gathered last night, you have plenty to go around."

"No one can have too much," I retort, placing the gems into my pocket before walking back to lean against the iron bars of the cell.

"Speaking like a true dictator," she mutters under her breath.

To this, I laugh.

"What's so funny?!" she shouts, finally losing her composure.

"You. You're what's funny. Calling me a dictator is like the pot calling the kettle black." I continue to chuckle.

"I'm not as ruthless as you are. But believe you me, every hour that you keep me locked in this jail cell is one less hour you'll have on this earth. I promise you that. I'll have you beheaded for treason for the way you're treating me."

"Like I told you last night, you should be worrying about your own slender neck, not mine, princess," I rebuke after my laughter dies down.

"Don't call me that," she says through gritted teeth, her cheeks growing red by the second.

"And what exactly should I call you?" I taunt.

"You know damn well what."

"Enlighten me. I haven't the foggiest notion, princess."

"I am your queen!" she shouts. "Not a princess!"

"Not from where I'm standing. You still sound like the bratty spoiled princess from back in the day to me."

Her face turns lethal, so much so that my smile only grows wider.

"You know what? There is no reasoning with you since it's obvious that you have lost your goddamn mind. Release me at once, and I'll show you leniency. A crazy person shouldn't be made accountable for their actions. Release me this very instant!" she orders, pulling at her shackles, the iron cutting into her flesh along the way.

"Stop. Just… stop," I command with a thunderous tone.

She stops immediately, my voice terrifying her still.

"Are… are you… going to set me free or not?" she stutters in fear.

"Is that what you want? To be set free?" She nods hesitantly as I announce with a deadly tone, "Then freedom you shall have, after…"

"After? After what?"

"After you've been sentenced."

"Sentenced? Does that mean I'm to be put on trial?" she asks, still holding onto hope.

I shake my head, causing her breathing to halt.

"Guilty people don't deserve trials," I add with a noncommittal grin.

"I see. So that's how the west works," she says, chewing on her bottom lip. "Fair enough. And just what kind of punishment am I to have for my so-called crimes?"

"Either I hang your head up high on the tallest of my tower for all of Aikyam to see, or I sell you to the highest bidder. Believe me when I say death comes as a mercy to the latter." I shrug unapologetically.

"The north will come for me," she utters with steel back in her voice, trying desperately to mask her fear.

"Oh, I hope so. In fact, I'm banking on it." I continue to smile sinisterly, showing that war with the north has always been part of my plan.

"They won't be the only ones. Levi and Teo will come for me too," she retorts, the mention of my childhood friends wiping the maniacal grin off my lips.

In four long strides, I reach the wicked queen, her breath hitching as I grab her throat.

I lean into her, so close that we're breathing the same air, and growl, "Do you think death scares me? That death intimidates my men? Unlike you, death is a friend to us. We welcome it. We yearn for it."

"You're not that brave. Everyone fears dying."

"You can't be afraid of something that has already happened to you. This is where you and I differ, princess. The west died a long time ago. Now it's the north's turn."

I snatch my fingers off her and stand back, my nostrils flaring in rage.

But unlike me, anger refuses to possess her now, sadness preferring to coat the silver in her eyes.

"What happened to you?" she whispers, staring deep into my eyes as if trying to see if the boy she once said she loved still lives inside me.

He does not.

She made sure to kill him long before I ever could.

Instead of answering her, I turn my back on the heartless queen, vowing to never set foot in this jail cell again while she still lives.

"Atlas!" she calls out, stopping me before I'm able to reach the gate. "Please. Tell me. Talk to me. What happened to you?"

I turn around and see that her eyes are heavy with unshed tears for a boy who no longer exists.

Lies.

All lies.

The prettiest liar to ever live.

"You want to know what happened to me? Who made me this way?"

She nods.

"It was you. You happened to me. You turned me into this. But damning my soul is just the tip of the iceberg of your crimes. Crimes that I fully intend to punish. So sleep well, princess. For the day of reckoning is fast approaching. I promise you that."

And with that promise hanging in the air between us, I leave her to her doom.

Chapter 7
Katrina

I'm unsure of how many days have passed since the awful night we arrived in Huwen. Days and nights seem to fuse together in this jail cell, becoming one tortuous, long hour before fatigue finally sets in and exhaustion lulls me to sleep.

The only thing that keeps me sane is the knowledge that Levi and Teo will come for me.

I may not be certain of many things, but I have no doubt my kings will come to my aid.

All I can do in the meantime is wait.

Wait for them to arrive north and see that I'm not there. Once that happens, they will quickly realize that my visit west didn't go according to plan and that I'm in great peril. My uncle, Adelid, will gather all the able-bodied troops we still have at our disposal in the north while Levi and Teo call their own men to arms and set west to save me from this mad man of a king.

For that is what the rebel king is—mad. Unhinged and completely lost to logic and reason.

Atlas.

Once my dearest and closest ally.

What horrible event could have happened to the sweet boy I grew up with that could have turned him into this—a cruel soulless king who doesn't bat an eye at chaining up his sovereign, knowing full well that he's damning his own people to death?

Because that's exactly what awaits every westerner once the truth is out of my capture. Neither the north, east, nor south will have pity on them for what their king has done to me. Ensuring their death is the only outcome of his actions.

Atlas.

Even though his treatment of me deserves my wrath and vengeance, the first second I laid eyes on him—seated on a throne made of human bones and skulls—my heart twisted in my chest in excruciating pain. The same light-blue eyes that once held such sweet tenderness for me now blankly stared back at me with no emotion whatsoever, as if we shared no history at all.

All it took was me staring into his eyes to know that *my Atlas* was lost to me.

He's no longer the frail boy that struggled for breath after the smallest run, nor is he the submissive child who didn't dare break a rule for fear of the repercussions.

But worse still, Atlas is no longer the loyal confidant I could tell my deepest darkest secrets to. Where before he had been the only one in our pact that understood what it felt like to be overlooked and underestimated, now he's the type of man who would crush such weakness in the palm of his hand.

The king I met bears no similarities to my long-lost friend.

This king only has one goal in mind—my ruin.

Even if it costs him his kingdom, he will make sure I die here.

But why?

Why?

These are the thoughts that run rampant in my mind when I'm awake, trying to figure out what foul crimes my father could have committed in the west, that I should be the one to be punished for them. Even my restless dreams are tormented by such thoughts.

Argh.

Damn the gods for my reckless temper.

I could have had all the answers to such questions if I had only kept my cool. When Atlas visited me a few days ago, I should have handled him differently. I should have kept my fury in check and tried a more strategic approach. Maybe if I had done that, I could have gotten some intel out of him. Or at least have the opportunity to ask him about what he's done with my entourage, most importantly Inessa. If this is the treatment he offers his rightful queen, then I shudder at the thought of what he's done to my sharp-tongued sister.

"She's fine. Inessa is clever. She'll know exactly what to say and do to keep herself alive," I tell myself, not wanting to think the worst.

With each passing day that I have no news of her, the more I'm convinced that Inessa is, in fact, safe from the mad king's prosecution. Whatever she's doing must be working since Atlas doesn't suspect how much she means to me. I'm sure if he did, he would have made it a show of killing her in front of me as I helplessly watched.

For that is what evil men do—they strip you of the people you love most just to weaken your resolve.

I shake my head, trying to push those ill-conceived images of my best friend's last breath out of my mind.

Stop it!

Inessa is alive.

She's alive!

I would feel it in my bones if she wasn't.

Wouldn't I?

'I will strip you of your arrogance and higher-than-thou attitude. Then I will steal your dignity and break your spirit. And once you are nothing but a shell of your former self, then, and only then, will any mercy be given—at the end of a noose.'

My sullen thoughts are briefly broken by the familiar sound of my cell being opened. I raise my head to see a small figure walking inside, carrying a bucket in his hands.

"Hi there," I say sweetly when the young boy's face comes into the light.

He must be twelve if he is a day. Wearing a large vest bearing an orange marigold crest over his dirty brown clothes, he looks even smaller. Focused on his task, he waddles closer to me, water spilling over the bucket with each step he takes.

"Is that for me? Are you here to bathe me?" I ask, confused as to why Atlas would give such an assignment to a boy, even one as young as this one.

The boy nods, letting go of the overflowing bucket in front of the cement block.

"My name is Katrina, but you can call me Kat if you want," I say overly sweetly, hoping that by introducing myself he'll be more inclined to talk to me.

"I know who you are," he mumbles, head bowed to the bucket as he submerges a washcloth into the water.

"You do, huh?" I smile. "Well then, since you know my name, it's only fair you tell yours, don't you think?"

The boy shrugs, still unwilling to make eye contact with me, much less tell me his name.

"Do you need to use the shit bucket? I can call Da to release you from your chains if you do," he says instead.

I look at the dirty bucket on the opposite side of the room with flies swarming around and shake my head. As much as I'd love nothing more than to stretch my aching limbs and feel a moment of relief from my shackles, the alternative isn't appealing to me either. I have previously suffered the humiliation of using the so-called *shit bucket* under the guards' scrutiny, so I don't intend to undergo such embarrassment more than I positively must.

"So, your father is one of the guards, is that right?" I probe, desperately needing to pull my attention away from my dire living conditions.

"Aye," the boy replies, still more preoccupied with his work than offering me any type of small talk.

I let out a frustrated sigh, sensing that I'll get little to no distraction from him.

No matter.

Even if he refuses to talk, there's no rule that says he can't listen.

"You know, as dungeons go, this isn't so bad," I try to joke. "I get two hot meals a day, plenty of alone time for me to collect my thoughts, and every so often, someone like you comes down here to pay me a visit. Not the worst arrangement, if I do say so myself."

This gets the boy's attention.

And not in the playful way I was hoping for.

"They call you a witch," he says scornfully as he plunges the rough soaked cloth onto one of my legs, scrubbing my bare skin until it's red. "People say that everything you touch perishes and dies," he adds, switching to my other leg to give it the same coarse treatment.

"You shouldn't believe everything you hear," I tell him, squinting my eyes in pain.

"Doesn't make it any less true. I know who you are, witch. Everyone in Huwen does. You're the evil witch of the north that preys on the weak and sells them off for a hefty price just so you can live in your white tower filled with diamonds and jewels. You're a plague that King Atlas will save us from."

I swallow dryly, both troubled by the words coming out of his mouth as well as the vehement belief he has in his words.

"I'm not a witch," I explain patiently once he's stopped scrubbing my legs.

"Liar!" he shouts, his whole body trembling. "I know you're a witch! And evil one at that."

"You're mistaken, little one. I promise you that I am not a witch. Just a queen that wants to go home."

The boy shakes his head furiously with his eyes shut closed as if trying to erase me from his sight.

"Da told me not to talk to you. That you'd tell all sorts of lies to confuse me. But he didn't have to warn me. All I have to do is remember what you've done to us to know what type of witch you are. You see, I remember," he says in a wild frenzy, stabbing his forefinger into his chest. "Some of my friends don't, or pretend not to because it hurts too much, but not me. I remember what you did to us. To all of us! I'll never forget it!"

My throat becomes parched at the sight of the murderous intent in his young, innocent eyes.

He hates me.

Nay, it's more than hate.

Just like Atlas, he won't rest until he sees my head up on a spike.

But there's immense suffering in his glower too. A pain so intense it consumes him from within.

Oh gods, what kind of hell did my father impose on these poor people?

"Listen to me, little one," I say calmly, "Whatever you believe I've done, I swear to you I have not. If the west is suffering, then you have my father to blame. Not me. I promise that if you give me a chance, I will right the wrongs that he's done. I vow to you that much."

I feel a fist strangle my heart when the boy standing in front of me begins to cry while still holding onto the harrowing expression on his face.

"Lies! You can't take back what you've done. Da says they're already dead or wish that they were."

"Who? Who's dead?" I ask, heartbroken just witnessing the suffering pain of this young boy.

"My ma and baby sister," he stammers, wiping the tears and snot away from his face with his forearm. "Men with blue roses on their chest came to our house throughout the dead of night and took them away from us, then shipped them off to gods know where. I'll never see them again. None of us will."

Suddenly, the jail cell grows that much colder at the boy's alarming confession.

'Where are all the women?'

That had been Inessa's first observation when we first entered the great hall.

At the time, I didn't give it much thought. I assumed Atlas kept them away for their own protection in fear that a fight would ensue.

But now…

No … he couldn't possibly have done … my father wouldn't … no.

"Why… why are you… the one here to bathe me?" I ask, fearful of his response.

"Because there is no one else," the boy replies loathsomely.

"No one? Not one woman?"

"The ones that escaped that night or were rescued are too frightened of you to come down here. They think you'll somehow use your witchcraft to set yourself free and then come back for them with your army. But I'm not scared. King Atlas will kill you before he lets anything like that ever happen again."

I'm still coming to terms with his confession when the boy picks up his bucket and throws the water at me, soaking me from head to toe.

"There. You're bathed," he says scornfully before retreating his steps and leaving me alone with my hellish thoughts.

But all too soon, his father comes down to the dungeon to pay me an unsolicited visit.

"What did you say to my boy?" the guard asks, mimicking the same odious tone his son had used just minutes ago.

Before I'm able to answer, he slaps me across the face, my teeth slicing my lower lip in the process. I'm still catching my breath when he plunges his fist into my stomach, taking the wind out of me. He grabs me by the hair, pulling at it so fiercely that strands come out from their roots.

"Don't talk to him. Don't even look at him. If you do, my fist will be the least of your worries," he threatens before releasing me.

He then pulls down his pants, making me turn my head away as he aims his cock at my body and pisses on my knees down to my feet, leaving a foul stench of urine to infiltrate my nostrils as it drips down my skin.

"That's the only type of bath you'll get from now on," he says. "Get used to it."

The minute he leaves, bile rises to my throat, coaxing me to throw up all the contents in my stomach. Drenched in cold water, urine, and my own vomit, my head hangs low as the tears—for all the souls my father condemned into slavery—weigh me down.

How can I call myself the rightful ruler of Aikyam, when I had no inkling whatsoever of how much my people were suffering?

I am not a queen, but the spoiled sheltered princess Atlas accused me of.

How could I dare call myself anything else?

A true queen would have seen through the lies of her father. She would have gotten to the root cause of the problem of why her vassals had turned their backs on her, instead of trying to manipulate them with games of royal matrimony.

Yet, I stayed blissfully ignorant, too proud of my crown and too eager to follow in my father's footsteps to see that I was part of the problem. For I cannot think of anything more dangerous than sincere ignorance, nor anything more evil than being kept that way.

The next time the boy and his father come into my cell, I don't instigate conversation. I don't say a word when the man releases me from my chains to use the shit bucket, or when the boy spits into my soup and hands it over to me to eat.

I'm all out of words.

None of them could ever bring back what they have lost.

Nor save my own soul from eternal damnation for my father's sins.

And my own reckless ignorance.

Chapter 8

Katrina

Sixteen years old

My father's loud, boisterous laughter can be heard above everyone else's as he makes another joke at the expense of his brother-in-law. Uncle Adelid takes it like a champ, unbothered by my father's attempts at comedy, laughing on cue with the rest of the drunken crowd.

And why wouldn't he be?

No one in this court holds the king's ear more than my uncle.

How I wish he'd use that power to whisper into my father's ear that this grand banquet is in poor taste, considering his sister—my mother—is getting sicker by the day.

'The physicians know what they are doing, girl. Don't you worry that pretty little head of yours. By the time my birthday arrives next week, your mother will be well enough to dance in my arms and celebrate the occasion like she's always done for the past twenty years that we have been wed. Fret not, child, for the gods favor the north. No harm will come to any of us. Especially your kindhearted mother. A true royal rose if there ever was one.'

That had been my father's answer to me when I conveyed my concerns about my mother's declining health. I wish I could place my faith in the gods and physicians alike as my father has done, but something inside me tells me that whatever illness my mother is suffering from isn't earthly bound or heaven sent, but man-made.

I've never seen such a temperamental illness before.

One minute my mother looks well—strong enough to get out of bed and take a stroll with me through our garden—and the very next, she's suffering one seizure after another, with fevers so high, it's a miracle her brain doesn't turn to mush.

Of course, Father is optimistic about her recovery. He hasn't seen firsthand the damage the illness has done to her. Not when every physician in Tarnow Castle has absolutely forbidden him to make any contact with his wife for fear that whatever ails her might be contagious.

An ailing queen is one thing.

A sick king is quite another.

For a kingdom can survive the death of its queen since a woman, no matter her rank, is deemed expendable. But should a king fall—the man who people believe was crowned by the gods themselves to lead the great kingdom of Aikyam—that would be catastrophic. Especially since the only living heir in line to the throne is a woman.

No.

My father must be kept safe and away from such a potential threat at all costs. For he can still bear sons, even if my mother cannot.

Hot tears sting my eyes at the somber thought while the rest of the great hall lift their cups with cherry wine, celebrating the health of their king.

I don't want to be here.

I want to be anywhere but here.

When I feel a hand on my knee below the table, giving it a consoling squeeze, I quickly dry my eyes before turning to face my best friend.

"Hey," Atlas says with a sad frown stitched to his lips. "Do you want to get out of here?"

I nod, thankful for having a friend in this room that knows my heart so well. I am in no mood to celebrate anything tonight. Not when my mother is upstairs locked in her bed chambers being slowly bled out by physicians, bloodletting being their go-to answer for any ailment of her body or soul.

Atlas stands up from his seat before discreetly pulling back my chair, allowing me to make my great escape. I don't miss how Levi and Teo quickly begin to rise from their seats, Atlas shaking his head, silently ordering them to stay exactly where they are.

"I got her," Atlas affirms, lacing his fingers through mine.

As Atlas pulls me away from the table, Levi offers me a commiserating nod, his gaze looking almost as miserable as I feel. Teo, however, looks uneasily restless, unhappy that he has to stand down and let Atlas be my solace.

I'm not sure why he's so upset, though. It's always been this way. We all share different dynamics between us, and it's never been a problem before. With Levi, I'm able to broaden my horizons, learn from the wisdom he's accumulated over the years, and better myself to become more worldly too. With Teo, it's the butterflies in my stomach that take the lead, letting me feel empowered in my femininity. Through his eyes, I feel beautifully strong, armed to enchant any heart, even if it's only his I wish to keep.

But with Atlas…

He's the one I can just be.

There is no pretense of grandeur between us, nor do I have to act stronger or wiser for his benefit. I don't have to worry if I'm beautiful enough or concentrate on what words to use to be even more appealing and desired.

I can just be… me.

I'm enough for Atlas.

And he's enough for me.

He's more than just a mere shoulder to cry on. He's my support system—the one I can relax and just breathe with. We can spend hours in complete utter silence and never get bored with each other's company. Atlas might be a year younger than me, but age means very little when it comes to finding your soulmate. Atlas is the opposite side of the same gold coin I have been burdened with, making him the only one who truly understands what it's like to be me. Like me, he's also had to face the trials and tribulations of being considered the weak link of his royal line.

Me because I was born female.

Him because he was born with a defect.

Since the moment King Faustus and Queen Rhea of Narberth brought him to Tarnow to introduce him as the heir apparent to the western throne, people have told me not to get too attached to the young prince since he wouldn't survive another winter. Sooner or later, his malfunctioning lungs would give up the arduous effort of keeping him alive, and I'd be setting myself up for heartbreak by giving sway to our friendship.

But like me, Atlas is resiliently stubborn.

Even though the naysayers still make bets on his demise, I have no doubt that Atlas will outlive them all just to gloat over their graves.

And one day, I, too, will silence the wagging tongues of everyone who insists that only a male heir could ever be competent enough to rule over Aikyam.

But that is in the far away future.

And as it stands, we are the only ones who see that future even happening.

A testament to that is how easy it is for us to leave right in the middle of my father's banquet. No one really cares when they see us retreat from the great hall. No one stops us to ask where we are going or tell me how inappropriate it is for a princess to be seen holding hands with any boy who hasn't been officially named her betrothed.

No one cares about either one of us.

So when we start running through the corridors of Tarnow castle, no one even bats an eye.

"Come on," Atlas says, the dark rings under his eyes telling me that my mother isn't the only one who's had a taxing night.

"Slow down, Attie," I beg upon hearing the familiar wheezing sound coming from his chest.

"I'm fine. Just hurry up. I want to show you something," he urges, pulling me to accompany his quick steps.

Atlas has never been faster than me, but since his last visit north, he's grown a good foot taller than me, his long legs making it easier for him to gain speed on me.

"Attie," I grumble, annoyed. "I said slow down. If you don't, I swear I'll turn around and leave you here alone."

"Argh. Fine." He pouts, finally slowing down his pace .

"Thank you." I smile gratefully, hugging his arm to me so I can lean my head against it. Last year I was able to rest my head on his shoulder. This year, the best I can do is his forearm.

We walk like this in silence, the echoes of the partying crowd downstairs bouncing off the walls, making me feel even sadder than when I was among them.

"You want to talk about it?" he asks.

"Not right now."

Atlas nods, releasing his arm from my grip to wrap around me and cradle me to his side.

"I get it. I'd be a mess if my mom ever got sick like yours is."

"Your mom is 'The Lioness of Narberth'. I doubt Queen Rhea has suffered even a cold in her lifetime."

"Hmm. Cruel, isn't it? That the gods have gifted her with such inner strength only to then give her a weakling for a son?"

I immediately stop in my tracks and face him head-on.

"You know how much I hate it when you talk like that, Attie. It isn't true."

"Isn't it, though?" he mutters, the light-blue hue of his eyes dimming before me. "Everyone says I'm like my father. That I'm his son through and through. While my mother sails the seas, captaining our fleets to exotic foreign lands, he cowardly sits at home on a throne with no real power to speak of. The west will always kneel for the lioness. Never for a craven's cub."

"Attie," I whisper, cupping his cheek in my palm. "You are more like your mother than you give yourself credit for. Don't let anyone measure your worth when you are absolutely invaluable to me."

He places his hand on top of mine for a minute, his eyes closed to take in my words. Sometimes that's what we do for each other—

remind ourselves that even if the world is against us, we always have each other.

He gently pulls my hand off his cheek and places a sweet kiss on the inside of my wrist before releasing my hand. My cheeks heat up of their own accord, even though they have no business blushing.

This is Attie.

My Attie.

He's kissed me like this plenty of times. I'm not sure why such an innocent kiss on the wrist has me so flustered.

I blame his growth spurt.

That must be it.

At a little over six feet, you could easily mistake him for a grown man. But Attie has a lot more growing up to do at fifteen.

And at sixteen, so do I.

"Hey, you still with me?" he asks, searching my face. "I'm sorry. Somehow, I managed to make this all about me. I'm here for you. Not the other way around."

"We're here for each other. Always." I smile sincerely.

Atlas's bright smile blooms on his face, making my heart suddenly pitter-patter.

"I… um… you said you wanted to show me something."

His smile widens, throwing in a conspiring wink to get me even more tongue-tied.

What the hell is happening to me?

Did I sneak in too much cherry wine and get myself drunk?

"I brought you something. I think you're going to like it," he says before locking his fingers through mine to lead me to where the said gift is.

When we reach the doors of his bed chambers, I can't help but hesitate.

"What? What's wrong?" he asks, his forehead creasing in confusion.

"I... um... what if someone sees us?"

"So? They see us. So what?" He shrugs, still not following my train of thought.

And how could he?

Since we've known each other, we've been almost inseparable. So much so that when we were younger, we would sneak away from our rooms and have sleepovers downstairs in the library. Levi and Teo used to come down, too, until our fathers put a stop to it. Apparently, at eleven years old, it was no longer acceptable for young boys to sleep on a rug next to their future queen.

Levi and Teo never dared to attend one of our cherished sleepovers again. However, Attie and I were more rebellious.

Instead of meeting downstairs in the library where anyone could catch us, we started sneaking into each other's rooms. Even with all our efforts to hide it and keep our sleepovers a secret, I'm sure everyone in court knew about them.

They just didn't care.

Levi and Teo were a threat to my maidenhead.

Atlas was not.

"Are you coming or not?" he asks impatiently.

"Open the door, why don't you? I want to see what exotic gift you brought me," I reply excitedly, uncaring if someone does see me entering Attie's room.

"Well, it's not exotic per se, but I know you are going to love them."

"Them?" I ask curiously while stepping inside his room.

Atlas is all smiles as he walks over to a table holding a large crate with a blanket covering it. Once I'm close enough, he pulls the blanket away, making a show of it.

"Voila!" he utters enthusiastically.

"You brought me pigeons?" I ask, unable to mask the disappointment with his gift.

"No. I brought you carrier pigeons."

"Is there a difference?"

"Yes, princess, there is." He grins, bowing down to peek at them and urging me to do the same. "I know how lonely you get here in the north when we're gone. How the months seem never-ending. These little birds are the answer to all that loneliness."

"Am I to keep them as pets and name them after you?" I laugh.

"No, silly. With these, you and I can exchange correspondence whenever we want. We can talk about everything and anything, and no one will know."

Suddenly these birds seem more important to me than anything else.

"How? How do we use them? Show me."

"Here," he says, handing me a scrap of paper and a quill. "Write something down. Something that you only want me to read."

I nod, turning my back to him as I write on the small piece of paper.

You're standing right next to me, and I miss you already.
I hope this works because I don't think
I can survive another winter without you.
Come back to me soon, Atlas.
Please.
K

"Done," I say before handing him the note and swallowing down the sudden tears trying to resurface.

"Are you okay?" Atlas asks, always in tune with my inner workings.

"Just anxious for you to teach me how this all works." I force a reassuring smile.

As Atlas starts to show me how to use the birds, he also begins to explain how, for the last three years, he's been training them to fly between the west and the north, using one of my father's stable boys as his accomplice.

He also explains that he got the idea when Queen Rhea—in one of her many voyages—told him that other kingdoms don't use riders to send messages like we do. They use carrier pigeons like the ones Atlas was able to obtain from her after months of begging and wearing his mother down.

I very much doubt Atlas had to beg for long since it's a known fact that his mother would go to the moon and back just to make her son happy. But I keep those thoughts to myself and pay close attention to his instructions. I voraciously make mental notes of everything he does, determined to keep every crucial detail in my head.

Once Atlas has firmly tied a piece of string onto the pigeon's leg and over the scrap of paper I gave him, he walks toward the closest window, carefully tucking the bird in his hands.

"Open it for me, princess, will you?"

I quickly do as he so lovingly commands, excited to see the pigeon take flight.

When Atlas opens his palms, the pigeon swiftly flaps its wings and soars through the night sky.

"In two weeks' time, that bird will reach Huwen."

"Two weeks?" I parrot in shock. "But it takes a full month to ride west from here."

"What can I tell you? Birds are faster than men on horseback ever will be. Also helps that they don't have to stop and take a leak every so often," he jokes.

"You're disgusting." I laugh.

"True, but you still love me." He grins before wrapping his arms around me from behind to keep me warm from the cold, both watching in awe of the small bird flying away.

"I envy that pigeon. He can just fly away and leave everything behind without a second thought."

"Is that what you want, princess? To leave?" Atlas asks, placing his chin on my shoulder.

"If I could leave, where would I even go? Tarnow is my home."

"No, Katrina. Aikyam is your home," he replies steadfastly. "And this kingdom is so much more than the white mountain tops you see outside your window. There," he points to the east, "lies lush green land, with meadows and fields so green they look like emeralds sprouting up from the ground. And to the south," he points towards Teo's homeland, "miles and miles of sand so fine that a grain could easily fall through the eye of a needle. And there you have Huwen," he points west. "A city so vibrant and full of life that the ocean that runs along our coast is so covetous that its waves constantly kiss our shores. Aikyam is full of wonders, and one day, you, Levi, Teo, and I will go on a grand adventure and bask in its glory."

"I like the sound of that," I say, offering him a noncommittal smile because deep down, I know there is no way I'll ever leave Tarnow.

Not with Levi.

Not with Teo and most certainly not with Atlas.

I'll be caged, much like the pigeon was. The only difference is that my cell will be made of diamonds and sapphires. My prison will be the crown on my head, sentencing me to a life of politics and little else.

Sure, I'll see my friends again.

But then, they will be the ones traveling north to pay homage to me on my birthday, with their wives and children in tow.

That is the only future that awaits me.

I know I must make peace with it, but in the meantime, I'll pretend that the future Atlas envisions for me is real and within my grasp. I'll pretend until I can no longer afford to do so. Until reality is forced upon me, leaving me with no place to even dream of such an existence.

Then, and only then, will I pack up and store away such childish notions and be the queen my father dictates I become. A queen the north will be proud of.

But until then… I'll pretend.

I'll just pretend.

Chapter 9
Atlas

After slightly heating the orange beeswax to make sure it's as soft as plasticine, I press the matrix onto the parchment and seal the letter with the marigold crest. Once it cools down, I get up from behind my desk and walk over to the center of my royal office, where one of the winter queen's loyal guards awaits, along with two of my men standing at either side of him just in case he tries something stupid.

"Here," I say, handing him the parchment, unbothered by his murderous glower.

It will take much more than that to intimidate me, I assure you.

"What is this?" he asks, waving the letter in his hand.

"This, soldier, is your freedom." I smile sinisterly. "I want you to take this decree north and read it to the entire court. I want everyone to know that I hold their precious winter queen captive and that I have no intention of ever releasing her from my chains. As far as the west is concerned, her rule is over," I explain, gaining cheerful smiles from my own men while the soldier continues to stare at the parchment in his hands.

"However, I am nothing if not a benevolent king," I add. "Should the north accept that they no longer have a foot to stand on in regard to who reigns over Aikyam, I can be persuaded to show leniency to Tarnow. If they fail to accept my leadership, then the north will fall before they see another winter."

"You're sending me home?" he asks suspiciously, still unable to grasp my intent.

"Does that surprise you?" I arch a brow.

"A bit, Your Grace," he retorts, still distrustful of my motives.

"Don't be. I'm letting you go for my own selfish reasons. I would much rather have you deliver the message than one of my men, as you are sure to keep your head after giving such harrowing news. But if I sent one of my own, I doubt he'd be shown such charity. I have promised my men that no more western blood will be spilled by the north, and I'm fully intent on keeping that promise."

"And what of *my men*?" the northern soldier asks, referring to the fifty-odd men and women his queen brought with her west and are currently being detained in the east wing dungeon—far away from her prying eyes and ears. "What's to happen to them?"

"I have given them a choice. Those who wish to renege their oath to the north and vow their allegiance to the west will be spared."

"And those who choose to remain loyal to our queen?"

"Then they shall share her fate."

The soldier's face turns as pale as the white-driven snow he's been accustomed to all his life.

"The north will not abide by this. We will come for our queen," he has the nerve to threaten once he's gathered his bearings.

"Then I guess this isn't a farewell but mere goodbye, for we shall meet once more… this time on the battlefield." I smirk.

The soldier nods in understanding, trying his best not to be intimidated by my own threat to his life.

"Good. Then we are in agreement," I add, already tired of his presence. "Now go and ride like the wind, for I am anxious for the wheels of justice to say their peace and use its gavel to crush the north's arrogance once and for all. Go!"

My men begin to escort the soldier away, but he remains planted in his spot, refusing to budge an inch.

"Is there something you wish to say?" I ask, bemused by his stubbornness.

"Yes, Your Grace. If I can be so bold, I would prefer that this task was given to someone else," he humbly retorts, his earnest request instantly piquing my curiosity.

"Are you saying you would like to bend the knee to me now and battle your northern brethren on the field behind the west's banner?"

By the disgusted scowl imprinted on his face, it's clear he would rather die a cruel, terrible death than ever fight for me, much less raise a hand against his own countrymen.

"No, Your Grace. I am more than content in sharing my queen's fate, for I am her loyal servant, through and through."

"So you'd prefer death than be free to return home?"

"If those are my only choices, then yes, Your Grace. All I ask is one thing. That I may name the person who would take my place to freedom."

"I must admit, I'm curious as to who is this person you'd willingly sacrifice yourself for," I retort, genuinely interested in who may merit such a sacrificial gift.

"Her name is Inessa of Bjørn. She is more than qualified to deliver your letter north in my stead."

"Is she now?" I counter, intrigued. "Is this Inessa of Bjørn your woman?"

It's his hesitation that gives me pause.

"Yes, Your Grace, she is," he finally replies.

"You're lying. Careful, soldier, for I have little tolerance for liars. Tread lightly and think on your next words, for they can be your last."

He lets out an exhale, his shoulders slightly slumping in defeat.

"No, Your Grace, Inessa is not mine. Nor have I ever viewed her in such a way."

"Much better." I grin upon hearing the truth in his statement. "However, I'm still confused. If this woman is not yours, nor have you ever had such romantic inclinations, why sacrifice your freedom in exchange for hers?"

"Though I have not spoken to my queen since you stole her from us, I know her mind well enough. If she could, she would have asked me herself to make this sacrifice. I would rather die in this foreign land and be loyal to my queen's wishes than rebuff her last dying wish," he replies, standing up as straight as he can, determined to accept his fate.

"I see," I mumble, rubbing my chin whilst taking in this tidbit of information.

The winter queen's soldier might be loyal to her, but he is far too green when it comes to court politics. By making it known that this Inessa of Bjørn is of importance to his queen, he has just sealed her fate.

Still … she could prove to be useful.

"Thank you for your honesty, but your request is denied," I tell him, feigning boredom as I flick imaginary lint from my shoulder. "You, and only you, will deliver my message north. Now leave my sight and get on with it. I have more important things to attend to. Go."

"Your Grace," he pleads as my men grab him to usher him away. "I beg of you—"

His pathetic pleas hit a nerve, making me order my men to stop and keep him still.

"Beg, you say?" I fume while eating the distance between us, forcing him to look deep into my dead-cold eyes. "You have no idea what the word even means. To hear the cries of mothers, sisters, and daughters plead for mercy, only for their outcries to fall on deaf ears. The north has no idea what true begging implies, but once I'm done with it, it will. I promise you that, soldier. Before we see each other again, you will know the true meaning of the word."

His eyes grow wide in terror, realizing that his death, along with his bannermen, is imminent. His freedom is only temporary, as all of Tarnow is.

"Take him away and accompany him to the northern border. Make sure he rides north or kill him if he so much as refuses," I command. This time, the soldier abides by my order, needing to put himself as far away from my presence as possible as if he faced the devil firsthand.

Little does he know that such a monstrous creature is currently in chains in my dungeon.

It's his beloved queen who is the true monster to ever plague Aikyam.

I'm just the instrument forged to eviscerate such evil from our lands.

A truth that will be known by all soon enough.

Inessa …

Inessa …

The name is familiar to me.

I rack my brain to remember where I have heard the name before.

'If you harm one hair on my handmaiden's head, I'll kill you myself, Atlas!'

Ah.

That Inessa.

I was so consumed with my own vengeful plans coming to fruition that I completely missed that honest moment of vulnerability. It's a lapse in judgment, a mistake I won't be making again. It's obvious that her handmaiden is important to the heartless ice queen, which makes Inessa's value increase tenfold.

"Squire," I call out to one of the orphaned boys that call Huwen Castle home.

"Yes, my king?"

"I want you to go to the east dungeon and ask one of the guards to bring me Inessa of Bjørn."

The young boy nods and hurries away in his task.

However, an hour later, he returns accompanied by a slew of guards and five women in tow.

"What's the meaning of this?" I ask, confused as to why I ordered an audience with one woman and gained five instead.

"Our apologies, Your Highness, but finding the woman you wanted proved to be harder than we expected. They all claim to be Inessa of Bjørn, every last one of them," one of the dungeon's guards explains, disgruntled, seemingly irritated with the predicament at hand.

"Is that so?" I retort, somewhat amused that, even in chains, these northern roses refuse to wilt.

Hmm.

On the night of my grand feast, I paid little mind to the winter queen's handmaiden since she wasn't the prize I had waited for all these years. An error that now will prove challenging to remedy.

But not impossible.

"Very well then. Let's remove the wheat from the chaff, shall we? Put them all in a straight line for inspection." The words have barely left my mouth, and already half the women have lost their nerve, beginning to shake and cry profusely. "Now, now, ladies. Do not fear. I don't intend to punish your defiance in the same way I'm punishing your queen," I coo, running the back of my knuckles on the cheek of the first woman in line.

Unable to look me in the eyes, her gaze instantly cowers in fear, giving away that she's not the one I'm looking for.

I step to the next woman—this one appears not to have seen her twenty autumns yet—and grip her chin softly while still forcing her to look straight at me.

"And believe me when I say that your queen is thoroughly being punished," I announce proudly, making the young maiden turn her head away from my stealthy gaze.

Nope. Not this one either.

I turn my attention to the next woman, this one with hair spun in gold, much like her queen, making me dislike her already.

"I have her strung up in a cell, the rats feasting on her toes," I add whimsically with a maniacal grin, painting a pretty picture of their queen's current circumstances.

The blonde woman whimpers, a waterfall of tears streaming down her cheeks.

Wrong one again.

"But the rats are the least of her worries." I shrug off as I walk over to the next woman in line. "You see, I have a favorite dungeon. One that was built, brick by brick, under Huwen Castle, so when the high tide comes, it is engulfed underwater. You think snow is cold? You haven't felt true cold until you've tried the freezing temperatures our ocean provides in the dead of night."

My nose flares in disgust as the woman standing before me loses control of her bladder, pissing on her already dirty clothes. But my annoyance quickly simmers down to elation when I see the last woman in line white-knuckle her fists with every word I utter.

With two short steps, I reach the raven beauty, her deadly black stare betraying her identity. I tilt my head to the side and draw a grin that would terrify even the bravest of men.

"But neither the rats, chains, or dire temperatures can compare to the humiliation and suffering my men want to shower your queen with," I forewarn, leaning into her ear to whisper, "All it would take," I continue in a low tone, bringing her hateful glower to focus on my middle finger pressed against my thumb, "would be a snap of my fingers to give them consent to fuck and rip her apart."

"I'LL KILL YOU FIRST!" Inessa shouts, lunging at me with her catlike claws.

My loathsome smile widens further on my face as my men are quick to subdue the winter queen's most loyal friend and confidant.

"Well, hello there, Inessa. So happy to finally meet you." I continue to grin as she tries to wrestle my men off her just to gouge my eyes out. "You don't know it yet, but you and I are about to be best friends."

Chapter 10

Katrina

I'm not sure how long I've been down here in this prison cell anymore. Be it a couple of weeks or a month, I wouldn't be able to say either way. I've completely lost track of time, no longer able to differentiate night from day.

Before, I was able to make a calculated guess just by the meals the guards fed me. Two meals every day—one in the morning and another in the evening. But after my unfortunate mishap with the guard's son, my meals have been cut in half and given at random times.

No more sponge baths have been given to me either, which is lamentable since I desperately need one. Especially since no one comes down to my cell when I call in need to relieve my bladder or bowels anymore. I seem to no longer merit the privilege of using the nasty shit bucket, left to suffer the humiliation of soiling myself.

But my punishment doesn't end there.

My guards have also ceased to unchain me from my shackles, ensuring that my aching body and limbs become atrophied, utterly weary from being in the same position all the time. The act of keeping the balance with my feet planted on the small cement block, my arms stretched high above my head while the iron handcuffs chafe into my wrists, has become a full-time job.

It's a wonder that my drained mind can focus on anything else.

Even the few minutes of sleep I used to be able to get have become a rare occurrence. No matter how tired or sleep-deprived I am, or how much every limb in my body screams for rest, my mind refuses to switch off and give in to exhaustion.

Not that I care much for sleep anymore.

In fact, being awake is one of the small reprieves I still find down in this jail cell.

Because whenever I close my eyes, that's when the nightmares come, and my true torture begins.

I dream of soldiers in royal blue garb kicking down doors and stealing sleeping babies from their cribs.

I dream of mothers being pulled away from their crying infant children as they offer themselves willingly as long as their young ones' lives are spared.

I dream of wives being kidnapped from their homes, watching helplessly as swords plunge into their husbands' bellies as they fight until their last breath to keep them.

But those nightmares don't hold a candle to the ones that come after these godless abductions.

My mind takes me to horrifying places of how these women and young girls were later used and mistreated.

'Man is a vicious beast, Your Highness. There are no limits to his cruel imagination. Nor how far the lengths an evil man would go to just to feed his ruthless ambitions.'

Those were some of Inessa's last words when we first arrived in this cursed place.

How right she was in her counsel—men *are* vicious beasts.

And I cannot think of a worse monster than my own father—the first man I ever truly loved and admired.

He forced young boys to march to their graves in the east and die for his own greed. He starved the whole southern kingdom just to ensure his own food dispensary was full. But worst of all, he abducted innocent women and girls, stole them from their loving homes, and sold them off into slavery, uncaring of the dreadful future that awaited them.

So while my treatment in this dungeon hasn't been the highlight of my journey, my heart doesn't condone their action, fully accepting the abuse bestowed upon me.

How could I not, when their loved ones have suffered a worse fate than the one I'm currently living?

My only remorse is that time is running out on their vengeance.

It's cold in the dungeon below the sea.

Too cold.

As cold as the highest mountain in Tarnow.

So cold that my lungs have struggled to function lately, making erratic sounds that I've only heard once in my infancy.

My body is slowly shutting down.

I feel it every time I try to take a breath.

I'm losing the battle to keep myself alive.

I'm not sure what Atlas has prepared for me, but I doubt he'll have time to put it into practice.

The cold will kill me first.

Ironic, isn't it? That it's the cold that will end up killing the legendary winter queen of the north?

The gods sure have a twisted sense of humor.

Be that as it may, everyone ultimately has a date with death.

I can see mine on the horizon.

It's so close that sometimes I can feel the cold breath of the god of death before he presses his lips against my cheek.

Every time I feel his deadly kiss, my mind wanders off to the people I love most in the world, and I quickly whisper a prayer to the gods to keep them safe and whole after I'm gone.

A single tear falls down my cheek as I try to picture them in my mind as I bid them farewell.

Elijah.

Salome.

Inessa.

Anya.

Levi and Teo.

And surprisingly enough, it's Atlas's face that always comes to me last.

Though it's not the image of the terrifying king that had imprisoned me that flashes before my eyes, but the young shy boy I shared my soul with in my youth.

"I'm sorry, sweet friend. Forgive me," I manage to wheeze out, my breath nothing but a white cloud of air in front of my face.

I hope my death brings you peace, Atlas, for I fear nothing else will.

Chapter 11
Atlas

I sit back in my chair, unbothered by the lethal glower the winter queen's handmaiden is currently giving me at the opposite side of my dinner table.

"Is the food not to your liking?" I ask before taking a sip of ale.

"I refuse to eat until I'm certain my queen is being fed also."

"I give you my word that your queen has seen more meals in her stay here than you and your friends have."

"If that's the case, then you wouldn't mind me hearing it directly from her lips," she counters.

"Is my word not good enough?" I arch a brow.

"The word of a madman seldom is," she rebukes, crossing her arms over her chest just so I can get the message that she will not be eating a single morsel of her food unless she gets her way.

"Hmm. I've been called many things in my lifetime, but madman is new to my ears. Your queen is also fond of the word."

"You've seen her?" Inessa asks, unintentionally giving me a glimpse of her underbelly and demonstrating how worried she is for the vile queen being held captive in the dungeon.

I offer a noncommittal shrug before bowing my head to my plate, pretending that cutting up the meat is more important than the discussion at hand. From the little time I've known Inessa, I can tell she can smell a liar from ten feet away. And though I saw my prisoner when she first arrived, I have yet to make another visit.

One time was more than enough for me.

"It's obvious you are loyal to your queen," I start after chewing a forkful of steak, "but I am curious as to why. You don't strike me as someone who would blindly follow someone as wretched as her."

"Queen Katrina of Bratsk is not wretched. She has more integrity in her little finger than you hold in your whole body."

"Careful there, my lady. Those are fighting words. I may be many things, but I'd never lay a hand on a woman."

"No, you'll just order your men to do it," she mumbles under her breath.

Rage bubbles under my skin, but I temper it down before she notices how her words insult me. Although I did insinuate that my men would take carnal advantage of the evil queen, even I know it was a bunch of bullshit. I'd never let anything like that happen to a woman on western soil. I've seen with my own two eyes how a woman doesn't survive that kind of assault. A part of her dies instantly, never to be the same again.

No.

I'm more than happy to wear the label of a madman, but I will never be called a fucking rapist.

There is a special place in hell for men who have committed such a sin—one that I'd be all too happy to send them to.

Still, I don't take back the threat, allowing Inessa to fear the worst. It's the only way to keep her honest.

"You haven't answered my question. It's your loyalty that intrigues me. Is her feeble act of integrity the only thing that grants her such devotion? You can tell me. Like I said, I wish for us to be friends."

I swallow a chuckle when she outright scoffs at my attempt at friendship.

This one has fire. A rare thing in the north.

"I doubt a man like you knows the meaning of true friendship. If you did, you wouldn't have turned your back on the girl who you once called your best friend."

"What do you know about it?" I grunt, displeased with her assessment.

"I know enough. In fact, I know everything. Because that's what true friends do. They share their most precious memories and divulge all their wants and desires. I know everything there is to know about Kat. And no matter what you do to me, I will never betray that sacred trust."

The mention of the winter queen's name—spoken so openly and affectionately—sets my teeth on edge, so much so that I punch the table, jolting the porcelain plate and silver cutlery in front of me.

"Eat! That's an order!"

Inessa's nostrils flare in contempt, but she does as I say, taking the first bite of her meal.

For all her stubbornness and arrogance, at least she's not blinded by those attributes to know when she's been bested.

We eat the remainder of our dinner in silence, long enough for my fury to de-escalate.

My mission tonight was to get some insight into the winter queen's rule over the north. I wanted to see if Tarnow was as faithful to its queen as her handmaiden appears to be. Unfortunately, my ill temper has gotten away from me, leaving me with no alternative but to postpone my task to another day when I'm more in control of my mood.

After I've ensured that Inessa has cleaned her plate, I order one of my men to take her back into her room since the dungeon isn't fit to house such a force of nature.

"Get someone to bring her some fresh, clean clothes and hot water for a bath. A lady like her deserves no less."

When my guard pulls her chair back, a sudden bout of sadness accosts me. The west hardly had the opportunity to shower a woman with such politeness. It's a true testament to how these small things are still ingrained in our subconscious, eager to live that type of reality again.

Unfortunately, the west is already lost.

King Orville made sure of it when he enslaved the better part of us.

A woman is so much more than just someone who brings life into the world.

They're our conscience. Our beacon of light and hope.

Without the sound of their melodic laughter and joy, the world turns an ugly shade of gray, preventing light from even passing through such a gloomy existence.

Boys without their mothers become lost.

Men without their partners become soulless.

That is what the west has become—a lost soulless place where extinction is all but inevitable.

How ironic that it was a woman who, along with her father, had a hand in ruining us.

I'm so lost in my own thoughts that I don't even realize that my reluctant dinner guest has yet to excuse herself to her room.

"Yes, Lady Inessa? Is there something on your mind?"

Her expression no longer holds the malice she had a few minutes ago but genuine worry for her queen.

"I'm not sure what kind of king you have become, but I can only hope that the young prince my dear queen loved so much still exists inside you somehow. I beg of you. Please do not hurt her in a way that she won't be able to recover from."

"Do not fret, my lady. I will not lay a finger on her pretty head. And I can vow that, when the time comes, her death will be quick."

She swallows hard but still does not leave.

"I believe you," she admits, disheartened. "However, at times, certain things happen to prisoners that even an all-knowing king like yourself cannot prevent. Men are more likely to take… some ill-fated liberties," she adds, measuring her words carefully, "forgoing asking for permission entirely, preferring to beg for forgiveness once the deed has already been done. My question is… how confident are you in your men and their loyalty to you?"

"I can guarantee that no man of mine will defy my orders."

"Even if such an order hasn't been officially given?" she counters sternly. "Please forgive my insistence, but how are your men to know what you want them to do or not if you haven't given proper instruction? As far as I can tell, they share your mindset—punish the north by any means necessary. Are you so sure their views of torture measure your own?" With those words of caution, she curtsies and turns to follow the guard to her new chambers.

Fuck.

I purposely set up this meal to get information about my enemies in the north, not to cause me to doubt my own men at home.

But the sharp-witted handmaiden played her part perfectly by planting the seed of doubt in my head. I know my men are true to me and me alone. However, like me, their hatred of the north has festered into this ugly thing that has consumed us all. Where I show restraint, some men may not be so inclined to do the same due to their weakness.

Fuck these royal blue roses.

They sure know how to get inside a man's head.

Damn the gods!

With one quick slide of the hand, I throw my plate to the floor in blind fury before standing up from my seat to do the one thing I've been avoiding doing for these past two weeks. I had no intention of visiting the winter queen until I had her army at my doorstep. Then, and only then, would I pull her out of her cell and kill her in front of her troops.

Such an act would spur them into war—one they would end up losing.

But alas, because of Inessa's serpent tongue, the poison of doubt is already flowing through my veins. If I'm to have a moment's peace, I'll have to see the wicked queen for myself.

As expected, two men stand guard at the door leading down to the dungeon. As I approach, they share a secret glance between them which raises my hackles.

"Your Majesty…" one starts to say, panicked, only amplifying my anxiety. "We weren't expecting you tonight."

"Do I need an invitation to see my own prisoner, soldier?"

"No, my king." He quickly shakes his head.

"I didn't think so," I grumble, pushing them away from the door.

They both hurry behind me as I race downstairs, praying that they weren't foolish to do something that will end up getting themselves killed.

Make no mistake—any man who dares so much as lay a finger on her will die an excruciating death by my hands.

Once I reach the last step, I pick up a nearby torch and rush to her cell, only to be confronted with a scene so gut-wrenching that it takes everything in me not to slice open the throats of the guards standing behind me.

Kat's head is hung low, her once glorious pale golden mane in complete disarray as it covers most of her face. The rest of her is flesh and bone. Her flimsy white undergarment is covered in vomit, urine, and feces, while her boney arms and legs hold a grayish hue reminiscent of a corpse.

"Open the fucking door!" I growl, handing out the torch to one of the guards. "NOW!"

Fearing the repercussions of my wrath, it takes two tries for the guard to successfully open the iron-barred door. I push him away and charge inside, the foul stench of her environment causing my anger to increase so that black spots begin to blur my vision. I bridge the gap between us and gently lift her chin up to face me, her once full red lips holding a sickly shade of blue.

My black heart sinks to the pit of my stomach as she tries to open her eyelids, the light from the torch too much for her to bear.

"Attie?" she whispers in a confused daze.

My chest tightens at the forgotten nickname, causing me to unlatch my grip on her chin.

"Take her down," I order with such vehemence that my men quickly jump to the task.

Before she has a chance to fall on the floor—her legs too weak to hold her up—I slide my arm around her and pick her up, cradling her safely in my arms. Her freezing limp form immediately molds itself to my warmth, uncaring that I'm the one that got her in such a predicament.

She will not die by the elements.

The gods have given her to me for a purpose.

Her death will be by my hand and no other.

"Move!" I order through gritted teeth. "I'll deal with both of you later."

"But my king," one of them has the nerve to protest.

"I swear if you don't get out of my way this very instant, I will gut you like a fish. I said MOVE!"

This time he hears the threat loud and clear, clearing the path for me to take Kat away from this ungodly place.

I run up the stairs, careful to not unsettle her more than she already has been.

"Attie, I'm cold. So cold," she wheezes in my ear, indicating that the illness has already reached her lungs.

I bite into my cheek, the taste of iron filling the roof of my mouth. I meet some of my men on the way and shout out orders for them, uncaring how puzzled they are by the frail package in my arms.

"Get me Ulrich! Get me the physician!" I scream at one. "And you," I yell to another. "Go to Inessa's room and retrieve the hot water boiling from the fireplace and bring it to my chambers. Tell her that another pot for her bath will soon be sent to her room. And in no way should she be made aware of why I need hers. Is that clear?"

"Yes, my king," they say in unison, doing precisely as I commanded.

"Attie," Kat calls out again as if trying to revive that part of me that should remain dead.

"Shh, princess. Tonight's not the night you die."

"I think the gods don't agree with you." She forces a grin, a smile so hopeless that it physically hurts to look at.

"I do not fear the gods. They should be the ones to fear me if they dare to kill you before I get the chance."

"Then I'll use my last breath to pray for the latter. For I'd rather die in your vengeful arms than be taken from them by merciful gods."

Fuck!

Fuck!

Fuck!

"WHERE IS MY FUCKING PHYSICIAN?!" I shout as I knock down my bedroom chamber's door.

"He's coming, Your Grace," one of my young squires explains, making me aware of his presence. "What can I do?" he asks hurriedly.

"Pull the bedding down," I command.

"But she's filthy, Your Grace," he utters in confusion, throwing a glance toward my clean bed and then to the foul-smelling woman in my arms that is sure to defile it.

"Does it look like I give a fuck?! Just do as you're told, boy!"

Is everyone in this castle intent on defying me?

Argh!

But before he has a chance to do as commanded, my room is suddenly bombarded with men, two holding a large pot with boiling water and two others with the very man I was waiting for.

"What took you so long?" I growl at the clean-shaven bald man wearing his traditional black robes.

"I have yet to gain the power of flight to be any faster, Your Grace," he mocks me in jest, his smile disappearing completely when his eyes land on the soiled queen. "By the gods, what hell has befallen this young maiden?"

"Ulrich, I need your help, not your accusations."

"Fair enough. I'll hold on to those for later. As for now, take those dirty clothes off her at once and place her in the tub."

"Get out!" I tell the guards once they have poured the hot water into the tub. "The physician and the boy are all the help I need right now."

"Yes, my king," they say before retreating from my bedroom.

"Wait," I call out to one of them. "Go to the dungeon. I want the guards that have been watching over her since she arrived locked in chains. Put them in separate cells and show them the same hospitality they chose to give her without my consent. That means no light, no food, and no bucket. Understood?"

One look at the fallen queen in my arms is enough for him to know where my mindset is at.

"It shall be done," he retorts with the resolve I expect from my men at arms.

Good.

At least not everyone has lost their minds.

"Close the door, boy, and lock it behind you," I tell the squire while I walk over to the tub. "Hold on," I tell her before trying to place her at the center of the tub, but she's too damn weak to stand, much less keep her hold on me.

"I... can't... Attie. My... legs...," she tries to explain, the wheezing coming out of her chest worrying me even further.

"Shh, princess. Save your breath for your prayers," I reply softly, kicking off my boots and stepping into the water with her in my arms.

I slide back and bring her to rest her head against my chest, my arm snaking around her waist to keep her from going under. Once I have her steady, I twirl my finger to the physician and the boy in the room, silently ordering them to turn their eyes away from the tub so I may undress her from their prying eyes. The water is already filthy just by touching her clothes, but it will have to do for now.

"Boy, give the king some soap. He'll need it to scrub her clean," I hear Ulrich say.

With his eyes closed shut, the squire turns to us and hands me the soap, almost falling into the tub himself when his knees hit the border.

"I'm sorry, Your Grace," he immediately apologizes for the mishap.

It's only when he's back at a safe distance, with his back turned around, that I get the nerve to peel the see-through wet undergarment off her skin. My throat clogs at the sight of the swell of her breasts, two pink studded nipples at their center. My eyes scan the rest of her body, her rib cage more pronounced than it should be, giving way to a flat stomach and dusty blonde hair hiding between her thighs.

I hate how my body reacts to her.

Even frail and weak, she is still a sight to behold.

"Your Highness," Ulrich calls out, reminding me of the task at hand. "Time is of the essence. We need to warm her up. If my assessment is correct, then the queen is suffering from an acute state of hypothermia."

"And how exactly have you come to that assessment? Just by looking at her?" I ask, trying to keep a dialogue with him just to get my head off how my soaped-up hands run over her body.

"Did I not do the same with you when you found me all those years ago?" Ulrich retorts smugly. "Aye, Your Grace," he adds. "One look is all I need to make my evaluation. From the blue hue of her lips and skin, and the dilation of her pupils, I can surely determine that she's suffering from hypothermia. Left untreated, it can lead to complete failure of the heart and respiratory system, and eventually… death. Judging by her breathing, I also fear that her lungs may have a touch of pneumonia, too, probably brought on by stress, exposure to cold weather, and lack of nutrition. Right now, we must put all our efforts into warming her body back to its normal temperature."

"And her lungs?" I croak out, panic obliterating my hard-on.

"Do you still have some of the potion I gave you for your own illness, or should I make a fresh batch?"

"I still have some," I reply hurriedly. "It's on my bedside table."

"Good. As I said, time is of the essence. Is the queen now clean?"

"As best as I could get her."

"Then be quick about it and place her in the bed. Boy, get me a clean shirt from the king's wardrobe for her to lay down in."

While my squire busies himself with his task, I step out of the tub, holding in my arms a now unconscious Kat.

"She's asleep. Is that normal?" I ask, concerned, running my knuckles softly against her wet cheek, hoping my caress will get a reaction out of her. Even if only disgust.

"I'll see soon enough. Just get the queen dressed and in bed so I may make my full assessment."

Both the squire and Ulrich wisely remain silent with their backs turned to me as I carefully lie Kat down on my bed after pulling one of my white shirts over her head.

"There, tend to her," I order, unable to mask my feelings.

Ulrich places his black bag—full of medical tools and herb potions—to the side and puts his knee on the bed, pressing his ear to her chest. I despise the way he shakes his head and forcefully plies Kat's unresponsive eyelids open.

"Is that really necessary?"

"Yes," he deadpans before standing up and facing me.

"It's as I feared. Hypothermia combined with pneumonia. All we can do is keep her warm and pay close attention to any fever she may have during the night. Then it will be a game of cooling her down just enough to keep the fever at bay while still keeping her warm enough to prevent her organs from shutting down."

"Nothing of what you just said sounds like a game to me," I grunt, running my fingers through my hair.

"I'm sorry Your Grace feels that way." He sighs before continuing on. "For that is exactly what this is—a game with the gods on who gets to keep her."

"The gods have no say in the matter. She is mine."

I pretend not to see the little smirk tug at his lips with such a bold statement being grunted by his king.

"Then I suggest that you get out of your own wet clothes. The gods have a funny way of playing with people's fates. They could easily take you in her stead."

I snarl at the remark but tell my squire to fetch me some dry clothes just the same. However, I can't help but fixate on the physician's counsel.

It's true.

The gods do have a peculiar sense of humor.

When I woke up this morning, in my mind, the winter queen was as good as dead.

Now here I am, desperate to keep her alive.

No matter the cost.

Kat must live.

She just has to.

For too many queens have died on my watch as it is.

I will not helplessly watch another be taken from me.

Chapter 12
Atlas

Fifteen years old

"You found me," my silver-eyed princess declares at the precise moment she sees me walking toward the alcove she's been hiding in.

I slide in and sit beside her on the cool, tiled floor and nudge my knee playfully against hers.

"I didn't realize we were playing a game of hide and seek," I joke with a coy smile.

Kat hugs her arms around her legs, resting her left cheek on both knees to face me.

"Aye, and yet you still found me anyway." She sighs. "Sometimes I think that if the gods were to make me disappear somehow, you'd be the only one to even miss me."

"Don't say that," I mumble in sadness, not liking where her melancholy is taking her to. Especially when such a statement is furthest from the truth. "Both Teo and Levi have spent the better part of the day trying to find out where you have been holed up," I explain without fail, needing to squash such thoughts from her pensive mind. "Even though they weren't successful, it wasn't for the lack of trying on either of their parts, I assure you. I guess I just got lucky." I widen my smile, even if it does nothing to lift her spirits.

"Stop being modest, Attie. We both know if there is one soul in all of Aikyam who genuinely knows mine as perfectly as he does his own, it's yours. Otherwise, how would you explain the fact that it was so easy for you to have found me when they could not?" she counters, her eyes briefly going to the closed door at the end of the long hallway.

For all my brothers' failed attempts, the answer had been so obvious to me. It didn't take a genius to know that if Kat was hiding anywhere in this castle, it would have to be close to her mother's bedside.

Unlike Levi and Teo, I didn't go looking for her at first light, though. If Kat didn't come to us, then that could only mean that she needed some time away to be by herself and her thoughts. The least I could do was respect her wishes. But once the sun began to set, and no one in court had laid eyes on her, I began to worry.

Some reflective time alone to collect your thoughts is healthy.

Self-imposed isolation to wallow in one's grief and misery is not.

"How is she?" I ask, knowing that her mother, Queen Alisa, is the only person occupying her every thought and action.

"I'm not sure. Yesterday she was well enough to receive visits, but today the physicians refuse to even open the door for me. They won't tell me why, and the door is just too thick for me to eavesdrop on their conversation. Believe me, I tried."

"So no one has gone in or out?" I ask curiously.

"Just a few servants to bring in fresh linens since hers have been soaked through by her fever," she recoils, rubbing her arms as if she could physically feel her mother's cold sweats.

I'm about to ask something else when the navy door at the end of the hall suddenly swings open, stealing our attention away from each other and onto it. A man in long dark robes and a pointed hood—wearing the most macabre long beak face mask I've ever seen—leaves the room in quick haste, but not before locking the door behind him, trapping his patient and colleagues alike in the queen's chambers.

The way he hurriedly sprints down the hall gives me an unsettled pause. However, it's when he pulls down his mask—revealing black tired rings under his eyes and a fearful expression on his face—that really raises my hackles.

"How long has she been like this?" I ask, trying to recall when last I saw Queen Alisa as the physician disappears from our view.

"Since the day everyone arrived for Father's birthday celebration," she whimpers, wiping away a stray tear. "I don't understand it. She was fine before then. She was strong and healthy, and then overnight… it's like something decided to suck all her life force dry."

"Sometimes I feel like that too, you know?" I try to comfort her, throwing my arm over her shoulder. "Some days I wake up with all the energy in the world, and others, I feel like I'm in a constant struggle with my own body, battling for breath. But I'm still here. Whatever is making your mother sick, she won't give in without a fight."

"How can you be so sure?" my teary-eyed love asks, looking completely lost in her misery.

"Because she has someone to fight for. Like I do," I confess, hoping my words of unrequited love reach her heart.

But all my princess does in return is cry even harder, too consumed with her own pain to be able to read the message I've been—not so subtly too—trying to convey since the first day we met.

"I've witnessed her fighting, Attie. I've seen it with my own eyes. I don't think there is anything in this world strong enough to keep her here," she sobs, placing her head on my shoulder. "I'm losing her, Attie. I can feel it in my bones. I'm going to lose her."

"Shh, Kat. Shh," I coo, wrapping my arms around her and pulling her to sit on my lap. "It will all be okay."

She shakes her head furiously, slapping my forearms before burying her head into my chest.

"Don't lie to me, Attie. Don't say pretty words filled with hope when neither of us believes them. We're not like that. We tell each other the truth. Always. Even when the truth is ugly and awful."

I hold her close to my chest, placing my chin on the top of her head.

"You're right, princess. You're right. We're not those people." I heave a sigh. "But you can't fault me for trying to unburden your heart. It hurts me to see you like this. It hurts me even more knowing there is nothing I can do to ease your suffering."

"Just hold me, Attie," she says in between sobs. "Just be here with me."

"Always, princess."

I let her break in my arms—this girl who has made it her mission to always seem unbreakable.

I let her cry her fill, knowing she feels secure enough in my arms to show me her weakened, vulnerable state.

Because the world—like the truth she is living—is ugly and awful.

But not when we're together.

Together, we are invincible, even if we break.

Even when the world views us as weak.

Even when no one thinks we will ever be able to meet the expectations doled upon us.

As long as we have each other, we can surpass any adversity—even illness.

Even death.

"Let me through!" I hear a familiar loud growl coming from down the opposite hallway.

"Father," Kat stutters, wiping her tears with the sleeve of her gown before pushing herself up and bursting into a run.

I quickly do my best to follow her, Kat already tugging at her father's winter coat to get his attention when I reach her.

"What is it, Father?" she asks, her voice still hoarse from crying.

"Step away, girl," he replies harshly, forcibly pushing her to the side, making her knock into the man who is back to wearing his demon-like mask.

Behind his back, I scowl at my lord and liege for his brutish treatment of his own daughter, but when Kat looks like she's about to follow him and his accompanying physician inside, I grab her wrist and pull her back with equal force.

"Let me go, Atlas!" she shouts, furiously shaking her wrist to make me release my grip.

"No! You are not going in there."

"I was in there just yesterday! I'm ordering you to let me go! NOW!" she continues to shout, but it's only when the door slams in our faces that I finally relent.

"Let me in! Father! Let me in!" she yells, frantically banging at the door with her closed fists.

King Orville, as well as anyone inside, must hear her pleas, but none of them come to her aid.

"Kat," I call out and wince when she throws me an ugly sneer.

"Why did you stop me? Why, Attie?!"

There is so much hatred and suffering in her stare that I end up swallowing any apology I could come up with.

Truth be told, the only reason I didn't let her follow in her father's footsteps was because I didn't want her to catch whatever Queen Alisa has been afflicted with. If Kat's inklings are correct, and her mother truly is on her deathbed, then by the gods, I will not let Kat suffer the same fate.

I'd sooner die than let her come to harm.

She was right earlier—no one in all of Aikyam knows her soul as well as I do.

But that goes both ways.

If there is anyone who can see inside me, through bone and flesh, above crown and title, it is her.

We share a bond like no other.

And while I may be jealous that Teodoro has won her amorous affection and Levi her wide-eyed admiration, our bond runs so much deeper.

We are the same, she and I. We share the same fears and hopes.

We're symbiotic.

Where she ends, I begin.

Nothing will ever sever that.

And because I know how her mind works, how her heart beats, and her soul breathes, I force myself to take a step back and wait. I patiently wait, knowing that nothing I could possibly say at this moment will stop her from trying to bring down the door that stands between her and her beloved mother.

But when exhaustion finally makes an appearance and Kat's voice strains to whisper a word, much less shout it, I go to her. I entwine my fingers with hers and remind her that she isn't alone—she will never be alone as long as she has me.

This time, my fearless princess lets me pull her away from the door, seeking my embrace to keep her steady.

"It's okay, Kat," I whisper, running my fingers through her hair and pressing a kiss on her temple.

"It's not. Nothing will ever be okay after... Nothing will ever be the same after..." she chokes on her tears, unable to say the words we both fear to be true.

Nothing will ever be the same after her mother perishes.

For a king who loves his queen, as much as King Orville loves his, can never survive such pain.

Either his heart shrinks until there is only a gaping hole in his chest, or his mind maddens, needing others to feel his loss just as deeply.

Either way, life, as we have lived it up to now, will forever change.

I just pray to the gods that we're ready for it.

Chapter 13
Atlas

*W*e weren't.

No one was ready for the repercussions of Queen Alisa's death.

None more than me.

My sight had been so blurred by the veil of optimistic puppy love that I failed to see the danger we were all about to be faced with.

Levi got a taste of it first.

Teo sold his soul to keep clear of it.

But me?

I held steadily in denial, honestly believing that the shared bond I had with the young winter rose would be my kingdom's saving grace.

How wrong I had been.

How careless and idiotic I was to have believed anything being told to me at the time.

The only one who saw the writing on the wall before anyone else even deemed to look was my own mother—the Lioness of Narberth. But back then, a coward ruled the west. A weak spineless man who was too scared to fight his own shadow, let alone defy his king.

I am no such coward.

I vowed I'd never be anything like that pathetic worthless craven.

Yet, look at me now.

Cowering in a dark corner of my own bedroom as I watch over the woman who took part in destroying the west, while simultaneously arguing with the gods on who gets to keep her. Death by their hands, although excruciating, won't have the same showmanship I had planned for her.

That's the only thing that keeps me up at night. The only reason I vigilantly look after her, making sure that she survives the night.

At least, that's what I keep telling myself—that it isn't the fact that she's dying right before my very eyes that has me in this panicked state, but not being the one to claim such a righteous death.

For it will be righteous to see her limp body sway left and right from a tower, the noose slung around her neck being the only thing that keeps her from falling down toward the ocean.

It's the one death my men have longed for. Even sang songs about it.

The winter queen's demise by the west would silence the wails of their sorrows. It would end the nightmares of their mothers, sisters, wives, and daughters being abused and tortured by foreign hands who just see them as acquired goods.

One woman's death would end my kingdom's long-lasting grief.

Then, and only then, would our souls finally be rid of such misery.

And afterward, should the god of death deem that we, too, must perish for such a crime, we'd be all too happy to shake his hand and be enveloped in his embrace.

For in death, the west will finally be united with the ones we lost.

That is the only true peace that awaits us.

It's what our hearts yearn for.

What kind of king would I be if I denied my people's wishes?

Just another coward who refused to do right by them.

Ney.

The west has been wronged enough.

The time for retribution has come.

Unless she dies tonight.

Just as the ominous thought pops into my head, the winter queen starts kicking the blankets off her body, restless in her sleep.

"Damn the gods," I curse under my breath as I get up from the floor and walk over to the bed to cover her up.

Ulrich was clear in his instruction. Keep her warm at all times.

' *Unless she gains a fever,* ' his words suddenly whisper back in my ear.

Fuck.

I walk up to where her head lays on the pillow and press my open palm to her forehead. Another curse leaves my lips when I attest that she's burning up.

I have half a mind to call for her handmaiden and let her be the winter queen's caregiver. But I don't trust Inessa farther than I can throw her. Her loyalty is beyond question. Knowing her, Inessa would save her queen from death's door and find a way to escape my clutches with her in tow.

Ney.

Best keep Inessa in the dark for the time being.

I could call one of my squires or even Ulrich to attend to her needs, but even this frail and weak, the northern queen hasn't lost her beauty. Even the most innocent and loyal of minds could easily be corrupted into doing things they never dreamed of doing with such a gorgeous specimen in their midst. Especially horny young boys who have never gotten their dick wet or old men who might believe it may be the last chance they ever get to.

"Fuck, princess. Even completely out of it, you still manage to be a pain to my backside," I grumble after concluding that the task of bringing her back to health lies solely on my shoulders.

I grab a washcloth and dip it in a basin filled with cool water, and then press the cold compress to her forehead and begin to wipe the sweat off her brow, cheeks, and neck.

"Attie... don't... don't hurt... Elijah," she mumbles in her fever dream, her head thrashing left to right.

Who the fuck is Elijah?

My forehead creases as I try to recall any and all the information I retrieved from my spies on her voyages east and south. More importantly, the mention of the so-called Elijah. Unfortunately, after wracking my brain, I come up empty-handed about who this man that is so important to her could possibly be.

When I was a boy, I might have been prone to jealousy where she was concerned.

Now… not so much.

Especially given the fact that my spies have told me that this queen has a vast appetite, one that cannot be satiated by one man alone.

My own dearest brother Levi—the one man I thought to crown king of Aikyam once my plan was complete—fell headfirst into her web of lies and tongue second into her drenched pussy.

Teodoro's reaction to her came less as a surprise than hers did to me. I knew Teo would do whatever he could to bed the one woman that had escaped his clutches all those years ago. However, I never expected her to slip into his southern bed so quickly after leaving Levi's.

But it's not their names that she calls out in her fever—it's the mysterious Elijah.

Hmm.

Maybe this lover resides in the north.

Gods know that was the only territory I was unable to spy on. No matter how hard I tried to send my spies north, their heads always ended up being delivered back to me. Even after King Orville's death, any man I sent would return home to me in pieces.

"Attie… Elijah…" she continues to mumble.

I don't know what pisses me off more—her calling for her lover or insisting on calling me by that fucking nickname.

"Attie—"

"Yes, yes, yes. I heard you the first time," I grumble, cutting her off, gently running the cool cloth against her skin. "Your precious Elijah is safe."

She lets out a small, content sigh, her tense body instantly relaxing but not cooling down as quickly as I would have liked.

"Fuck," I groan as my eyes scan her feverish body, still mostly covered with one of my shirts. "Okay, princess. Believe me when I say that I take no fucking pleasure out of this either."

Before I lose my nerve, I pull my shirt off her body and throw it across the room. I avoid fixating on her creamy, smooth skin or the goosebumps springing forth upon lavishing it with the cool cloth. Instead, I keep busy at work, going back to the basin to soak the cloth when it becomes warm to the touch. I lose count on how many times I do this, but when I turn around to face her again, and find her wincing, as if death's cold fingers were strangling her, I rush to her.

"The fuck, Kat?! What am I to do with you now?" I blurt out in frustration, my frazzled nerves getting the best of me.

How the fuck am I to bring down the fever while keeping her warm?

Ulrich was right—this is a game with the gods.

They're toying with me.

Making me believe that I could save her, only to pry her out of my fingers after.

Over my dead body, will anyone take her away from me ever again. Not even gods.

I quickly strip my clothes off—until I'm as naked as she is—and slip into my bed to lay beside her. Without any coercion on my part, she molds her body next to mine as if it were the warmth that she had been craving all this time. I bite into my cheek as her head nestles between the crook of my neck, her ample breasts pressing up against me while her leg hooks over mine. My eyes squint as I try to breathe from my nose when the feeling of the featherlight hairs of her hot pussy scorch my outer thigh.

Even at death's door, she is a temptress.

Not wanting to be sucked in by her uncalculated seduction, I keep pressing the cold compress on her skin while still offering her some kind of warmth. The heavy weight on my chest only lightens when her shallow breathing evens out, a deep, peaceful slumber finally taking hold of her.

The minute I'm sure she is no longer in danger, every fiber of my being begins to shout for me to get out from under her. To jump out of this bed and get as much distance as possible from her.

But when I try to move, Kat's hold on me increases.

"Attie…" she whispers adoringly in her sleep, the name of her northern lover now replaced with mine.

I look down at her face, her silver eyes thankfully still hidden under her eyelids, confirming her deep slumber. I wait a few seconds before I attempt to move again.

"Attie…" she utters again, her nose wrinkling in annoyance when I try to shift her off me.

Curse the gods.

"You're not fucking making this easy, princess. You know that?"

Kat just sighs and snuggles in closer as if taking joy in my suffering.

"Fine. You fucking win. This time," I grumble, and instead of pushing her away, I wrap my arms around her and pull her closer, my nose diving into her hair, taking in her flowery fragrance.

"You are the bane of my existence. How I loathe you," I coo after a beat, gently pressing my lips on the top of her head, wishing she was awake to feel them.

Kat all but purrs at the remark, her satisfied sighs straining my already fragile sanity.

Yes, Levi.

I understand now, brother.

How effortlessly you could have been corrupted by such a beauty.

Even at her frailest, she doesn't make it easy on a man.

Not even on a king who has vowed to be the instrument of her destruction.

Luckily for me, I'm not so easily swayed.

Not while my memories still haunt me.

And as I close my eyes, I wait for the nightmares to come and remind me of why my hate is justified—even as I hold her tightly to me and breathe her in, her very essence soothing my black soul.

Chapter 14

Atlas

Fifteen years old

I freeze in my spot when I hear a loud crashing noise coming from the great hall. Curiosity gets the better of me, coaxing me to see what all the commotion is about.

"Have you lost your mind?!" I hear my mother shout from the top of her lungs, her angry tone alone making my spine shoot up straight.

"Rhea—"

"Don't you dare Rhea me, Faustus! What you're suggesting is lunacy!"

I silently hide behind one of the pillars, listening to my parents' not-so-private conversation since I'm sure that my mother's contempt can be heard all throughout Huwen Castle.

"It's not lunacy, Rhea. It's simply doing one's duty," my father retorts hesitantly, afraid of my mother's building temper. By the shattered glass on the floor, I can tell she's already thrown something at him. I wouldn't be surprised if she tried again, this time not missing her intended mark.

"Duty? You dare speak of duty?" She scoffs. "Where is the duty you professed to me on our wedding day? That you would be my champion and keep me safe from harm?"

"You're being preposterous," my father retorts, sounding annoyed. "What harm can you come to at the hand of our king?"

My mother grows silent, so much so that I have to venture a peek around the pillar I'm hiding behind to make sure she's still there. My brows furrow when I see her standing in the center of the room, staring at my father with a pitying look on her face.

"Are you that naive, husband? Can you not see that Orville, now without his Alisa, is a threat like no other? Can you not see how he will wish to punish us all for his grief?"

"Again, you exaggerate, woman," my father rebukes, shaking his head in denial. "Orville has always been a just king. I do not see how his queen's untimely demise will alter that."

My mother pinches the bridge of her nose in utter aggravation. But even from where I'm hiding, I can tell there is a sliver of sadness in her demeanor too.

"Aye, I know all too well that not every husband would go mad at the loss of his lady wife. The gods know I married such an apathetic man."

"Don't be cruel, Rhea," he's quick to retort, this time sounding pained. I watch in silence as my father gets up from his throne to eat the distance between him and my mother. Ever so gently, he rests his palm on her cheek and stares deep into her light eyes. "I have given you more cause to believe in my love than most husbands ever do. Have I not satisfied your every whim? Let you sail off into this great world and have every adventure your heart desired? Have I not done the unthinkable of letting a woman—even one as formidable as you— captain my fleets while I waited patiently for your return?

"Oh, dear husband," she starts, cupping his hand with hers on her cheek. "You did not do that out of love for me but out of cowardice. For we both know you would never set foot on a ship for fear of drowning, nor do you hold enough steel in your spine to lead our fleets."

"Stop it, Rhea," he says, pulling his hand away from her. "I know what you're doing. You want to hurt me because my decision has hurt you. But in the end, it is *my* decision, wife. And, once made, a king's decision cannot be undone."

"And what of a husband's?" she pleads. "What of a father's? What lies will you tell our son? What justification could you possibly give him that would rationalize him being without his mother?"

"You exaggerate," he says, rubbing his thumbs at his temples. "Atlas will not be without his mother for long. In fact, he may not even notice your absence at all, for I doubt your visit north will be longer than any voyage you've ever taken."

"It's not a visit, Faustus! I'm not to be welcomed to Tarnow as a guest! I'm to go as a prisoner, and you're too blinded by this unfounded sense of duty and honor to know the difference."

"Again, with the theatrics! You will not be a prisoner but rather be given the respect and grace of a queen. King Orville will undoubtedly treat you as such."

"If that is true, then why has Krystiyan refused the king's command of sending Daryna north?" my mother counters knowingly, crossing her arms over her chest.

"How am I to know what goes on in Krystiyan's mind?" My father scoffs. "You have no qualms in calling me a fool, but it's Krystiyan who should be deemed one in your eyes. His blatant refusal to send his queen north only makes him look guilty. Maybe Orville is right. Maybe someone did poison his beloved. And maybe that is why Krystiyan won't send Daryna because he fears his wife has done the misdeed. Have you ever considered that, wife?" my father explains, arching his brow as if proving his point.

But my mother doesn't seem convinced. Not by the way she shakes her head profusely.

"Again… you are wrong, my dear naive husband," my mother explains sullenly. "Daryna loved Alisa like her own flesh and blood. She would have rather drank poison from a cursed vile herself than ever offer such a thing to Alisa. No matter your reasoning, even you can't deny that. The two were like sisters. They were family. If Alisa's death was somehow provoked, Daryna would have been the last person to have had a hand in it."

My father turns his back on my mother, his expression now pensive. I watch him chew on my mother's words and become disappointed for finding no fault in them.

"Aye. I don't see Daryna being capable of such a betrayal. Her love for our departed queen was well-documented. But then again, what other explanation is there that the King of the East should refuse to comply with our sovereign's order? There must be a reason behind his decision," my father muses out loud, almost as if he were trying to figure out the answer to an equation that has stumped him at every turn.

"Look at me, Faustus," my mother urges, her facial features losing all their fighting quality.

My father turns around to face her, his gaze turning sad at how defeated she looks.

"There is a reason why Krystiyan has taken this stand against our king. He knows as well as I do that sending Daryna north is a sure death sentence. The same sentence you're so eager to bestow unto me."

"You will not die, Rhea," he retorts with the same dejected tone. "You will go north and prove your innocence to our king. He will see that you had no hand in his wife's death and then return you home, safe and sound. Do you not trust your own king to do right by us? Do you not trust that I know what I'm doing? That I would never put you in such peril?"

Again, my mother shakes her head.

"I don't trust anyone right now. Not even you, sweet husband. The man I have vowed to love with all my heart."

"Rhea," he supplicates, rushing toward her to envelop my mother in his arms. "Please don't say such words. I'm just doing what I believe to be right. How can anything go awry when a heart is pure?"

She pulls away from his embrace, misery coating her usually extraordinary fearless features.

"Do not talk to me about purity of heart. If you had one, you wouldn't forsake me so."

"Rhea—"

"Stop, Faustus. You've said your piece. Now hear mine. I will not be going north as you've ordered me to. I will gather my men and be on the first ship out tomorrow morning. You can deal with your king once I'm gone."

"I feared you'd say such a thing," my father mumbles, dispirited, as he turns his back on her again in favor of walking over to a nearby table to retrieve a small parchment from it. "Here, Rhea. Read for yourself what King Orville has written and what he stipulated should you wish to sail away instead of riding north with his men in the morning."

My mother snatches the decree from my father's hand and begins to devour every word.

Her eyes grow wide in horror.

"This is... he wouldn't dare..." she stammers while rereading the document.

"Someone must go north, Rhea. If not you, then—"

"Atlas?!" she finishes his sentence for him. "You would send your own son to die? Your only son?"

"I do not see it that way. I see it as sending a young prince to pay homage to his rightful ruler in place of his reluctant mother. Unlike you, dear wife, our boy will be thrilled to return to Tarnow. We both know how he worships Orville's daughter and how crestfallen he was that this year's visit was cut short. Should you sail away to god knows where, Atlas will take your place and ride north."

"Over my dead body, Faustus!" my mother yells, balling up the royal decree in her hand. "I'll sooner take Atlas with me than send him to his death!"

"If you do that, then you'll be the one who has killed our son," my father rebukes, with the same vehemence to his tone. "Or do you honestly believe that Atlas will survive even the smallest voyage out at sea?"

My throat clogs as I watch my mother hang her head down low.

Neither of them believes I can survive.

I'm the rightful heir to the eastern throne, a kingdom that was built on salt and iron with the sound of the waves as our tribal song. Yet, neither one of my parents believes I'm strong enough to survive even the simplest of voyages.

All this talk of death, and they don't even realize that they just killed my spirit.

"If you loved us, you would sacrifice yourself and go in our stead," my mother whispers loud enough for both of us to hear.

"It's because I love you and our people that I do not. Someone needs to stay at Huwen and rule, wife. Make sure that our kingdom persists. How am I to do that if I have a wife who would rather spend her time on a ship than do her duty as a queen? Do you wish me to go and leave Atlas seated on the throne? A boy so frail that a small wind could take him from us? For these are my choices, Rhea. These are my only choices. I've made my decision. What's yours to be, wife?"

My mother stands there completely immobile, reminiscent of a god-like granite statue. She doesn't move. She doesn't so much as blink. And for the briefest of moments, I begin to believe that the gods have frozen her in their likeness. Taking her away from her agony and preserving her fearless beauty for future generations to be in awe of.

"You do not have to decide tonight," my father adds once he realizes my mother won't say a further word. "But should you be here in the morning, then I will assume you have come to your senses."

He then walks over to her and places a tender kiss on her frozen lips.

"You may not believe that I love you or our son at this moment, Rhea. But my life means nothing without the pair of you. I'm just trying to do the right thing here. Be the honorable strong man you need me to be. I wish you could see that."

With the world on his shoulders, he leaves the great hall and my mother to her grief.

"Mother," I call out, my voice barely above a whisper.

She turns around and sees me standing in front of the pillar I had been hiding behind all this time.

She falls to her knees and opens her arms out for me. I run as fast as possible into her arms and hug her tightly.

"I don't understand," I begin to sob, trying to connect the dots of their conversation. "Why is Father forcing you to go north?"

"Because your father has a politician's heart instead of a king's. He believes polite discourse will solve his problems when it's a show of strength that is needed," she replies, her own tears flowing freely.

"Is it true? Will you be sailing off in the morning?"

She shakes her head and wipes her tears away.

"Nay. Your father has made his decision, and so have I, little lion. No harm will ever come to you as I live and breathe."

"But I don't understand," I repeat, confused. "Why would I be in any danger? Father's right. I'd be in safe hands in the north. Kat would never let any harm come to me."

"Katrina of Bratsk is still very much a child, even if she has seen her sixteen autumns. But most importantly, she is her father's daughter. She lives for his praise and approval. Someone so easily influenced can never be a true friend to you, sweet lion. Not when it means going against her father's wishes."

My forehead creases at her statement.

Kat is much more than just my friend.

She's half of my soul.

She would never turn her back on me.

Not even for her father.

Never.

I open my mouth to say as much, but my mother silences me with her next words, "I need you to pay close attention to me now, my little lion. For it might be the only way to save you."

I nod, even though I don't feel the same imminent danger that she does.

"Tomorrow, I ride north, but before I go, I will leave precise instructions to my best captains. If something should happen to me, I want you to sneak away to the harbor and get on the first available ship. I'll make sure that there is one fully equipped at all times waiting for you to sail away."

"But…" I stammer, "aren't you afraid that I'll end up dying?"

"If that be your fate, then better you die free at sea than a prisoner on land."

She wraps her arms around me, almost suffocating the air out of my lungs. But no matter how difficult it is for me to breathe, I hug her back just as fiercely and make a vow of my own, "I won't let anything happen to you, Mother. I swear it."

"Oh, my sweet, sweet little cub. The gods have already decided my fate." She smiles while leaning into my neck. "Do not be scared, for I'm not afraid. I'll seek out my destiny with my head held high. Make sure that when the time comes, you do the same. Do not cower, Atlas. Be the king Huwen deserves, for I fear the one it has now just cursed it with his cowardice. Do not waste your time on pretty words but be a king of action. Huwen needs a leader, not a diplomat. Do you understand?"

I nod, even though I'm still struggling to fully comprehend what she's trying to teach me.

My mother then pulls back and cups my face in her palms, and says, "Whatever happens, Atlas, remember this. My greatest adventure was never sailing around the world. It was being your mother. I could not be prouder of my little lion. You have given me more joy in a lifetime than I could possibly merit. No matter what happens, Atlas, know that I will always watch over you and keep you whole. The gods owe me that much."

"I love you," I sob.

"I love you, too," she cries, the sound of her tears feeling like paper cuts slashing away at my heart.

She then stands up and kisses the top of my head before turning away and vanishing from my sight, never to return whole again.

Chapter 15
Katrina

My mouth feels as dry as the Nas Lead desert at the peak of a southern summer. It's with much effort that I force myself to pry open my heavy eyelids, praying for a pitcher of water to quench this unforgivable thirst. Unfortunately, when I do manage to open my eyes, I'm unable to see a thing in front of my face as the room is immersed in pitch-black darkness.

But as I stretch my aching limbs, some things do come to light.

I'm no longer in chains in Atlas's dungeon.

I'm in bed. A very large bed, at that. One fit for a king.

How did I get here?

I pull up the last memory I have and confirm that I was still a prisoner of the west before everything went hazy on me.

I also remember the freezing cold.

How I never experienced such sub-zero temperatures even growing up in Tarnow.

I remember how difficult it had been for me to breathe, my lungs struggling with the declining temperature, my chest tightening every time I gasped for air. Like an afterthought, I place my open palm on my chest and listen as I breathe in and out, the persistent wheezing sound barely audible now.

But that's not all I realize.

I swallow the lump in my throat at the realization there isn't a piece of clothing on me save for a bedsheet and a large, heavy blanket that lies on top of my body. My shaky hand travels down my chest throughout my naked form to verify if any damage was done while I was out of it. I let out an exaggerated exhale upon recognizing there's no cause for concern. Although my muscles feel sore and tired, nothing indicates that certain unwanted liberties have been taken on my body without me knowing.

Gods be good.

But my gratitude is short-lived when I hear a small chuckle coming from somewhere in the dark room.

"Who's there?" I ask while hurriedly pulling the covers all the way to my chin.

When another smug, arrogant laugh rings out, I get my answer.

"I know it's you, Atlas," I mutter, unsure if I should be relieved or frightened about him hiding in the shadows.

My eyelids squint when a flick of light illuminates a corner of the room. However, I still manage to see my abductor blow out a wooden splint after lighting the wick of a candle perched on the side table next to him. When my eyes become fully acclimated to the light, I just stare at the silent king who remains seated in his chair, glaring back at me. Neither one of us says the first word as we take stock of each other— me in complete helpless disarray, him looking like a vengeful god amongst men.

Even though Atlas carries that hard edge of his like a shield, the boy of my past has turned into a remarkably beautiful man. Bad men like him shouldn't merit such a word. Yet it's the only one I can find to describe him.

The long waves of his dirty, blond hair hit his broad shoulders as if needing to praise them with their touch. My eyes scan his impressive muscular arms and large veiny hands, the same ones that threaten to strangle the very air in the room. His whole demeanor oozes strength and power. Nothing about this man resembles the frail best friend I once had. Though his face still holds the kiss of youth on his clean-shaven apple cheeks, his jaw is cut like fine glass, and his deep pink lips look like they have been drawn on by the gods themselves. Yet it's his light eyes that serve as a stark reminder that this is not a celestial being.

They're cold in their beauty.

Lifeless.

Soulless.

As if their stare could see right through you and find you wanting.

Much like they are now.

I try my best to slow down my accelerated heartbeat, desperate to show that I'm in no way intimidated by him. But as I watch his upper lip lift at the corner of his mouth, it's clear that he sees right through my pretense.

"How long have I been here?" I ask, needing to break this tense-filled silence between us.

"Four nights and three days," he replies with a monotone voice.

143

I try to do the math in my head, but unfortunately, there are too many blocks in my memory to know if I've been held prisoner for over a month or not.

If I have, then someone must be coming for me.

If not, then I'm still at Atlas's mercy.

Not that he knows the meaning of the word.

How could he when none was shown to him?

My tense shoulders deflate when I remember what my father has done to his kingdom.

It was he who turned my best friend against me. Who corrupted his soul and turned him into this—a soulless king with a justified vendetta against the north… and me.

My throat starts to constrict and scratch at the thought, reminding me of my punishing thirst.

"Can I have some water?"

I swallow dryly as Atlas remains anchored in his seat, making me believe that his willingness to nurse me back to health has finally hit its limit.

But just as I think it, that realization comes to me like a slap on the face.

Atlas nursed me back to health.

There is no doubt in my mind that I would have died in that dungeon cell if he didn't intervene.

But why?

Should I be grateful that I'm still alive?

Or should I be wary of his intentions?

'Either I hang your head up high on the tallest of my tower for all of Aikyam to see, or I sell you to the highest bidder. Believe me when I say death comes as a mercy to the latter.'

Maybe death in chains would have been kinder to the alternative he has in mind for me.

My breath hitches when Atlas suddenly springs up from his seat and turns his back to me, the sound of water being poured into a chalice. My fingers cling to my blanket as I watch him turn around and walk toward me with a cup in hand. Though my brows furrow in confusion when he unexpectedly stops midway.

"Your water, princess," he announces, holding the cup halfway from me.

I bite into my cheek at his incessant refusal to acknowledge me as his queen, but I'm too thirsty to argue with him now.

"Can you come closer?" I ask since I'm unable to reach the cup in his hand.

"No," he replies with a bored tone.

My teeth grind in frustration as I fix the blanket under my arms so as not to slide down when I raise halfway up the bed just to grab the cup in his hand. I hate the smirk displayed on his lips when I grab the cup away from his grip and begin chugging its contents down to the very last drop. I wipe the droplets of water from my lips with my forearm and hand the chalice back to him.

"More," I order, but by the look in his dead eyes, I'm going to have to be more submissive in my plea. "Please," I add as he just stands there staring at me, unwilling to take the cup out of my outstretched hand.

"Who's Elijah?"

My eyes widen for the briefest of seconds, stunned by hearing my baby brother's name come out of his mouth so unexpectedly.

"No one that concerns you," I reply steadfastly. "Water. Now. Please." I pronounce each word with false sugary politeness.

His jaw ticks before snatching the cup away from my hand, only to grab my chin with his other.

"I won't ask again. Who. Is. Elijah?"

His fingers dig into my flesh as his eyes stare into mine, his face so close that I can smell the mint of his breath.

"I'm waiting, princess. Need I remind you that patience isn't my forte."

I almost scoff at the lie. He's been nothing but patient when it came down to avenging his people. He waited for me to travel all the way west before putting his plan into action. An impatient king would have kidnapped me the minute I set one foot out of Tarnow.

No.

Atlas is more than patient when he so desires to be.

But apparently, knowing who Elijah is doesn't fall in that category.

He's safe.

Elijah is safe.

No harm will come to him while he remains north.

Not even Atlas can do him harm from here.

"My brother," I finally reply.

"Don't lie to me," he commands, his nostrils flaring in contempt.

"I'm not."

"You are. Your father never remarried," he says, his voice holding that eerie, calming tone even when his fingers bite deeper into my skin.

"And since when does a man need to be married to father a child?" I retort, staring him coldly in the eyes.

Atlas takes a beat and then releases his grip on me.

"A bastard?" he utters with his brow arched up high in amusement.

"Don't call him that," I spit out, hating that word. "Elijah is the queen's brother and deserves to be respected as such."

Atlas's smirk stretches.

"You care for him." It's not a question. Just an uneasy affirmation.

I try to keep my facial features as inexpressive as possible, but I'm unable to cloak the fear in my eyes when talking about my brother. Especially with a man who has all but assured me that I'm to die for my father's disgusting actions against his kingdom.

"He's just a boy, Atlas. A child. He's innocent to all of this."

"Is that so?" he says, pinning me with his glare. "What about the children of the west? Weren't they just as innocent when your father came for them?"

I refuse to give him a reply.

How can I when he's right?

But by the gods, I will not place Elijah in the same danger. Not while I still have life in me.

"I've answered your question. Can I have my water now?" I ask instead, needing to diffuse the situation and move the topic of conversation as far away as I can from my baby brother.

Atlas's lips thin into a fine line before turning around to fill the chalice again, briefly giving me a moment of reprieve to breathe easy, since I'd all but stopped with his impromptu interrogation. However, my spine goes ramrod straight as soon as he turns to face me again, this time coming closer to my bedside. And when he sits beside me, it takes everything I have not to flinch at the close proximity. Sadness immediately wraps itself around my heart at the thought.

This is Atlas.

My Attie.

The one I used to run to share all my doubts and fears, knowing I'd be safe and find solace in his arms.

And now?

Now I feel like he would use those strong hands of his to snap my neck in a heartbeat if he so chose.

"No longer thirsty?" he asks, carefully shaking the chalice in my direction.

I take it from his hands and, this time, slowly drink its contents, my gaze never leaving his, just in case he tries something funny.

As if reading my mind, he lets out a low chuckle.

"What?" I ask, wondering what he finds so amusing.

"You're too trusting," he says as if taking notes of my flaws.

"Am I?" I sneer. "And just exactly what have I done to make you think that?"

When his malicious gaze drops to the cup in my hands, taking it away from me, my eyes widen in horror.

"You… you… poisoned me?"

He lets out another chuckle, placing the cup on the bedside table and shifting further on the bed. He leans against the headboard, placing his arms behind his head and crossing his legs by the ankles.

"If I wanted to kill you, I would have left you in that cell," he explains without remorse, his eyes now closed.

I fight the urge to crawl up his body and strangle his neck.

Not only would it be easy enough for him to stop me, but what he said is true.

If he wanted me gone, he could have just left me in his dungeon to die. He could be celebrating with his men right now, dancing and drinking over my freshly dug grave.

But instead, he's here, looking more like he's ready to take a nap than kill me.

"Why didn't you?" I ask, the question burning in my mind. "Why keep me alive?"

"You're here to serve a purpose, princess. And until that purpose is completed, you'll live to see another day."

Purpose.

I've only known one purpose my whole life—to be queen.

What other purpose is there?

"Atlas – "

"It's been a long couple of nights, princess," he cuts me off, before turning his back to me, making himself comfortable. "Even a king needs to rest."

"You're going to sleep? Here?" I ask in outrage, completely appalled at the idea of sharing a bed with him.

He turns his head over his shoulder and silences me, yet again, with his soulless eyes.

"It is my bed, princess. If you have a problem with that, I suggest you use the floor."

He turns around again as if that fact is all the explanation I need.

I'm completely naked under these blankets, so there is no way I'll be moving anytime soon with Atlas in the room. Instead of arguing with my abductor, I fall to the other side of the bed, making sure there is sufficient distance between us.

Sleep, however, refuses to come to me as his last words still play in my mind.

"What's my purpose, Atlas? What do you expect of me?"

A stretch of silence passes by, making me believe he fell asleep the minute his head had hit the pillow. But then I feel the mattress dip behind me, alerting me that Atlas is now staring at my back. A shiver runs down my spine when his fingers gently play with a strand of my hair.

"Be it in life or death, you will make my kingdom whole again. I'm just of two minds on which to choose."

My heart hurts at his words, hearing the truth in them.

"I can't bring back the ones you've lost, Atlas," I whisper, overcome with helplessness that I can't turn the hands of time back and remedy what has befallen the west.

"Then death it is."

Chapter 16
Katrina

Sixteen years old

"EVERYBODY OUT!" my father shouts, slamming my mother's bedroom door behind him and bypassing me and Atlas like a destructive tornado.

I pull away from Atlas's embrace, my tears still stinging my eyes as I rush toward my father.

"Father! Father!" I call out frantically, desperate to get his attention, while he storms the halls, yelling and shouting at everyone that crosses him. "Father! What happened? Is Mother alright? What did the physicians say? Father?!"

"Move, girl!" He discards me, looking straight ahead as if I weren't even there. "I want every last piece of vermin out of my castle! They have murdered me!" he continues to shout to anyone who can hear him, sounding like an unhinged madman.

"I don't understand," I stammer, panicked by his deranged behavior.

In all my sixteen winters, I've never once seen my father this way.

It's almost as if something has possessed him, turning him into this lunatic of a demented man, so blinded by rage that he sees little else.

"If there is a soul that doesn't belong to Tarnow by sunrise, it will be the last one they ever see!" he carries on, pushing servants and soldiers out of his way.

"Atlas!" I hear a familiar voice urgently call out behind me.

I turn my head over my shoulder and see Queen Rhea pleading with Atlas to follow her. But he just shakes his head, preferring to run behind me as I follow my father down toward the great hall.

"I said, OUT!!!" My father persists in shouting, looking ready to take down everything in his path.

His fury is so intense that he doesn't even see or seem to care that I'm running right behind him. So much so that Atlas has to grab me by the waist, forcing me to jump back or risk being hit with the fragments of a broken vase that he's successfully plummeted to the floor, leaving stems of our royal blue roses decorating the very ground we walk on.

Atlas turns me around and locks me in his embrace.

"Let me go, Atlas!" I yell, trying to wrestle out of his arms, needing to follow my father.

"Atlas! Now!" Queen Rhea shouts behind us, looking just as manic as my father.

But Atlas doesn't pay his mother any mind, too focused on me to listen to her pleas.

"Listen to me, princess. I have to go."

"What?" I ask, still struggling to make sense of what's happening around me. I try to turn my head to see where my father is, but Atlas pulls my chin to face him. "I need you to listen to me, Kat," he begs with despair in his tone.

I feel like I'm being pulled in every direction, but ultimately, my attention chooses to be on Atlas.

"Stop following King Orville and go to your mother," he orders, his voice sounding more adult than ever before. "She's the one who needs you right now, not him," he adds, his chin pointing to where my father has run off to in a furious rampage.

I offer a small nod, my confusion and panic bringing forth a new wave of tears.

"I don't understand what's going on," I admit, letting them free fall down my cheeks.

"I know, princess," Atlas replies in sadness, gently wiping my tears with his thumbs while cupping my face in the palms of his hands. "I'm still trying to connect the dots too. But one thing is clear, I have to leave you," he adds, strained.

"What? No! I need you," I exclaim, closing the small gap between us by wrapping my arms around him and placing my cheek on his chest.

My world is violently crumbling around me, but the sound of his heartbeat is even louder than any curse my father belts out in the distance. Atlas keeps his tight hold on me with his nose in my hair, and for the briefest of seconds, I feel the chaos dissipate, feeling safe in his arms.

"Atlas! Come!" Queen Rhea calls out again, reminding us she's just a few feet away.

We begrudgingly pull apart, if only by a little, as Atlas keeps his light grip on my chin.

"Use the birds I gave you. You can write to me every day. Promise," he says, the desperate tone of his voice feeling like daggers digging away at my heart.

"Don't leave me. Not now," I stutter through my tears.

"I don't want to. Fuck, I really don't want to," he retorts, his expression just as pained as mine. "Promise me, Kat. You'll use the birds. Promise me."

"I promise," I vow, feeling his tense muscles instantly relax somewhat.

"ATLAS! Now!" his mother urges behind us.

"I have to go," he says, never taking his light blue eyes off me. "But even though I'm leaving, I need you to remember that you are never alone. You have me, Kat. Mind, body, and soul. You'll always have me."

And before I'm able to stop him, Atlas lowers his head and kisses me.

I'm too heartbroken to tell him I'm in love with someone else and that he shouldn't be kissing me like this. But Atlas's kiss is sweet, filled with the tenderness I long for. I let myself get lost in his kiss, his lips warm and comforting, pressed against mine, easing the knot in my chest with his love.

For that is what this departing kiss is—a vow of his undying love.

I should be taken aback by it.

I should place my palms on his chest and push him away.

But I don't.

Instead, my body leans into the kiss as if needing to make a vow of my own.

And when he groans with the way I deepen the kiss, my lower belly constricts, igniting a flame inside me that I had no idea even existed. The world around me stops spinning as if I were tethered to the earth by this one kiss. Confusion lifts from my eyes, and suddenly, I see things so devastatingly clearly.

Atlas loves me.

Truly. Unconditionally. Loves me.

And although I was sure I loved another, my soul seems to love Atlas right back.

But just as that clarity pulls the veil away from my heart, Atlas breaks our kiss, the maddening world crashing in full force down on me.

"Atlas," I open my mouth to say, but he silences me by pressing his forefinger on my lips, his temple kissing my forehead.

"I'll come for you," he whispers breathlessly, his gaze still heady. "One day, I'll come for you, princess. I promise."

All I manage to do is nod, still lightheaded with our kiss.

"Atlas!" Queen Rhea shouts, losing her patience with her son.

"Fuck. Now that I have you, I don't want to let you go," he mutters under his breath, still holding me close.

I'm so confused with these rampant new feelings that I'm unable to argue that he doesn't have me. That I've promised my heart and hand to Teo. But even when I try to string that sentence along, it feels like a lie on the tip of my tongue, one that refuses to come out.

Atlas presses a chaste kiss on my creased forehead and releases me from his embrace, leaving my body painfully bereft of his warmth.

"Go, Kat. Go to your mother," he orders, sounding more in control of his feelings than I am.

"What about you?"

"Don't worry about me. I'll be fine." He smiles assuredly even though it never reaches his stellar blue eyes. "Now, go. Go to her."

I look to where my raging, mad father has gone and then to the stairs that lead me back to my sickly mother's room. My heart is split down the middle, but in the end, I make my choice.

I hug Atlas to me one more time before running in the opposite direction toward the great hall. I don't have to turn around to feel the heat of his disappointed gaze graze my back.

But Atlas has given up.

And I refuse to.

No matter what has befallen my mother, my father should not be treating his vassals so callously. They are not at fault here, and someone should remind my father of that. He needs to be pulled away from the cliff of madness before he does something we will all regret.

When I reach the hall, I see my father still shouting absurdities to anyone willing to hear. Tarnow is in complete disorder. Everyone is dashing every which way, trying to keep their distance from their king, fearing his wrath will be brought down on them.

"Father!" I shout, but before I'm able to take another step toward him, two strong hands pull me away from his view.

Gray piercing eyes—so like my mother's—stare disgruntled at me.

"Uncle, I need to see Father," I beg, trying to pass through him while he remains blocking me at every turn.

"You will do no such thing," my uncle Adelid proclaims menacingly, with a lethal glint in his eyes. "Your father is not in his right frame of mind right now for you to pester him so."

"I can see that, Uncle." I grit my teeth. "That's why I need to speak with him. I need to know why he's acting this way and sending everyone home."

"I thought you were smarter than that, niece." My uncle tsks disapprovingly. "Your mother is very ill, and choices need to be made. Would you rather have him use up all his energy to entertain guests, or would you prefer him to be at your mother's bedside in her greatest time of need? For he cannot do both."

He's right.

Wasn't I the first to chastise my father for his aloof behavior recently?

Hadn't I been angry with him for preferring to celebrate his upcoming winters with his guests than spending time with my mother when she was so bravely battling whatever sickness has consumed her?

Seeing that reason has finally paid its visit to me, my uncle places his hands on my shoulders and gives them a gentle squeeze.

"Go to your queen, niece. Take care of my beloved sister while I deal with your father."

I offer him a clipped nod and follow my uncle's instructions.

If there is anyone that can talk sense into my father, it will be him.

Uncle Adelid offers me a comforting smile as he watches me slowly walk away from the hall. Each step feels heavy as I gain distance from my raging father and grow closer to my ailing mother. The corridors are hectic, with people running up and down, carrying large cases and luggage or whatever they can take to make their hurried escape. I pass easily enough through the erratic commotion, no one paying me much attention as I walk up the stairs that lead to my mother's bedchamber. This time, no one tries to stop me as I open her door and walk inside.

"Katrina," she whispers joyfully, but her gaunt sickly face pierces through my already broken heart. "I'm so glad you came."

"They wouldn't let me see you," I confess, shifting my weight from one foot to another when I realize she's all alone in her room—a telltale sign the physicians no longer see a reason to be here.

"Aye. Well, you're here now, thank the gods." She smiles weakly. "Come here, Katrina. Let me look at you."

I take a step closer, still unwilling to admit what's so painfully evident.

"You're going to be alright, aren't you? There must be something someone can do."

"I'm afraid not, sweet girl. I fear death has its unholy grip on me, and soon it will snatch me away from this mortal coil."

"Don't say that," I sob, taking another step closer to her bedside.

"None of that. There will be no tears, sweet Kat. I shall not look the reaper in the eyes and let him see that I'm frightened. I need ice in my veins for what's to come. But for me to do that, I need to make sure that you, my dearest daughter, are well equipped to handle royal life. I fear I have sheltered you too much to see the dangers that bite at your heels."

"I don't understand." I shake my head, taking another step closer.

"It's okay. One day you will." She offers me a thin smile. "Now, come close, so I can say what I need to." She pats the small space at her side.

I eat the small distance between us and plant myself on her bedside, leaning in further when she urges me closer.

"Trust no one," she whispers in my ear. "Not your father. Not my brother. Not even those three young boys you dote on. Not a soul, Katrina. For even love can grow cold with time, but ambition for power never dwindles its flame. Men are flawed that way and are capable of unimaginable cruelty to get what they want. Even lie, kill, or betray those they love most. Trust no one."

My forehead creases as I pull away to stare at my mother's pale face.

"I don't understand. You don't want me to trust Father?"

"No, I don't," she deadpans with resolve.

"But… don't you love Father?"

"With all my heart." She sighs. "But though a woman can love a bad man, that doesn't mean her love can change him. It only domesticates him for a spell. I fear that once I'm gone, the father you know will also perish. And the man that will rise in his place will listen to no one but his own grief."

"Not even me?"

"If you were born a boy… maybe," she admits sullenly. "As it stands, my love for your father and his for me was the force that kept the vile beast that dwells inside him in its cage. Do not be fooled, child, for a wild animal can never truly be tamed. It can only be contained by a force stronger than himself. In our case, it was love. Once my body is cold and buried, there will be no cause to keep him docile and civilized. Especially when even bigger monsters whisper in his ear, taunting him to do his worst. Take care, my sweet daughter, and heed my warning. Trust no one. Not even your own heart, for I am proof that even a heart can be blinded to the truth."

I swallow dryly, the warning in her eyes prickling the back of my neck.

"And what truth is that?"

"That love isn't enough to save a tortured soul. And eventually, all it will do is condemn our own."

Chapter 17
Katrina

The next morning when I open my eyes, it's not the veil of darkness I encounter, but the familiar gaze of my best friend, the rays of sunlight beaming at her back.

"Inessa!" I shout, rising halfway from the bed and wrapping my arms around her. "You're alive! Thank the gods, you're alive!"

"You sound surprised," she jokes, but her hold on me tightens as if needing confirmation that I, too, still live.

"I was afraid I'd never see you again," I confess between joyful sobs.

"Aye, Your Highness. I must admit, for a second there, I thought the same."

When we pull apart, Inessa grows silent as she begins to run her hands up and down my still-weakened frame. She then pulls down the blankets on top of my legs as if they, too, need to be thoroughly inspected.

"I'm fine, Inessa. Truly." I wave her overprotectiveness away and pull the blankets up again.

"You're not fine," she rebukes. "From what I've heard, you were basically at death's door not three moons ago."

"That may be true, but as you can see, I'm fine now. I wouldn't say that if I didn't mean it."

Inessa leans back from her perched position on the side of the bed and scans my face up and down.

"You do look good. Healthy even." Her brows furrow in confusion.

"Now it's you who sounds surprised." I laugh, wiping the happy tears out of the corner of my eyes.

"Forgive me, Your Highness. I just didn't know what to expect. King Atlas hasn't been very forthcoming with his news of you. I only learned this morning that you were ill," she mutters through gritted teeth, angry that our abductor would keep such news from her.

But it's with the mention of the inhospitable king that a myriad of questions begin to bombard me all at once.

"What about you, Inessa? How has the king treated you?" I ask, my eyes doing their own inspection of her, needing to make sure no harm has come to her.

But as I examine her more closely, new questions begin to form.

Her raven hair smells like her favorite lilac flowers, as if she's seen more than one bath since we arrived. She looks just as strong and fearless as ever, her cheeks pink with good health and nourishment. She's even wearing one of her favorite green gowns with sapphire jewels at the waist, looking like she's taken court here. Inessa doesn't look like a prisoner—she looks like a guest.

"How are you here, Inessa?" I ask, adding to the slew of questions I've already asked her.

"I'm alright, Your Grace. And to answer your question on why I'm here, it was King Atlas who gave me permission to stay with you while you're still recovering. He said he had spent enough of his precious time babysitting you as it is and that someone else should do the job. I've never met a pricklier king, and that's coming from me. Out of all your men, I dislike him the most."

"He's not mine," I chastise sharply, my cheeks blushing at the absurd insinuation. "Just tell me what has happened since we last parted," I demand urgently. "Are my people safe? How long have we been here? And why do you look like a guest rather than a hostage?"

"Easy there, Kat. We have plenty of time to discuss all of this. First, you should break your fast and eat something."

I shake my head and place my hand over hers on the bed.

"Food can wait, Inessa. This cannot. I need to know exactly what has happened since we last saw each other."

"Very well," she answers sullenly. "But it brings me no joy being the bearer of such dire news. What do you want to know first?"

"Are my people okay? Are they alive, or has Atlas killed them all?" I question, holding my breath for the inevitable answer that he may have killed everyone on the train except for the pair of us.

"Out of the fifty souls you brought on this journey, only two soldiers have gone to the gods. The ones who wielded their swords to protect you at the feast," she starts, saddened. "Everyone else is currently stationed in a dungeon, waiting for the king's justice. He's given them all an option to spare their lives. If they vow their loyalty to the west, then they shall be pardoned. If not, then I fear their death is all but guaranteed."

Damn the gods.

"Has anyone taken Atlas's hospitable offer yet?" I ask, fearing that all of them will perish if they remain loyal to me.

"A few. Mostly young girls and boys," she answers with a disappointed glower.

"Do not be cross with them." I smile, thankful that a few are now safe. "I hold them no malice for wanting to live and see another day."

"Well, I do. Cowards, the lot of them," she grumbles, unpleased that anyone would be disloyal to me, even when faced with sure death.

"Not everyone is like you, sweet friend. Which is why I'm so confused to see you here at my bedside, donned in your finest garments no less."

"To tell you the truth, I'm not sure either," she says, sounding just as baffled as I am. "At first, I thought he pulled me out of the dungeon to gain intel on you, but he has yet to interrogate me. Aside from an awkward dinner we shared one night, we've only been in the same room once. Today was the second time I saw him and only for the few minutes it took for him to order me to your bedside. I guess he has no need of me anymore if he can get his precious information right from the source."

"You two had dinner?" I arch a brow.

"Please don't tell me that was the only thing you heard me say just now." Inessa frowns.

"No, of course not." I shake my head, burying the unexpected feeling of jealousy deep into the caverns of my soul. "Whatever Atlas's intentions for us, I'm sure they will be revealed soon enough. Whatever they may be, we'll handle it. I have total faith in our abilities to foil whatever plan he might have concocted." I feign a smile.

"I'm not sure it will be that easy. He's a man with many secrets and… well… the west… they hate us here. They hate everything about us. And though it pains me to say so, for a good reason too," she begins to explain, the trepidation in her eyes clear as day.

She knows.

She knows what my father has done to Atlas's kingdom.

"Kat." Not wanting her to have the burden of having to tell me all the horrors the west has endured under my father's rule, I give her hand a little squeeze to stop her from saying another word.

"I already know, Inessa."

"You do? Everything?"

"Yes." I nod. "The young boy who took care of me in my cell beat you to it. He told me the gist of it. It was enough for me."

Inessa's shoulders slump.

"I'm so sorry. This is all my fault. I felt in my gut that something was off when we first arrived at Huwen. I should have listened to it. Made you turn back or head home instead of coming here."

"You had no way of knowing what was to come. You may be exceptional, my dear Inessa, but even you do not have the gift of foresight. Nor do you hold the ability to spy into the past. We had no way of knowing about the horrors that were done here. Nor can we blame the west for their hostility toward us."

"Aye, maybe you and I couldn't have known, but there must be someone in Tarnow who does," she states with a sneer before collecting herself. "Forgive me, Your Grace, but I would be even more ignorant if I were to believe that your late father did this all on his own. A king can only be that ruthless if he has people around him to aid him in his cause."

"What are you saying?" I ask, completely taken aback by her words.

"I'm saying that most of Tarnow, as well as you, my queen, were kept in the dark on purpose. There is no way the north would abide by such cruelty. We may have ice in our veins, but that does not mean we would stand idly by and do nothing if we learned about the atrocities done here."

I take her reasoning, the fog suddenly lifting from my eyes as if the truth was always there, right beyond my grasp.

It's true.

The north would have revolted if they knew what was happening across the land. Maybe some could stomach knowing that young boys were being forced into battle in the east, and maybe others could live in blissful denial that the south was starving just to keep their bellies well-rounded. But there is no way they could turn a blind eye to women and young girls being taken from their homes to be sold off as slaves. There would have been chaos in the streets of Tarnow, revolution on the tip of everyone's tongue demanding that their king was no longer fit to reign over Aikyam. The kingdom would have wanted my father's head on a spike to appease the millions of lives he so happily sacrificed.

"We have been deceived," I whisper, the pieces of the puzzle falling into place, painting a horrific picture of deception and conniving masterminding.

"Aye." Inessa nods. "We have. *You* have, Kat," she points out strongly. "Your father is no longer here to explain himself, nor is he here to pay for his crimes, but there must be others who are as much at fault as he was. One man alone cannot cause such destruction. He needed help. Help from men who were as ruthless as him. Loyal to the crown, above gods and countrymen, uncaring who got in their way or who they had to deceive to reach the ultimate goal of tricking an entire kingdom into believing their well-spun lies."

"Monad," I belt out my chief of arms' name. "He must have known. To do such a thing, my father needed soldiers to act on his orders. Monad must have headed such an assignment. He has held the title of chief at arms for over two decades. He must have been involved."

"That's one." Inessa holds up a finger and nods. "Who else?"

I rack my brain and come up with a few other names of men in court who would be too willing to line their pockets to keep such a secret from being spread. Despicable little men who have smiled to my face while secretly hating that a woman now sits on the throne. Half of my court is still loyal to my father instead of me, and I have to question if that loyalty was earned or bought with slave-trading gold.

"Otto," I grumble, disappointed when my reasoning spins to land on him. "Plenty of money was earned with the slavery trade in the west. Money needed to be accounted for and then carefully hidden in the treasury ledgers. Otto must have been brought into the fold and told the truth of how Tarnow was suddenly swimming in riches. If there is anyone who could have manipulated the numbers, it would be him. He's been our treasurer for as long as I can remember, and there was no one my father trusted more with his money. He must have known where it was truly coming from."

Inessa nods again, coming to the same conclusion I have.

"What about Salome?" she asks pensively as if she, too, is running down the names of all the suspects in this nefarious list.

"No. Never." I shake my head. "Salome would never betray me like that. If she knew anything, she would have told me."

"How can you be so sure? She shared your father's bed for the last seven years. He must have confided in her."

"No. Not Salome," I snap, refusing to believe her capable of such duplicity.

She cared for me even when I had been so painfully cruel to her at the beginning of her clandestine courtship with my father. And after Elijah's birth, our relationship bloomed from there. Salome loves me as much as any mother loves their child.

Of that, I'm sure.

I'd bet my own life on it.

The same cannot be said for everyone else in my court.

"Okay," Inessa treads carefully, seeing that she's hit a nerve. "If you are sure that Salome was left as clueless as we have been, then I believe you. But there must have been someone else, then. Another woman, perhaps."

"If I'm to go through all the servants my father has bedded since my mother died, we'll be here all day," I grumble in annoyance. "Not that it would do us any good. Aside from Salome, he never particularly took much interest in any one of them."

"Not one?" Inessa asks suspiciously.

"No. Why?"

"Because it doesn't make sense. Someone must have been your father's confidante. If not a woman, who?"

"Maybe he had no use for one. Maybe he kept as much as he could close to his vest so as not to endanger his secrets," I counter with a noncommittal shrug.

"Look at me, Your Highness," Inessa commands, pulling my attention to her face. "I have been at your side ever since your godly mother perished. Have I not?" I nod. "And in that time, we've learned many secrets about each other. You and Anya may be the only people on this god's earth that know my every weakness and aspiration. All my fears and hopes combined."

"As you do mine." I squeeze her hand comfortingly.

"I know I do," she deadpans. "You know why?" I shake my head nervously. "Because everyone needs to share their burdens with someone. Everyone needs that one person who truly knows and accepts them for who they are. You have me, which begs to conclude that your father must have had someone too."

"He had my mother," I reply in earnest.

"Yes, and she brought out whatever goodness was inside him. Now think, Kat. Who could have replaced her? And more importantly, who do we know had the capacity to feed his monstrous ways, convincing him that he was righteous in his actions?"

'Trust no one,' she whispers in my ear. 'Not your father. Not my brother. Not even those three young boys you dote on. Not a soul, Katrina. For even love can grow cold with time, but ambition for power never dwindles its flame. Men are flawed that way and are capable of unimaginable cruelty to get what they want. Even lie, kill, or betray those they love most. Trust no one.'

My mother's last words ring in my ears as my uncle's name becomes lodged in my throat, unwilling to be pulled out.

My father trusted my uncle above anyone else.

I trusted him.

No. It can't be.

'Once my body is cold and buried, there will be no cause to keep him docile and civilized. Especially when even bigger monsters whisper in his ear, taunting him to do his worst.'

"How long have we been here?" I ask, still unable to come to terms with the blatant truth staring right in my face.

"Kat—"

"How long, Inessa?" I forcefully interject, unwilling to believe that my own flesh and blood could be capable of such vicious savagery and cunning deceitfulness.

"Four weeks. Give or take a day," she finally replies.

"That's good. It means that any day now, Levi and Teo will arrive in Tarnow. Once they see that I'm not there, they will head west searching for me, which leaves another month for them to rescue us. And once they do, I'll march north myself and get to the bottom of this. Then, and only then, will we learn who my real enemy is. For anyone who could have aided my father so maliciously is no friend of mine."

When Inessa's face falls, my hackles rise.

"What?"

"You don't know," she murmurs, disheartened.

"Don't know what?" I question impatiently. "What are you not telling me? I am tired of always being the last one to know about everything and anything of importance."

"Better I show you instead, My Queen," Inessa says with a lamentable tone, holding out her arms to pull me out of bed.

I let her help me up, my weakened body still needing to lean on hers for support as she leads me across the room to one of the windows. I lick my dry lips, suddenly excited to see the ocean for the first time, but when Inessa pulls the crimson velvet curtain to the side, the ocean is the last thing I see. Thousands upon thousands of ships, bearing flags from distant lands, all align the western shore. My heart drums madly in my chest as my gaze falls to the horizon, showing yet more ships sailing in our direction.

Speechless with the formidable sight, I turn to Inessa for answers, only to have the hairs on the back of my neck stand on end, watching her beautiful facial features morph into despair.

"There will be no rescue, my queen," she affirms. "Only slaughter."

Chapter 18
Atlas

"I s it true?" Cristobal asks, far too eagerly for my liking, unable to hide his feline smirk from his face.

"Is what true, Cristobal?" I reply, feigning boredom while running over his ledgers, which lists the various weapons and merchandise that he brought with his fleet from Shefcour.

"No need to be coy with me, young cub. I just want to know if it's true what every single soul in Huwen is saying? That you spend your days meticulously plotting the demise of the winter queen's reign while, at night, you torture her in more *pleasurable* ways." He suggestively wiggles his onyx eyebrows at me.

"If you spent half the time you waste listening to idle gossip and focus on your ledgers, you'd be a better commander and king for it than you currently are. Here." I point to the ledger spread out on the table. "You promised me five thousand bows and arrows, and yet my men only counted three thousand. Explain."

Cristobal rolls his eyes as if scamming me should be the least of his cares. But then again, pirates tend to be that way—far more interested in rum and women than worrying about little details like math or swindling a friend.

"Five thousand… three thousand… who gives a fuck?" He rolls his eyes, his black curls bouncing away on his head.

"I give a fuck, Cristobal. Since I'm the one paying for all of it."

"Semantics. Besides, we all know you're good for the money once you've sacked Tarnow. Now come, young friend, and tell me about the girl you have locked in your room," he singsongs like an anxious child ready to devour his dessert.

"Cristo," I grumble, annoyed.

"Oy vey, Atlas." He swings his arms in the air in pure frustration. "Life cannot be only about war and weaponry. Especially when young beauties lie nearby. Have you learned nothing from me?"

"Aside from not fucking the same barmaid his whole fleet has or risk his dick falling off?"

"One time, Atlas," he grumbles, holding up one finger. "That happened one time."

"You were pissing fire for a month. Excuse me if I found that memorable."

"Sometimes I question why we are friends," he retorts with a chuckle.

"Are we friends?" I arch an accusing brow. "Because friends don't try to pull the wool over their eyes and cheat them out of their money or weapons," I counter, pointing at his ledger.

"Yes, yes. Fine." He waves his hands in the air. "I'll give you the five thousand bows and arrows—"

"You mean three," I interject, crossing my arms over my chest.

"Yes, yes, three. I will give you the *three* thousand bows and arrows free of charge with one tiny condition—all I want in return for my generosity is that you let me take just a little peek at you know who. Legend has it the winter queen favors her late mother Alisa's beauty while inheriting King Orville's temper. I'd like to see for myself if the rumors are true." He licks his lips excitedly.

"Oh, is that *all* you want?"

He nods, his catlike smile stretching on his face with the mere possibility of laying his eyes on my prisoner. But with Cristobal, his eyes alone won't satiate his curiosity. He'll want to touch her creamy skin too. Lick it with his tongue. Feel the softness between her thighs with his hand, the slickness of her.

Like fuck would I ever let that happen.

I lean back in my seat and place both my heels on top of the table, crossing my boots at the ankle.

"I must say, Cristobal, generosity suits you." I smile sinisterly as I wrap my clasped hands behind my head. "Tell you what. I'll keep the weaponry free of charge, as you so graciously offered, while you, *my old friend* , get to keep your balls. How does that sound?"

Cristobal's smile vanishes as quickly as his good disposition.

"I was wrong," he curses under his breath, snatching the ledger off the tabletop and placing it in his satchel.

"As we already concluded, you've been wrong about a great many things. Care to enlighten me on which error you're referring to now?" I offer him a goading grin.

"I thought that once you fucked her out of your system, you'd grow a heart."

Now it's my turn to scowl.

"Me being heartless never troubled you before," I retort, my jaw locking in place.

"Aye. But it hurts knowing the young boy I met so many years ago still prefers to hold onto his anger than appreciate the simple beauty in life. I was sure that once you captured who you truly ached for, that would change. That if you just took her to your bed——"

"If that's how you feel, then why come?" I interrupt him, not wanting to hear the rest. "Why help me wage war on the north?"

"For the same reason the other kingdoms have sent their fleets." He frowns in sadness. "Because we made you a promise that we would stand by you in avenging the Lioness's murder. That has not changed, even if her cub has forgotten."

I jump out of my chair and rush at him, my ornery face just inches away from his disappointed one.

"I have not forgotten. My mother's memory is branded to my skull," I growl, digging my fingers into his temples. "Talk not to me about promises when I was the first to vow vengeance."

"You pain me, my young friend. As you would surely have pained Rhea with such talk if she were here."

I take a step back, my nostrils flaring in contempt at his audacity.

"And what would you know of her pain?" I snap.

"I know that she loved you more than she loved just about anything else in this world. I know she spent many a night looking at the stars while out at sea, wondering if you were seeing them too, just to be connected to you." He lets out an exhale and then places his hands on my shoulder. "I know that Rhea wanted you to live a life full of happiness and wonder. She wanted you to find a woman to love and bed and make little blonde cubs with. She wanted you to have a life,

Atlas. This… is not a life. If she saw how you lived now, it would have pained her far more than anything done to her by the north."

My back molars grind at his words, despising the very sound of them leaving his lips.

"And as I look at you now," he adds, disheartened, "it's not a thirst to live that I see in your cold eyes but a hunger to die." He frowns, tightening his grip on me. "Tell me, young friend. Have we all traveled all this way to be accomplices in your glory or to be witnesses to your funeral?"

"Go, Cristobal. We've had enough talk for one day," I say before turning my back on him and pinching the bridge of my nose to alleviate the migraine that is fast approaching.

"That wasn't an answer, Atlas. I will not leave until I get one."

I don't want to give him an answer. Mostly because I'm not sure he won't see through the lie and take his ships with him. The others would follow if he left, and I can't risk that happening. Not when I've come this close to accomplishing my goal. So I give him the only answer that matters. The only one that will mollify him.

"Katrina of Bratsk is the most stunningly beautiful creature any man has ever dared to lay his eyes on. The gods must have wept when they made her."

Cristobal stares me in the eye, and after a pregnant pause, the corners of his lips begin to lift into a glowing smile.

"Good. That's good." He beams, his tense shoulders relaxing. "And have you tasted such beauty yet? Is she as mouthwatering as you say?"

When I don't give him an answer, he looks to the heavens as if arguing with the gods themselves.

"Please tell me you've at least kissed the girl?"

"I'm still trying to choose between hanging her by the neck or placing her head on a spike. Excuse me if neither scenario calls for courtship."

"You won't kill her," Cristobal assures, his wide smile fully planted on his lips.

"Really? Care to make a wager on that?" I hold out my hand for him to take.

Cristobal walks toward me, clasps his hand to mine, and pulls me to his chest.

"You won't kill her, Lion," he whispers in my ear. "You want her too much."

I pull my hand away from his grip and take two steps back.

"Stay off the rum, Cristobal. It's messing with your head."

"Aye, that may be true, but I would bet my entire fleet that before we sail north, the winter queen will have moaned out your name more than once."

And with a conspiring wink, he leaves.

Fucker.

Out of all my mother's friends, Cristobal has always been the one who knows exactly what to say to get under my skin. As flamboyant as he may be and with his devil-may-care attitude, he sure has a knack for seeing the truth in people, even when they refuse to see it for themselves. Maybe that's why my mother liked him so much. Though, right now, I can't think of a single reason why I do.

A knock on the door pulls me out of my aggravated thoughts, bringing me to the here and now.

"May I come in, Your Grace?" Ulrich asks underneath the door frame.

I wave him over and pretend to be busy studying the various scrolls all spread out on the table.

He steps inside, scanning the large library before venturing a word.

"I don't think I've ever seen you work here."

"That's because you haven't," I retort, keeping my gaze still on the paper in front of me.

"Ah, that's right. You prefer to conduct business in your bedchambers. But seeing as it's currently being occupied, I can understand why you've had to relocate."

"Hmm," I mumble, not hearing a question in his sentence.

"I'm curious, though. Why haven't you moved the queen into another room? Gods know Huwen Castle has many that can accommodate her."

"I'm quite busy here, Ulrich. Is there a reason for your visit?" I ask, bypassing his question altogether.

He nods and replies, "You asked me to give you a report on the queen's health. As I have just left her room after examining her, I thought you might want to know the results."

This gets my attention. "And?" I interrogate.

"The worst has passed, as you well know, but she should continue to take the medicine for her lungs for another couple of days just to make sure there's no relapse. With pneumonia, you can't be too careful."

"I'll make sure that she gets it," I reply, feeling the small weight on my shoulders ease somewhat.

"I'm sure you will, Your Grace." He smiles knowingly.

"What does that mean?" I counter with a snarl.

Did everybody have a meeting behind my back today and decide it was a good idea to piss me off?

"I'm not sure what you are referring to." He shrugs, his smile still intact. "If that is all, Your Grace?" He bows, the moonlight coming through my windows shining on his bald head.

"That is all. You may go."

He begins to turn around to leave but stops midway.

"Oh, I forgot." Ulrich spins around to look at me. "I've ordered her handmaiden to be escorted back to her room since the queen needs her rest. She's alone now, Your Majesty. Just thought you might like to know."

My jaw ticks with the sparkle in his eyes, but I offer him a curt nod just the same.

After he leaves the room, I let out an exhale, suddenly feeling exhausted with the day's workload. I knew from the get-go that preparing for war would be a tiresome endeavor. Yet, I always assumed that my zealous eagerness to see the north burn would energize me. But then again, I have spent most of my nights tending to the hostage currently tucked in my bed.

Fuck.

Ulrich is right.

There are plenty of rooms in my castle that I can keep her in. There's no need for her to spend whatever limited time she has on this earth in my room.

'She's alone now, Your Majesty. Just thought you might like to know.'

It is late. A few hours of sleep will do me good.

Fuck it.

Not wanting to second guess myself, I head toward the door and begin walking the corridors up to my bedroom. I pass by a few servants and soldiers alike, each one with a different expression on their faces as they greet me. Some of my men think I should have let her die in that dungeon cell, while others take pride in my depraved ways. These believe that I've taken her to the brink of death only to bring her back to health and have more time to torture her. Then there are those few souls that believe I'm doing to her what many of our fallen sisters had to endure on foreign soil. That leaves a bad taste in my mouth that they believe me capable of such a monstrous act. I may no longer have a soul, but there are just some lines that even I refuse to cross.

When I finally reach my chambers, I place my hand on the knob, only to freeze in place. I lean in and listen for any sign of life coming from inside the room. After making sure that none can be heard, I open the door and walk in, only to find the bane of my existence looking fucking majestic in a simple white slip of a sleeping gown, staring out a window.

"I thought you'd be asleep by now," I grumble, closing the door behind me and alerting her of my presence.

When she doesn't turn around, obviously preferring to ignore me, I do the same. But when I begin to walk over to the other side of the bed, she turns and stops me, placing her delicate hand on my chest.

"I want to live, Atlas," she says softly while I stare at her hand, feeling her fingers burn through the fabric of my shirt.

"Everyone wants to live, princess. What makes you so special?" I ask, grabbing her wrist ever so gently to pull her hand off me.

"I hate when you call me that," she replies with the same forsaken soft tone.

"What? Princess?" I goad with a malicious smirk.

"Yes," she replies, locking her gaze with mine.

"You never hated it before."

"That was when you said it with tenderness. Now the word sounds bitter coming from your lips," she says, bowing her head, unable to maintain eye contact with me.

"Do I not have reason to be bitter?"

"More than most," she mumbles under her breath before holding her head up high. "But that doesn't mean I'm any less your queen. For that is what I am, Atlas—your queen. Even if you refuse to acknowledge it."

"All I will acknowledge tonight is how bored I am of you," I retort before trying to sidestep her.

"If that's the case, then why keep me here?" she asks, blocking my passage. "Why keep me in your bedroom, of all places? Why let me sleep in your bed?"

"I was hoping for a little entertainment. I hoped wrong," I answer, trying to pass by her other side, but she quickly steps in to block that side too.

"I want to live, Atlas," she repeats with steel resolve, this time placing both of her palms on my chest.

I grind my teeth and take a step back, her arms instantly falling to her sides.

"Give me one good reason why I should let you?" I ask, crossing my arms over my chest to create a barrier between us. Still, the damn woman won't give me an ounce of space as she eats up the small gap between us until her slender frame is all but a hairbreadth away from mine.

"Because..." she starts, licking her dry lips, coaxing my gaze onto her decadent mouth. "Because I will personally avenge all the souls that have been stolen from you.

My lips form a sneer as I push her away from me.

"I'll do just fine on my own," I growl, losing my patience with her.

180

"Maybe," she counters loudly behind my back as I walk toward my side of the bed. "With the vast army you have at your disposal, I'm inclined to believe you."

I smile ominously when her gaze flicks toward the window. It was only a matter of time before she saw all the ships carrying men and weaponry that I intended to use against her.

"Then I ask you the question again—why should I let you live when your death is far more meaningful?"

"Because I am the Queen of Aikyam," she replies steadfastly. "Not just of Tarnow, but of Arkøya, of Nas Lead, and of Huwen. I am the queen of the north, east, south, and west, Atlas. What has been done to all kingdoms has been done to me. And I should be the one to avenge such cruelty. To right the wrongs of my father and bring my kingdom the peace they have been denied for all these years under his rule."

"Pretty words from a girl who not two weeks ago was locked up in chains. One might suspect that you would say just about anything to keep your head."

"Aye. I won't deny that is true. But I'm more than willing to accept any punishment the west needs to heal its scars."

"Scars from wounds you helped create," I growl, pulling down the bed sheet before sitting on the bed to take my boots off. Silence falls in the room as I begin to strip my shirt off, leaving only my brown leather trousers on. It's so deafening that I have no choice but to turn around and face her.

"What?" I snarl, throwing my clothes on the floor. "You have nothing to say now?"

"You won't believe me either way," she mutters so softly that I almost don't catch it.

"Try me. What won't I believe?"

She chews on her bottom lip as if considering her options.

"Princess—"

"I didn't know," she blurts out, cutting me off. "I didn't know. I didn't know any of it. Not what my father did to the other kingdoms. I just… didn't know," she adds the last part sullenly.

"Liar."

"I am not a liar, Atlas!" she balks in outrage.

"Then you're a fool," I snap, making her wince. "And so am I for keeping you breathing for as long as I have."

Her furious, raging temper raises its ugly head, making her jump knees first to the center of the mattress.

"You want my blood, then have it. You want my misery and suffering, I'm all for it. Do your worst, Atlas. I don't care what you do to me as long as you let me bring the culprits of the savagery done to Aikyam to justice. If my death is still the only thing left that will heal my kingdom, then you can have that too."

I tilt my head to the side, staring at her, and realize she means every fucking word she's saying.

"Tell me why I should grant you any favors?" I ask, suspicious of her intentions.

"Because there was a time when we were friends. When you knew my soul better than anyone." I can't help but scoff.

"Please tell me you have more in your arsenal than that? Is this really the technique you used to fool Levi and Teo to do your bidding?"

"I didn't fool anyone!" she shouts, her silver eyes turning into sharp glaciers, enough to cut a man down.

"No. You just fucked them to get your way."

Her eyes widen in both embarrassment and what looks a lot like guilt, but the complex emotions quickly disappear to be replaced by fury. She quickly shifts herself off the bed, grabbing a pillow on the way.

"You're right. I am a fool. A fool for believing that my best friend might still live inside the empty shell of a man before me. I won't make that mistake again," she spits out, dropping the pillow on the floor and making her bed on it.

I run my hands through my hair to keep myself from losing it completely.

"Just what the fuck do you think you're doing, Kat?" I grunt, balling my hands into fists.

"Oh, now you remember my name!" she belts out angrily, turning her back to me. "Funny, because you haven't said my name once since I got here!"

Curse the gods, but the woman is making me insane.

My feet move to where she's lying on the floor before I order them to.

"Get the fuck up, Kat. And get into bed."

"No."

"Kat!"

She turns just enough to pierce me with those fucking gorgeous gray eyes of hers.

"I said no!"

My nostrils flare as I charge at her, easily lifting her body up in my arms and swinging her onto the bed. Before she has a chance to get out of it again, I pin her wrists above her head, my body carefully hovering over her.

"Stay put, Kat," I growl. "I'm asking nicely."

"Right... like this is nice."

I have to bite down an unwanted chuckle when she rolls her eyes at me.

"Are you going to behave?" I cock a brow.

"Are you?" she counters with a scowl.

"Haven't decided yet." I smile.

She starts blinking rapidly, staring at me like I've grown an extra head, when I realize the smile on my lips is too reminiscent of the genuine one I used to gift wrap to her as a child.

I pull myself off her and roll to my side of the bed.

"Go to sleep, Kat. I'm sure to kill you in the morning."

And with that threat hanging above us, I close my eyes and pretend that sleep is on the horizon, even though it never is.

Hours pass by, and I remain wide awake, turning restlessly on the bed in utter frustration. As much as I try to relax, it feels like an impossible feat to accomplish since the king who has vowed to kill me is almost within arm's reach.

"Kat," Atlas grumbles in exasperation, turning on his back with his forearm covering his eyes. "I'm starting to regret not letting you sleep on the floor. If you continue on like this, then neither one of us will get enough sleep tonight."

I pull the blanket up just high enough to hide the pleased smile on my face. I'm not sure if it's because Atlas has finally succumbed to calling me by my rightful name or the fact that I'm troubling his rest that pleases me. Either way, I'm surprisingly content.

"I'm too restless to sleep," I admit after a long bout of silence.

"You've made that painfully clear."

I turn toward him, placing both hands under my cheek, the rays of moonlight making it easy for my gaze to land on his face.

"Maybe if we talked for a bit, it would help."

"We don't talk, Kat. We argue. There's a difference."

I bite the corner of my lips, my smile always trying to pop out whenever he uses my name repeatedly, like he's tired of fighting it.

"Fine. Then let's argue. I'm sure you'll bore me enough that sleep is sure to come."

"Funny." He fakes a laugh. "No, go to sleep."

"I don't remember you being this stubborn," I taunt him.

"Well, I remember perfectly well how spoiled you are. Always trying to get her way. Even if she has to annoy a man to death to get it."

"Is that what I'm doing? Annoying you?" I goad.

"Yes. Now go to sleep, princess. That's an order."

When there is no taint of malice in his preferred nickname for me, my stupid heart does a small backflip in my chest and dares to do the most moronic thing of all—have hope. Fueled with an idiotic sense of bravery and misguided affection, I inch in closer to him, bringing my pillow to kiss the edge of his.

"You did it," I whisper, my heart beating erratically in my chest. "You really did it."

Atlas sighs before turning to his side, his face now inches away from mine.

"You have to be more precise than that. I've done plenty of things in my life. A great... number... of... things," he all but purrs. I don't miss how my cheeks heat up under his scrutinizing gaze or how his breathing suddenly turns shallow as his eyes take in every small curve of my lips. "What exactly have I done to please you so?"

"You sailed the seas just like you always said you would," I answer him, unable to hide the pride in my voice. And when his stellar blue eyes soften, I melt into the mattress.

I'm fully aware that this man lying in front of me has sworn to be my enemy. That he hates everything about me and wishes to cleanse the world of my very existence, but by the way he's staring at me right now, you wouldn't say that. He's completely oblivious to the fact that the shadows are not his friend tonight but mine, showing me the myriad of conflicting emotions swimming in his light gaze.

It reminds me too much of my Attie.

And for a brief moment, I convince myself that he is.

My palm reaches out to him of its own accord and gently presses against his cheek.

"You truly did it. Against all odds, you did it," I whisper in utter adoration, my heart full of awe and pride that he was able to accomplish his dream.

My heart stops when he leans into my caress, his heavy eyelids closing for a second. Again, I feel my soul soaring into the heavens, the wind of hope blowing at its sails.

"Your mother would have been so proud of you, Attie," I add wistfully.

The words have barely left my lips when his eyelids spring open, the cruel, menacing glower back in his perfect ocean eyes. My breath hitches when he pulls me closer by my wrist, my chest pressed to his.

"My mother isn't here to be proud of anything I do."

"Attie—"

"Don't. Don't call me that."

My chest tightens at the visible misery he's in. I should want to prolong his suffering. I should want him to feel the same agony I've been in since I stepped foot in Huwen. But the gods must have another purpose for me since I'm incapable of inflicting more pain on him than the one he's already experienced.

"I'm sorry. I'm so… sorry."

I'm sure my apology falls on deaf ears, being completely meaningless to him, but sorry is the only word I can find to convey how I truly feel. I am sorry for all he had to endure. For what his kingdom had to go through. But I could spend the rest of my days apologizing for the wrongs that have been done to him and still not come close to the remorse I actually feel.

There's still bitter spite in his gaze, but I don't shy away or cower from it. I let his hate pollute my veins and poison my bloodstream, praying it's enough to ease some of his pain away.

"You're sorry?" he says, with that eerie monotone voice he likes to use to unsettle his opponents.

I nod, biting my lower lip, making his eyes lock in on my mouth again.

"Just how sorry are you?" My brows pinch together at the center of my forehead, my confusion about his question blatantly apparent. "Earlier, you offered me your misery, your suffering, as well as your blood as compensation for letting you live. I'm curious to see how resolved you are in giving up such gifts."

"If they keep me alive long enough for me to make Aikyam whole again, then yes… they're all yours," I confirm with conviction.

That's all I want now.

Just enough time to heal my kingdom.

If he wants to kill me afterward, then it's his right.

"Hmm. Let's test that, shall we?" he coos, his nefarious smile kicking up at its corners.

"Like I said before, do your worst, Atlas. I'm ready for it."

My head swarms with a plethora of ways he could hurt me, mentally preparing myself for the worst.

But nothing could have prepared me for what Atlas does next.

He releases my wrist in favor of cupping the nape of my neck and pulls me to him, crushing his lips against mine. Air leaves my lungs with the brute force of his kiss, but too soon does my shock give sway to something different—something far more dangerous to my soul.

Atlas's mouth molds perfectly to mine, his warm tongue teasing the entrance of my mouth and forcing its way inside. He tastes every hidden nook and crevice, his tongue taunting mine into a seductive game of cat and mouse. And before I know what I'm doing—and against my better judgment—my mouth begins to kiss him back with the exact same fervor.

Atlas's kiss breathes life into my weak body, coaxing it to rub up against his hard chiseled chest. My fingers find themselves in his hair, pulling at the strands as he deliciously tugs at my lower lip. A breathless moan leaves me as I feel his hard edges soften under my touch, the leather of his pants grazing my already fevered flesh, further igniting a flame that should not exist.

And when Atlas bites down hard on my lower lip, my eyes roll to the back of my head with heady desire. He takes his time smearing the small droplets of blood along my bruised lip, teasing and sucking at it until the ache travels down between my thighs.

I'm a wanton mess, needy and anxious for more.

Begrudgingly, I let Atlas break the maddening kiss, his heaving chest mimicking my own.

"Fucking Cristobal was right." I hear him curse under his breath.

I'm about to inch closer for another kiss when Atlas surprises me yet again, pulling my hands off him and rolling over to his side, leaving me nothing to stare at but his back.

"Good night, princess. You'll live to see another day."

The next morning when I wake up, my arm stretches to his side of the bed, becoming immediately disappointed when I verify that Atlas has already left.

"Curse the gods," I mumble, staring up at the high ceiling, recalling our kiss from last night.

I have imagined many things happening to me under his tyrant rule, like being forced back into that dank dungeon, chained and alone with nothing but my horrible thoughts. I have even visualized being paraded naked on the streets of Huwen while westerners curse out my name, throwing rotten vegetables at my head. I've even contemplated how the noose would feel on my neck, the scratchy rope grazing against my skin, indenting it with its mark, before the rebel king kicked the world from underneath my feet.

But not once did I ever imagine that Atlas of Narberth could leave me in such utter turmoil with just one kiss. If his goal was to mess with my sanity, then he's done one hell of a job.

ARGH!

I pull his pillow over my head and scream into it, his lingering sandalwood scent not making it any easier for my frazzled nerves. I end up throwing the damn thing to the floor, preferring to jump out of bed than stay another second in the same place where *it* happened. I begin to pace the room, needing to find something that will get my mind off that damned kiss. My irate gaze lands on Atlas's desk, my triumphant smile finally making an appearance as it crests my lips. I start to open each drawer, pulling out every scroll and piece of paper I can find to read its contents.

Atlas has the largest army I've ever seen. One that the east, south, and north combined will not be able to overpower. There must be some sort of correspondence indicating who all these kingdoms are and why they stand by Atlas instead of me—the rightful queen of Aikyam. It's in this deranged state that I stumble into a small wooden box hidden away beneath his desk. I cross my legs on the floor, tracing the marigold symbol carved at its center with my fingertips.

Whatever Atlas keeps inside, it must be very important for him to go through all the trouble of hiding it amongst his personal things. I hesitantly stare at the box for a while as if there might be a snake inside, ready to bite me if I dare open it.

"Don't be ridiculous," I say out loud, even though no one is here to hear me.

But that will change.

Soon, Inessa will come to check up on me, and if she sees the box, she'll demand that I open it, or she'll do it for me.

I push my irrational indecision to the side and unhook the piece of string keeping the box locked. My stomach twists, and the fist around my heart tightens when I see what Atlas wants to keep secret.

Inside the box is the first wooden boat Levi ever carved for him, looking like it has been recently polished and well taken care of.

Right at its side, there are four paper mâché dolls that I had completely forgotten Teo made for us at a time in our young lives when we still played with such childish things. Each one is branded with the color of our distinguished kingdoms and our names written in a delicate cursive font.

And right beneath the cherished toys of Atlas's youth, a stack of the notes I had sent him through his gifted courier pigeons, bound by a stunning blue silk ribbon.

Every note I have written is here.

Every one, except for the last.

The one that never made it to Huwen.

Chapter 20
Katrina

Sixteen years old

Everyone I love has abandoned me.
First my mother, the plague forcing her to leave me behind.
Then my father, his overwhelming grief making it impossible to even acknowledge my existence, much less my own suffering.

Even my uncle Adelid has been oddly absent from my life.

But the cut that slices the deepest is how Levi and Teo have so easily forgotten about me, not even bothering to send a rider up north to convey their sorrows and condolences regarding my mother's passing. I thought their feelings were stronger than that, but apparently, I was wrong.

No one cares.

Everyone has forgotten about me.

Everyone… but Atlas.

His letters come to me every week, airborne by his majestic pigeons.

It's his words of solace that make me get out of bed in the morning. His little notes of wisdom and courage give me the fortitude I need to go through another day. It's Atlas's kind and beautiful soul that reminds me that I'm still loved. That even from afar, he's at my side, urging me on, being the pillar of strength and the perseverance that I need.

It's because of Atlas that I don't get lost in my grief.

That I don't let it consume me as it has done my father.

I need to stay strong.

Because one day, Atlas will return to me.

And when he does, I want to be worthy of his love.

What a fool I had been. To think Teo was the one my soul longed for when it already belonged to Atlas all this time. It took me going through this ungodly strife to see who truly would stick by me through thick and thin.

It still stings.

And though I'm hurt by his indifference, I can't help the intense feelings that bubble up inside me every time I recall Teo's gorgeous face.

Or Levi's.

They both haunt my dreams.

It's only when I wake up that clarity comes sweeping in, shaking sense into me.

They have abandoned me.

Atlas has not.

"Your Grace," my new handmaiden, Inessa, calls out, pulling me away from my troubled thoughts.

"Yes, Inessa?" I stare coldly at her, remembering why I no longer have a governess, only a slew of handmaidens to tend to my needs.

After Mother passed away, my father beckoned me into his chambers one night. Hope settled in my chest, thinking he wanted to share his pain with me so that we might pass this miserable hurdle together. Of course, I should have known better. The conversation lasted but five minutes, if that. He didn't so much as look at me as he relayed the message that I was now the lady of the castle and, therefore, no longer a child in need of a governess. From that night on, I would have handmaidens to tend to my every whim, as well as tutors to teach me the ways of the world and Aikyam traditions. He then went on to say that his high expectations of me needed to be met and that I should start conducting myself as his rightful heir. Disappointing him was not an option.

He talked of disappointment as if he were the only one to have the right to the sentiment, oblivious to the fact that I have been festering in mine for his recent conduct.

I'd have to be blind and deaf not to be aware of the rumors circling Tarnow. It's widely known that the minute my mother left her mortal coil, my father was all too eager to leave her cold bed to seek a warmer one. He spends his days raging and warring with everyone that crosses his path, while at night, he becomes a ghost, disappearing into the servant quarters only to come out when the sun rises.

I've heard the name Salome being whispered in the halls, and though I have not yet met her, I already despise her. Not only has she replaced my mother in my father's eyes, but she's also robbed any attention I could get from him.

But resentment seems to be my go-to feeling these days.

Much like I resent the raven beauty standing before me now.

Inessa's stare doesn't waver under my cold scrutiny and instead takes a step closer to me, head held up high.

"Your math tutor shouldn't be kept waiting, Your Grace. It's well past the hour, My Lady."

"Are you saying my time is of less importance than Otto's?" I cock an intimidating brow, but Inessa maintains her blank expression, unbothered by crossing her future queen.

"I'm merely reminding you of your schedule and duties, Your Grace. Your time is your own." She bows, taking a step back to the handmaiden's lineup.

I've been given four handmaidens since, apparently, my father didn't agree with me that two were more than enough. There's Kari, Ebbe, Anya, and of course, their ringleader, Inessa. I was already well acquainted with Kari and Ebbe, as they used to be my bedchamber servants, only recently promoted to the title of handmaiden.

It's Anya and Inessa that are new to me.

I'm unsure if they are genuinely here to aid me in becoming the distinguished heir my father so desires me to be or if they are just his eyes and ears, keeping tabs on everything I do. I wouldn't put it past Inessa since she has the arrogance of royalty, even if she is a low-born.

Anya is harder for me to read. Like her wild red hair, her personality is quite untamable, always speaking out of turn and uttering the silliest things, which usually lands her in a world of trouble with Inessa. But it's the genuine smile that is always planted on her face, that almost makes me believe she cares for me. But I have been fooled before, and it would set a bad precedent if even my handmaidens could so easily deceive me.

"Thank you, Inessa, for the reminder," I reply curtly. "Otto can wait just a while longer. I need to do something first."

Sitting in my desk chair, I pull out a small parchment of paper from a drawer, retrieving the ink and quill as well, only to stop when my handmaidens begin to whisper behind me.

"What was that?" I ask sternly, turning my attention back to them.

"Nothing, Your Grace. Please continue," Inessa speaks on their behalf.

"That wasn't nothing. It's obvious that you were all literally whispering behind my back. Now, what was it?"

Inessa opens her mouth to placate my temper, but Anya beats her to the punch, taking a step forward.

"It was me you heard whispering, Your Highness," she admits, unembarrassed for being caught. "I was just telling Inessa to loosen up a little. That you writing to your boyfriend is far more important than being stuck in a dusty library being bored to death by all those ledgers and numbers." She pretends to yawn to push her point across.

"Anya!" Inessa scolds, pulling her by the sleeve and forcing her back in line.

My cheeks heat up at her insinuation that Atlas is my boyfriend.

"I'm sorry, Your Grace. Anya doesn't seem to have learned her place yet," Inessa chastises, side-eyeing her friend.

Instead of reprimanding the redhead, I turn my back to the group of girls, my hand shaking as I pick up the quill.

Is Atlas my boyfriend?

Can a princess even have one?

I shake that nonsense out of my head as quickly as it came.

Of course, I can't.

I'm to be betrothed to a prince of my father's choosing.

And Atlas, for all his wonderful attributes, will not be on my father's list of acceptable suitors. Atlas's ill health prevents him from being on any list a king would make for their daughter. Why marry their child to someone whose days are numbered on this earth?

But then again, aren't we all that fragile?

Can anyone truly know their death date?

My own dear mother was in the prime of her life when the gods decided to take her from us. Who is to know when any of us will join her?

It's true. Maybe my father wouldn't approve of such a match between Atlas and me, but that doesn't mean my feelings for him are any less valid. Any less real.

Time is short for all of us.

And because it is, we shouldn't waste it hiding our true feelings from the people we love most.

With new resolve, I pick up the quail feather and dip it in ink.

If there was a world where I could be yours, would you have me?
Would you love me with the same intensity that I pray you do now?
Because I would, Attie.
I would have you.
I would keep you.
I would love you.
Always.
K

The parchment in my hands trembles as I blow onto it, drying the fresh ink.

It is awfully frightening to write down such words, being that vulnerable and exposed to another human being. But my tense muscles begin to relax when I remember who they are meant for—Atlas. He will keep such words of love a secret and will cherish them all the same.

For that is what we do for each other, be strong when the other cannot.

My smile crests widely across my lips as I jump out of my seat and rush out of the room, toward the horse stables where Atlas' carrier pigeons have made their home. I don't slow my steps for the handmaidens, too excited to send my love note to my blue-eyed prince.

With each step I take, there is this nagging tug at my heart that screams out for being disloyal to Teo's love. It loosens slightly when I inwardly yell at it that Teo has forsaken me and that I do not owe him such loyalty. But just as I clear my mind of Teo, Levi's strong, masculine face flashes before my eyes as I continue to run through the castle's corridors. Again, I bash the image away, telling myself that a man like Levi is probably entertaining himself with women his own age right now. Women that are far more experienced, and that's why he's forgotten about me.

No.

Atlas is the only one that deserves my affection.

His love for me isn't conditional.

It isn't vain or superficial.

It's deep and raw. Stronger than any distance that can stand in our way.

My soul sings with the epiphany, needing him to urgently know that I feel the same.

The cold winter wind cools my flushed cheeks as I dash toward the stables to find the dovecot. I gently pick up a pigeon as Atlas taught me and wrap my note to its leg, binding it with string. I give the bird a little pet on its head and whisper in its ear, "Be safe, sweet thing. Come home soon with news of my love."

I walk back to the courtyard and open my palms, the bird instantly batting its wings and taking flight.

"What the hell are you doing, Katrina?!" I hear a familiar voice shouting behind me.

I turn around and see my uncle Adelid jump off his horse, pulling his crossbow from his back. I watch in horror as my uncle pulls back the shaft on his bow and aims it at the sky, the steel arrowhead slicing the pigeon mid-flight, his small body plummeting to the snow-filled ground.

"NO!" I scream as Inessa and Anya pull me back from my irate uncle.

"Stupid, stupid child!" he scolds, throwing the crossbow on the ground and marching toward me.

"What have you done?" I sob hysterically.

"What have I done? What have I done? What have *you* done, niece?" he castigates, pulling me away from Inessa and Anya just to shake me by the shoulders. "Do you want to kill us all, niece? Is that your intent?"

"What?" I stammer, confused by his accusation. "How can I bring death to our house with a note to a friend, uncle? Tell me how?!"

His angry features school themselves into softening, but his silver eyes still hold fury in them.

"Your father is at fault here. I shouldn't be so harsh on you when he's the one to keep you in the dark. Apologies, dear niece. I did not mean to hurt you."

"You killed my bird," I continue to sob, pained that my Attie will never read my love note.

"Aye, I did. And I'll have to kill the others you have hidden in the stables."

My eyes widen in outrage.

"What? No! You can't!"

"I can and I will, Katrina. Your father has given me the task of protecting Tarnow at all costs. Your birds are too much of a risk."

"How? How are they a risk? They are just birds!" I shout, using my balled-up fists to punch his chest.

"Those carrier birds carry much more than just little notes between friends. Like vermin, they carry diseases too. They are nothing but rats with wings, spreading death all throughout the land. I wouldn't be surprised to learn they were the culprits behind my beloved sister's death since they arrived at the same time she fell ill."

I shake my head, unwilling to believe that Atlas's thoughtful gift was what made my mother sick. She had no contact with them at all. And how does my uncle know about the carrier pigeons and when they arrived in Tarnow anyway?

Seeing all the unanswered questions I have swimming in my gaze, my uncle pulls me to the side, away from the handmaidens and any other ears that may want to eavesdrop on our conversation. Though I'm still furious at him as well as hurt, I let him lead me onto a nearby bench. He sweeps the snow off it and then pulls off his coat, spreading it across the bench before urging me to sit down.

"I have been so consumed with work these past few months that we haven't had a chance to talk." He smiles, grabbing my hand in his. "And there is much to be said, I'm afraid. Against your father's wishes, I'm going to confide in you, for I believe you are stronger than he gives you credit for."

I wipe the tears away from my eyes and swallow down my misery, sensing that whatever my uncle wants to tell me is extremely important.

"What is it, uncle?"

His forehead creases in sorrow as I inch closer to him.

"I'm afraid that a plague has fallen on our land, sweet niece. The same one that stole my sister—your beloved mother—away from us has also taken more precious lives in its wake."

The hairs on my neck stand on end as I wait for him to tell me who else I love has perished.

"King Krystiyan of Thezmaer and his lady wife, Queen Daryna, have both fallen victim to it. Queen Nahla has also died, though news of her cause of death is still unclear. However, it's a safe bet to say the dark plague is responsible for her untimely demise too."

"Oh, by the gods! Levi! Teo!" I shout, my heart shattering for them.

"Aye, the princes are well, even if in mourning for the loss of their loved ones. But that's not all," he continues on. "It seems the plague has also reached western shores, to which the Lioness of Narberth has fallen ill."

Atlas!

"But... Atlas didn't mention anything in his letters that his mother was sick," I mutter more to myself than to my uncle.

"The young prince probably didn't want to worry you. You've been grieving yourself. He most likely didn't want to pile onto your suffering."

I don't want my love and soul to feel the same pain I'm in. If his mother were to die, I'm not sure Attie could cope with it.

"What can we do? There must be something we can do?" I beg, needing to protect Atlas from the pain of losing a parent.

My uncle's tender smile widens as he engulfs his arm around my shoulder and pulls me into a side embrace.

"King Faustus, in his wisdom, has sent Queen Rhea to a nunnery in the northern mountains of Cleinia just at our border, where our best physicians await her in the hopes that we can save her. We can't risk her coming here to Tarnow any more than he can risk keeping his queen in Huwen. Your father has ordered me to travel swiftly to Cleinia to make sure the plague is contained in that one spot. Too many lives have already been lost to it as it is. I promise to do my best to keep an eye on your beloved prince's mother and vow to do everything in my power to return her home in perfect health."

I instantly jump into my uncle's arms and hold him tightly.

"Thank you, uncle. Thank you for telling me the truth as well as helping Queen Rhea."

"Of course, niece." He smiles, breaking our embrace.

His eyes then land on the stable, fixing on the dovecot.

"Your birds will have to be killed and burned. You understand that, don't you?"

I nod, even though it feels like I'm suffering their death already.

"Your young prince won't be able to send you any more correspondence for a while. Neither of them can. We have to limit who travels through our borders if we want to contain this plague and be rid of it once and for all."

"I understand." I force a smile.

"Good. I'm glad we got a chance to talk and settle this," my uncle says, getting up to his feet. "Now, if you excuse me, niece, I have a long ride ahead of me."

"Safe travels, uncle."

He smiles again and turns around to head back to his horse, only stopping to call out one of the stable hands to give them the order to kill my precious birds.

But it's okay.

Atlas will find a way to send a word out to me. He's more than resourceful.

Besides, he made me a promise—one I know he will keep, no matter what.

Atlas will come for me.

He will.

I just need to be patient.

All I have to do is wait.

Just wait.

Chapter 21
Atlas

"Y ou seem antsy today, young friend," Cristobal gloats as he fills his chalice with his favorite rum before taking a seat at the table. "If I were a betting man, which we all know I am," he laughs, coaxing the other kings at the table to do the same, "I'd say you didn't sleep well last night. Maybe a certain someone made it impossible for you to grab some much-needed shut-eye? Hmm?" He wiggles his obsidian-colored eyebrows and pretends to bang at the empty air with his crotch.

Some of the kings laugh at his not-so-subtle insinuation, but I don't miss the few who do not find him so amusing.

"I slept just fine, Cristobal. Now can we please continue with our arrangements? We're wasting precious time as it is," I grumble, eyeing the map of Aikyam spread out on the table.

I'm about to point to the safest route from here to Tarnow when someone at the table clears his throat, interrupting my train of thought yet again.

With my hands planted on the table, I lift my head just enough to see who wants my attention now. Regrettably, the man in question is one of the few that didn't laugh at Cristobal's crude joke.

"Yes, Taurasi." I direct my question to the king of the Melliné Isles. "Is there something you wish to say before we continue?"

"I do," he is quick to reply. "I'm not comfortable with the way we are dealing with Queen Katrina. She is still of royal blood and should be treated as such. This insistence you have of keeping her caged in your own bedchambers is unbecoming. Especially to a noble lady who is not yet wed."

The low murmur in the room from the agreeing kings makes my jaw click in aggravation. My tongue runs over my upper teeth as I stand up straight, piercing the island king with my unrelenting gaze while simultaneously silencing the others.

"First of all, Taurasi, *you* are not dealing with her. I am. And excuse me if your comfort about how I deal with my prisoner is not at the top of my list of concerns. We're here to discuss battle plans, not my lack of hospitality."

Taurasi's face turns all shades of the rainbow, but he's smart enough not to pursue the topic. Unfortunately, not everyone is as keen to move on from the issue he brought to the table.

"Taurasi is right, young lion. The girl *is* of noble blood, and we should not push that fact to the side so easily," Halfdan, King of the Maffei Kingdom, interjects. "And though I curse the day King Orville was ever born, my sources tell me that she is not the devoted daughter we all initially took her for."

"When you say sources, Halfdan, I suspect what you really mean is spies?" I arch both brows.

"Oy vey, young cub," Cristobal interrupts with a roll of his eyes. "We all have spies. How else would we keep tabs on our enemies and our *friends* ." He has the audacity to wink. "But tell me more, Halfdan. I'm curious to learn everything there is to know about this girl who has ruffled my young friend's feathers."

Fuck the gods.

Now that everyone has his attention, Halfdan begins to relay his intel on Kat, going into fine detail about her upbringing right down to the day of her capture. Resentful that Kat dominates the room even here, I sit down in my chair and wait for the gossip to end.

"So she's signed a decree that the east is no longer required to send children off to fight?" King Lefevre asks in amazement, sounding just as impressed with Kat's recent actions as all the other men sitting at the table.

"Aye." Halfdan nods. "And before she left Nas Laed, she also signed a law that both the north and the south shall have equal portions of food and that no nation should starve in benefit of another."

"Both acts are commendable and very unlike anything King Orville would do," Taurasi chimes in, finding his voice again, now that he's gained the support of the other kings.

"Did you know about this, young lion?" Cristobal questions accusingly, his carefree demeanor taking on a more serious look.

I nod nonchalantly.

Of course, I knew.

How could I not?

Cristobal and the other kings aren't the only ones who rely on spies for their intel. I'm just pissed that Halfdan's men were able to infiltrate the north when mine could not.

"This… changes things," he mumbles, disappointed in me.

"Does it?" I cut in assertively, needing to take back the room. "What does it change? Will her good deeds bring back the western women that were sold into bondage? Will it somehow miraculously bring back my mother? Enlighten me, Cristobal? Just exactly how does this change things?"

The room grows quiet, no king brave enough to say another word after my enraged spiel. I'm so worked up that it takes me a minute to regain my composure.

"Now that is settled, shall we continue with our plans to sack the north, or will I have to add another enemy to my list?"

This time no one dares to interrupt me as I go over my carefully laid-out plans to gain justice for my mother. Their hearts may have softened for the winter queen, but their sense of loyalty to the late Lioness of Narberth prevents them from going back on their word. Gods know it took me seven years of visiting each of their kingdoms to gain their sacred oaths in the first place. A dangerous feat to accomplish since there were other neighboring kingdoms that were loyal to Aikyam and its mad king. If anyone so much as caught a whiff of my plan, they would not only have alerted King Orville, but they would have also sent their fleets to aid and protect him. All that effort and time spent away from my home could not have been in vain. It was just dumb luck that Orville's heart stopped working the minute it was decided that I should sail back to Huwen to put my plans for war into action. With a new queen sitting on the throne—one that the other kingdoms did not owe such loyal allegiance to—they would be less inclined to meddle with my plans.

Thankfully, for the next eight hours, everyone remains well-behaved, and we spend the day strategizing without so much of a mention of my prisoner again. But that all ends when the kings at my table excuse themselves to go back into their rooms for a well-earned night of rest while Cristobal refuses to move an inch from his seat, his yellow eyes throwing daggers at me.

"A word, young cub?" he says with a disappointed scowl marring his flawless ebony features.

"If I say no, will that stop you?"

"No."

"I didn't think so. Say your peace, Cristobal. I am far too tired to argue with an old friend."

"It pleases me that you still feel that way about me, young lion, for I'm sure that what I'm about to say won't be to your liking."

"Pour me some rum, then. Maybe it will take away a bit of the sting you're about to deliver," I tell him, feeling physically and mentally exhausted after such a long day.

He offers me a genuine, friendly smile and pours us both a glass.

"Here," he says, handing me the chalice. "Drink up."

I hold the cup in my hand and raise it up high into the heavens.

"To my mother. May she continue to give me the strength I need to avenge her."

"To Rhea. The fiercest woman I had the honor to call a friend," Cristobal adds, clinking his glass on mine before chugging its contents.

He then sits back down and lets out a long exhale.

"She was, you know? Rhea was a formidable woman. Fierce as much as she was loyal," he says fondly. "Loyal to a fault, some would say. In all the years I knew her, she never once strayed from Faustus's bed, considering she had good cause for it," he adds with a disheartened sigh. "I met many a king who became instantly enamored with her, promising all the riches she could ever dream of if only she abandoned your father and chose them instead. Fuck. Half the kings at this table are still in love with her and would be all too happy to fuck her ghost, given half the chance."

"Is that why you're here? Because you loved her?" I ask outright since I always suspected as much.

"Aye, I am," he admits with a sad smile. "If it's true that the gods let our departed souls visit the people we love after our death, then I want Rhea to see that I have never left her cub and that I will protect him until my very last breath. She might not have let me love her in life, always so loyal to her beloved Faustus, but I hope she sees how hard I'm trying to win her heart in the afterlife since your father is no longer worthy of it."

"The dead can't love, Cristobal. They're gone. Erased from this world. Therefore, your gesture is useless to her now."

"Then my heart hurts for the living. For the boy I love, as dearly as if he were my own, believes in nothing, cares for nothing except his thirst for vengeance."

"Cristo—"

"No, young cub." He shakes his head sorrowfully. "Halfdan says this young woman you have stashed away in your bedroom is not the monster we believed her to be. That she is making great efforts to undo what her demon of a father did to Aikyam. Now, I know no matter what she does cannot bring Rhea back, but can't you see that the girl is trying? Trying to be the queen this kingdom so sorely needs?"

I thin my lips, refusing to utter a word and give him any more ammunition to use against me.

Mostly because I know he's right.

Whereas before, I firmly believed Kat's attempt to fix the east and south's ill-gotten wrongs was just her manipulative way—of strategically moving the chess pieces across the board in the hopes of gaining favor with both Levi and Teo so neither one would find a reason to dethrone her—now I'm not as certain.

Not that it matters.

It still doesn't change the past or her previous callous actions.

And one thing that the west knows by heart is that actions have consequences.

She won't be able to escape her reckoning—the west will all but demand it.

Even if its king is faltering somewhat.

The west never forgives or forgets.

Justice will be served.

Whether I wish for it or not.

I take a deep breath, preparing myself for what lies on the other side of my bedroom door. If I had half a brain, I would have stationed her somewhere else, but apparently, it's not my head making the decisions right now.

Unwilling to delay the inevitable, I swing the door open and pretend that I don't see her standing by the window staring into the sea of battleships. I rush toward my side of the bed and begin to take my clothes off, except for my leather pants. Those fuckers can't come off, no matter how uncomfortable sleeping in them is. If I were to strip myself bare and slip into bed with Kat, then I'm not sure I could stop myself from having my way with her. Hence why I need the leather garment—a reminder not to give in to temptation.

Once I've sat at the edge of the bed to take my boots off, my sore muscles scream in agony. All I did today was strategize, and yet I feel like I already went to war, the built-up pressure in my shoulders and neck confirming how tense I've been lately.

"Rough day?" she says softly behind me.

"You can say that," I mumble, trying to ease the knot in my neck. I try to rub the ache away, to no avail. I make a mental note to visit

Ulrich in the morning. I'm sure he has some potion that can ease the discomfort.

"Here. Let me help," Kat says as she comes closer, positioning herself behind me and kneeling on the bed.

The minute her hands touch my bare skin, I grab one of her wrists.

"Just what the fuck do you think you're doing?" I snap, my black heart accelerating in my chest with just one touch.

"If you let go, I'll show you," she replies, unintimidated.

When I hesitate for a second, she pulls a Cristobal and rolls her eyes at me. "I'm only strong of will, Atlas. Not of body. I'm not going to snap your neck if that's what concerns you."

I'd have her on her back if she so much as tried.

I slowly release my grip on her but remain vigilant just in case. I try not to flinch when her delicate hands touch me again as they begin massaging my stiff neck and shoulders. She starts gently at first, giving me ample time to get used to her touch. I begin to relax, her hands magically easing the tension away. My eyes close, making the world around me disappear, save for her. I'm lulled into a relaxed state as I listen to her breathing and smile at how it hitches when her hands run down my muscular forearms. But all too soon does my cool skin begin to heat up with each caress and feather-like touch. And when her chest grazes my shoulder blades, her diamond-studded nipples pierce through her flimsy nightgown and poke my back, springing my cock to life. I fist the blanket at my sides, trying to control my body's reaction the best I can. Kat gently sweeps my hair to the side, exposing my neck so she can lavish it with attention. Her breath touches my skin and wreaks havoc on my nerves, rushing blood to my cock. It takes everything I have not to palm the stiffness between my legs and subdue my hard length into submission. By the way that Kat begins to hum, she has no clue how my body is on fucking fire with every little touch.

Or she does, and she's just fucking with me.

"That's enough," I snap, jumping off the bed.

"Are you sure?" She bats her eyelashes and gives me an innocent look, biting her lip when her gaze falls to the bulge in my pants.

She knew exactly what she was doing.

Curse the gods.

I grab her chin and crane her neck back, the satisfied grin on her lips making it impossible to keep my scowl in place.

"You think you're clever, don't you?"

Her smile stretches in response.

I lean down just enough for my lips to graze her earlobe, goosebumps instantly rising on her flesh.

"Don't toy with me, princess. You have no idea what clever games I can play too."

When I pull back, Kat's eyes are just as heady as she has left me.

"Go to sleep, Kat. I'm sure to kill you in the morning."

She does as ordered and slips inside the covers on her side of the bed. I blow out all the candles in the room, shrouding us in darkness, save for the moonlight streaming through the window. I walk over to my side, lie down on my back and start counting in my head, only reaching the number fifteen before Kat snuggles in closer to me, like a moth to a flame.

"You made a lot of friends in your expedition," she starts, running circles with the pad of her finger in the small gap left between us.

"I've made a few." I smile.

"How many kingdoms have you seen exactly?" she asks curiously.

"Too many to count."

"Hmm," she hums. "I wish I could see them one day."

"Hard thing to accomplish if you're dead," I snicker but stop when I feel her intense eyes on me.

"My misery. My suffering. My blood."

It's the way she repeats the words from the night before that has me turning to my side, my gaze finding her lips in the shadows.

"Do your worst," she whispers on bated breath, her chest already heaving with anticipation.

This time I don't vacillate, grabbing her by the waist, pressing her body to mine.

"I almost forgot about my gifts," I tease, running my thumb over her fat bottom lip.

"Am I so easily forgotten?" she counters, unable to hide the sadness in her voice.

In one quick hoist, I fling her on top of me until her legs are wide open and straddling my waist. My hand grabs her throat and pulls her down to me, just enough for us to be face to face.

"If I knew of a way to forget you, I would have done it by now."

"I don't want you to forget me," she says, revealing her underbelly.

"Then give me something worthy of remembering you," I whisper, my low, hoarse tone completely foreign to my ears.

My heart beats rapidly as Kat leans further down to place a chaste kiss on my Adam's apple. Her lips then find the crook of my neck, followed by the line of my jaw, all the way up to my cheeks and closed eyelids until her tender kisses aren't enough to satiate my hunger. With one hand still at her throat, I use the other to pull her long, pale hair back and crash my mouth on hers. We both groan in unison as our tongues meet for the second time in as many nights. We're all teeth, tongues, and lips as we give sway to our desire and let it overwhelm us.

Our hands travel up and down our bodies, too impatient to stay in one spot for long. She whimpers in despair when I break our kiss and then purrs when they begin to suckle at her neck. Kat rubs her pussy on my hard length needing to ease the ache building inside of her. My teeth nibble at the soft spot of her throat, my tongue licking its way down toward her chest. My hand grabs hold of one covered breast hard, the soft gasp that leaves her lips like music to my ears. I begin to needle her sensitive nipple with my thumb and forefinger while my mouth finds its twin and wraps my lips around it, painfully aware that she's still fully clothed.

Kat wails out loudly, her head falling back over her shoulders as her rhythm picks up speed on my dick. She is fully fucking me over my pants now, her hot pussy scorching me over the hard material. I continue to suck her studded nipple through her nightgown as my fingers dig into her bare waist, maddened by the friction she's creating on my cock. She pulls at the strands of my hair, causing a delicious burn on my scalp. Her other hand keeps its grip on my shoulder for balance, just as her nails sink into my flesh, successfully breaking the skin.

She offered her misery, suffering, and blood to me, but it looks like she won't be satisfied until she has mine too.

"Attie," she croaks out, dry-humping her way into an orgasm.

She's so close to coming that all it would take is a little spark for her to burst into flames.

I feel the head of my cock leak its arousal as her pussy walls tighten. Her scent is so fucking intoxicating that it takes all my restraint not to free my cock from its prison and fuck her like she deserves to be fucked.

"Attie," she sobs again, her eyes squinting in pain, begging me to push her over the edge.

And to my own disbelief, I'm all too happy to show Kat mercy by biting into the swell of her breasts, trickles of blood tainting her gown. She screams out my name, riding me until I have no choice but to follow her off the cliff, our euphoria a tangible thing that can be touched and cherished.

She falls down on my chest, our erratic breathing taking forever and a day to calm down. The euphoric bliss takes its sweet time to evaporate from my system. Though I'm not bothered. I'm perfectly content with keeping her in my arms for a few seconds longer.

But it's when she places her chin on my chest, looking freshly fucked and so goddamn beautiful, that reality seeps back into me.

"Attie," she starts, but I place a finger at the center of her lips, stopping her from saying another word.

"Good night, princess. You'll live to see another day."

A delicious shiver runs down my spine, and I instantly smile at my body's reaction.

I don't have to see Atlas to feel him standing outside his bedroom door as if he needed some time alone to mentally prepare himself for battle. But it's not the threat of an army that has him so frazzled. It's not the prospect of coming face to face with soldiers, all geared up in their coats of mail and holding sharp swords, that has him hesitating to turn the knob.

No.

There is probably very little in this world that could intimidate the rebel king. However, there seems to be one opponent that he is hesitant to face—me.

On featherlight feet, I quickly make my way to bed and hurry to bury myself under the blankets. I close my eyes and hide my smile when Atlas finally finds his courage and ventures into the room. I only open my eyes when there is no other movement except for the sound of his breathing.

"Are you ill?" he asks, unable to mask his concern.

"No, I'm quite well. Thank you."

His blond brows pull together suspiciously as if not believing my word.

"Have you taken the potion I left out for you?"

"I have. Your physician was very clear on his instructions." I smile, hoping to ease his worry.

"Then why are you already in bed?"

"Well, that is where people usually go when they are tired. Isn't that why you are here?" I taunt.

He offers me a curt nod and proceeds to walk over to his side of the bed.

Atlas is a creature of habit as he takes off his shirt first and then sits down to take off his boots and socks, always leaving his pants exactly where they always are. Those never come off. He then begins to stretch his muscles, rubbing at the soreness of his neck for a second. He must think better of it, though, because he quickly drops his hand while the memories of last night's massage are still fresh in his mind.

No matter how hard he tried to hide it, I saw how his body responded to my touch. His lips may curse my very existence, but his body thinks very differently—a fact that I fully intend to exploit tonight for my own benefit.

I don't so much as move from my spot as he continues with his nightly routine of blowing out all the candles in the room before getting into bed. When he's finally lying on his back with his arm covering his eyes, I hold my breath, awaiting the familiar words to spill from his luscious mouth.

"Go to sleep, Kat. I'm sure to kill you in the morning."

My heart flutters in my chest as if those words signal me to make my move.

"What was it like?" I whisper. "Life at sea?"

"Exhilarating. Magical. Lonely."

The corner of my lips dips into a frown.

"How come? I would imagine a ship to have over a hundred souls on it."

He turns on his side to face me, and I follow his cue and do the same.

"One thing I've learned about loneliness is that a person can be surrounded by a mob of people and still feel its pain dig at your soul. It's not numbers that ease that ache. Sometimes all it takes is the memory of the right person to ease it a little. Does that make sense?"

"Yes." I nod.

Like Atlas, I have spent most of my adult life surrounded by crowds of noblemen, courtiers, guards, and servants, deprived of even one moment's peace. Yet, I've never felt more alone than I was in Tarnow. For nothing could replace the empty space in my heart when Levi, Teo, and Atlas left. Maybe that's why I tried my best to ice their memory away, making my heart rock-solid just so the pain of my loneliness was somewhat bearable.

But tonight, neither one of us is alone.

And if I listen hard enough, I can almost hear the current of energy trying to reconnect our souls together, eager to morph into one, as they always were meant to. I know that it is only under the veil of darkness that they are free to kiss and intertwine, unburdened by the ills of our tragic past. Though Atlas is still resisting its pull, I've more than given up the fight, unable to stay in this torturous limbo a second longer.

"I've missed you, Attie," I confess in a low whisper, my soul sprawled out naked for him, just like my body is under the covers.

"Did you?" he asks, his voice dropping an octave. "How much? Show me how much?"

My hand stretches to his face and softly caresses his cheek.

"My misery. My suffering. My blood," I reply, parroting the words that will surely break his restraint. "Do your worst."

Atlas pounces on me in an instant, and I sigh in relief before his mouth captures mine with his lips, claiming them as his. The weight of his body feels like heaven on top of mine, his brisk movements making the blanket underneath him rub against my sensitive nipples, giving them just the right amount of pain to make me moan into his mouth. Atlas steals every moan that falls out of my lips and swallows it with his kiss. He takes his sweet time devouring my mouth, leaving me a wanton mess of a woman when he relinquishes his hold on me. He tugs at my lower lip before nibbling away at my chin, throat, and neck.

It's only when he pulls the blanket down my chest that he freezes in place, his eyes taking in every last inch of my bare skin.

"Fuck."

Still unable to believe his eyes, he sits back on his heels, slowly pulling the blanket down, inch by tortuous inch. I stew in my own impatient and overwhelming desire, his lengthy perusal feeling almost unbearable to withstand.

"Fuck, Kat. You sure know how to play dirty," he curses.

"And when has anything in our lives ever been fair?" I counter, lifting my knees and spreading my thighs to prove my point.

He remains perfectly still as he watches me fondle my right breast with my hand while the other travels down to ease the ache of my swollen clit. My fingers are almost there when Atlas grabs my wrist, preventing me from getting closer and easing this delicious torture I find myself in.

"Your misery, your suffering, and your blood are mine, are they not?" he says with a nefarious smirk tugging at his lips. "That was the deal, correct?"

I nod.

"Then I shall do my worst."

And before I even have an opportunity to reply, he dives in between my legs and sinks his teeth into my inner thigh. My back lifts from the bed, but Atlas pushes me down with his open palm spread wide on my stomach.

He lifts his head a smidge and pins me to the spot with his sharp-edge stare.

"Don't fucking move, princess. I promise this won't hurt… much."

His head disappears from my view, his nose grazing against my clit before he takes his first audacious lick.

That's all it takes for me to roll my eyes to the back of my head, completely unaware that the worst was still to come. Atlas becomes ravenous, the pad of his thirsty tongue lapping up my juices like they were some exquisite summer nectar. His tongue is soon followed by his lips and teeth, all needing a little taste of their own. His mouth is relentless as it continues to eat me out with such fervor that all I can do is squirm, fisting the bedsheet beneath me to keep me still like he ordered. My legs begin to shake profusely, too, overwhelmed with the fire burning me. It feels like Atlas has set a torch to my insides with the sole intent of seeing me burn from within.

I muffle my cries by biting down on my knuckles, needing a release more than air in my lungs. Atlas takes pity on me as if the gods themselves were coming down from their celestial thrones to whisper mercy in his ear. I feel a pinch at my entrance as two fingers slide ever so easily inside my wet core, curving themselves in a way that I begin to see stars. Atlas sucks the very marrow out of my clit while his diligent fingers fuck me into the high heavens. I scream out my release as if being savagely ripped apart and then lovingly glued back together all within the same breath. I'm still feeling the flame of my orgasm searing through my veins when Atlas bounces up into bed, palming his hard shaft right in front of my face.

"Take it out, Kat," he grunts, making my pussy convulse with his wicked order.

I lick my lips, wide-eyed, at the gift he's offering. But then it hits me—if I refuse to do as he says and pull his trousers down, Atlas won't take things further either. He needs this barrier to keep himself guarded. It's the only way he's found to protect his heart from me. If I do this, then he'll be able to rationalize in his head that he did everything humanly possible to safeguard his fractured soul.

Now that I know what the stakes are, I pull myself together and rise to my knees, unaffected by their wobbliness from the intense orgasm he just gave me. My eager fingers pull at the leather strings keeping his pants secured on his waist, and I salivate when I finally free his cock. My head cranes back just a little, seeing the turmoil and lust all marring his beautiful features. He's hungry for my mouth and yet hates himself for being so weak. There is a plea in his eyes. A desperate plea to end his suffering.

I wrap my hand ever so gently around his girth, his needy veins pulsating with just one touch. My gaze locks on his as my tongue takes one long sweep from base to tip. His groan of pleasure is immediate, encouraging me to continue licking his smooth, velvet skin and tease the crown of his cock. I lap the droplets of precum before wrapping my lips around his head. My rhythm is slow at first, needing to acquaint myself with his hard length, but I quickly pick up the pace, cupping his balls in my hands and toying with them as I bob away at his impressive manhood. His whole body vibrates with need, and yet he refuses to touch me, giving me all the control.

Unhappy with that scenario, I begin to hum, knowing the vibration will set him off into a tailspin that will leave him unable to control himself any longer. His fingers weave themselves into my hair as he starts fucking my mouth with sheer abandonment. I take all of him in, relaxing my throat muscles to control my gag reflex. His cock hits the back of my throat with a decadent and harsh repetition, my taste buds singing with the salty taste of his length. Tears sting my eyes, and I'm becoming so turned on that I could come just like this, with him dominating my mouth.

"Princess," he grunts in despair, so close to climbing the stairway to the gods and tumbling down from the high heavens.

My nails bite into his thighs, drool and spit streaming down from the corners of my mouth.

He just needs a push. And the gods help me, so do I.

I pull a hand away from his waist and find the slick heat in between my thighs. All it takes is a few flicks of the wrists to be gone, coming while Atlas beautifully fucks my mouth as if his life depends on it. My orgasm coaxes his own, and a wave of ecstasy rushes through us as I swallow him whole. His cum is still dripping down my face when he drops to his knees and gives me an earth-shattering kiss. Our chests heave in exertion, and yet no one can deny the smiles of utter happiness cresting both of our faces. His temple kisses mine, his hand cradling my neck as we fall from grace back to the cold, harsh reality of our lives. I pull away to look him in the eye. I get lost in the blue of his eyes and open my mouth to say all the words that I long to say.

But just like the nights before, Atlas places a soft finger on my lips, silencing me.

"Good night, princess. You'll live to see another day." He smiles and presses a chaste kiss on my lips as if reluctant to bid them farewell, even if only to sleep.

I let him roll to his side of the bed, knowing that he needs the safety of the added space between us. And as we lie there, still reeling from what we've done, I come to three conclusions.

The first one I learned earlier after rummaging through his room and finding his box of secret keepsakes. There is no question in my mind now that *my Attie* is still very much alive underneath the rebel king's perfectly cruel facade.

The other thing that I have learned is that he will never take me unless I force him to.

He might still hold the air of a tyrant, but again, that is all it is—a clever pretense to keep himself guarded. No matter how vicious he wants to be perceived, there are just some lines he'll never cross.

And the final lesson, the one that I'm tucking away in the confinement of my soul, is that Atlas still loves me—even if he hates himself for it.

Chapter 23

Atlas

This past week has been both tortuous and the happiest I can recall living. I long for the days of preparing for war to pass swiftly by just so I can enjoy the sweet spoils that my sworn enemy has to offer at night.

As soon as the sun sets and the moon rises, I rush to her side. Like a young boy with a new toy, I spend my every waking hour counting down the minutes until we can play our wicked games with each other.

Every night, they always start the same.

'Go to sleep, Kat. I'm sure to kill you in the morning,' I whisper, knowing those words are all it takes for her to rub up beside me, tempting me with her usual response.

'My misery. My suffering. My blood. Do your worst.'

And gods help me, but it's with great restraint that I don't give in to such an appetizing offer and take her at her word. My cock has seen my hand more times this week than it has these twenty-two autumns I've been alive. Just the taste of her drives me mad as she slips her tongue into my mouth, teasing me to take a bite.

And bite her, I do.

There isn't an inch of her body that my teeth have not marked.

Just the memory of how they grazed her swollen clit as I sucked the nectar straight from the source of her drenched pussy, has me hard as eastern steel.

And fuck me, that mouth.

That mouth was made to turn sane men mad.

However, no matter how much I enjoy our playtime, I haven't let myself take our seductive games too far. An impossible feat to accomplish when just the scent of her arousal spurs me to take all of her. Every time I so much as lick my way up her thighs, her essence floods my senses, begging me to rip the cord and fuck her already.

But even the strongest of men can only hold out for so long, and I'm not sure how long I'll be able to restrain myself from taking what she is so willing to offer.

Each night my will weakens, overrun with desire for her.

And just as I'm close to coming undone, I somehow find the fortitude to stop, hurling myself to the other side of the bed, needing to put as much distance as I possibly can from temptation.

'Good night, princess. You'll live to see another day,' I always say, officially ending our game and pushing us to our respective fighting corners.

I wonder who the victor will be tonight.

Will I be strong enough to keep to the tradition of leaving myself so unsatisfied, or will Kat finally break me, releasing us both from this agony?

Only the gods know what they have planned.

But I fear that not even the gods are worthy adversaries for the winter queen.

When she sets her mind on something, not even the heavens can stop her.

"King Atlas! King Atlas," a boy shouts, running in my direction, successfully hoisting me from all the wicked fantasies starring the winter queen.

The instant he reaches me, he bows his head, venturing a peek from his dirty brow hair every so often, waiting for my command.

"Yes?"

"May I speak with you, Your Grace?" he asks hesitantly.

"You already are." I grin. "What's your name, boy?"

"It's Branson, Your Grace."

"Well, Branson, what can I do for you?"

The boy, now holding my complete attention, fidgets left to right, wringing his sweaty palms behind his back.

"Go on, Branson," I encourage with an assuring smile.

"It's my father, sire. I wish to speak to you about my father."

"Fair enough. And, pray tell, who is your father?"

"One of your most loyal subjects, Your Grace. He's been a loyal servant to the west since the Lioness of Narberth herself ruled our shores."

"Then he has my complete gratitude, for any friend of my mother's is mine."

But my confusion rises when the boy begins to frown.

"If that's true, then why has he been locked up in chains in the very dungeon you ordered him to guard?"

My smile immediately fades.

"Hmm. I see. Your father must have been one of the men responsible for watching over Ka… the queen, when she was first sent there."

The boy nods.

"He did nothing wrong. Nothing, Your Grace. And yet you punish him," he curses while giving me the evil eye.

"Careful, Branson. You are still talking to your king," I explain curtly. "And your father is exactly where he needs to be. Everyone in the west must be made accountable for their misdeeds. Your father went against my orders and treated the queen as he saw fit. Now he's reaping the consequences of his actions."

I square my shoulders to look impenetrable, but the rage in young Branson's eyes is far too familiar for me to ignore. It's almost as if I were looking into a mirror. I had the same hue of hatred bleed from my own blue eyes not that long ago. Where did all that poisonous hatred go? And when did it disappear so completely from my black heart?

When she started sharing your bed, that's when.

My jaw tics as the boy in front of me begs for my attention.

I let out a sigh and place my hand on the boy's shoulder.

"I'm still a fair king, Branson. Your father will return to you shortly. The queen was in his care for two weeks, so he will suffer two weeks under mine."

Branson chews at the corner of his lip, looking unrepentantly displeased with my ruling.

"You know," I say, leaning down a smidge to be at eye level with him, "my brother once told me that character is defined by how we react to those who have wronged us."

"Brother," Branson parrots back, sounding confused, which is expected since I've always been an only child.

"Aye. King Levi of Thezmaer was more than a friend to me growing up. He was like an older brother that I never had. He taught me everything there is to know about honor. He drilled it in me so that one day I could be not only a fair king but an honorable one. Hence why my judgment of your father remains intact. How we treat our prisoners says as much about us as it does about them."

"Your *brother* sounds weak," he grumbles under my watchful eye.

Weak.

Hadn't that been the precise word I used to describe Levi?

The exact word?

"One day, you will come to understand my reasoning, Branson. I promise you that."

"Just like you promised the witch's head on a spike. The west doesn't forget or forgive," he spouts furiously, pulling his shoulder away from my hand.

From the mouths of babes.

"She murdered my mother and baby sister! Her men stole them from us! And you talk of honor?!"

229

My spine goes ramrod straight at his enraged words, taking a step back from the young boy's wrath.

"Forgive me, Your Grace, if I don't find any honor in keeping the witch alive while my father remains in chains for being loyal to the crown." He sneers, spitting at my feet.

I grab the young boy's chin, panic quickly replacing his fury.

It's the fear mixed with rage in his eyes that calls to my old demons, reminding me that his family wasn't the only one to be destroyed by the north.

And how eager I was to neglect all that painful history just so I could keep her for one more day in my bed.

My fingers dig into the young boy's chin as I pull his face against mine.

"The west doesn't forget or forgive," I tell him. "You shall have your vengeance. And so will I."

Fifteen Years Old

My wrist aches as I struggle to write another letter to my beloved princess, urging her for some news about my mother. She's been in Tarnow for the past two months now, and I still haven't heard one word from either her or Kat. No courier pigeon has arrived to reply to any of my letters, and what's more concerning is how some of them never make it back to Huwen, as if they were plucked from the sky by the gods.

It's the not knowing part that has me so tormented.

I can't shake this ill-gotten feeling that something is terribly wrong. My anxiety and fear increase every time I remember the conversation I overheard my mother having with my father and how she accused him of sending her to her death.

I shake that notion out of my head, unwilling to believe in the worst. Still, it's a hard thing to do when the only rumors coming from the north say that King Orville has lost his mind, fully given himself over to his grief.

The only hope I have is Katrina.

That she somehow finds a way to reason with the king and keep my mother safe.

Katrina will protect her.

Somehow.

Some way.

Unless she can't.

Unless my Kat is also in peril.

With that terrible thought burning a hole in my chest, I pick up my quill and put ink to parchment.

This must be my hundredth attempt at reaching you,
asking you to beg your father to return my mother home to me.
But your silence has me fearing for your safety as much as I fear for hers.
Please, princess, please write to me.
I cannot bear another second of living with this uncertainty.
My soul cannot bear it.
A

"SMOKE! SMOKE!" Servants begin to yell outside my bedroom, forcing me to discard the letter. "SMOKE! SMOKE!"

I kick the chair beneath me and rush to see what all the commotion is about.

"What's happening?" I ask the first person I can find, but he just follows the herd of people, all scattering through the castle's corridors like a hill of ants about to be stepped on.

Seeing as no one will stop long enough to tell me what's going on, I go to the one person who is still in charge of this madhouse. I find my father easily enough, as he never leaves his throne anymore since my mother left us.

Not to eat, bathe or sleep. He just sits there, staring into the empty space of the hall's entrance as if waiting for my mother to pass through its doors. Even with all the loud disorder heard throughout the castle, he doesn't so much as move.

"Father?" I ask, slowly approaching him as one would approach a frightened animal. "Do you know what's happening? Is the castle on fire? What's going on? What's happening?"

My father doesn't even flinch at the urgency in my tone, his blank stare remaining intact, as if his mind is too broken to register me standing in front of him. My lips dip into a frown as I take stock of the dark rings under his eyes and deep sunken cheeks. He looks as if he's aged twenty years in the last couple of months. I should sympathize with his suffering, but there's a part of me that feels he's reaping the fruits of his labor. If he had just stood his ground like Levi's father did against King Orville, then we would still have my mother with us, not having to live in this constant uncertainty that we may never see her again.

I step closer to him, my nose twitching at the stench coming from his filthy clothes, reeking of both sweat and desperation. Even sitting on his throne, the king of the west looks weak and frail, in contrast to the fierce Lioness he married.

"Father?" I call out again, this time placing my hand on top of his and giving it a light squeeze.

The unfamiliar affection pulls his attention toward me as he blinks once, then twice, trying to clear the fog from his vision.

233

"Atlas?" he whispers, his voice sounding just as feeble as he looks. He reaches out for me, laying his hand on my cheek to make sure he's not hallucinating and to feel that I'm made of flesh and bone.

"Yes, Father. It's me," I assure him, covering his hand with mine.

"You look so much like her. It's like staring at a ghost."

My forehead creases at the fatidic remark, making me take a step back away from him, his hand instantly falling to his lap.

"Father, can't you hear the shouting? There is smoke, but for the life of me, I don't smell any coming from inside the castle."

His shoulders slump back into his seat, tilting his head toward the large windows to the right of our hall facing our shores.

"It means they're coming," he states, disheartened.

Confused about what he means by that vague statement, I follow the direction of his stare and walk over to the closest window to the throne. There I see what everyone has been shouting about—a ring of thick black smoke rising from a hilltop, not a day's ride away, polluting the air above it.

It's a warning signal.

But warning us of what?

I rush back to the catatonic king, ignoring the cold shiver that runs down my spine.

"Who's coming, Father?" I ask forcefully, and when he doesn't answer, I shake his shoulders and yell in his face. "Who is coming?"

His empty gaze bypasses me altogether, back to staring at the front door.

"Father?! What are we to do?!"

"Now we wait."

Instead of my mother, the north brought an army.

I stand by Father's side on his throne, throwing daggers at all the men in blue rose vests crowding the great hall. But the one that holds my particular interest is Adelid of Leikrland, King Orville's right-hand man and the late Queen Alisa's older brother.

The minute he walked through our castle's doors, he began shouting out orders to the servants, demanding food and ale for him and his men, as if he were the one wearing a crown and not the king who sat before him. To my chagrin, my father said nothing of his blatant audacity and instead told the staff to do as Adelid requested.

For the past two hours, I've been stewing in righteous anger while silently watching the arrogant asshole eat and drink his fill. The fucker doesn't even have the decency to pause long enough from his meal to offer us news about my mother's whereabouts or her good health.

No.

Instead, he forces us to watch him and his men cheer and laugh the night away as if this were some kind of laid-out banquet done in their honor. My patience is at a breaking point, and if someone doesn't tell me where the fuck my mother is, I'm going to lose it.

"Atlas," my father whispers at my side, somehow lucid enough to pretend he's fine in entertaining our uninvited guests. I begin to turn to the side to face him, but he discreetly shakes his head, silently ordering me to not move an inch from my spot. My back goes ramrod straight, and I do exactly as he commands, feigning that my attention is solely on the army in front of us and not on my father sitting beside me.

"Before your mother left us," he starts to whisper with pain in his voice, "did she say anything to you? Give you any set of instructions to follow?"

I offer him a curt nod in response and get hit with a tidal wave of relief that washes over him.

"Good. That's good," my father replies, and just as he's about to say something else, I watch him, from my peripheral, swallowing his next words with the sound of Adelid's boisterous laughter ringing in his ears.

But while Adelid's laughter irks me to no end, my father remains completely passive to it. Almost as if none of this fazes him, and therefore, no longer insulted or hurt by it either. I'm not as apathetic. If I were king, I'd have the fucker locked up in a cell with only the rats to keep him company until he told me where my mother is.

But that would mean I needed an army as big as the one he brought with him.

The west doesn't have an army.

We have sea merchants and sailors.

We have innkeepers and fishermen.

Why would we need an army when the west is meant to be protected from domestic and foreign enemies alike by our sovereign king in the north?

Levi has an army, but even they obey King Orville's command.

I wait for my father to do his due diligence of scanning the great hall, needing to make sure that no one is paying us any mind before we can continue with our clandestine conversation.

But as I wait and scrutinize the room, a more unsettling question begins to surface in my mind. In the mob of men dining at our tables, not one of them belongs to the north or east. They may wear Tarnow's royal blue crest colors, but by their peculiar accents, they were not born and bred in Aikyam.

Which can only mean one thing—they're mercenaries. Bought and paid for.

But for what purpose?

If King Orville's intent was to invade the west with his troops as an intimidating show of strength, then why not use the eastern army already at his disposal? Why hire mercenaries to do his dirty work?

"Atlas," my father whispers, snapping my attention back to him.

I straighten my spine and inch closer to him so I don't miss anything he has to say.

"I need you to discreetly excuse yourself and follow your mother's instructions. Can you do that for me?"

My jaw tics in frustration at his order, and I do the unthinkable of going against it by shaking my head and refusing to do such a thing. I will not flee from my own home like a coward in the night. I need to know where my mother is and refuse to move from my spot before I get some answers.

My father frowns in defeat, but thankfully he doesn't waste the precious little time we have by insisting on the matter.

"Ah, little lion, you are so much like her. Your will is so strong that even the ailing body that insists on betraying you is no match for it," he whispers after a pregnant pause. "It will be your saving grace in the years to come. Of that, I have no doubt."

The pride in his voice is quickly replaced with a tone of regret.

"Don't be like me, son. If you are to be loyal to anyone, let it be only to the woman you love. No king, crown, or country deserves such fealty. Learn from my cowardly mistakes, Atlas. Learn from them, son. And maybe one day, Huwen will have the king it so richly deserves."

Hot tears sting my eyes at his words, but I temper them down with all my might, not wanting the enemy in our midst to see any weakness in me.

My father has already shown them more than I can stomach.

As if the stench has reached his nostrils, Adelid rises from his table and struts over to us, wiping his greasy lips with his forearm.

"Thank you, King Faustus, for the lovely feast," he says with a smug beaming smile, but it's the fresh marks on his left cheek that fixes my gaze. Four deep scratches are now marred on his face, ugly, deep, and red as if some wild animal tried to claw itself from his grasp and lost.

"I'm glad you approve," my father retorts with little feeling to back up his statement. "Now that you and your men have been fed, maybe you can answer me this—to what do I owe the pleasure of your visit to our shores?"

The mercenaries in the room begin to laugh, raising my trepidation with how they all seem to know more than we do. Adelid swiftly controls his men by placing a finger on his lips, silence instantly befalling our great hall. His arrogant smile is back on his lips as he stands just a few feet away from us, elated that every eye is on him.

"King Orville has sent me to relay a message to you."

Hope swells in my chest, thinking he's about to give us news about my mother.

"Our great king is no longer happy with some of his vassals and their respective kingdoms. He feels that Aikyam needs a restructuring of sorts since it's become apparent that the west, as well as the east, have shown him little reason to believe they are loyal to him and only him."

"Only the west and east?" I interrupt, confused as to why the south has been shown mercy.

"King Yusuf, as well as the young prince, Teodoro of Derfir, have more than proven their fealty to the north. Now it's time that the east and west do the same."

"The west has done nothing for King Orville to have doubts about our loyalty," my father affirms with little heat behind his words.

"Maybe not your loyalty, King Faustus," he says, pining my father with his malicious stare, "but what is that really worth when it is not you that the west follows, but its queen?" Adelid arches a brow. "It's a well-known fact that it's the Lioness of Narberth who your people follow. At her side, you are nothing but a weak little man, unworthy of your title."

Blinding fury bubbles inside me when my father remains resigned to his seat after such an insult.

"And when shall the west expect her return?" my father asks instead, bypassing Adelid's offensive remark altogether.

"We'll come to that soon enough," the villain replies nefariously. "Now, where was I? Ah, yes, King Orville's decree for the west," he adds nonchalantly. "Against my own counsel, our fair king believes that you, King Faustus, are still worth saving. And with enough encouragement, you may be able to rectify the transgressions of letting a woman rule in your stead."

"I didn't realize my life was in peril in His Majesty's eyes, nor has he ever had an issue with my queen before," my father cuts in. "Can I ask what has changed for him to see threats where there aren't any? Your counsel, perhaps?"

When Adelid's grin stretches on his face, my father gets his answer.

"I am nothing but King Orville's humble servant. As he expects you to be."

"And how shall I serve this new king?" my father counters.

"I'm glad you ask." He continues to grin. "The king will appoint someone to aid you in ruling Huwen, as it's obvious you have not been up for the task for a while now. I'd offer to stay here myself, but my services are more valuable back in Tarnow. In regard to your fleet of ships, I will personally see to it that they are captained by men of my choosing since your queen's captains don't inspire much confidence, especially considering the precious new cargo we expect to start shipping."

"What new cargo?" I ask, holding my indignant pose.

Adelid's beady eyes cut to mine for an antagonizing minute before shifting his accusing gaze back to my father again.

"This is precisely what I mean, Faustus. You let women and children speak on your behalf, giving them room to ask questions when they are not entitled to any answers. Very disappointing."

With balled-up fists, I take a step toward the prick, but my father holds out his arm and stops me.

"Atlas is my heir, Adelid, and one day he'll be sitting on this very throne, wearing this very crown. He's entitled to more than you will ever be."

Pride fills me with my father's uncharacteristically passionate outburst, and I can't help the smile that pulls at my lips when Adelid's stare turns a lethal shade of silver.

But all too soon, my smile fades when Adelid's enraged gaze turns victorious.

"How inconsiderate of me," he says, feigning sympathy. "I all but forgot that my dearest niece, Princess Katrina of Bratsk, has sent the young prince a gift." He then proceeds to snap his fingers, coaxing one of his men to rush to him with a large box in his hands, tied with a silk blue ribbon. "Well, boy? Aren't you curious as to what my niece has brought you?"

My forehead creases in confusion as I take the three stairs down to them both, wondering why Kat would send me a gift through her despicable uncle instead of responding to my letters.

Why didn't she warn me he'd come with an army to invade my home?

Why did she use him, of all people, to deliver any kind of message to me?

Why now?

"What is it?" I stare apprehensively at the box as if it had sharp teeth just waiting to spring out and bite me.

"As I said, it's a gift from Princess Katrina," he repeats with that sinister smile. "The princess also wanted me to tell you that she received your letters and that this gift is her response to all of them. It should be self-explanatory."

With shaky fingers, I grab the box from his man's hand and place it on a nearby table.

I pull the ribbon and slowly lift the box's lid, only to find my mother's severed head inside it, a knife stabbed into her forehead with a single note.

You wanted your mother back.
Now you have her.
K

I fall backward to the floor, my eyes almost coming out of their sockets at the horror.

"NO!" I scream back, crawling away from the cursed gift.

"Hmm," Adelid pretends to pout. "My niece will be so disappointed you didn't like her present. Especially with how much thought she put into it."

Tears stream down my cheeks as I turn my head toward my father, his blank expression giving nothing away. There is no pain. No sorrow. There is just emptiness in his eyes. Almost as if he already knew this would be the outcome of tonight's events. As if he's spent the last two months preparing himself for this very thing. And now that it's here, he's as dead as my mother before me.

My soul feels like it's being ripped apart.

Even as I close my eyes to control the waterfall of tears consuming me, the memory of my beautiful mother's face never comes, fully replaced with the ruthless image of her decapitated head.

"Atlas," I hear my father call out above my wails of misery. "Please recuse yourself from the hall. Adelid is right. There is no room for a child when business is being discussed."

There is no negotiating in his tone.

I'm both stunned and hurt that this is his reaction to my mother's head being so savagely put on display.

"Listen to your father, boy. It's the wisest thing he's said all night," Adelid adds his two cents.

I want to fucking kill him on the spot, but I'm too weak to move. My trembling arms can barely pull me off the ground, my lungs feeling like they have been torched, begging for air when there is none to have. The horror of seeing my mother's beloved face like that, brutally severed and stabbed, is wreaking havoc on my lungs. It adds such pressure on my chest that I fear I'm about to pass out at any moment.

"Atlas! Now!" my father yells, jumping from his throne for the first time in two months. In three strides, he's on me, forcibly pulling me from under my arms and hauling me up off the floor. And just as he has me on my feet, he places his lips on my ear, my eyes widening when he whispers, "Run."

He then spins me around and kicks my backside, provoking a loud ruckus of laughter from the very mercenary army sent here to destroy us.

I'm in too much shock to go against his wishes and reluctantly begin to walk slowly out of the great hall, my tears continuing to fall down my cheeks, suddenly realizing that this might be the last time I see its walls if I do as he says. If my mother's instructions hold true, there will be a ship at the harbor, ready and waiting to sail off with me. I may make my grand escape and travel to whatever foreign land my mother deemed safe enough for me to flee off to.

For all his cunning, Adelid doesn't give me a second thought, completely oblivious to me heading toward the two large doors of my home's great hall instead of retreating to my bed chambers upstairs. And why would he when he's far more focused on announcing his plans for the new cargo the west is about to export.

My blood grows cold as I hear him tell my father that from this day on, all the women of the west, be them old maids or newborns, will be taken from their homes and sold off to King Orville's most trusted allies across the sea.

"Since it's obvious the west pulls its strength from their women, it's time their gifts be sampled by men more worthy of them. Men with deep pockets that will enrich Aikyam for years to come."

This is the final nail in my father's coffin, all but guaranteeing the ruthless destruction of my mother's beloved kingdom.

With one foot out the door, I venture a look back at my father and see the truth in his eyes.

This is the last time I'll ever see him again.

The north has killed him without so much as laying a finger on him.

And as I pass the doors that will lead to my freedom, I make my own solemn vow.

I will return.

And when I do, I'll bring with me an army ten times the size of the one currently taking my home hostage.

The north will pay for its sins.

King Orville.

Adelid.

And even the girl I swore to love for all my days—Katrina of Bratsk.

Any love I had for the north and its princess died this night.

In one blow, they successfully murdered me and both my parents.

Not content with that, their plans of enslaving every western woman will kill the very heart of my kingdom.

And for those crimes, the north will suffer my wrath.

The west may fall on this day, but soon it will rise again with a king worthy of its title—for I am the Lion of Narberth, and by the gods, I swear that a day of reckoning will come for all our enemies.

For the west will not forget or forgive what has happened here tonight.

The north will burn for this.

On my blood, I vow it so.

When Atlas storms into our shared bedroom, forgoing his usual back-and-forth hesitation of seeing me, I immediately know that something isn't right.

"Atlas, what's wro——" I don't have the chance to finish my question, as his hand is already lodged at my throat.

"I'm going to ask you a few questions, princess, and if you value your life, you'll tell me the truth, understood?" he asks with that emotionless monotone voice that I despise. "Is that understood, Kat?" he repeats sternly, and all I can do is nod in reply.

Sorrow fills my heart as I see that the unhinged king I met on the first night of my arrival is alive and well. I honestly believed that my Atlas was slowly returning back to me with each night we spent together, but it seems I was just lying to myself.

The real Atlas—the one my father created—is currently staring me down, his nostrils flaring with rage.

"When you were locked away in my dungeon, what did my guards do to you?"

His question comes as such a surprise that I fumble my reply.

"I… I… don't… understand."

His fingers tighten around my throat, but not enough to leave their mark or make it difficult for me to breathe. It's almost as if he's controlling himself not to hurt me with his intimidation tactic. It's enough for me to cling to the fragile string of hope that this is just an act and that my Attie is currently hiding underneath this imposing king's frame for a reason.

"The truth, princess! I already know that they refused to feed or bathe you, considering the lamentable state I found you in. I want to know if there is more. If they did anything else to you."

Memories of how one particular guard—calling me every name in the book as he relieved his bladder on me—come to the forefront of my mind. But so does the image of his young, tormented son. The way the boy hated me just because he believed me guilty of stealing his mother and sister away from him broke me in ways I'll never fully be able to mend. Not in this lifetime or the next.

"They did not touch me, if that's what you're worried about," I reply, keeping to myself the truth about the callous treatment of the boy's father.

The gods know I deserved every smidge of his wrath.

I might not have ordered the fall of Huwen and the destruction of so many western families, but my ignorance cannot protect me from sharing in the blame for my father's ruthless actions.

Not only for what he did to the west but for all the strife he brought down to the east and south as well. Nothing will ever absolve me of my guilt, for I should have fought harder for the truth. I should have suspected something wasn't right when the boys I loved so dearly in my youth suddenly decided to turn their backs on me. Now that I have had room to dwell on the past, I see how there had been so many signs that my grief and melancholy refused to see.

I thought Levi, Teo, and Atlas had all abandoned me when I needed them most, but it was I who abandoned them first.

Instead of tearing down the sheltered walls my father had built to keep me caged in blissful ignorance, I chose to let them harden me. I let ice fill my veins and turn my heart into stone to be spared the pain of their rejection. If my father hadn't died so unexpectedly, I'd still be in Tarnow now, completely unaware of anyone's pain except my own.

I wonder what my father's thought process must have been in the last seconds of his life.

Did he really believe that once I was crowned queen, I would follow in his footsteps so diligently?

Was I that cold-hearted for him not to doubt my willingness to continue his reign of terror?

Or was he just as ignorantly blind to the truth as he desired me to be?

The irony is that my father might have been successful in making me as cruel and as empty as he was inside, if it wasn't for one fatal mistake that ensured my humanity remained intact—Elijah.

If it hadn't been for the birth of my little brother, I'm sure I would have forgotten how to love altogether, and my father would have won by creating a monster in his own image.

But as it stands, I refuse to rule Aikyam with the same iron fist and tyranny he was so fond of using.

My reign will not be based on fear or prosecution. It will be based on love. And that starts with my empathy for my people's anger, suffering, and sorrow.

Atlas's dungeon guards don't owe me any loyalty, for I have not given them any reason to be. But I owe them more than what I'll ever be able to repay in one lifetime. I owe them justice.

That stark truth of that is what has me holding my head up high, my strong gaze steady on Atlas's scrutinizing one.

"Next question," I say steadfastly.

His brows pull together in suspicion, not believing that his men only kept water and food from me and did not take other liberties with me.

But I don't waver.

Seconds pass as he continues to stare into my eyes, trying to establish if I'm lying or not. I breathe out a sigh of relief when he releases his grip on me, accepting me at my word.

But before I'm able to ask what has brought on his sudden change in behavior, Atlas walks over to his desk, lowering himself just enough to pull out his hidden box of secret keepsakes. I try to school my features to pretend that I've never seen the box before as he places it on top of his desk and begins to ransack it. My notes fly to the ground until he finds what he's looking for.

"Did you write this?" he asks gravely, handing me a piece of parchment to read.

I feel my forehead crease as I take the letter from his hands. But the second I do as commanded, so many questions bombard me at once, considering I've never written such an ominous note to him or anyone else in my life.

You wanted your mother back.
Now you have her.
K

"I don't understand. What is this?" I hold the note up high.

"Kat, answer me! Did you or did you not write me this note?!" he shouts in utter desperation.

With wide eyes, I just stare at him, seeing how close he is to unraveling. Whatever the meaning behind this mysterious piece of paper is, I know it's of great importance to Atlas. I read the note again in case I've misread it and shake my head once I finish to confirm that I haven't.

"I didn't write this. I swear to you I have never seen this note before in my life."

Unable to keep still, Atlas begins pacing the room back and forth while my eyes remain glued to the parchment in my hands. Whoever wrote this must have been an expert forger because the handwriting looks uncannily similar to mine. I almost second-guess myself into believing I must have written it somehow.

But then I see it—the subtle curve of the K. It's just a little thing that I would have missed if I hadn't been staring at it for the past five minutes.

"I can prove it," I belt out, going to my knees to pick up a few of the various notes Atlas had dropped on the floor in his mad pursuit of finding this note.

Atlas stops his pacing long enough for him to kneel beside me.

I spread out all the notes, side by side, so that he, too, may see the difference and prove my innocence.

"Here. See? The K's don't match. There is a small curve upwards in this one. You see these others? They don't have that curve. None of them do. I did not write you this letter, Atlas. I swear on my mother's soul that I had no part in writing it."

Atlas stares at the notes for what feels like an eternal minute, his finger running over each K to make sure he is not seeing things.

"I missed it," he whispers under his breath, pain and sadness tainting his every word.

I'm about to ask who gave him such a thing when he slides his hand to the nape of my neck and pulls my face to his, crashing his lips on mine.

My heart breaks at the desperation of his kiss, so unlike the passion in his previous ones. There is too much pain in it. Too much suffering. So much so that tears begin to sting my eyes, threatening to spill at any given second.

When he breaks the kiss, he leans his temple with mine, his breathing as erratic as my own.

"I'm sorry. I'm so fucking sorry," he whispers before standing up.

Trepidation falls down on me as I watch from my kneeled form, Atlas's desperate demeanor change into steel resolve.

"I have finally decided what to do about your punishment, princess. One that will satisfy the west and its need for retribution for all it has endured these past seven years. Tomorrow, at noon, you will be taken to the town square, where my people will finally be able to watch justice unfold. Go to sleep, Kat. For tomorrow is reckoning day."

When he starts walking toward the door, my heart stutters in my chest.

I hear the threat in his words well enough. The chance of me surviving whatever punishment he has concocted for me tomorrow is slim to none. But it's not the threat of death that scares me beyond measure. It's watching Atlas walk out of this room and never having the opportunity to tell him how I feel.

How I have always felt about him.

Because even at his cruelest, there is no denying how my soul yearns to be with his.

If tonight is all we have, then he needs to know it.

"Atlas!" I shout, scrambling up from the floor to my feet. "Will you not stay with me tonight?"

With his back still turned to me, he shakes his head.

"My misery. My suffering. My blood," I whisper, needing him to stay with me more than I need air to breathe.

He turns his head over his shoulder to look at me, his face giving nothing away. Except for his eyes—those hold the same longing and sadness I will feel if he walks through that door.

"Tomorrow, my people will have all of that and more. Good night, princess. You'll live to see another day, just like you wanted. If you see another, that's up to the gods to decide."

And on that somber note, Atlas leaves.

"I should have stabbed his black heart with a table knife when I had the chance," Inessa curses out the next day as she helps me into a white backless dress Atlas has provided specifically for today's event. "This is no way to treat his rightful queen."

"It's fine, Inessa. Nothing that will be done to me today is without merit."

She stops what she's doing and stares at me like I've grown an extra head.

"How can you be so calm right now?" she blurts out, accusation heavy in her tone. "That man is about to do gods know what to you in front of so many people, and you look like he's just invited you to tea? How are you not losing your mind right now?"

I smile affectionately at my best friend and grab her hands in mine.

"You are riled up enough for the both of us. One of us should keep their wits about them, don't you think?" I joke, even if my attempt to lighten the mood falls flat on the ground.

Inessa pulls her hands away, her stern expression imprinted on her face.

"This is not a joking matter, My Queen," she scolds. "The west will not be satisfied until they have your head on a spike. And King Atlas is all too willing to satiate his people's thirst for revenge."

"Atlas will not kill me today, dear friend," I state with conviction. "Whatever is in store for me, I willingly accept it as my penance for everything the west had to endure. But hear me now, Inessa, I will survive whatever punishment is inflicted on me. I will hold no malice or thoughts of revenge against the west for doling it out, and I order you to do the same."

Inessa frowns, unhappy with such a command.

"I don't see how sacrificing yourself for something you had no knowledge of will do any good either," she replies, still holding onto her resentment. "The whole thing is barbaric nonsense. You have more than proven your innocence. Why should you be the only one punished for the crimes committed here? Why do you have to suffer for *his* people?"

"If my spilled blood can somehow break the horrid cycle of misery and pain the west has suffered, then it's a noble sacrifice as any other. If I truly want to heal Aikyam and be a queen that is worthy of ruling it, then I need to do this. I *must* do this. For *my* people, Inessa."

Inessa's frown deepens, still not on board with my wishes. But even if she can't see my reason behind it, I know it's the right thing to do.

Inessa continues to help me prepare myself, combing my hair into one long braid while keeping her thoughts to herself this time. I'm grateful for the silence as it gives me time to think.

Although my mind has accepted my fate, not knowing what that fate is causes some concern. My brain comes up with innumerous ways that Atlas may call upon to hurt me, but my gut tells me that whatever punishment he decides won't be more than I can bear to take. And the reason he won't hurt me any more than he needs to, comes down to one—Atlas loves me.

He may not have come to terms with that fact yet, but he does. With every fiber of his being, he loves me. And because of that, no matter what happens today, Atlas will make sure no actual harm comes to me. I will live to see another day because the contrary is unacceptable to him.

Of this, I have no doubt.

Chapter 26
Katrina

I was wrong.

Terribly, terribly wrong.

As I'm led by two guards to the whipping post in front of me, I realize I've made a huge mistake in judgment.

I was sure that Atlas's love for me would keep me safe and that he would find a way to protect me while still being able to quench the west's hunger for justice, but that had been a fool's prayer from the start.

Cold sweat drenches my brow as I get closer to the hooded henchman and priest in charge of this afternoon's proceedings. Once I've stepped foot onto the makeshift stage built at the very heart of the town square, the priest tolls his large bell by his side, announcing to everyone gifted with hearing that the time of reckoning has arrived.

I block out most of what he says since half, if not all, of his spiel is derogative by nature, but I do pay close attention when he finally doles out my sentencing. My heart rattles in its cage when I hear that I'm to suffer one strike of the henchman's whip for every hundred souls that have been sold off in favor of the north's greed. The words have barely passed his lips when the crowd cheers in elation, eager to see me bleed.

There is no way I'll ever be able to survive such punishment.

I may live long enough to suffer every blow, but I'll never survive the wounds.

It's not anger that I feel for being tricked so viciously by the rebel king—it's sadness.

Sadness for the love my own father had taken away from me in my youth. And sadness for the one being stolen from me now by the very man I'm in love with.

I was a fool for believing Atlas's love for me was stronger than his need for vengeance.

A blind, lovesick fool.

As the guards take me to the whipping post and bind my hands around it, I turn to face the crowd, my eyes searching for any sympathetic face I can find. I'm glad Inessa was ordered to stay in her room back at the castle, and that she is spared from having to watch her sister and queen being so savagely beaten. But there is a weak part of me that wishes she was here. If she was, I'd at least be able to look upon her beautiful face and pull the much-needed strength I yearn for to see me through this somber hour.

It's with this thought that my sight lands on pale blue eyes, so light they remind me of a sky on a summer's day.

With all the commotion, I didn't realize that Atlas was right in front of me, standing in the first row alongside men who look too regal to be commoners. His jaw tics as his guards tighten the coarse rope around my wrists, giving it a good tug to make sure I'm secure to the post. His eyes never leave mine as the guards and the priest walk down the small flight of stairs of the stage, leaving me alone with the henchman and his whip.

This is it.

This is how I die.

Gods forgive me.

Just as I have given in to my torturous fate, I watch in bewilderment as Atlas breaks his stance and takes a step toward the stage. My confusion multiplies when the man standing at Atlas's side grabs him by the shoulder, preventing him from taking another step. The crowd is too alive with excitement for me to hear whatever interaction they are having, but whatever words are spoken between them, it's obvious that Atlas won the argument.

No surprise there.

I've never met a more stubborn man in my life.

What is surprising is watching the king—who vowed to ruin me— walk up to the stage and turn the attention to his people. Everyone falls silent, his presence alone quieting the jubilation of the crowd.

"My fellow brothers and countrymen," he starts in an even tone, "I have asked you all here today to witness justice being served. Too long have we waited for such words to be spoken. Too many nights have we dreamed of punishing those who have stolen our loved ones from us. Like you, I have prayed to the gods, begging them for this day of reckoning to arrive. I have cursed the name Katrina of Bratsk with the same venom I used to curse her father, the late mad king—may he rot in the pits of hell," he adds with a sneer, spitting to the ground to drive his point home. "It's no secret I have no love for the north. That the tyranny we have endured was enough to sever all ties of loyalty the west might have once professed for Tarnow. How could a dynasty ever expect our submissiveness when all they have shown us is misery? No.

The north doesn't deserve an ounce of mercy. Doesn't deserve an inch of our pity. The north deserves nothing from us."

The loud cheers that ring out are less hurtful than the words coming out of my true love's mouth. Atlas waits for his mob of loyalists to calm down before continuing his rant.

"Huwen, on the other hand, deserves this day of retaliation. Our painful past can only be cleansed by the blood of those responsible for it."

My chest tightens as Atlas points the finger at me before addressing his people.

"But if Katrina de Bratsk is to suffer for the crimes of her father, then I, too, must suffer her fate. For her father might have cut us down with his sword of cruelty, but it was my father who cast the first blow. He was the one who went against us and sent the Lioness of Narberth to her death. If the daughter is to be found guilty of her father's sins, then the son of your king is equally to blame."

Suddenly, there is a shift in the crowd, murmurs of confusion and alarm replacing their previous cheer.

"Our quarrel is with the north, my brothers. Not with its queen. And if any blood is shed here today, then it will be mine."

Atlas breaks from his stance and marches toward me.

"What are you doing?" I ask, horrified as he begins to strip off his shirt and throws it to the ground.

"What I must, my queen. What I must," he replies, wrapping the ends of the brown rope around both of his wrists, his chest now covering my bare back.

"Atlas," I begin to protest, but he silences me with a chaste kiss on the lips.

"My misery. My suffering. My blood." He smiles softly, rubbing the length of his nose on mine. "They are yours for the taking, my queen. Don't deny me now."

"But I don't want this. None of it," I try to reason with him.

"This, my love, is how the west will start to heal. I need to do this, Kat. And you need to let me."

The fist around my heart tightens at the sincerity in his eyes, but all too soon does my fear kick up when Atlas orders the henchmen to deal out his sentence. When the hooded man hesitates, I begin to thank the gods for their mercy. Still, Atlas doesn't seem to want their gift as he orders his man to strike the first blow or suffer his wrath for his disobedience.

And then I hear it—the unforgiving slash of a whip cutting through the air and landing on flesh.

Atlas doesn't so much as flinch as he yells out, "Again!"

The whole crowd holds their breath as the henchman begins to strike down their beloved king, one blow at a time. I wince every time I feel the whip slash through his skin as if it were my own. Tears stream down my cheeks with each severe strike on his back, and I start losing track of time. The ringing sound of the whip connecting with his back churns my stomach. They come fast now. One hard blow followed by another more merciless one.

It's all too much.

The sound of flesh being ripped apart will forever haunt me.

"STOP! PLEASE STOP! YOU'RE KILLING HIM!" I cry out in desperation, holding onto his hands as his body begins to slide down my back an inch, unable to keep to his standing position.

"Shh, sweet Kat. This will all be over soon," he whispers lovingly, hiding his head in the crook of my neck, trying to conceal his pain from the crowd.

"I can't take it, Atlas. Please. Tell him to stop," I beg, but my love stays silent, perfectly content in taking my punishment for me.

No matter how much I cry and beg the henchman to stop, he keeps wielding his torturous whip on his king, too afraid to go against his wishes.

"Please! Please! Someone make it stop! Make it stop!" I yell as loud as I can, praying that one brave soul will hear my plea.

My vision blurs with hot tears when the crowd in front of us begins to mimic my earnest plea.

"Stop!"

"No more!"

"Save the king!"

"Save King Atlas."

"Stop!"

When the henchman hesitates, obliviously tired and spent from torturing his king, hope flutters into my heart for this to be over.

But then, to my chagrin and despair, Atlas still has enough strength to shout out one more word, "Again."

The cries of the crowd are in tandem with my own as the henchman pulls his whip back only to fling it again at Atlas's already tender and bleeding flesh. His breathing comes out in labored spurts as he takes each blow like they have his name on them. I count fifty more slashes done before someone finally comes to their senses. The man who had previously been standing next to Atlas jumps to the stage and pulls the whip out of the henchman's hand.

"ENOUGH!" he roars loudly. "You've done your duty, as has your king. Be gone from my sight before I use this fucking whip on you!"

The relief of everyone witnessing this horrific ordeal is so thick that I can almost taste it. Still, I won't be able to have the same respite until I'm sure Atlas will survive his wounds.

"The king!" I shout out to the closest guards standing by the stage. "Save the king!"

Atlas's champion rushes to me before his guards do.

"Please, please, you have to save him! You have to!" I shout as they pull him away while his friend unties the bindings on my wrists.

"We will, Your Highness. I'll make sure of it," the man says, but the promise never reaches his dark eyes, as if he, too, isn't so sure he'll be able to keep to his word.

No one stops me as I run after the guards racing back to the castle with their unconscious king in tow.

"Get Ulrich!" Atlas's foreign friend shouts to a passing servant once we step through the wide double doors of Huwen Castle. "By the gods, you assholes are slow in the west! Give him here!" he adds in frustration, snatching Atlas out of the guards' arms and hoisting him over his shoulder.

The stranger takes two steps at a time, reaching Atlas's bedroom before anyone else can keep up. When I finally reach the room, breathless and shaken, Atlas is already on his stomach, the whole of his back disfigured to a pulp.

"Oh, gods!" I shout before dropping to my knees beside the bed. My eyes scan every ugly red piece of flesh clinging to his back by a mere tendril of skin. "What have you done, Attie? Why? Why?"

"Because the fool wouldn't listen to reason," the dark-eyed man curses under his breath.

"He rarely ever does. He's stubborn like that," I mumble, wiping the tears away from my cheeks to prevent causing him more pain in case one manages to slip into his cuts.

"That he is," Ulrich interjects behind me as he walks into the room with two young boys—one holding a pitcher of hot water and the other his black bag of herbs and potions.

"Fucking took you long enough!"

"Apologies, King Cristobal, but my healing potions needed time to stew. King Atlas only told me last night that he'd be needing them. If I had a little more forewarning, then you wouldn't have needed to wait."

King Cristobal cuts his eyes at the bald physician, but he doesn't interrupt him as he examines Atlas's poor back.

"I must admit, I didn't expect this," Ulrich grumbles, unhappy with the condition of his patient. "I thought you, of all people, would have talked sense into the boy."

"As if Atlas ever listened to anyone's opinion except his own. I fucking pleaded with him not to do this, but he felt it was the only way the west would forgive the queen and welcome her into the fold."

My eyes widen at who I now know to be King Cristobal.

"He did this... for me?"

Both Ulrich and Cristobal eye me with sympathy.

"From what I saw this afternoon, you were more than willing to do the same for him. Does it surprise you that much that he'd rather die than see you in pain?" King Cristobal says with tenderness in his voice.

"He can't die," I retort with a pained wail. "He just can't."

"Well, that's up to Ulrich here and the gods. Mind you, my money is on the bald one." He winks.

I wipe at the tears that keep on coming and stare at the man in black robes who is already busying himself cleaning Atlas's wounds.

"What can I do? What do you need me to do?"

Ulrich's gaze bounces from me to Cristobal with a worried frown on his face.

"Pray."

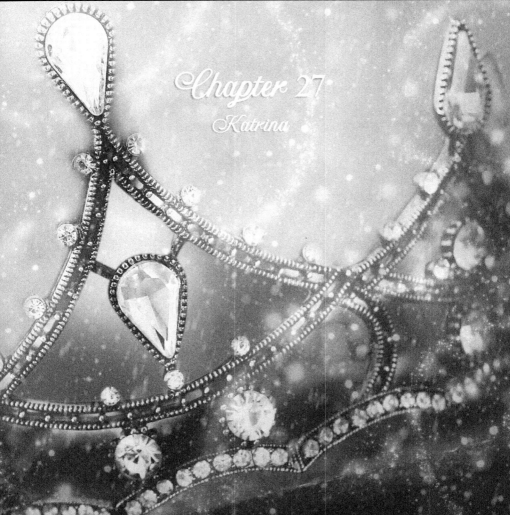

Chapter 27
Katrina

Two days have passed since that horrid day in the town square, and thankfully, just as King Cristobal professed, Ulrich has been nothing more than a miracle worker. I watched in awe as he used a simple needle and thread to stitch Atlas's flesh together. Once that was done, he rubbed his special ointment on the wounds before applying bandages, explaining how its purpose was to prevent infection and to provoke Atlas's injuries to heal faster. Although Ulrich took great care in healing Atlas's wounds, his back will always tell the story of that day. Atlas's scars will be a lasting reminder of his sacrifice, but at least he won't have to carry the weight of his people's suffering on his shoulders any longer.

There has been a clear shift in the mood of the castle and Huwen as a whole. I'm no longer considered a prisoner here and have been given free rein to roam the grounds and corridors. But even though I'm grateful for the west's forgiveness, nothing could pull me away from

Atlas's bedside. I've remained in our room, diligently looking after him and changing his bandages every few hours, just as Ulrich instructed.

Atlas has yet to wake up, though.

Ulrich says that's a good thing—while he sleeps, his body is healing.

But with each passing hour that he doesn't wake up, the more I fear he never will.

"You need to rest, my queen. You haven't slept in over forty-eight hours," Inessa cautions beside me.

"I can't. I'll rest when he wakes up," I explain, holding his hand in mine.

"Your handmaiden is right. Atlas will be livid with me if he learns I let you exhaust yourself this way," Cristobal adds, concerned. "You must not forget that not too long ago, you were the one battling for your own life."

"Yes. And Atlas took care of me when I needed him most. I won't abandon him now," I rebuke with conviction.

"Oy vey, but you two are really made for each other." Cristobal smiles. "Fair enough. But at least take a little break to wash up and eat. Even the young lion did that much when you fell ill."

"An hour at the longest," Inessa chimes in. "I can have a bath and some clean clothes sent to my room so you can have some privacy. The king will still be here in an hour."

"Aye," Cristobal agrees. "Besides, he's on so much poppy milk that I doubt he'll wake up anytime soon."

I chew on my bottom lip, my gaze fixed on Atlas's sleeping face.

"Fine. An hour. But no more."

I almost feel guilty at the relieved expressions on their faces after I've given in to their coercion.

"Will you stay here, Cristobal? And call me if he wakes up?"

"Of course, Your Highness." He smiles affectionately.

I rise from my chair, wincing from the screams my sore muscles make. Neither Inessa nor King Cristobal utters a word as I lean down to kiss Atlas's warm lips.

"Wake up soon, Attie. We have unfinished business to talk about."

I venture one more look at him before I let Inessa pull me out of the room. But as we both walk down the hall that leads to Inessa's room, I can't help but notice the difference Atlas's sacrifice has made. Everything feels so distorted as his guards and servants all bow down to me, paying their respects whenever I pass them by. It's as if Atlas's blood gave me a clean slate in their eyes.

"Just think, a few days ago, these people would have danced over your grave," Inessa whispers in distaste as she fakes a smile to one of the passing guards.

"Hush now, Inessa. I don't want them to hear you say such things," I scold, rubbing away at the soreness of my neck.

"I'll keep my tongue in check if that is your wish. Doesn't make what I said any less true, though."

"Inessa," I begin to scold, not wanting anyone to be offended by her scathing remark.

The west has found it in its heart to forgive me.

The least I can do is to follow their lead.

"Yes. Yes. I heard you well enough the first time. These lips are now sealed," she interjects, annoyed. "Besides, your new friend talks more than enough for the both of us. The man sure likes the sound of his own voice, doesn't he?"

"You mean Cristobal?"

"The one and only. That one is so full of himself that it's a wonder he doesn't get lost kissing his own ass. Not only that, but he's an incorrigible flirt."

"Is he? I hadn't noticed."

"That's because you have been otherwise preoccupied with King Atlas. I, however, have had to endure his company. And you would not believe the filth that comes out of his mouth. He even had the audacity to say that once the north was won, he would take me back to his Kingdom of Shefcour as his prize. A northern rose to add to his harem. It took everything in me not to snap his royal neck right there and then."

I swallow the giggle that wants to come out when I acknowledge that Inessa would indeed kill the King of Shefcour if he so much as tried to steal her away.

"Most women would be flattered by gaining the attention of a king," I instigate, knowing full well that Inessa is not like most women.

"Please. I'd rather give myself to a nunnery than be with a man who loves looking at himself in the mirror more than he does looking at me. Besides, I doubt he will be troubling me much anymore. To cease his incessant flirting, I told him that I was already spoken for."

"And are you?" I nudge her shoulder with mine. "Spoken for, I mean? Maybe by a red-haired general that is fond of writing you love letters?"

"If I'm to hold my tongue, then I'd appreciate it if you held yours," she grumbles, rushing her step in such a way that I almost have to run to catch up with her.

Though these past few days haven't necessarily been propitious for making jokes, I must admit that this small exchange with my dearest sister has been a welcomed reprieve. And after I've been bathed, clothed, and fed, I feel like a brand-new woman, ready to tackle anything that comes my way.

I leave Inessa in her room and walk back to Atlas's bedchambers. As I'm about to open the door, I hear Cristobal's voice in such anguish that I instantly freeze in place, remaining rooted in my spot.

"You have to wake up, young cub. I do not think my heart could survive losing you. Not only would Rhea have my ass if I let anything happen to you, but I would miss you terribly. And I wouldn't be the only one—that woman you have been obsessed over all these years loves you just as fiercely as you love her. So please, for your old friend's sake, wake up. Wake up, Atlas."

I give him a few minutes to collect himself before I knock on the door, alerting him of my return. Cristobal quickly wipes his eyes, getting up from the chair next to Atlas's bed so that I may retake a seat.

"Are you okay?" I ask sheepishly, not wanting to overstep.

"I'm fine, Your Highness. Just an old man acting the fool." He tries to force a smile.

"It's not foolish to love someone. I can tell that you care a great deal for Atlas."

His eyes soften as his stare lands on the king in question.

"Aye. The young cub might not be mine, but I love him as if he were my own," he admits shyly.

"I'm curious. How did you two meet anyway?" I ask, needing to learn every detail of the life Atlas led before I came along.

"That's a story for another time," Atlas mumbles. "Now, if someone would be so kind as to give me some water, that would be great."

"Atlas!" We both shout in excitement.

"Yeah, yeah, I'm alive. Now how about that water."

I can't help the happy tears streaming down my face as I lean in closer and place his hand against my wet cheek.

"You gave us quite a fright," I chastise, unable to hide my happiness.

"I'm sorry for that, princess. It wasn't my intention."

"But tricking me was?" I frown, remembering how he made me believe that I was going to be punished.

"Did you ever really think I'd let anyone hurt you?"

"It crossed my mind. You had done it before."

"And I will spend the rest of my life begging for your forgiveness for that," he counters, gently running the pad of his thumb on my cheek.

"The rest of your life?" I ask, hope swelling in my chest.

"If you'll have me."

We just stare at each other for the longest time before Cristobal clears his throat, reminding us of his presence. I lean back into my chair, giving him enough room to sit at Atlas's bedside to help him drink his water.

"You didn't kill my henchman, did you, old friend?" Atlas asks between sips.

"Believe me, I was tempted. But the poor man feels guilty enough as it is. Besides, you're the one I should be mad at, not him."

"Did it work?" Atlas whispers to his lifelong friend.

"Aye, young cub. Against my better judgment, you were right to do what you did. It worked."

Atlas's smile is so wide that it physically hurts him to maintain.

"Damn the gods, that hurts. Turn me around and help me up, will you?"

"Ulrich said you have to stay on your stomach," I tell him, not pleased with him going against his physician's orders.

"Ulrich isn't here, now is he?" He throws me a cocky smirk as Cristobal carefully turns him on his back.

"Motherfucker!" Atlas grunts, squinting his eyes in pain.

"Careful now. Your great plan still had its flaws. All the bloody bandages Katrina and I had to change in the past two days are a testament to that," Cristobal explains as he tucks two pillows behind his head so that Atlas's back barely grazes against the headboard.

"Shit. Two days. I've been out for two days?" Atlas parrots in irritation.

"What did you expect? That you'd get the living daylights whipped out of you and that you'd be right as rain in no time?" Cristobal rolls his eyes at him. "Aye, young cub, you have been asleep for two days straight. And if we are to go by Ulrich's predictions, then you'll be on bed rest for at least ten more."

"Curse the gods," Atlas grumbles exasperatedly, running his fingers through his long hair. "That doesn't give us much time, now does it?"

"No, I'm afraid it does not," Cristobal agrees.

"Time for what?" I interject, reminding the two men I'm still in the room.

"You've taken a bath," Atlas says, eyeing my wet hair and trying to move off-topic. "I'm kind of jealous. This hair definitely needs a wash."

"Don't change the subject, Atlas. What did you mean about not having enough time?"

"How about I ask Ulrich if you can have a bath? I'll go and find him," Cristobal says, wanting to make his great escape.

"Don't even think of stepping one foot outside this room, Cristobal," I warn, hating them both for trying to evade my question. "What doesn't give you enough time, Atlas? And don't you dare even think of lying to me," I order, pinning him down with a stare.

They grow quiet as if neither wants to come clean.

"Answer me!"

"Fuck," Atlas mumbles under his breath. "Fine. Here it is, princess. My plans haven't changed. The north is still my enemy, and I won't rest until I see it burn up in flames."

"But…" I croak, not expecting such blind hatred to still live inside him.

"But nothing, Kat. You might not have known what your father had done to my kingdom, but he sure as fuck had help. I cannot live in a world where these villains remain free and impugned of their crimes. They need to be brought to justice so that all of Aikyam learns that sins like theirs have dire consequences and that King Orville's reign of terror will no longer be tolerated."

"My father is dead, Atlas. He can no longer hurt you. I'm queen now."

"That might be true, but even you were kept in the dark of your kingdom's suffering. Which means you're not the one pulling the strings. Someone else is standing in the shadows and ruling in your stead, keeping your father's legacy alive and well."

"And your answer is to wage war on the north?" I stammer, still coming to grips with all of this.

"Aye, it is," he deadpans, with no remorse.

"You would wage war on innocent people who had no fault in my father's actions against you?" I rebuke, just as angry as he sounds. "Do you honestly believe that I was the only one kept ignorant of what was going on in the other kingdoms? Tarnow alone holds more than eighty thousand souls within its walls, and I can guarantee you that no one there knows of Aikyam's hardships aside from the ones they deal with on a day to day basis. They can't be held responsible for something they had no knowledge of."

"Just goes to show you how powerful the bastard is," Atlas retorts, his nostrils flaring in burning rage.

"Atlas," Cristobal interjects, shaking his head. "You've said enough, young lion."

"No, he hasn't. Who are you referring to, Atlas. Who?" I shout while my mind goes to every name on my suspect list of possible accomplices.

Monad.

Otto.

Adelid.

A cold shiver runs down my spine as my beloved uncle's face flashes in my mind.

Could he have betrayed me so calculatingly?

Could he have been that deceiving?

"If you have to ask that question, then he's done a better job at concealing his true nature than I thought," Atlas explains despondently.

I feel the weight of both Atlas and Cristobal's pitying gaze on me, and I don't like it. Not one bit.

"I will not let you slaughter innocent lives in your quest for vengeance, Atlas. But I will help you seek out justice for those who have had a hand in destroying so many lives."

"And how do you suggest doing that?" Cristobal asks curiously.

"If anyone is to wage war against those who profited from my kingdom's strife, it will be me. Make no mistake, my lords—I *am* the queen of Aikyam, and it's about time everyone knew it."

Chapter 28
Katrina

"Good evening, my lords. Apologies for waking you all up at this ungodly hour, but I assure you it couldn't be helped," I announce the second I walk into Atlas's library, and what I can only assume to be his command post for the past few weeks, if not months.

"Queen Katrina," they all greet, and I count eleven half-asleep kings rising up from their respective seats to pay their respects.

My smile is nowhere to be found as Cristobal pulls out a chair at the head of the table so that I may sit down.

"Are you sure about this?" Cristobal whispers discreetly behind me.

"Only one way to find out," I reply, taking my seat.

I take my time and glance over every royal blue blood here, immediately noticing how each one is so different from the other, and yet they all came together with one sole purpose of destroying my home.

That's not happening.

Now or ever.

"Any news on the king?" one of them asks, his cheeks turning pink when my eyes fix on him.

"And you are, sir?" I counter with an even tone.

"King Taurasi of Melliné Isles, Your Royal Highness." He bows his head. "At your disposal."

"I pray to the gods that the last part is true," I tell him with an unmistakably sharp edge in my voice. "As for King Atlas, I can assure you that he is in good health. We should expect him to join us in a few days' time when he feels more up to the challenge. As it stands, I will be taking his place and heading this expedition north."

Every man sitting at this table begins to stare in confusion and whisper at each other.

"Is there something wrong?" I snap, pulling their attention back to me.

"Not wrong, per se, Your Highness," another king responds. "Just a bit confusing."

"How so, King…"

"Beg your pardon, Your Majesty. I'm Halfdan, King of the Maffei Kingdom."

"Pleased to make your acquaintance, Halfdan. Now, if you could be so kind as to explain exactly what is the cause of such confusion, then maybe I'll be able to clarify it for you."

"Well, Your Highness, your mere presence in this room is *unexpected.* We have all been called to Huwen in the service of King Atlas to wage war against the north, not go on an expedition as you referred to it."

"I'm well aware of your intentions, my lords." I frown. "However, I've called you all here tonight to tell you that there has been a slight change in plans. Yes, we will march north, but there will be no war waged against it. Not unless we can't prevent it."

This time, their murmurs are louder than before.

"And how are we to take Tarnow without actually *taking* it?" King Halfdan queries with a scowl on his face.

"I'm glad you asked. It has come to my attention that there is a small group of men in the north whose power has gone to their heads. They believe they are the true ruler of my kingdom. And gentlemen, I can assure you that they are not," I explain with such vehemence that even my father would be proud. "When we ride north, I want every man in your armies to know that no blood should be shed except for theirs. I will not sit idly by and watch one innocent life be lost. Too many lives have already been ruined by their greed. I refuse to be responsible for ruining more. Our numbers alone will be enough to scare these men into submission. I have no doubt that they will surrender themselves when we reach Tarnow's gates and spare all the lives within its walls. To put it plainly, I don't need your swords, but I do need your numbers. It's the peaceful resolution I can see happening."

Another onslaught of whispers bursts in the room, this time the kings sitting in front of me having no qualms in showing their hesitance in being part of such a plan.

I let them squabble with one another as I lean back in my seat and turn my head to whisper over to Cristobal, who is still standing beside me.

"I don't understand. They were all ready to go to war, and now that I tell them there is no need for such bloodshed, they falter?"

"I don't think they are seeing the big picture, my queen. You'll need to give them some incentive," Cristobal whispers back.

"You mean riches?" I arch a brow.

"It's what makes the world go round. Do you really think these men would sail so far away from their homes if there wasn't anything they could gain from it? Atlas has made a lot of promises over the years. You telling them that he's inexplicably changed his mind and that peace is the end objective now won't fill their pockets."

"Is that why they all came west? Because Atlas promised them money?"

"That and because they want to see the man who killed Rhea burn," he explains, his own dark eyes turning into a bottomless abyss.

"Someone killed Atlas's mother?" I blurt out, as this is the first time I'm hearing of it.

No, that can't be right.

She was sick.

Sick with the same plague that took my mother from me.

The last thing I remember before receiving news of her death is how King Faustus sent her to the nunnery up in the northern mountains of Cleinia in his last attempt to save his queen. Unfortunately, Rhea was too far gone to be saved and died within a month.

Shortly after, news broke out that Atlas had decided to sail across to the other side of the world, leaving his poor father alone with his grief. Within a span of three months, after being abandoned by both his wife and son, King Faustus passed away.

I remember that day perfectly. I hadn't seen my father in weeks, but I could hear him just fine, ranting and raving like a man gone mad. Somehow, he got it into his head that my uncle had been to blame for the king's death. But I knew better—King Faustus had died of a broken heart. At least, that's what I believed at the time, but now all my memories feel like lies planted in my brain to keep me submissive and clueless.

"Who? Who killed Atlas's mother?"

"Focus, my queen," Cristobal replies instead. "And keep those sorts of questions for Atlas to answer, as it's not my place. Right now, you are losing his army—a fact that he will not be pleased with. If I were you, I'd give these kings a reminder of why they are here in the first place. These men want two things—vengeance for Rhea and inexplicable wealth. You'd be surprised how a promise of jewels and payback can motivate a man."

"Nothing surprises me anymore," I mumble, rising from my seat and gaining once again the attention of all the kings in the room.

"I know that Atlas has promised you the sack of Tarnow. But what you lords fail to comprehend is that there is no need for such violence to be well compensated. I will personally make sure that you'll all swim in diamonds and sapphires before you return back to your kingdoms."

But even after promising them riches beyond their imagination, half the table still looks wary and unconvinced.

"I'll tell you the same thing I told the young lion—keep your gold and jewels. I'm here to run my sword through the man who killed the Lioness of Narberth. He's the head I'd like to see on my spike," Taurasi roars, plunging his fist into the table.

"And so you shall," I promise. "Stand with me and march to Tarnow, and I vow that you will get your vengeance."

Halfdan snorts.

"Yes, King Halfdan? Is there something you wish to add?" I question, my gaze pinning him to his seat.

But the king of the Maffei is not the least bit intimidated by my glower, as proven by how he rises from his chair to look me dead in the eye.

"First, I'd like to say how pleased I am that the young lion has finally come to his senses in regard to your stay here. I was never comfortable with the idea of keeping a woman of noble birth imprisoned. But alas, Huwen is not mine but his to rule over. Therefore, I could do nothing but announce my concerns," he begins to explain. "I've heard a great many things about you, Winter Queen. How your heart burns for justice even if born from ice. I knew it when I heard of the changes you were making in the east and then again with the ones done in the south. And as I've sat here, listening to you speak about taking the north without having to result to violence, I can't help but admire your idealistic nature. Having said that, I refuse to send my men to Tarnow on a fool's errand."

"Halfdan," Cristobal warns menacingly.

"No, no. Let the king say his piece and explain himself," I interject. "Tell me, King Halfdan, is it my non-violent approach to a problem that offends you, or is there another reason why you won't follow me north?"

"Aye, there is," he affirms assertively. "I was all too happy to stand by Atlas because I trusted him. I trusted his hatred. And I trusted his anger. I would eagerly march to my own death if those two things remained on the table. But now you ask me to bow a knee and have faith that you will accomplish all that we desire without bloodshed. And here is where the problem lies. I want nothing more than to see blood taint the pure white snow of Tarnow. I want to see the streets of the city covered in a crimson veil of blood. Give me that, and you have my men."

"I can't give you the blood of the innocent to satisfy your war lust, King Halfdan," I tell him assertively, unwilling to concede to his demands.

"And what of the guilty? Will you give me their blood?"

"Yes."

"I wish I could believe you." He shakes his head in disappointment. "I've heard too many stories now of your good heart to believe you

280

capable of killing even the guiltiest of men. Especially when you've made it a point of wanting only their surrender. Tell me, what will you do if or when they refuse? What action will you take when they barricade themselves behind Tarnow's safe walls and refuse to wave the white banner of surrender? Will you charge then, or will my army's life be forfeited to the cold, harsh winter of the north? Think long and hard, Your Highness, because those will be the only choices you have when the time comes."

I stew in his words as the other kings begin to second-guess their willingness to follow me.

"As I said, no innocent life will fall victim in the north. That includes your army as well as my people. If the cowards refuse to give themselves up to us, then we will take appropriate action." I square my shoulders and plant my hands on the table, leaning my body in his direction. "And the only way I can prove my resolve is if you come with me north and see with your own eyes how determined I am to save my kingdom by any means necessary."

"And if Tarnow falls, what will you do with the prisoners? What sentence will you give the men you have accused of conspiring against you? Will you show mercy and keep them locked up in chains to rot, or will you be the sword of justice that the Kingdom of Aikyam needs?"

"If blood is what you thirst for, then I'll be more than happy to give you theirs," I reply with conviction while my rapid heartbeat rings in my ears at the unexpected standoff with the King of Maffei.

A deafening silence falls in the room as the other kings hold their breath, waiting for King Halfdan's decision, which will undoubtedly affect theirs.

"Very well," he finally concedes, sitting back in his seat. "You have my men. I will remain true to my word as long as you remain loyal to yours."

Relief washes over me as each king begins to fall in line after Halfdan fully commits himself to the cause. But my gratitude is short-lived when the King of Maffei decides he hasn't said all he needs to.

"I do, however, have one stipulation."

"And that is?" I arch a brow, aggravated at this king who insists on being a thorn in my side.

"It's nothing, really. A simple technicality that both King Atlas and I agreed upon years ago."

"If King Atlas has given you his word, then I have no issue with giving you mine," I assure, wanting to silence this king once and for all.

"I'm glad you said that." He smiles. "All I ask in return is that you carve out the heart of the man who killed our fierce Lioness of Narberth and that you hand-deliver it to Atlas and me as payment for my army's service."

"A heart? That is all you want? Not diamonds or jewels. Just a heart?" I repeat, trying to make sure I understood him correctly.

"Yes, My Queen. That is all I want."

"Very well, then you shall have it. May I ask whose heart will I be gift-wrapping for you?"

When Halfdan's smile widens, the hairs on the back of my neck stand on end as he pronounces his next words with such hatred, I almost choke on them.

"Your uncle's."

I close the door behind me and find Atlas in the middle of the room, soaking in his tub without a care in the world, while mine feels like it's crumbling apart.

"By the look on your face, the meeting with the other kings didn't go as you expected."

Instead of piling on to his remark and telling him every tiresome detail of the night's events, I go straight to the root of my misery.

"Did my uncle kill your mother?"

Atlas's blue eyes widen with rage at the very mention of my uncle.

"I don't think now is the time to talk about this," he replies in that monotone voice I hate.

"If not now, when?" I throw my arms in the air and march toward him. "When do you think is an appropriate time to talk about it? How long will you be an accomplice to keeping me oblivious to everything that has happened in my own life? I'm tired of all of it, Atlas. Tired of racking my brain for a smidge of truth when all I find are lies and deception. Do you know how frustrating that is? To be unable to recall one memory of the past and wonder if any of it is true? How maddening it feels to not be able to count on your judgment since it has failed you over and over again? Are you really going to let me live like this? With doubts and uncertainties? Are you that cruel?!"

"Fuck," he curses, holding on to the sides of the tub to keep his balance. "Just give a man a minute, princess. I know you have questions. Believe me, I understand where you are coming from. I do, but can you find it in your heart to give us at least one night to catch our breaths? To just be still and grateful that we are both alive? Can you do that for me, princess?"

"It all depends. Will you be postponing this conversation for just tonight, or will you come up with another excuse to avoid it tomorrow, too?"

"Just tonight, Kat. Just give us tonight," he replies in earnest.

"And we'll pick this up first thing tomorrow morning?"

"Yes. Whatever you want. I'll tell you everything. Just as long as I'm not buck-naked while doing it," he says with a crooked smile, trying to lighten the heavy tension in the room.

It has been a long night.

In fact, it's been a hectic couple of nights.

Atlas asking me for a reprieve from our current reality isn't without its merits.

I'm too exhausted to think or argue right now, anyway. So if he wants to ignore our problems and just concentrate on us for a few hours, then I guess I can concede to that much.

"I see that Ulrich caved to your demands of a bath. Here, let me help," I say softly, leaning down beside him to take the wet, soapy cloth from his hands.

"Thank you," he says, letting out the pent-up exhale that he was holding.

I carefully run the wet cloth over his back, ensuring I don't add any pressure on his stitched-up wounds.

"Talk to me, Kat. I want to hear your voice," he says with his eyes closed, his tense muscles relaxing under my touch.

"You've made a lot of friends. Though I don't think all of them like you," I tease, gaining a smile from him.

"Adoration is overrated. All I need from them is their respect and loyalty."

"Well, you have that in spades," I retort, bringing the washcloth away from his shoulders and onto his chest.

"Hmm, this reminds me of something," he whispers, his voice dropping an octave.

"Oh? Do I want to know what it reminds you of? Have you had many queens on their knees giving you a bath?"

Atlas groans and shifts himself in the tub.

"This is the first time I've had the pleasure, princess. However, it does remind me of the bath I once gave you." He wiggles his brows suggestively.

I can't help the giggle that bursts out of me, feeling the laughter soothe all my worries away.

"You gave me a bath? Are you sure you've not mistaken reality for one of your salacious fantasies?"

"Nay, my queen. It happened in this very room and in this very tub. Your fever might have blocked out that memory, but I will never forget it."

My heart swells with love as Atlas's eyes soften and stare lovingly into mine.

"I never did thank you for nursing me back to health. You hated me so much back then, yet you still ensured I'd survived the pneumonia. Most kings wouldn't think twice about letting their prisoners die in their jail cell."

"That's because most kings weren't in love with their prisoners," he whispers, love swimming in his blue-ocean eyes. "Even when I told myself I hated everything you represented, I still loved you just as fiercely. I'm sorry it took me so long to see it."

"That's okay. I didn't make things easy for us either." I sigh, dipping the cloth in between his legs.

"Well, you sure have a knack for making things hard," he grunts before covering my hand with his so we're both palming his cock.

"Behave, Atlas. Or need I remind you that you should be taking it easy and not overly exerting yourself?"

"Fine." He pouts, releasing his hold on my hand. "Then how about a kiss? A kiss to show how appreciative I am for you nursing me back to health," he says with a wink.

"Are you honestly trying to flirt with me to get your way right now?" I laugh.

"I wouldn't dream of it," he coos, crooking his finger so I can lean in closer to him.

"Don't be cute."

"Oh, so I'm cute now, am I?" He laughs and then winces at the pain of his back muscles moving in tandem with his chuckle.

"Stop, Atlas. You need to take it easy."

"I'll take it easy after you've kissed me. Just one kiss, Kat. That's all my body will allow me anyway."

My soul longs for him too much to deny him such a simple request.

Ever so carefully, I lean closer and press my lips on his. My heartbeat stutters in my chest with how perfectly our mouths align with each other. As if his lips were sculpted by the gods themselves to fit mine and breathe life into my lungs. And when Atlas groans into my mouth, his tongue tentatively trying to deepen the kiss, I have to grab the rim of the tub to physically pull myself back.

"Curse the gods, but you taste sweet," he grumbles, his hand sliding back to his cock and giving it two languished strokes to ease the ache. "I guess the secret is out. You can't kiss me without me getting hard for you," he tries to joke, but his half-mast eyes give him away.

"Is that so?" I ask, sounding just as breathless as he is.

"Hmm. Can't you tell?" he asks, stroking his hard cock again to prove his point.

"You sure played it coy when we were fooling around," I whisper, licking my lips at the beads of pre-cum coating his mushroom head.

"Aye. But that was when I still had some will in me. As you can see, my will to keep you at arm's length has officially flown out the window. I'm too tired and exhausted from pretending that I don't want you.

You are all I ever wanted, princess. Only you. And fuck do I want you now."

His words are filled with so much love and desperation that they hit me right at the center of my aching core.

"I want you too," I confess in a whisper.

The heady gaze of his molten blue eyes reflect my own need for him.

"Let me show you how much," I tell him.

His stare flares with unrestrained desire as I get to my feet and slowly begin to pull at the laces in front of my dress. Atlas continues to stroke his cock as I let my gown drop to the floor, leaving me only in my undergarments, corset, and panties. My fingers work double time at the strings of my corset, flinging the dreadful thing to the corner of the room when it's finally off. Atlas's hungry gaze never leaves mine as I pull the remaining white undergarment over my head and sashay out of my panties. Now completely bare to him, I dip my feet into the warm water, holding on to his broad shoulders to keep my balance while lowering myself down to straddle him.

"Now, you heard Ulrich. You have to take it easy. That means you need to remain perfectly still or risk busting one of your stitches," I remind him, just as my wet hot pussy runs up and down his hard shaft.

"Easier said than done," he grunts before biting down on his lower lip, white-knuckling the tub's edges.

"Don't move, my king. Let me do all the work."

"Fuck me," he groans.

"Oh, I intend to." I lick my lips. "Thoroughly."

His Adam's apple bobs away at the tempting threat, all too eager for me to put it to the test. I lean down as low as I can and begin to lick my way up his formidable chest until I'm close enough for my lips to hover on his. His breathing comes out in spurts as he feels my hand grasp the base of his cock and align it to my entrance.

"If I start hurting you, tell me so I can stop."

"It's hurting like a mother fucker already," he murmurs, aroused. "But don't you dare fucking stop." He snakes his hand around the nape of my neck and pulls my lips closer to his, leaving only a hairsbreadth between us. "My misery. My suffering. My blood. Do your worst, princess."

My lips instantly tug into a smirk with his words.

Atlas is greedy for another kiss, yet I don't give in, needing to torture him just a little longer. My tongue traces his bottom lip before my teeth bite into it while simultaneously rubbing his crown against my pussy lips. My resolve to stretch this sweet torture snaps like a brittle twig when Atlas releases his gentle grip from my nape and wraps his fingers around my neck.

"Either kiss me or fuck me, Kat. Whatever you decide, do it soon. If you hesitate for even a second, I'll have you on your back and be inside you before you can even say 'stitches'."

I don't even think twice.

Panting, and with our eyes in a locked stare, I fling myself down on him, and in one thrust, he's balls-deep inside me, my lips crashing down on his in sweet surrender.

"Gods," I moan with the feel of his girth hardening inside me.

"Don't fucking call the gods into this. I'm the one you're fucking, princess. And don't you forget it," he growls in between kisses.

My body turns to molten lava as Atlas bites down on my lip before wrestling with my tongue to show who's really in charge. With his hand still on my throat, he adds just enough pressure to set me off. Each kiss becomes more decadent, leaving me breathless and wanting with each flick of his tongue. I keep riding his cock, the slow rhythm no longer scratching the itch underneath my skin.

Reluctantly, I break our kiss and grab his shoulders to use them for balance as I increase my speed.

"I feel every inch of you, Atlas. Every inch," I moan out, my head falling over my shoulders with the exquisite feeling of him finally being inside me.

"So fucking beautiful. Fuck me, but I never stood a chance," he roars, digging his fingers into my waist, helping me keep my furious tempo.

Water splashes to the floor as we endure fucking at a maddening pace. My breasts ache to be touched, my nipples hard like fine-cut diamonds. As if hearing my silent plea, Atlas releases his hand off my waist to grab my right breast, pinching my nipple to the point of pain.

"Atlas!" I cry out, fully losing all sense of self as his cock thrusts deep inside me, hitting that one pleasure point that drives me insane. "I'm almost... I'm almost..."

"That's it, princess. Come on my cock. Let me see how beautifully you shatter on it."

And even though it must hurt him, Atlas takes over and drives his cock deep inside me, each repetitive thrust more punishing than the last. It's no small wonder that I do as he orders and come undone, my soul and body shattering before him, knowing they are safe in his hands.

"Fuck. Fuck. Fuck," he curses as he, too, is pushed off the cliff, the heavens opening up and welcoming him home.

I fall on top of him, our heaving chests in sync with one another. Atlas runs his fingers delicately through my wet hair, giving me more than enough time to collect myself after such a whirlwind orgasm.

"You've ruined me now," I whisper into his chest, the sound of his rapid heartbeat mimicking my own. "There's no turning back. Not now. Not ever. And I don't know what to do."

"Hate to break it to you, princess, but it looked like you knew exactly what you were doing. No complaints here," he jokes.

"That's not what I mean," I whisper, lifting my head off his chest to rest against his shoulder.

Atlas lets out an exhale, his soft blue eyes doing nothing to soothe my shame and guilt.

"I know what you meant, princess. Or more importantly, *who* you meant."

"They'll never understand. Levi was heartbroken when he learned of my feelings for Teo. And Teo basically threatened that he wouldn't come to Tarnow if Levi was who my heart belonged to. And now—"

"You've gone and fallen in love with me, too," he finishes my statement.

"Yes. I have. I love you, Atlas. I love you with every inch of my soul."

His knuckles softly caress my cheek before wrapping his arms around me and pulling me into an embrace.

"We'll figure it out. Somehow, we'll find a way."

I wish I could be that optimistic.

But deep down, I know that happily-ever-afters only occur in made-up fantasy folklore and children's fairytale books. My life has never been touched by such magic.

It's always had heartbreak in its center.

Why should the fates change their minds now?

"The fuck?" I shout when something hits me across the head, successfully waking me up from my slumber.

"Put your pants on, Atlas. It's time we had that talk," Kat orders, standing at the end of our bed with her arms crossed over her chest to show she means business.

"What? No good morning kiss?" I taunt, carefully pulling myself out of bed so I don't bust a stitch.

"Don't be cute, Atlas. Get dressed and meet me in the library in ten minutes. I mean it. You're not going to sweet-talk me out of this one."

I watch her storm out of our bedroom, my teasing smirk falling the minute she slams the door.

Fuck.

Every muscle in my body screams in agony while my back feels like it's on fire. I hurriedly look for the small bottle of poppy milk and take two large gulps. But even though today I'm in excruciating pain, I don't regret a single thing that happened last night. I had my princess in the tub and then fucked her again twice on our bed. I would have been more than happy to spend the rest of the night fucking her brains out, but the last couple of days had exhausted all her energy. So when she fell asleep in my arms, I didn't have the heart to wake her up so we could go for round four.

Unfortunately for me, Kat isn't in the same love-dovey mood that she was in last night.

No.

Today she wants answers.

Answers that will dig up old wounds that I've yet to heal.

Fuck.

The scars on my back will heal faster than those on my heart.

But I gave her my word, and though it gives me no satisfaction to look back at that time in my life, she deserves to know the truth.

Now, if only I could get myself dressed.

"Come in," I say, relieved that someone is knocking at my door.

"Morning, young lion," Cristobal greets as he waltzes into my room.

"Give me a hand here, Cristo. My woman will throw a fit if I'm a minute late."

Cristobal walks over to the other side of the bed and helps me get dressed. I try to walk on my own but falter and end up falling on my side on top of the mattress.

"Shit," I grumble as he helps me up to my feet again.

"You're in a bad state, young cub. You should be resting in bed, not frolicking about in the castle," he scolds with a deep-rooted frown.

"And give a reason for wagging tongues to call me weak?"

"Oy vey, Atlas. No one will think that. Not after the beating they saw you take for the woman you love. All of Huwen can't stop talking about it."

"And just what, exactly, are my people saying?"

"Most say that the act was a noble one. That it showed the winter queen was to be trusted, and like you had no fault in her parentage," he says before pulling my arm around his shoulders to use his wide frame to support my steps.

"Most, but not all?"

Cristobal shrugs defeatedly.

"Hate is funny like that. When you spend so many years despising someone, it's hard to stop. Even if confronted with the fact that there was no reason to hate them in the first place. Just give the people time, young lion. Soon enough, they will fall for her charms just as you have," he says, holding onto his sincere soft smile. "Now tell me, where are we going?"

"The library. Kat is waiting for me there so we can have *the talk* ."

"I would have assumed you being slashed by a whip over a hundred times to be enough of a sign of your commitment to her," he adds, so confused that I can't help but laugh.

"Shit," I grumble. "Don't make me laugh, old friend. It hurts too damn much. And it's not *that* talk I'm referring to. It's the one that involves her prick of an uncle."

"Ah, aye. Halfdan is to blame for that one. He gave the winter queen hell last night. The minute she came to him with talks of a peaceful siege, his eyes started to bug out of their sockets. For a second there, I honestly believed he'd take his men right there and then and leave Huwen. Luckily for us, your Katrina was able to temper his vengeful mood. Still, he couldn't help himself from bringing up Adelid's name. Like I said, hate is a powerful thing, young cub. Not everyone will find it easy to let it go."

"You think I have?" I cock both brows up to my forehead.

"Forgiveness isn't a sign of weakness either. It takes far more strength to forgive an enemy than to strike one down," he retorts, shifting my weight further onto him.

I thin my lips since I'm done with this conversation.

Some hatreds only grow with time. They don't diminish with it.

"He's her flesh and blood, Atlas. Remember that when you paint your picture of the past to her. She's struggling as it is. Be kind, young lion. For her sake," he adds before we reach the library.

"Oh, gods!" Kat shrieks when she sees me holding onto Cristobal for support. "Why didn't you tell me you couldn't walk?" she adds, helping him to lay me on a sofa.

"You were far too angry for me to say anything. Besides, you'd probably think I just wanted an excuse for us to stay in bed all day." I feign a cocky smile.

"Cristobal, call Ulrich so he can examine the king," she orders, but I wave it off.

"Cristobal, you will do no such thing. When I'm done here, I'll go to him myself and not a minute sooner. What you can do is ask one of the squires to fetch the queen and me some breakfast. After the night we had, I'm sure she is just as famished as I am."

Katrina's cheeks turn pink, but she doesn't put up a fight with me ordering us some food. Cristobal excuses himself, and twenty minutes later, our breakfast arrives, along with the unanswered questions in Katrina's gaze.

"Where do you want me to start?"

"Are you sure you don't want me to call Ulrich?" she asks, still concerned for me.

"That's not the question you want to ask me," I reply, throwing my arms behind the couch. "Don't beat around the bush, my queen. Just ask me what you want to ask."

Katrina takes a deep breath, forgoing her fruit plate, and kneels on the couch beside me.

"Is it true? Did my uncle really kill Rhea?"

"Yes." I nod, the empty space inside me overwhelmed by the pain in her silver gaze.

"I want to know. I want to know everything."

I cup her cheek, seeing the pain in her eyes.

"Once you know the truth, there is no going back. You know that, don't you, Kat?"

"I've been kept in the dark for too long. Tell me everything. Please."

So I do.

I tell her how her father sent a decree demanding for the queens of his vassals to go north. I tell her how my father, in his naive ignorance, sent my mother to her death. I tell her how I wrote to her every day, begging for news of my mother and hearing nothing but silence from her. I tell her how her fucking uncle rode in through Huwen's gates on his white horse with an army of mercenaries behind him. I tell her how he made a mockery of me and my father, only to kill us both with his niece's supposed gift to me—my mother's severed head.

"The note that I showed you the other night... it had been plunged in my mother's forehead," I tell her as shame accosts me for being so foolish to believe my princess would ever write such words.

Tears stream down her cheeks, but she never wavers her gaze from mine, intent on seeing this through.

"That was also the night Adelid told my father that our ships would start exporting western women instead of the usual coal and jewels the north would send us to trade. It was the last thing I heard that bastard say before I ran. And Kat, I fucking ran like a coward. Just like my father ordered me to. Just as my mother instructed. I didn't think twice. I ran. And every day, I feel shame for it."

"No... don't," she sobs, resting her head on my chest and placing her hand on my heart as if needing to make sure it's still beating. "If you stayed, then who knows what my father and my uncle would have done to you."

"They left Levi and Teo well enough alone. They got to rule after their fathers died. I couldn't do that stranded at sea, miles away from my home. All I could do was bide my time and plan my revenge."

"Where did you go?" she asks softly, her not-so-subtle way of trying to move off-topic since it's evident this one strikes too much of a nerve for both of us.

"To Maffei, to see King Halfdan."

Katrina cranes her neck back to look at my face, the look of astonishment imprinted in hers.

"You look surprised." I chuckle softly, amazed for being able to, considering what we are talking about.

"I just assumed you went to Shefcour first since you seem to have such a strong friendship with Cristobal."

"As much as anyone can with a pirate and conman." I laugh again.

"Don't say that." She smiles. "It's clear as day that he loves you dearly."

"Aye, I know. And I love him too, though I will deny it if you tell him so." I continue to laugh, thankful for the poppy milk to finally kick in, successfully numbing most of my back and taking the pain away. "But no. My mother had been very clear with her instructions to her ship's captain. He was to sail to Maffei and hand me over to her cousin, King Halfdan."

Katrina rises back and sits down on her heels.

"Halfdan is Queen Rhea's cousin? I thought your mother was born here in Huwen? How did I not know this?" she asks, genuinely intrigued by this revelation.

"I'm not sure why it wasn't common knowledge that my mother was born in Maffei. I think that once she married my father and took over the fleets, the people began to view her as their own." I shrug. "Hopefully, one day, they'll do the same with you."

"I hope so too, though I'm not sure how. However, I now understand why Halfdan hates me so much."

"He doesn't hate you, princess, any more than I do. It's just that when he looks at you, he sees the man that killed his beloved cousin."

"Adelid," she curses as if that name now holds poison. "I was so stupid. So naively stupid to have believed one word he said to me. To rely on his counsel even. I should have known something wasn't right when he tried to change my mind about traveling through my kingdoms. He must have known that I'd find out the truth of what he and my father had done to Aikyam and put a stop to their tyranny."

"Maybe he did, maybe he didn't. Maybe he believed you were brainwashed enough to believe him no matter what you heard. All I know is that you now hold the future of your people in your hands. It's up to you—and only you—to decide how we go from here."

Her forehead creases in confusion, and it takes everything in me not to kiss the lines away.

"What are you saying?"

"I'm saying that if you don't want an army to march north and prefer to take a more diplomatic stance, I will back up your decision," I reply, Cristobal's advice still ringing in my ear.

"If I do that, then the other kings will leave. The west would never forgive you for such leniency."

"Aye, I know." I sigh. "But it has come to my attention that I love you more than I hate your fucking uncle. Which means if you want to show him mercy, then I won't stand in your way."

Kat stares at me wide-eyed and speechless for the longest minute.

"You would sacrifice your revenge for me? Because you love me?"

"Princess, I have a back marred in scars that proves there is no sacrifice big enough that I wouldn't make for you. If mercy is what you want, then so be it."

"And what if I want Adelid dead?" she asks sheepishly.

"Then I've never loved you more than right now," I reply truthfully.

"Then that's what I want. I want to cut out his black heart and his lying tongue," she says arctically, her silver eyes turning cold.

"Then it shall be done," I promise, as I pick up her hand and kiss each of her knuckles before admiring how beautiful she looks with vengeance in her eyes. "His misery, his suffering, his blood, in exchange for those he stole from us."

"We will do our worst." She smiles menacingly, and gods help me, but she's never looked more beautiful than at this very minute.

"You have no idea how much I want you to sit on my face right now," I groan, feeling my erection harden in my pants.

"Behave, Atlas." She giggles, jumping off the sofa and sashaying that peach ass in front of me to grab our now-more-than-cold breakfast.

"I changed my mind. I think I'd rather eat your ass first," I groan as she leans down to pick up her fruit plate, showing off those ample breasts of hers.

"Nope. Scratch that. I want to fuck those tits of yours and see them all covered in my cum."

I lick my lips, famished.

She giggles again, as if me losing my mind with want is nothing to be concerned about. She walks back to the sofa and carefully plops the plate of food right on my lap, hard cock be damned.

"Eat your food, Attie."

"I'd rather eat you. Every inch of you," I growl, stretching my arm to grab her throat and keep her next to me. But the damned vixen is too fast for me, and she quickly slides over to the floor, making sure a wide berth is kept between us.

"None of that. Not until you visit Ulrich, and he gives you the green light."

Fuck my life and blue balls.

"I'm serious, Attie. You can't even walk without someone helping you. How do you expect me to let you fuck me in good conscience?

"Shit. Say fuck me again, princess." I muffle my moan by biting down on my knuckles.

"Why are the men in my life so incorrigible?" she complains, then thinks better of it and seals her lips tight.

But it's too late.

The off-the-cuff remark has fully succeeded in throwing ice water into my libido.

Surprisingly enough, not for the reason she suspects.

"I'm sorry," she says, chewing her bottom lip nervously.

I lean forward as much as I can and lift her chin with the tip of my finger.

"Don't be sorry, princess. I don't want there to be any secrets between us," I coo lovingly. "I knew before you even reached my shores that you had fallen in love with them. But if we are really being honest with each other and with ourselves, we both know you were in love with them long before you ever set one foot outside of Tarnow."

Her cheeks turn crimson as she inches closer to me so that I can cup her cheek.

"It's true. I think I've always been in love with Levi and Teo. Just as I have always been in love with you, Attie."

"I know, princess. I know," I whisper, saddened. "That still doesn't change things for me, though. News of your capture is bound to have reached the east and south borders by now. Soon they will come for you, Kat. And when they do, they'll kill me, and maybe I should let them, after all you had to endure."

"That's not funny, Atlas," she scolds, slapping my hand off her cheek.

"I wasn't trying to be, princess. I'm just trying to prepare you for the inevitable. How do you think Levi and Teo will feel when they learn that their beloved queen has shared the same bed as her kidnapper? How do you think they will react to another king trying to steal your heart away from them?

"These are not strangers aiming to win my heart, Attie. These are your brothers. Levi and Teo love you. They'll find a way to forgive you, just as I have."

"If you say so. However, that only solves one of our problems. As I recall, I don't remember Levi and Teo ever being the sharing kind. Not when it comes to you."

"What about you?" she asks hesitantly. "Are you the sharing kind?"

"If it meant that I could have you, then yes," I confess without delay.

Her features soften at the admission, picking up both of my hands so that I may cup her cheeks.

"We're on the brink of war, princess. My friends, who I love like brothers, are probably planning how best to kill me. I'm still healing from the scars from being whipped within an inch of my life. And yet, I have never been happier. And that comes down to you, princess. Down to your love for me. If I have to share your love to keep it, then by the gods, so be it. I wouldn't care as long as I had you."

Her silver gaze turns to lava as she places her hand on my chest and pushes me back onto the sofa.

"I just poured my heart out, and you shove me?" I chuckle.

But the minute Kat begins to lift up her skirts and place one foot on each side of me on the sofa, my laughter dies on my lips, my hunger for her coming toward me like an avalanche.

"I love you too, Attie. Now be a good king and make me come on your face."

"As you wish, my queen."

Chapter 30

Atlas

My eyes squint in agony with how her greedy pussy swallows my cock whole. The wails she moans out every time I drive my cock into her dripping cunt only spur me on to pump deeper and harder than she's ever been before. When I see the top of her head banging on my headrest, I pull her by the braid, craning her neck all the way back while keeping to my punishing rhythm.

I don't care who knows it, but my princess on all fours taking my cock up to the hilt is the prettiest damn sight the gods have ever presented me.

"Attie! I'm coming! I'm coming!" she shouts, playing with her clit as I hit that soft spot inside her walls.

Scratch that.

Seeing Katrina of Bratsk come like a firecracker with my cock in her pussy and my thumb playing with the rim of her ass is the best sight in the world.

Not that I can enjoy much of it since my eyes close when her pussy strangles my cock in such a way that it's impossible not to come.

Fuck me, but I never get tired of fucking this woman.

Under Ulrich's strict orders, that day we spent in the library was the last day I left my bedroom for the remainder of the week. Luckily for me, Katrina was all too eager to entertain me while I healed. Though the pain from my wounds is more manageable now, I'm sure I would have healed a lot faster if I didn't spend my time fucking my princess raw every chance I got.

I wasn't lying when I told her I was happy that day.

I almost forgot how good it felt to love and be loved in return.

My heart and soul preferred to cling to vengeance than seek out such pleasures.

But now, with my princess at my side, I almost believe we could live in a world where happiness wasn't a scarce commodity but a certainty.

With my cum still dripping down her thighs, Kat turns her head over her shoulders and gifts me that heartbreaking, beautiful smile.

"I love you," she says with a naughty smile, playfully wiggling her ass at me.

"I love you too, princess," I reply, pulling my dick out just so I can bite that tempting ass of hers.

"Argh!" she half-wails and half-moans when I slap her other cheek.

I'm still hard as shit, and when I see my teeth marks on her flawless creamy skin, I'm ready for round two.

"Atlas! Atlas!" Cristobal bangs at my door like a raging lunatic, but I just ignore him since I have more pressing things to do—like fucking Katrina's pretty little ass.

I drop to my knees and pull her ass to my face, hungry to have a little taste.

"Atlas! Atlas! Atlas!" he continues to shout, banging on my door like he's going to break it down.

"It sounds important, Attie," my princess whispers, apprehensively eyeing the door, afraid it's not strong enough to sustain Cristobal's abuse.

"Shh, princess, and don't make a sound. Nothing is more important than me eating your ass right now."

My tongue is about to take its first lick when the sound of cracking wood stops me.

"Motherfucker! This better be life or death, Cristo!" I shout, hurriedly covering Kat with a bedsheet before he walks in and gets a chance to see her naked.

Not that I'm not going to kill him for interrupting me from my meal either way.

"Gods, Atlas! Have you grown deaf, boy?" he shouts, his face red from beating the door in.

"No, but you are about to lose the gift of sight if you don't turn around so my queen can get dressed."

"Oh, fuck! Apologies, Kat," he stutters hurriedly when he realizes what he just interrupted.

"Cristo! Turn the fuck around! Now!" I shout, my hard dick hitting my stomach as I jump off the bed to physically make him move.

"Sorry, Kat. Sorry," he repeats.

THE WINTER KISSED KINGS

"Stop calling her Kat. She's Your Highness to you, asshole."

"That's quite alright, Cristobal," Katrina defends behind me. "This is all Atlas's fault since he should have opened the door the minute you knocked."

"All dressed up. You boys can turn now," she says after tapping twice on my shoulder.

I frown when I see that she only put on a robe.

"That's all you could find?" I chastise. "Isn't there a dress somewhere in here?"

"This from the man who still has his dick out," Cristobal mumbles beside me, throwing a discarded towel my way.

I wrap the damn thing around my waist before returning my fury to my pain-in-the-ass friend.

"This better be important, Cristobal. And you better pray that my door is fixed by nightfall, or it's your ass."

"Unfortunately, young lion, you have more important problems than a broken door," he says, flinging a letter in my hands. "A rider just arrived with it. A message from Tarnow."

I don't even scold him when I verify that the blue rose seal has already been broken and that Cristobal was the first to read its contents.

"What does it say?" Kat asks, looking pale all of a sudden. "Read it, Attie."

I nod and proceed to open it to read it aloud—word after terrifying word.

The north no longer recognizes
Princess Katrina of Bratsk

as its sovereign ruler.

Aikyam has a new king.

Elijah of Bratsk is the only true legitimate
male heir of the late great King Orville.

His rule is without question.

All hail the king of the north.

Fuck.

The war I wanted so badly to happen has just turned into a hostage-saving mission.

"Oh, by the gods!" Kat shouts agitatedly, snatching the letter from my hands to read the ill-gotten message for herself. "They have Elijah! Attie, Adelid has my brother!"

"Calm down, princess. Calm down. No one will lay a finger on your brother's head while he can be useful to him. Just calm down."

"How can you expect me to calm down?" she sobs, her eyes wide in panic. "Who knows what Adelid will do to him? What if he's torturing him? Or keeping him locked away in a dungeon and only pulling him out when he needs to? Oh, gods! He's going to kill my brother. He's going to make him sign some decree that empowers him as his proxy, and once the north has accepted Adelid's rule, he's going to kill my baby brother. With no one else of Bratsk bloodline, and with Adelid already proving to be a fair ruler, the people won't think twice about it," she says in a manic trance.

I grab her by the arms and keep her still.

"Your imagination is getting the better of you," I lie, hoping it's enough to calm her down.

"Don't do that." She shakes her head. "Don't lie to me, Attie. Not you."

I let out an exhausted exhale and say the words I never wanted her to hear, "You're right. You're absolutely right. If I were in Adelid's shoes, that would be exactly what I would do."

My heart hurts from the misery swimming in her eyes.

"But there is still hope. Time is on our side. He won't hurt the boy until he's proven himself as a worthy ruler. We just need to accelerate our plans to charge north and spoil his plans. Okay?"

She nods as I wipe away a sole tear from her cheek.

"That's not all. I wish that was the only bad news I had for you both, but unfortunately, I have more," Cristobal interrupts with a hard tone. "Look outside your window, Atlas."

My brows pull together in confusion, but I do as he says, and when I see the thick black smoke on the horizon, my chest tightens.

"Your rider said he passed a large train on his way here. He's not sure, but he estimates at least five thousand soldiers are riding west and should be here by dawn tomorrow."

"Let me guess? All of them carrying green and gold banners?" I ask, turning around to see Cristobal nod.

"Blue too. North, east, and south, Atlas. What do you intend to do?"

Instead of answering him, I bridge the gap between me and the woman I love and lift her trembling chin upward.

"It seems to me, princess, that your boyfriends have finally put two and two together and have come to rescue you. How about we give them a good welcome?"

Chapter 31
Levi

A month ago

Something is wrong.
I should have received some kind of word from Kat by now.
If not from her, then at least from Atlas.

But instead, all I get is silence coming from the west.

Something is not right.

I can feel it in my gut, and my gut is rarely ever wrong.

I fist the heart-shaped necklace in my hand as I stare at the marble statue of my parents in front of me, wishing the stone could come to life so they could whisper their counsel in my ear.

"I don't know what to do, Father," I whisper to a ghost. "Should I wait the rest of the month out and ride north like Kat expects me to, or should I follow my instincts and march west to ensure that Atlas didn't lose his goddamn mind?"

Instead of my father's loving voice, all I get in return is the gentle swishing sound of rustling leaves provoked by a light spring wind.

"Father, help me. Give me clarity to distinguish between what's real and what are just my insecurities wreaking havoc in my heart," I beg, fiddling with the heart-shaped diamond Kat gifted me to prove her love for me. "This woman is my heart, Father. Please help me protect it. Please, give me a sign on what to do."

Another gentle wind blows through the trees and kisses my stubbled cheeks, proving that the dead are still unwilling to shed any light on my current predicament.

I blame Teodoro for this.

If it wasn't for him, I wouldn't feel so uncertain… so anxious.

I would have trusted the gods to hold Atlas to his word and bring Kat back to me.

But instead of certainties, all I have is doubt.

Would Atlas go against my explicit wishes and hurt my queen?

Is his hatred so strong that he would willingly turn his back on his beloved brother?

I was very clear in my last letter to him, explaining how Kat is not the villain he believes her to be. That she is the way for our kingdoms to finally be free from their chains and live in peace.

My words must have touched his heart.

They must have.

But what if they didn't?

What if Atlas kept true to his original plan to take Tarnow and make a show of killing my heart in front of every northern man, woman, and child?

Gods, be merciful and make it not so.

Breathe love and forgiveness into my broken brother's heart.

For if he lays one finger on Kat, I'll have no choice but to kill him.

After I've said all my prayers and come to terms with the fact that dead kings and queens can't mend an aching heart, I get up from the stone bench and make my way back to my castle.

Unfortunately for me, the first person I run into is my overly nervous general, Brick, manically pacing back and forth outside my office chambers.

"Fuck! Finally! Where the hell have you been?!" he shouts when he sees me.

"Remind me to give you a crash course in etiquette, Brick. I believe there is a 'Your Highness' missing somewhere from your outburst," I grumble, opening the door and walking into the room.

"Fuck etiquette! Can't you see I'm going out of my mind here!" he shouts, following me in, but when I raise a menacing brow at him, he controls his panicked state himself long enough to add, "Your Highness," to the end of his statement.

"I need you to calm down, Brick. Maybe some wine would do you good," I tell him while pouring some into two goblets and handing him one.

"I don't need wine, my king," he says but drinks every last drop of the chalice before continuing his rant. "What I need is Inessa."

"You've made that evidently clear these past few days with your repetitive raving and grumbling. And like I always tell you, you'll see her soon enough when we reach Tarnow next month."

"That's not good enough, Levi. I need to see her now. I can't sleep at night. I can't eat. I can't even think straight. I can't do anything with this boulder pressing down on my chest. It's not like her to take so long to respond to my letters. Usually, I would have received some kind of word from her by now. Even if only a simple note telling me to fuck off and shove my letters where the sun doesn't shine." He smiles wistfully.

"You two are very odd." I snort.

"Just the way we show our love." He beams, only for his smile to dip into a concerned frown a second later. "Just hear me out, my king. I say, instead of us marching north at the end of the month, we go west. Now. We can even say that we are there just to ensure Queen Katrina and her train arrive up north safely."

"Atlas won't like that," I mumble, running my fingers through my beard.

"Who gives a fuck what that madman likes or not," he shouts, causing me to pierce him with a menacing gaze.

"Careful, Brick. That is my brother you are talking about. I've been loyal to him longer than you've been loyal to me. Tread carefully, general."

Brick's cheeks turn as red as his hair, but by the way that his nostrils are flaring, he doesn't look any closer to backing down.

"Beg your pardon, Your Highness, but your *brother* is as unhinged as they come. I've only met the man once, which was more than enough for me. His dead eyes still cause me nightmares. I know you love him. I do, and I sympathize with that, but I think your love is misplaced. You love the memory of the boy he once was, and that memory blinds you from seeing the soulless man he's become. Your little brother is long gone, my king. And I fear the king who rules the west is doing terrible things to the women we love."

"You said something similar about the winter queen. You were wrong then, and you are wrong now," I retort sternly, hiding the fact that Brick is poking at a raw nerve inside me that sees too much reason in his words.

"That might be true, my king, but I'm a big believer in being safe rather than sorry. Rally our men and march us all to Huwen instead of Tarnow. If I am wrong, there is no harm done, and we get to see our women sooner than expected. However, if I am right…"

"If you are right, then I must go to war with my brother to rescue my queen from his clutches. Is that what you are saying?"

"Wars have been fought for less, my king," he counters with steel resolve.

I stew in my own panic with his words, my heart dropping to the pit of my stomach, fearing the worst.

'Once you are married and crowned king, I will plunge my dagger into her cold heart on her very bridal bed as my wedding present to you. I swear it on the blood that was shed in her family's name.'

Hadn't those been Atlas's exact words to me?

Is what Brick said true? Is my faith in Atlas's loyalty to me unfounded? Have I been naive in believing no harm would come to Kat in the west once I confessed to him how much she means to me?

Am I that much of a fool?

Hate that deep doesn't just disappear in a blink of an eye.

No.

It festers.

It takes root inside a person's heart until it poisons the blood and blackens the soul.

A lone breeze, gentle and yet strangely foreboding, tiptoes into the room, causing a chilling shiver to run down my spine. Like an ethereal whisper, the breeze continues its clandestine journey, brushing against the faded curtains with a ghostly touch as if demanding my attention.

Even though I'm grateful for it, I no longer need a sign from the dead to tell me what needs to be done.

"Gather the men, Brick. The best we have. No more than a couple thousand, though. If you are wrong, I don't want to insult Atlas by bringing an army to his shores. But if you are right, I'll need men worth their steel. Atlas never fully divulged his plans to me on how he intended to best the north. However, he seemed certain in his capabilities, which means we have no idea what we are about to find."

"Thank the gods!" Brick shouts, eyeing the heavens.

"Don't thank the gods yet. I honestly want you to be wrong about this."

"I'm not," he retorts.

"Still, I want us to be cautious and not start a war over a misunderstanding. Too many of those have happened as it is. Go. Rally up the men and get them ready to leave by daybreak."

Brick sighs in relief and doesn't wait for me to change my mind, rushing toward the door to do my bidding.

I pull out Kat's necklace from my pocket and kiss it.

"I pray to the gods I'm wrong, my heart. But if you are in peril, stay strong. I'm coming, Kat. I'm coming.

For the past two weeks, my army of two thousand brave souls and I have marched westward with eastern steel determination. Our heavy metallic armor glimmers under the sun as we move in unison, our steps raising the dirt from the abandoned roads. Brick and I lead the way, while behind us, the bannermen keep the green hydrangea at the center of Arkøya's flag, fluttering proudly in the wind.

Five hundred footmen follow closely behind the soldiers on horseback, clutching their swords and shields tightly to their sides. Another five hundred archers and crossbowmen are ready, arrows and bolts firmly locked in place, always on alert for any potential threat.

My troops push forward, their resolute gaze fixed on the distant horizon, as we traverse rugged terrains and dense forests until we reach our target—the western shores of Huwen.

A journey like this would usually take a whole month to accomplish, but I'm determined to cut that time by a week at the least. Though tired and spent from the journey, my men are up before sunrise and only camp for the night long after the moon has found its home at the center of the sky, with very little breaks in between.

Brick is usually the first to caution me not to exhaust the men before a big fight, but since we left Arkøya, he's remained oddly silent to their plights. Not that I'm surprised. Like me, he has no patience to waste unnecessary time. If the man had wings, he would have flown west by now to see his beloved Inessa.

"Rider! Rider!" I hear one of the men shout, and sure enough, the rider I had sent as a lookout can be seen riding toward us at a hurried speed.

"Fuck. What now?" Brick curses under his breath.

"Easy, Brick. Maybe he's just riding back to tell us that the road ahead may not be suitable to pass through, and perhaps we need to find an alternative."

"Gods, I hope not. That will eat away at the time we've managed to gain."

"Would you rather he brings news that an enemy is afoot?" I tease to lighten his spirits.

"Fuck yes. A good fight would do me a world of good."

"Only you, Brick, could be happy with the idea of a brawl." I shake my head with a mocking smile.

But my grin slips off my face when the rider approaches near enough to see the hate in his eyes.

I square my shoulders and wait for him to stop his horse at my side.

"Your Highness," he greets breathlessly.

"Sten," I retort. "By the look on your face, I don't suppose you have good news for me, do you?"

"I'm afraid not, my king," he replies, bowing his head.

"Well, don't keep Your Highness waiting! Speak up, boy!" Brick shouts beside me.

"Excuse our friend, Sten. Brick has been a bit prickly lately."

"Nothing that seeing my beautiful Inessa's face won't solve," Brick interjects. "So be quick about it, boy. We are losing precious daylight."

"See what I'm talking about? Prickly," I taunt, slapping Brick's back hard enough so he knows to hold his tongue.

Not that it would matter any.

Everyone already knows the real reason why I commanded my best men to follow me west. It's not because I wanted to chaperone the Queen of Aikyam safely back to Tarnow after her visit to Huwen, but because I fear she's been taken prisoner there.

Just the image of my heart bound and tied up by chains has me just as impatient as Brick is for Sten to say what he has to say.

"What is it, Sten? What did you find?"

"There's a camp, Your Majesty, not five miles from here."

"A camp? Whose camp?"

Sten swallows harshly before almost knocking me off my horse with his next words.

"I saw the south's golden sunflower crest, my king."

"Teodoro-of-fucking-Derfir?!" Brick blurts out in outrage. "That's whose banner you saw?"

Sten gives him a curt nod.

"Fuck me! What are the odds of us crossing paths while he goes north and we go west?" Brick cackles.

"Infinitesimally small," I rebuke, finding no humor in this situation.

Something is not right here.

Why would Teo ride north weeks ahead of time before Tarnow expects him to?

It doesn't add up.

"Sten, which road is the king of the south taking?"

"Not north, my king. If I had to guess, he's on the same road we are, heading west."

Could Kat have somehow been able to send word to him advising she was in danger?

And if so, why would she pick the south as her savior, which only has farmers, and not the east, which boasts well-versed soldiers?

"Sten, go back," I order with a grave tone. "Ride back to Teo's camp under a white banner and tell him that I want to speak with him. I will be there within the hour."

"What?!" Brick asks, staring at me as if I had lost my mind. "When you say speak, I hope to the gods that you mean kill the fucker, right?"

"There will be no bloodshed tonight. If my suspicions are correct, then Teo is riding west for the same reason we are. And as the old saying goes—the enemy of my enemy is my friend. At least until I'm sure that Kat is safe. After that, all bets are off."

Chapter 32
Teodoro

The young soldier has barely left my tent with news from his king wanting to parley when Cleo jumps to her feet, ready to tear the world down before I give in to such lunacy.

"Don't do it, Teo. It's a trap. A ploy to kill you."

"If that was the case, then he'd invite me to his camp and not come to mine," I counter nonchalantly.

"Hello??? Do you think the great warrior Levi would think twice about shoving a dagger into your heart if he so much as got the chance?" she shouts, incredulous that I would think otherwise.

"Aye, but if he did that, he might find it challenging to leave my camp alive. Especially with you around seeking vengeance on my behalf."

"You better fucking believe it. I'd cut him up into tiny pieces and feed them to the dogs."

"Always with the dramatic visuals." Anya sighs, hugging Cleo from behind. "It's a good thing you're cute, babe, or I'd think I had fallen in love with a psycho."

"The jury's still out on that one," I pile on, throwing both girls a mischievous wink.

Cleo scowls at me while her lover skips in my direction like she has no care in the world—save for the one that pushed us out of our tropical haven in Nas Lead and brought us here to the rough terrains where the eastern border meets west.

"Don't pay her any mind, my king." Anya smiles. "You know how Cleo gets… how should we say… anxious, for lack of a better word, in situations that may be dangerous to Your Highness. But I assure you, King Levi is a just, honorable king. He would not break the sacred rules of a parley. No harm will come to you. I swear it."

"Remind me again why you fell in love with my hot-tempered right hand when you are far more levelheaded than she is?" I ask before tapping the tip of her little nose with the pad of my finger and returning her infectious smile with one of my own.

"You have a woman, Teo, so stop flirting with mine. Cherry, come here before he gets any funny ideas," Cleo grumbles possessively.

But Anya just laughs her lover's possessive nature away.

It helps that she knows my heart only belongs to one woman—her queen.

"Stop being so overdramatic. Besides, King Teo needs me to escort him to his meeting with King Levi." She beams proudly.

"Come again?" Cleo asks, like she's lost her hearing all of a sudden.

Anya walks over to my side and places her hand on my shoulder.

"You heard me well enough, Cleo. I'm going with our king."

"Oh no, you are not!"

"Yes, I am," Anya deadpans with a severity I didn't know she was capable of.

She then cuts her green eyes off her lover and onto me with the same iron-clad resolve.

"I'm going with you, King Teo, and I don't want to hear any ifs, ands, or buts about it. Is that understood?"

I swing my arm to my waist and give her a bow.

"My lady, I'm at your mercy."

"Oh gods, kill me now! Don't encourage her, Teo. She has no idea what she's getting into."

"No, love of mine, you're the one who doesn't seem to grasp the importance of this meeting. If Levi is here, then he must have come to the same conclusion as we have—Kat and Inessa are in trouble. And as much as I love you, Cleo, these are my sisters we are talking about, and I would march to hell itself if it meant that I could protect them. Now I'll repeat, I'm going with Teo. Is that understood?"

Cleo turns every color known to man as she fists her hands to her sides.

"They make them feisty in the north, don't they?" I taunt, but Cleo just flips me off with her middle fingers in the air.

"Then it's settled. You stay here and hold the fort while Anya and I go off to meet Levi."

"Over my dead body, you will," Cleo seethes through grinding teeth. "You will not put the woman I love in danger. I will not abide by this."

Now it's my turn to scowl.

"Every second that we wait, the woman *I* love continues to be in danger. I'm sorry, Cleo, but if by some miracle Anya can keep me alive long enough for me to see my love again, then by the gods, she is coming with me. She'll be my fucking shadow if need be, and there is nothing you can say that will change my mind."

Cleo's feline gaze bounces off of me, and her lover in a way that tells me she would love nothing more than to slap some sense in us.

"Fine. Then if you two are going, so am I," she says at last.

I let out a frustrated sigh, but thankfully Anya is already on her way, walking over to Cleo to calm her down. She flings her arms around Cleo's neck and stares lovingly into her eyes.

"You are going to follow the king's command and stay here, since you're not exactly known for being very diplomatic, babe. We don't want King Levi to feel he's being ambushed, now do we?" Anya then whispers something in Cleo's ear before giving her a passionate kiss.

Whatever Anya said was enough to calm Cleo down, for which I'm grateful, since it's one less problem I have to worry about.

Gods know it will be a miracle if I survive this night.

But Anya is right—Levi is a man of honor. Always was, always will be.

It's the only reason why I'm not fearful of accepting his offer to parley.

I just hope he's strong enough to put his hatred aside for me long enough for us to work together.

Our Kat is in trouble.

I can feel it in my bones, and if Levi has traveled all the way east to the same crossing point we're camped at, that means he feels it too.

I just pray to the gods that we're not too late.

"Are you nervous?" Anya asks, staring at how I keep wringing my hands over and over again.

"Can't you tell?" I try to joke off, even though this is no laughing matter.

The last time I saw Levi, I was a fucking asshole to him. And that was just because I didn't want him to see all the guilt I'd been carrying with me since his parents died.

"Let's just say that Levi and I have a difficult past together, and it might prove challenging for him to set all those feelings to the side."

"Then you underestimate me, Teo. I have more pressing concerns than to waste them on you," Levi's strong voice rings out in the tent, alerting us both of his arrival.

I turn around and instantly grow static when my eyes meet his cold, green gaze.

Anya, though, runs toward the red-haired man walking behind him.

"Brick!" she yells, throwing herself into his arms with tears in her eyes.

"Anya! What are you doing here, love? Is Inessa with you?" he asks, picking her up from the floor and twirling her around, just as happy to see her as Anya seems to be. But his excitement is short-lived when he places her back on her feet and sees the tears in her eyes.

"Anya, where is Inessa?"

"With our queen," she answers him, unable to disguise her anguish.

"Fuck!" he curses before taking his eyes off Anya and moving them to the king of the east. "Levi," he begins to say, but his king shuts him down with one cold stare.

When that same malicious glower falls in my direction, I stand tall, hoping he doesn't see the lost boy inside me who weeps to embrace his friend.

"Teo," Levi greets with a stoic air about him. "Thank you for agreeing to meet me."

Maybe it's the thank you that tilts me off my axis, or perhaps it's this whole fucked-up situation we find ourselves in that steals the rug from underneath my feet. Still, I suddenly feel my knees grow so weak that it takes great effort on my part to keep standing without any help.

"Levi."

That's all I say in return.

Not you're welcome or even a sorry for all the shit I had done to him in the past.

Just his name.

Just his fucking name.

If Levi is aware of how close I am to falling over the abyss headfirst into madness, he doesn't show it.

Instead, he just walks over to Anya, offers her his handkerchief so she may dry her eyes, and gives her shoulder a comforting squeeze.

"You look well, my lady. My heart is full just knowing you are safe."

Fuck.

This is what a real king sounds like.

A king that can command a room at will and still be able to show vulnerability when necessary.

How the fuck was Kat ever going to choose me, with him as my greatest opponent?

"Thank you, Your Majesty," Anya says while using his handkerchief to dry her tears. "May I be so bold as to ask why you've come here today, King Levi?"

"I came because I believe we are both heading in the same direction with the same purpose," he announces, his voice strong and poignant.

"You think Atlas has kidnapped Kat, too, don't you?" The words come out of my mouth before I even order them to.

I don't miss how Levi's stern green eyes morph into dark molten lava with the sound of my voice. My fingernails bite into my palms as I meet his gaze head-on, unwilling to show him how his anger rattles me. This is the older brother I looked up to for most of my life, and now... now he won't look at me without murder in his eyes.

Yes, I should be grateful that he's a man of honor, for if he was like me, I'd be dead and buried by now.

"Yes," he replies after a pregnant pause, and I try not to grimace when he walks toward me and stops just a few inches away.

"Hear me now, Teo, and hear me true," he begins to say, his gravelly voice barely loud enough to be heard above a whisper. "I despise the very earth you step on. I loathe the sun that kisses your cheek in the morning as you wake to greet a new day, as much as I hate any ray of moonlight that touches your skin as it lullabies you to sleep. You are my soul's hate, villain. And though I'd love nothing more than to snap your neck right here and now, I made a vow to my queen, to the owner of my beating heart," he growls, pounding his clenched fist on his chest. "That I would spare your life as long as she felt her happiness laid with you. Now, it's still unclear to me how you were able to seduce and charm her into your bed, but I know my Kat well enough that her love for me would grow cold if I so much as nicked that slender neck of yours with my blade. Her love, *hers* , Teo, is the only reason why you are still breathing right now. Is that clear?"

I tilt my head to the side and smirk at him. It's my go-to move whenever I feel my heart is in danger of shattering, and after Levi's passionate tangent on how much he abhors me, I feel like someone has just beaten my heart into a pulp.

"Tell me, Levi, do you have such an eloquent speech prepared for Atlas too? Are you practicing what you are going to say to him when the time comes?"

His nostrils flare in contempt as he takes two steps back from me and frowns.

"Is that a no?" I taunt, taking one step toward him. "Tell me, Levi, why are you really here? Why have you left your home to travel west all of a sudden? Is it because you think our little Atlas is no longer that frail little boy that used to look up to you like you hung the moon for him? Because I've heard the rumors, *brother*. I've heard how Atlas returned to Aikyam after being seven years at sea with a few bolts loose in his head."

"If that's true, then why did you let Kat leave Nas Lead?" he counters, his voice turning thunderous.

"For the same reason you let my kitten crawl all the way back to me from Arkøya," I taunt, my heart drumming wildly in my chest. "You knew that no matter whatever history might have taken place between us, I loved her and would never lay one finger on her glorious head. You knew it when we were kids, and you saw it again in my eyes when you delivered her to me in Braaka. That's why you let her go, and I did the same when she left me to travel west. You might have been too up your own ass to see it, but Atlas loved Kat just as fiercely as we did in the day, if not more."

"Don't tell me things I already know," he curses under his breath.

"Then don't accuse me of doing something when you would have done the same if you were in my shoes!" I shout back.

"Will you two stop?!" Anya yells at the both of us. "Just stop comparing dicks for a second, and remember why we are here in the first place."

"You tell 'em, Red," Brick encourages her.

"Gods! You two really need to discuss your issues, but that is neither here nor there. Right now, I wouldn't care if you killed each other as long as I could take both your armies and head west," she scolds. "My friends are in trouble. Real trouble. I knew it the minute their letters stopped coming, which only happened when they both arrived in Huwen. Now, I have never met King Atlas, nor do I know of his reputation, but I know my sisters. They would have reached out if they could. And since they haven't, that means their lives are in real danger. And I'm sorry to burst your bubble, but even though my queen loves you both with all her heart, you come second to me," Anya finishes by batting her eyelashes innocently at us.

"I don't doubt it, my lady," Levi laughs, the foreign sound bringing with it memories of a forgotten past where he and I were still brothers.

"My deepest apologies, Anya. You're right. We need to keep focused on our real goal. And that's rescuing Kat."

"And Inessa," both Anya and Brick say in unison.

"Yes, and Inessa," Levi adds before holding out his hand.

"What's this?" I ask, looking at his fingers as if they were already lodged in my throat.

"It's a peace offering, Teo. One that I will only maintain until Kat is safe and sound in Tarnow."

"And after Tarnow?" I arch a brow.

"Shake my hand, Teo," he orders, ignoring my question.

Reluctantly, I do as he says and shake his hand, only for Levi to cover our clasped hands with his and pull me hard into his chest. "Don't worry about Tarnow, Teo. Worry about surviving Huwen first."

Chapter 33

Levi

Five fucking days.
It's been five fucking days that I've had to endure Teo's irksome voice.

Seeing his smug, cocky face.

Hearing his boisterous laughter.

I'm not sure if I can take another day of this torment.

Still, I trail on.

For her.

This is all for her.

My heart.

The heart that he is bound to steal away from me the minute we rescue her.

Fuck Atlas.

If you only knew to which lengths I've succumbed just to remedy whatever scheme you've put in place. You'd probably be disappointed in me to see how far from your pedestal I've fallen. To pair up with my sworn enemy just to get our girl back.

Fuck Atlas.

Why didn't you just listen to me?

Why, brother? Why?

Even as I ask myself that loaded question in my head, I already know the answer to it.

The west suffered incredible horrors under King Orville's rule, and unbeknownst to Kat, Atlas blames her for all the sins her father committed.

I should have known Atlas wouldn't fall in line with my orders.

I should have known his hate could not be dissuaded just by a few words I wrote on a parchment.

I should have fucking known.

And now, as if the gods haven't laughed enough at the tragedy that is my life, they've gone ahead and added Teo to my daily dose of suffering.

Gods, give me strength not to slit his throat.

Give me the fortitude I need to keep my solemn vow to my queen.

"Look over there!" Teo shouts in glee, pointing to the horizon of sand and ocean. "We made it, brother! We fucking made it!"

My jaw clenches at the familiarity of the word, hating how my heart twists in my chest with faint affection for the boy I grew up with.

"I'll race you there. Last one on the beach has to kneel down to the winner in front of all his men." He winks and, to my chagrin, takes off on his horse, but not before slapping the rear of mine.

Motherfucker!

My horse begins to gallop at speed behind his while Teo's lighthearted laughter continues to ring loudly in the air.

Does this asshole actually believe he's off the hook for what he's done to me just because I let him live?

Rage and fury bubble up inside of me as I force my horse to ride like the wind just to catch up with him, uncaring for our train being left in the dust as we race toward the beach. When I finally reach him, I venture a look at his carefree face and am hit with a memory of two young boys happily racing through a field of freshly fallen snow. A fierce pang hits my chest at the forgotten memory, forcing me to look away from him to focus on the finish line.

But even though my steed is faster than his, Teo is much lighter since he refuses to wear any mail, giving him the advantage of reaching the ocean shore before me.

"I win!" He smiles cheerfully, his eyes filled with youthful glee. "Kneel before me, Levi. Let everyone see who bested the great King Levi of Thezmaer."

Blinded by anger, I push Teo off his horse; he does a backflip and lands feet first on the sand. My nostrils flare in disgust as I jump off mine and charge at him.

"What the fuck is your problem?" he says before pushing me back a step.

"You, Teo! You're my fucking problem!" I shout while shoving him.

The cold autumn sun acts as a silent witness to the escalating tension between us. In the midst of the tranquil coastal setting, where the rolling waves gently kiss the shore, a storm brews inside me—one that I cannot control no matter how hard I try.

"I was trying to have some fun, Levi! Remember fun? We used to have loads of it together, if you remember."

"I remember everything just fine. I especially remember how much of a snake you were."

His face blanches for a second as if hurt by the insult, but before I even have time to blink, that motherfucking cocky smirk is back on his face.

"Someone should really remove that stick up your ass, Levi. You've become boring in your old age."

"Fuck you, Teo!"

"You're not my type," he taunts, his smirk broadening on his lips. "My kitten, on the other hand…"

The idyllic ambiance is finally shattered by the sudden clash of my fist hitting Teo's face. His eyes grow wide in shock as he wipes the blood from his busted lip and just stares at it. There's a moment of silence that occurs, one that seems to stretch for an eternity before his amber eyes pull away from the specks of blood on his fingers and fix deadly on mine. A second later, Teo throws his first punch, which lands with a resounding thud across my cheek, further intensifying my already volatile mood. All too soon do we give into our basic animal instincts and begin to tear each other apart, blow by merciless blow. We become locked in a desperate struggle, grappling with fury and seeking dominance over each other on this sandy battleground.

"You punch like an old maid," Teo taunts further.

"Shut up! Just shut the fuck up!" I yell.

Harsh curses fly back and forth like seagulls fighting over scraps of food.

"It's all your fault! You killed them! You killed them!" I begin to shout, my accusations swirling in the air, highlighting all my past grievances against him and igniting new sparks of resentment.

"But that wasn't enough for you, was it? Not only did you have to wipe my parents off the face of the earth, you just had to find a way of stealing the woman I love from me too."

My hurling curses halt when Teo abruptly looks to the side and shakes his head at someone. That's when I see that our men have stumbled onto our makeshift fighting ring, where I'm adamant that only one king may be called the victor.

We face each other for a brief second with our fists clenched and eyes locked in an intense stare. Then the invisible string that kept me from losing control snaps, and we restart our exchange of furious punches, each blow landing with a vicious resounding thud. Sweat glistens on my brow as pure unadulterated hatred courses through my veins.

Not caring that we have an audience now, Teo strikes repeatedly with malicious intent, and I'm all too eager to follow his lead. Arms flail and feet stumble as the violent waves tumultuously continue to crash beside us, washing away the fresh blood absorbed by the sand. Our men watch with held breaths as the fight plays out against the peaceful backdrop of the ocean, infused with the fervor of each one of our blows.

Ducking, weaving, and counter-attacking, we both continue to battle fiercely for dominance over the other. My muscles strain with the strenuous effort as we trade powerful blows, the sound of tearing flesh and broken bones reverberating through the air. Determination etches Teo's face, unyielding in his pursuit of defeating me. But while Teo has spent most of his life indulging in every vice and pleasure known to mankind, I was born and bred to be a soldier.

This fight he will not win.

There are no tricks here.

No clever maneuvers or lies to safeguard him.

He has nothing but his fists.

And I've been using mine long before he knew what to do with his.

Even though Anya and Brick shout at the top of their lungs for us to stop, they don't dare to intervene, afraid that our wrath will spill onto them. Even if they tried, we're both too lost in our own pain and anguish to hear reason right now.

The only thing that catches me off guard is how Teo's smile just widens with every hit he suffers.

If I didn't know any better, I'd swear that Teo is taking as much satisfaction in me beating his face to a bloody pulp as I am.

Still, he never wavers as our fight rages on. Locked in a fierce contest of strength and willpower, neither of us backs down, refusing to give even an inch to the other.

I lose count of how many times my fists connect with echoing force into his stomach, jaw, and cheek, my rage intensifying with every passing moment. Each landing blow increases my determination, pushing me to unleash greater power. Fueled by sheer hatred and stinging pain, my movements become even faster, bringing the fight to its escalating pinnacle and dwindling Teo's energy. Exhaustion starts to take hold of him as his physical strength quickly begins depleting compared to mine. Bloodied and bruised, and now on his hands and knees, I just stare at him, panting loudly as my chest heaves profusely. Even from afar, I can almost taste the sense of collective relief washing over our friends that the fight is over, mingling with the dense scent of saltwater and adrenaline in the air. Yet I am still not satisfied. Not in the slightest.

"You fucking betrayed me, Teo. In the worst possible way. I loved you like my own brother, and you pissed that away like it was nothing. Like *I* was nothing!"

He cranes his neck back just enough for me to see much of his pretty face I ruined.

"Do it, Levi! Go ahead and do it! I know you have more in you than that," he taunts, spitting out blood, his eyes swollen beyond recognition. "Just do it!"

I swing my elbow back, ready to give him the final blow, when a woman who I believe to be Anya's lover by the way they have been carrying themselves for the past five days, suddenly rushes to the beach and places herself in between us.

"Don't! Don't," she shouts, tears streaming down her cheeks as she stretches her arms wide in front of him.

"Get out of the way, Cleo," Teo orders, trying to push her aside, but he's too damn weak to do more than hold himself up.

"He killed him! He killed him!" Cleo shouts frantically. "He did. I swear to you he did."

"Shut up, Cleo!" Teo yells.

"Killed who?" I ask, confused, my heavy breathing coming out in erratic spurts.

"Teo killed King Yusuf! I swear to you, he did. I sold him the poison to do it," she explains hysterically. "He did it! For you!" She points an accusing finger at me.

"What?" I stammer, baffled by what she's saying.

No.

No.

It's a trick.

"You're lying!"

"I'm not, you beast! Teo killed his father because of you!"

I shake my head, not wanting to hear her spin lies and confuse me, but the crazed woman continues on with her fictitious rambling.

"Teo couldn't live with what his father had done to your parents. He couldn't live with the guilt, even though he was just a scared boy who had no idea what his father's plans were when he took him to Arkøya. But you didn't care. You couldn't even see beyond your own grief to realize that a part of Teo died that day, too."

My jaw clenches at the way Teo's shoulders slump in shame, as if Cleo's words are digging up memories he'd rather keep buried. But to his chagrin, Cleo doesn't stop and continues on with her agitated rant.

"So one night, he came to me, looking like death itself. He said that either his father died that very night or he did. I didn't believe him until he grabbed my knife and aimed it at his heart. He told me that if I didn't give him something that would kill his father naturally, he would use my knife, carve out his own heart and send it to you. I couldn't let that happen, nor could I let anyone know Teo's intentions of killing his own father. If such news got out, King Orville would march his men south and kill Teo for treason. So I sold him the poison and insisted that I go with him back to his castle to help.

"While I entertained that pig Yusuf, Teo dropped the poison in his wine and gave it to him to drink. We both sat there and watched the monster gurgle every drop down. Then as Yusuf realized his mistake and started to grab his chest as if an iron pole were stabbing his heart, Teo stood over him, unwilling to miss a second of the life draining from his father's eyes.

'This is for Levi,' he said. 'This is for my brother.' Those were his exact words. Teo did it for you! And now you want to finish him? Give in to his incessant need of wanting to be punished for something he had no control over? You call that justice? You call that mercy? Shame on you, King Levi!" She spits at my feet. "My king told me stories about you. He told me there isn't a man in all of Aikyam who can compare to your just sense of honor. Even when you had no cause to hate him, he spent his whole life idolizing you, thinking you were a better man than he could ever be. But that's not what I just witnessed here today on this beach. I don't see an honorable king before me. All I see is another ruthless, petty man needing to hurl his pain onto others just so he can feel better about himself. Shame, King Levi! Shame!"

"Is this true?" I stutter, still overwhelmed with Cleo's version of accounts. "Did you really kill Yusuf?"

Teo falls on his back and stares into the crisp, blue autumn sky, tears starting to form at the corner of his eyes.

"Fucker died of a heart attack. Ironic since I didn't think the bastard had a heart to begin with," Teo answers, his voice heavy with grief.

I hold out my hand to Cleo, but she just stares at it as if I had daggers for fingers.

"Please, my lady. Give me a moment with my brother."

Cleo's forehead creases in suspicion, turning to her king for guidance.

"Go, Cleo. I'll be alright," he says with a bloody smile.

Cleo takes my hand so I may pull her up from the sand, but before she leaves us alone, she leans into my ear and says, "If you kill him, this beach will be your burial ground."

"Your loyalty alone demands I do no such thing. For a man to have gained such devotion from a fearless champion like yourself must be worthy of mine."

Begrudgingly, Cleo walks away to join the rest of the on-looking crowd. I drop to my knees beside Teo as he continues to stare at the sky through the small slit of his swollen eyes.

"That night when I went into your room," he starts, "I was trying to save you. I didn't know from what exactly, but my gut screamed at me that I had to try. So I stayed up late that night and sneaked my way into your room just so I could get you out of the castle without my father knowing about it. That's all I could think about. Your safety."

"Did you know?" I ask, my voice hoarse with unshed tears for the dead. "Did you know what he was going to do to my parents?"

He shakes his head.

"All I knew is what my father thought opportune to share with me. He told me Queen Alisa was dead and that King Orville believed one of his vassal's wives to be the culprit of their demise. Since my mother had recently passed away while giving birth to my baby sister Zara, King Orville demanded that she be handed off to him in my mother's place. I couldn't let that happen. I couldn't. So I begged my father to plead my sister's case and send me instead."

The ugly sneer that crests his face twists my heart further.

"But my father did no such thing. Instead, he told me he made another bargain with the mad king. We were to march to Arkøya, talk to King Krystiyan and convince him to hand over your mother. I knew your father would rather die than part with Queen Daryna, so I lied to myself, believing no harm would come from us going east and that his mission would prove fruitless. But deep down, I knew my father wouldn't give up so easily. That he had some sort of maniacal plan up his sleeve. I just couldn't fathom how monstrous his actions would be."

Memories of that night come at me like a tidal wave, knocking the very air out of my lungs.

'I can take the young prince back to his room so that you can continue your negotiations.'

'No! You can't kill him,' Teo had yelled out when his father charged at me with his sword.

I was so consumed with hatred and despair that I didn't even realize what Teo had done for me that night. My life was spared because he knew exactly which words to use to negotiate with his father without either one of us knowing his true intentions.

'Ask King Orville to send decrees across the eastern land, advising that King Krystiyan and Queen Daryna were slayed tonight for treason against him. Let him write that King Levi has been spared due to his loyal heart. And while it remains

that way, both he and every man, woman, and child born in the east will be protected by King Orville's merciful rule.'

Not only did Teo spare my life, but he prevented an all-out war from breaking out between the east and north. A war that I might not have been able to win due to my age and inexperience as king.

And just as that realization dawns on me, another one pierces my heart and shatters it completely.

'We remind him that death may sound like a blessing to him right now, but there are still people in Aikyam that he loves. Friends that love him just as much. Remind him that King Orville knows exactly who these friends are and wouldn't bat an eye at taking them from him. Remind him of the lesson his father just taught him tonight—that there are far worse things than death.'

At the time, I thought his words were a threat, but even back then, Teo had tried to tell me that he was still my brother, and though I may have wanted to die at that moment, I had to live to protect the ones I loved most since we were all facing the same kind of danger.

But I didn't see it.

I didn't see it.

Fuck! What have I done?!

"I'm so…" Teo tries to apologize but then turns to his side to cough up blood.

"Shh, Teo. Don't say anything else," I beg him, my eyes red with guilt-ridden tears.

"But—"

"But nothing, Teodoro. Just shut up so I can check if there is blood in your lungs," I order as I lean down on his chest, praying to all the gods who might be listening that I just didn't kill my own brother.

Relief swells in my chest when I confirm his wounds aren't life-threatening.

"Fuck, that hurts," he curses when I poke at his bruised ribs.

"It will for a while, but at least nothing is too severely broken."

"Tell that to my nose," he snorts out a laugh.

"You were too pretty to begin with. A broken nose will give you character."

"I don't know if I should be insulted that you think my character needs improvement or flattered for thinking that I'm pretty. I think I prefer the latter." He winks mischievously, trying to lighten the mood.

"You always were a vain fuck." I chuckle, needing the sound of our joined laughter to mend the fractured pieces of our painful shared past. "You need to see a healer. Can you walk?"

"I think I can manage if you help me." He displays that toothy, crimson grin of his, making me feel even more ashamed for what I just did to him.

Ever so carefully, I pull him up to his feet and wrap my arm around his waist, taking the brunt of his weight to my side.

"Tell you one thing, you sure pack one hell of a punch. There was a moment where my eyesight went all black on me."

"You're not too bad either." I chuckle. "My back molars are still aching from that one punch you threw at the beginning."

We both start laughing as we slowly walk to the bank of astonished onlookers.

"That's it? You both good now?" Brick asks suspiciously.

"Aye. We are. I'll explain later. First, get Teo a healer and some strong ale. He deserves it."

But before anyone can follow my command, the sound of hoofbeats in the distance pulls our attention back to the dirt road behind us—a

340

train of over three thousand riders rapidly approach us, displaying high in the air for all the world to see, a flag with one single royal blue rose imprinted on it.

Chapter 34
Teodoro

"He's gone mad, I tell you! Mad!" Monad, Katrina's chief-in-arms, shouts with eyes so big they threaten to pop out of their sockets.

"Anya, sweetheart, be a dear and hand some wine to the general. He needs something to calm his nerves to start making some sense," I chime in since, for the past half hour, all we have gotten from Monad is that someone has gone mad. And from where I'm sitting, he can be referring to just about anyone I know.

I shift in my seat, wincing with the pain caused by my bruised ribs as Anya dutifully hands Monad a chalice of wine, only for him to take the pitcher from her hands and chug it down instead.

"Stop moving," Cleo scolds as she and Levi's healer try their best to mend my wounds.

"Are you okay?" Levi asks, his expression filled with guilt from the beatdown he gave me earlier.

"Does he look like he's okay?" Cleo chastises, giving Levi a dirty look.

"Be nice, Cleo. That is my brother you're talking to." I smile, giving her hand a gentle squeeze.

She just cuts her eyes at both of us and thins her lips, not entirely on board with how Levi and I have settled things. The thing is, I would have gladly let him beat me to an inch of my life if it meant I would finally gain his forgiveness. Now that I have it, there is nothing that I would let stand in our way again. Not even my protective best friend.

But right now, we have more pressing issues to concentrate on.

Our uninvited guest for one.

Everyone inside the tent watches impatiently for Monad to drink his fill so he can finally explain why he and his men are marching west, just like the rest of us.

After a loud, disgusting belch, Monad wipes his mouth with his sleeve, looking like the wine has succeeded in calming his nerves.

"Where was I?" he asks, eyeing his confused audience.

"You were saying that he's gone mad," Levi coaxes with a frown. "But you have yet to tell us who."

"Isn't it obvious?" he counters as if the question didn't make any sense to him. "I'm talking about Adelid, Your Grace. It's our dear queen's uncle who has lost his goddamn mind."

Levi and I share a suspicious look since that was not the name we were expecting to hear slipping out of his mouth.

"Adelid? As in the late Queen Alisa's older brother?" I ask, needing to make sure we are talking about the same person.

"Yes!" he belts, slamming the pitcher of wine onto the table with a loud thud.

"I don't understand," Anya interjects, voicing our own confusion.

"What's not to understand, girl?!" he shouts in her direction, Cleo instantly stiffening beside me, her hand already at the dagger strapped to her thigh.

"If I were you, I'd be careful with your tone, my lordship," Levi's own general, Brick, reprimands, pulling Anya away from the half-crazed man. "And I'd start explaining myself instead of talking in riddles."

"Oh, for fuck's sake," he curses, "Have you not heard what's happening in Tarnow? Do you not know that our lady queen has been betrayed? That her reign is in danger in more ways than one? We are wasting precious time!"

"Gods be good, Monad, but if you don't start from the top, then we're not going to get anywhere with this conversation," Levi interjects with a harsh tone.

Monad slumps into a chair, taking a minute to compose himself, and lets out an exaggerated exhale.

"Fair enough," he mumbles. "A few weeks ago, a rider—one of my best sergeants—arrived inexplicably in Tarnow when his mission had been to accompany our queen in her travels through Aikyam. He brought a decree with him from King Atlas, and was adamant that it be read to her majesty's court. The message was chillingly clear. Queen Katrina of Bratsk had been taken prisoner by the west. King Atlas has proclaimed that the north's rule over the west is now forfeited and that our queen will remain in chains as long as he sees fit."

Fuck.

Fuck.

Fuck.

We were right.

Kat is in grave jeopardy.

A part of me didn't want to believe it.

I didn't want to believe that Atlas would be so cruel. That somehow the love he once had for our girl would prevail and keep her safe. But now, that whisper of hope has been entirely crushed with Monad's news.

"Oh, by the gods," Anya sobs into her hands, already fearing the worst for her beloved queen.

My eyes land on Levi, who looks like he's about to scorch the earth.

One of us needs to be clear-headed about this.

If Levi can't be, then I'm the one left with the burden to be so.

"You said Adelid had lost his mind, and yet it seems it is the king of the west to have gone mad," I announce, doing my best to temper my anxiety about learning that Kat is alone and scared, chained up somewhere in Atlas's castle.

"Aye, I remain true to my statement," he insists with a grave scowl. "Huwen may have our queen, but it is Adelid that holds Tarnow hostage."

"How so?" Levi counters, his bruised-up knuckles balled into fists at his side.

"After my man shared the horrific news with our majesty's court, he went into a tangent about how this was bound to happen with a woman on a throne. He called my lady queen weak and a danger to our northern way of life. I said that if we bowed down to the west and its demands of waiting to be a free kingdom, then it was only a matter of time before the east and south followed suit. Tarnow could not abide by such blackmail, and therefore we should renege our queen's claim to the throne in favor of King Orville's other legitimate child, Elijah of

Bratsk," Monad explains, his face growing red with rage by the second. "Now, I do not fault the boy for his birth, but all of Tarnow knew that he was just one of many of Orville's bastards, even if the queen herself had proclaimed him to be her brother. Yet when Adelid claimed that his mother, Salome, and King Orville wed in secret before his birth, the whole court just went along with the preposterous lie. It's almost as if Adelid had already whispered into the ear of the lords to back up his claim when the opportunity presented itself," he continues to explain, disgusted with his northern brethren. "Adelid then went on to say that since the boy is of young age, he would need a proxy to rule in his stead and claimed himself as King Regent," he adds, spitting to the floor as the very idea of Adelid ruling over Aikyam churns his stomach.

"If all you say is true, then why are you here, Monad?" I ask, suspicious of the man's intentions.

"Because I am loyal to the true winter queen," he retorts, squaring his shoulders and putting out his large belly forward as if insulted by my question. "Not all of us fell in line with Adelid's power-hungry grab for the throne. We remained true to our lady queen, hence why I traveled all this way here with my men. Our aim is to rescue our righteous queen from the clutches of one madman so that she can aid us in getting rid of the other that sits on her throne."

Though Monad isn't the most likable man, his words ring true.

"What are we going to do?" Anya asks, still looking overwhelmed by everything we just heard.

"Are you well enough to ride?" Levi asks, taking stock of all my injuries.

"Yes," I retort without hesitation.

"Then there is only one thing we can do. We march west," he announces with steel resolve. "Save our queen first so we may save her kingdom second."

But just like life, nothing is ever that simple.

Three days later, we come to the top of a hill, and while staring at Huwen Castle from above, Brick mutters under his breath, "It's a suicide mission."

"Fuck me," Cleo stutters in astonishment, eyeing all the armored ships lining the western shore.

"Gods help us," Anya prays on her horse beside Cleo.

"It'll be a massacre," Monad blurts out, just as amazed at the sight.

The only ones who remain silent are myself and Levi.

I tilt my head to him before galloping to a quiet spot on the hill where none of our friends can hear us. He follows my lead, his face giving nothing away.

"Did you know about this?" I ask when we are far enough from earshot.

"No." He shakes his head despondently.

"Don't give me that, Levi. You must have had some sort of inkling of Atlas's plan."

"I didn't," he insists. "All he asked was that I march my men to the northern border and await his instructions. He never once told me he had an army ten times the size of my own."

"Were you taking instructions from Atlas? Since when have you ever let anyone give you orders?" I rebuke, running my fingers through my hair.

"It wasn't like that, Teo. At the time, I thought taking down Tarnow was a combined effort. I had no way of knowing Atlas had this up his sleeve. I'm as surprised as you are. Trust me," he grumbles with a clenched jaw.

"Well, I gotta hand it to our kid brother. He doesn't half-ass shit." I sigh. "There is no way our army will be able to defeat his."

"We have to try. We can't just leave Kat with him," Levi states assertively. "She's been held against her will long enough. Who knows what Atlas is doing to her."

Fuck.

Would Atlas really hurt our Kat?

Is he that far gone?

"Stay strong, brother," I tell him, giving his shoulder a comforting squeeze. "If you lose your shit now, then we are as good as lost. You're our best hope in saving her."

Levi places his hand on mine and stares me straight in the eye.

"We both are."

He then tilts his head toward the castle, his green eyes taking a wistful gleam in them.

"Do you think she sees us up here?"

'Everyone can see us up here,' I think to myself.

Which means that Atlas sees us too.

The element of surprise is long gone, and now we are completely at his mercy.

But just as the somber thought begins to take root, whispering we will not come out of this alive, my eyes catch the flicker of a white banner carried by a fast-approaching soldier on horseback.

"Rider! Rider!" Brick screams at the top of his lungs.

Levi and I ride to join the head of our train and await his arrival.

Draped in the traditional orange colors of the west, with a marigold crest on his vest, the rider stops right in front of us, keeping his white banner hanging up in the air.

"King Levi. King Teodoro. My ladies and my lords," he greets with a bow. "Welcome to Huwen. My king and his lady queen wish to extend their well-wishes and greetings to our shores and request that you all follow me back to the castle so they may greet you in person."

None of us say it, but we all think it.

This is a trap.

But before I reject the not-so-generous offer, Levi beats me to the punch.

"Thank you. It will be an honor."

The soldier smiles and turns his horse for us to follow him.

"What the fuck are we doing, Levi?" I whisper at his side, not excited by the idea of riding toward my own death.

"If you have a better plan to get inside that castle without being murdered, I'm all ears," he whispers back.

"Shit. I have nothing," I mumble in frustration.

"That's what I thought. Now smile, Teo, and get ready to use that southern charm of yours. Something tells me we're going to need it."

Fuck.

No pressure.

May the gods save us all.

Chapter 35
Atlas

"Come here, princess," I coo, pulling my anxious girl to sit on my lap so I can kiss her sweet lips one more time before our guests arrive. When I feel her tense muscles start to relax and her body molding itself to mine, I gently pull my lips from hers while I still have the will to do so.

"Feel better?"

With her lips now beautifully swollen from our kiss, she throws me a tempting shy smile and rests her head on my shoulder.

"A bit." She sighs, staring at the large double doors at the end of my heavily guarded great hall. "Do you think they'll come?"

"Yes," I reply steadfastly.

She cranes her head back ever so slightly, fixing her piercing, silver eyes to my blue gaze.

"You sound awfully confident. You know that most people in Levi and Teo's shoes would probably think you were setting up a trap for them and therefore decline your invitation."

"Aye. Nevertheless, they'll come, and if I know my brothers like I do, they'll try to set a trap of their own to steal you away from me."

"That's not funny, Attie." She frowns, her nervous tension returning at full force, weighing heavily on her shoulders.

"I wasn't trying to be funny, princess," I tell her truthfully. "Levi and Teo are here to take you from me, of that I have no doubt. It comes down to you to decide if you want them to steal you away or not."

"You know that's not what I want," she whispers low enough so my guards don't hear.

I run my thumb over the worried lines on her forehead and press a chaste kiss on the tip of her nose.

"No. My greedy queen wants all three of us to worship her at the altar. Isn't that right?"

She looks at me expectantly, chewing on that fat bottom lip that always seems like it's begging me to bite it.

"If I say aye, would you think less of me for it?"

"If that is what you want, then there is nothing I won't do to make it so."

"Are you saying—"

"I'm saying if you want me, Levi, and Teo, then you shall have us. I'll find a way to get them on board. Although, I doubt they'll need much convincing."

"You'd share me with them?" she asks, amazed.

"As long as I can call you mine, I'm perfectly content in sharing you with my brothers."

The look of utter love that takes over her face has me hard as steel, so much so that I'm sure my dick is poking her ass. Suddenly, the idea of fucking my princess on my throne of skulls, right here and now, takes precedence over our guests.

"Oh, no. I know that look. Don't even think about it." She giggles, slapping my chest and pushing herself off my lap.

"Just what do you think you are doing?" I ask a bit too harshly as I watch her fix her gown, followed by the crown on her head as she positions herself to stand beside the throne.

"What does it look like? I'm getting ready to meet our guests."

Pissed that she would think so little of me, I get up from my seat and grab her by the waist to plant her perfect peachy ass on the throne. I then gently grab her chin and lean into her so there is only a small space between us.

"You are the queen of Aikyam, Your Highness. If there is anyone in this hall that should be seated on a throne, it's you."

"This from a man who insists on calling me princess," she retorts with a teasing smile, her cheeks turning a pretty shade of pink.

"Outside our bedroom's walls, you are my sovereign queen and therefore should be given every inch of respect that title affords you. But when we're alone and in our bed, that's a whole other matter. There you can be the spoilt, needy little princess I know you to be— the one who loves to gag on my cock before begging to be fucked with it." I wink.

She licks her lips, her eyes going half-mast with the pretty little picture I just planted in her brain.

If I'm hard, then it's only fair she be just as flustered.

I'm about to tempt her further when one of my squires rushes over to us.

"They're here," he says, breaking the spell we're under.

I stand back to give the boy my full attention.

"Are the kings alone?"

"No, Your Highness. They have two men and a woman with them."

"Very well. Let King Levi and King Teodoro in, but only them. Their entourage can enter after we've had a private audience with them first."

The boy offers me a curt nod and runs to do my bidding.

"Are you ready?" I ask my jittery queen.

"As ready as I'll ever be," she answers.

"Good. Now I know that it's going to be hard for you, but for the duration of our talk, I want you to stay seated exactly where you are. Don't get up, no matter what."

Her forehead instantly wrinkles in confusion.

"Levi and Teo's banners weren't the only ones we saw. The north has come for you too, and until I know who is accompanying my brothers, I'd rather keep you safe where my men can intervene in case of an attack."

She nods reluctantly and schools her anxious features to look cold and regal—like the true winter queen that she is.

With my arm draped over my throne, I lean against it as I wait to be reacquainted with my brothers again after so many years apart.

This reunion can only go two ways—in celebratory cheer or in bloody carnage.

"This should be fun," I joke, only to have Kat slam her arm across my stomach.

"Easy now, kitten. If anyone is going to hit the asshole standing beside you, might as well let us get a crack at it," Teo's whimsical voice rings loudly through the hall.

Kat and I turn our attention to the two men strutting in our direction as they walk down the makeshift corridor made up of heavily armed guards on either side. I'm unable to hide my crooked smile when my eyes land on my older stoic brother, Levi, looking like the great soldier king that he is as he marches toward us with conviction. But when my eyes shift to my mischievous brother, I see that their travels west must have had some mishaps on the way since Teo looks like someone used his face as a punching bag.

Kat begins to shift in her seat, the urge to run into their arms too strong to keep her rooted to her spot. I can't even chastise her for it since I'm having a hard time, too, with memories of our youth coming at me from all directions.

Still, we're not those boys anymore.

We're kings.

Kings who would do just about anything for the woman we love.

And unbeknownst to them, their unconditional love is about to be tested in a way it never was.

I wasn't lying to her when I said that if she wanted all three of us, I would do everything in my power to grant her that desire. But I can only do so much. In the end, Levi and Teo will have to come to the same conclusion I have. To claim Kat as ours, we will have to find a way to share her love. If even one of them refuses, then my princess will never be truly whole, and that is fucking unacceptable to me.

Only the gods know if they feel the same.

When both kings finally reach the end of the line and stand tall in front of us, it's up to me to break the tense-filled silence lingering about. And what better way than to ruffle their feathers a little.

"Levi, Teo, thank you for accepting our invitation. Welcome to Huwen," I greet them, taking two steps toward them while still keeping the advantage of higher ground. "By the looks of it, you two had a rough time getting here. Teo more than you, Levi. Let me guess?" I hum mockingly. "Did a little detour to settle some old scores, did you?"

"Aye. And we're here to settle another," Levi growls, eyeing Kat carefully to see if she's still intact.

"Whatever do you mean?" I taunt.

"You know damn well why we're here, Atlas. You lied to me. You said you'd keep Katrina safe, and yet you're keeping her prisoner," Levi seethes through gritted teeth, throwing daggers at me with his emerald eyes. He then turns his menacing gaze over to our queen, his expression immediately softening. "Are you well, my heart? Did he hurt you? Fuck, I'm so sorry you had to go through this. I should have never let you leave Arkøya. But I'm here now. *We're* here now." Levi turns to Teo to drive his point home. "I'll get you out of here. I promise. Even if it's the last thing I do, I'll get you home."

The misery in Levi's voice is too intense for Kat, and against my counsel, she rises from her seat to stand beside me.

Katrina laces her fingers with mine—not only shocking Levi and Teo, but me too—her silver eyes pleading with the two kings for understanding.

"I *am* home, my king. Huwen is as much my home as Arkøya, Nas Lead, or Tarnow. They all have a place in my heart, for they all belong to Aikyam and, therefore, to me as I am their rightful queen."

Though the message she just relayed is subtle, it still packs a hell of a punch—one that knocks my angry brothers off-kilter.

"Ah fuck, kitten. What have you done?" Teo mutters in disbelief, reading the writing on the wall before Levi is able to add two and two together.

To her credit, she doesn't so much as flinch at the accusation. Instead, she holds her head up high and squeezes my hand tighter.

"I'm sorry you came all this way believing I was being kept against my will. As you can see, I assure you that I'm not. Having said that, my heart is full seeing you both together. I cannot tell you how much I prayed to the gods to see such a union. If nothing comes out of this visit today, then at least I can take solace in the fact that you both have repaired your friendship and found each other again," she says in earnest, her silver gaze glistening with happy tears for Teo and Levi being able to heal their past trauma and find enough common ground to mend their friendship.

Teo's golden stare melts into liquid lava, her words meaning more to him than she could possibly realize. This time it's Teo's turn to shock the hell out of me when he decides to fall to one knee and bow his head to her.

"If there was anyone who could perform such a miracle, it was you, my queen. It was our need to save you that got us here, together. Now I'm not sure what exactly has transpired in these last few months, but I can see that you speak the truth and that you are well. That's all I need to know to settle my wayward heart."

Kat lets out her held breath and lowers her hand over to Teo for him to take. With eyes closed, he kisses her knuckles before standing back up.

But while she smiles lovingly at Teo, my scrutinizing gaze never leaves Levi's empty one. My older brother's cold expression is the real cause for concern here, even if my princess doesn't realize it yet.

"Levi, will you not bow to her majesty, the queen?" I ask, eyeing his every move.

With a blank expression on his face, he takes a half-assed bow, making no attempts to kiss his woman's hand.

Stubborn fucker.

When he gets back to his feet, his face is all business.

"Since you're in good health and in no need of saving, Your Highness, then I see no reason why my men and I cannot retreat back to Arkøya."

"But *I* need you," Kat blurts out, hurt, before she remembers she has an attentive audience. "I mean, I need your troops, King Levi. Although there is no fight to be fought here, there are still dangers lurking in Aikyam. Dangers that need to be snuffed out before they get out of control."

"If you are referring to the King Regent, King Atlas has enough men with him to assist you," he replies, scornfully looking at me as if my omission of the size of my army is just another betrayal he has to swallow down.

"King Regent?" Kat repeats, confused.

"You don't know?" Teo interjects, sensing that Levi is in no mood to calmly share any information they were able to obtain. "Your uncle has claimed the northern throne, kitten. He has crowned your brother king in your absence and gave himself the title of King Regent, acting as Elijah's proxy."

"Atlas." She squeezes my hand with fear in her voice. "It's starting."

"I know," I mumble, hating that my princess can't take a second to concentrate on matters of the heart when she's too overwhelmed with the thought her brother could be in danger. "Where did you hear this?" I ask Teo point-blank.

"On our way here, we came across a train from the north headed by your chief-in-arms," he explains, his eyes never leaving Kat.

"Monad is here?" she asks, surprised. "Bring him in. Bring him in at once!" she orders, releasing her hand from mine and walking back to sit on the throne.

I snap my fingers at one of my guards to do as she says, and two minutes later, Monad is escorted in.

"Your Royal Highness," he greets, not only surprised to see his queen sitting on a throne of skulls but also apprehensive about seeing me standing tall at her side.

"Talk!" she orders, bypassing any ounce of polite decorum. "I want to know why you are here and what my uncle has done. Now!"

Monad's jaw drops to the floor, eyeing Teo and Levi for support, because his queen looks ready to murder him where he stands. When he gets no such help from either one of them, he begins to tell us everything he knows.

He confesses that after receiving my decree from the northern soldier I set free, Adelid used it as a valid excuse to dethrone the queen and replace her with her younger brother. He also reveals how most of the northern court accepted such a *coup d'etat* without so much as a blink of an eye.

Disloyal-fucking-traitors.

"Yet, you are here. Why?" my queen asks suspiciously.

Monad's eyes can't tear themselves away from my throne as if each skull were whispering in his ear to be wary of his words.

"Your queen asked you a question, Monad. If I were you, I would answer it. As you can see by my throne, I don't take kindly to northern usurpers." I grin sinisterly, remembering the first thing I did after returning home from my seven-year voyage—kill every last northerner that Adelid had left to hold Huwen hostage and use their skulls to adorn my throne.

"Because I swore my allegiance to the one true queen of Aikyam. As did my men and many other brave souls who still breathe winter air back in Tarnow."

"If that were true, you would have brought my brother with you instead of leaving him at the mercy of a madman!" she yells, slamming her fist on the arm of the throne.

Monad drops to his knees, pleading for forgiveness.

"I tried, my queen. Gods know, I tried," he pleads, his face red. "But your uncle keeps the boy and his mother under heavy guard. I couldn't risk rescuing him without alerting Adelid of my intentions to flee Tarnow and ride out west to rescue you. I had to make a decision—either save my queen or the boy. To me, there was only one option."

"You chose wrong," she says with venom in her tone.

Accosted by shame, Monad lowers his eyes from his queen, gaining an immediate scoff from my eldest brother.

"If this is how you treat your loyal subjects, then I see the western shores have washed away your sense of mercy as well as logic," Levi states resentfully, making his disappointment clear.

"Levi," Teo tries to calmly interject, holding onto Levi's arm before he does or says something he will regret.

"No, Teo. The winter queen will hear me out," he rebukes, shaking Teo's hand off him so that he may take center stage. "For the past few days, I have ridden shoulder to shoulder with your chief-in-arms and heard of his struggle to get here. Against all odds, he managed to gather enough men to come to your aid, and this is how you repay his loyalty? If you want to blame anyone for what has happened in Tarnow and to your brother, look no more than to the man standing at your side, for it was he who started this avalanche of dire events. Had Atlas not kidnapped you—and don't even try lying to me that he didn't, for I won't believe a word—your uncle wouldn't feel like this was the perfect opportunity to grasp for your crown," Levi reprimands, never once losing the steam. "Or if your new lover has blinded you too much to see fault in him, then place the blame of your brother's predicament on your own shoulders, for that is what a true leader does—take responsibility for their subject's actions."

"Are you done, brother?" I bark at him, my own temper taking over.

"Don't call me that, Atlas," he growls, pointing an intimidating finger at me. "You have lost that right."

"And what about me, King Levi?" Kat chimes in, using the same harsh tone that Levi currently holds. "You've already accused me of losing heart as well as soul. Have I lost your fealty as well?"

Levi thins his lips and says nothing.

"I see," she mutters under her breath. "Very well, my king. Then I'll simplify things for you. I treasure my kingdom as I do my crown, but if I was hard on Monad just now, it's because there are just some things that are far more important to me than keeping my title as queen. The people I love, for one, my baby brother being at the very top of that list. So forgive me if my harsh resentment was too much for your delicate sensibilities to take. Believe me when I say that your anger toward me isn't easy to bear, either. Therefore, I'm going to give you a choice. I'm going to give you *both* a choice," she says, her arctic gaze sliding off Levi momentarily to Teodoro's. "Tomorrow, all those fleets you saw aligning the Huwen shore will sail north to Tarnow with the sole objective of saving my brother and restoring me back to my rightful seat on the throne. If your loyalties still lie with me, then you will come with us and fight by my side to make my dream of a unified, peaceful Aikyam a reality. If they are not, then I release you of your obligations as my vassals and deem each one of your kingdoms yours as sovereign free nations to rule as you please. The east, south, and west have suffered enough under the rule of one mad king. I will not be accused of doing the same."

She then stands up from the throne, takes two steps forward, and proclaims, "You have until tomorrow morning to decide, for we sail at dawn."

And with those words still hanging in the air, she leaves.

"That was quite an exit, princess. You should really consider a career on the stage," I tease when I enter the library to find Kat huddled on a velvet sofa with her handmaiden, Inessa.

"Do you think me mad, Attie?" she asks sullenly, lowering her eyes. "Having offered Levi and Teo such options?"

"I can't speak for Levi, but there is no way you'll get rid of me that easily," Teo says whimsically, trailing behind me.

"Teo?" she calls in astonishment.

"The one and only, kitten. Now, how about you come here and give me a proper welcome?"

Kat doesn't hesitate and springs to her feet, rushing toward him, instantly jumping into his open arms.

"Teo," she sobs, holding him tightly.

"There, there, kitten. You didn't think I'd scare off so easily, did you?" he taunts, holding her just as fiercely. After a few minutes, when she's cried her fill, he breaks the embrace just enough to palm his hands on her cheeks.

"You really are full of surprises, aren't you, kitten?" he says adoringly.

"I've missed you. I've missed you so much."

"Not nearly as much as I missed you," he retorts before crashing his mouth on hers.

My princess purrs as he slides his tongue into her mouth, his hands falling from her face to grab her lush ass just so that his body is perfectly connected to hers. I am more than happy to let the two have their moment when I realize that not everyone is as comfortable as I am in watching such a reunion go down. Inessa shifts in her seat embarrassingly, not knowing where to look, making me take pity on her.

I walk over to the pair of lovebirds and snake my hand around my princess's waist and pull her lips off of Teo's by tugging at her braid. But instead of cooling her libido, her heady gaze bounces off me and Teo's, her ass rubbing unashamed against my now hard cock.

"There will be plenty of time for us to play later," I whisper to both of them. "First, Teo brought with him a couple of people who want an audience with you. Now be a good queen and save that fire for later."

I tuck Kat safely behind me while Teo rubs his thumb over his lips, not hiding the hunger in his amber eyes.

"You," I tell him. "Play nice, and I'll let you play with your favorite pet later."

He laughs, placing a hand on my shoulder.

"Little Attie grew some balls, huh?" he jokes, and the familiarity of his teasing chuckle feels like a soothing balm to my soul.

When I was younger, I used to hate the sound of his laugh, but now? Now it feels like brotherly affection, which I didn't realize how much I had missed.

"So? Are you going to hug me or what, asshole?" he says with a teasing smirk.

I let him wrap his arms around me, my black heart mourning the fact that I may never have this type of moment with Levi. When we pull apart, Teo sees the flicker of sadness in my gaze.

"Give him time, Attie," he whispers softly so our love doesn't overhear. "Just hours ago, we thought we were here to drive a sword into your heart for hurting Kat. Give him room for his feelings to catch up with this new reality."

"You don't seem to have had much of a problem with it."

"Aye, but I'm not as prideful as our older brother," he retorts with a sigh. "Besides, I've made my peace with it long before now."

I'm about to ask him what he means by that when a loud shriek pierces my eardrum.

"Anya!" Both Kat and Inessa scream out with glee as they run over to a red-haired handmaiden Teo brought with him.

I watch the three women hug each other, their happy tears falling from their cheeks, as they all profess their sisterly love for each other. Again, there is a pang in my chest, hating that Levi's stubbornness is keeping us from having such a reunion.

The women are still holding each other's hands when another guest enters the room, clearing his throat to bring their attention to him.

"Your Highness," he says before bowing in respect. "I hate to interrupt such a happy moment, but if it would be alright with you, I'd like to speak with Inessa in private."

"I'd be more than happy, Brick, but it's really up to Inessa." Kat smiles.

With her head held high, Inessa walks over to Brick, her cold expression giving nothing away.

"My lady." He bows again, only this time his fixed stare remains on the raven beauty.

"General."

"My heart is happy to see you are well," he says nervously.

"Is that all your heart is? Happy?"

He stands up straight and stares lovingly into her eyes.

"Nay, my lady. My heart is a chaotic mess of longing and agony. It has suffered for months from not being able to look upon your beautiful face. It has longed for far too long to touch your creamy skin and breathe in your floral scent. My misery may have eased somewhat, knowing that you are in good health, but it still aches for more. So much more, my lady."

"You sound just like your letters. I'm surprised, since I assumed they were written by a hired poet and not by a hardened soldier like yourself," she retorts, still holding onto her icy tone.

"Aye. The letters were all written by my hand. I guess love has made a poet out of me." He shrugs shyly.

"And is that all you have to give me? Pretty words on a piece of parchment?" She arches a brow.

When he begins to grasp for the right words that never come, looking completely out of his depth at how to win his woman's heart, I almost pity the poor, lovesick fool for even trying.

"Oh, for fuck's sake, Brick. You sure are dense." She rolls her eyes before grabbing at his lapel and pressing her lips against his.

And suddenly, watching these two lovers kiss before us brings up the memory of another kiss I spied on—the one between Teo and my princess.

I was just a foolish teenager back then, still learning the ways of the world.

But it was on that day, when I watched Teo kiss my princess, that I learned the most important lesson of all.

I realized that no matter how much I wanted it, my Kat would never be solely mine.

Her heart would always be split in three ways between us.

At fifteen, I made peace with that stark truth.

I just pray that Levi finds the same wisdom and comes to terms with it sooner rather than later.

If not, he may risk losing her forever.

Chapter 36
Teodoro

"So, we are to sail north, not ride there?" I ask Atlas while Kat and her handmaidens catch up for old times' sake.

He just nods, his gaze never leaving our woman.

"It's clever. Adelid will naturally assume that if anyone is to march north, they will take the eastern border. He won't suspect us coming from behind."

"You sound surprised." He laughs, finally straying his gaze off Kat long enough to hold a conversation with me. "I have spent the better part of seven years coming up with this plan."

"Aye, but from what Levi tells me, it was to overthrow Katrina and not her uncle."

"Plans change," he retorts with a smirk before his attention slides off me to fix on Kat again.

"I can see that." I chuckle as my own stare follows his to find my kitten still enjoying her time with her best friends. But when Brick shifts in his seat at the corner of the room, impatiently counting down the minutes until he can get some alone time with Inessa, my mind wanders back to his king.

"Is it also true that you intended to crown Levi king of Aikyam if you had been successful in your coup?"

The minute I mention our older brother, Atlas frowns and gives me a curt nod as I reply.

"Now that surprises me."

"How come?" he asks, turning his attention back my way.

"Well, I would assume you would want the crown for yourself. You have the men, the power, and the cunning to achieve such a goal. So why risk life and limb to put Levi on the throne when you could have kept it for yourself?"

"Aye, I might have all those things, but I still lack the essential characteristics to be a fair and just king. To prevail, Aikyam needs a symbol of hope. A strong leader with integrity and a kind dutiful heart. Do you think me capable of such a thing?" He arches his brow.

"I think most of the west would disagree with you. Your people love you. That alone tells me you're a good king." I smile.

"It's different here. Huwen and I share a common trauma. I would never be able to see past my resentment of the north to lead it. Levi, on the other hand, could. His sense of honor wouldn't allow anything less of him," he explains with absolute conviction. "We both know he has always been the best of us. The only one we would follow blindly. He's the kind of king we model ourselves after. The one we inspire to become. Am I wrong?"

"No." I shake my head. "You're not. He is all those things and more."

"What did I tell you? He beat your ass black and blue, and you still look up to him. That's a king, Teodoro. We're simply understudies."

I can't help but laugh at his comparison, my hand rubbing at the small crook of my nose.

"True. He did do a number on my face." I laugh.

"It's an improvement. Trust me. No man should be that fucking pretty anyways."

"Levi said something similar." I laugh some more. "If I didn't know any better, I'd say you guys were jealous." I nudge his shoulder playfully with mine.

"Oh, fuck off, Teo." Atlas laughs, gaining the attention of our woman.

Katrina smiles at us with love in her eyes, happy to see us getting along after so many years apart. And when I wink at her, her cheeks blush crimson before she returns to her conversation with her friends.

"Levi might be all those things, brother, but he'd never be her," I tell him, watching my love giggle away with her girls. "She's the one with a heart big enough to fit all of Aikyam in. She's the queen that was meant to lead us all. The one that will make us whole again."

Atlas doesn't add anything to my comment and just watches her with attentive eyes instead.

He knows as well as I do that Katrina of Bratsk was born for this role—to be Queen of Aikyam. And our hearts.

"They're going to be here all night, aren't they?" Atlas utters, revealing his own impatience about waiting to get rid of his guests so that Kat's attention is fully on him again.

"Give the girls a little more time." I laugh. "You'll soon realize that those three are attached to the hip. Nothing could tear them apart."

He sighs, leaning against the wall and taking in their comradery.

"We used to be like that," he says with a nostalgic taint in his voice.

"Aye," I retort, my shoulders slumping a little. "But I could have been a better brother to you."

"Brothers fight, Teo. Don't go looking at the past and try to change it now."

"Still, it shames me that I didn't believe in you. Levi never doubted that you could be a captain of a large fleet one day. But I did. In fact, I even resented him for putting such ideas in your head. I honestly believed you wouldn't survive an hour out at sea, much less days on end. And for that, I'm sorry."

"There's no need to apologize, Teo. As much as I hate to say it, you were right," he states evenly. "I almost died a dozen times before I reached Maffei. I was half-dead when I reached Halfdan's shores. Hate and revenge were the only things that kept me breathing. As luck would have it, Cristobal arrived a few days later with Ulrich in tow. Unbeknownst to my mother, Cristobal had spent the better part of fifteen years searching all the kingdoms for a healer that could remedy my illness. When he found such a man, he brought him directly to her cousin, hoping that Halfdan would put him on a ship to Huwen. Cristobal couldn't do it himself, fearing my father would reject such a gift from a man who never hid his love for my mother. But if the physician was sent by her dearest cousin, my father wouldn't bat an eye and would welcome Ulrich with open arms. Unfortunately, neither one of them lived long enough to see me healthy."

"I'm sorry, Atlas. Levi told me what happened to the Lioness. I know how much you loved her."

"Aye," he retorts stoically, not wanting to broach the subject any further.

"I hate to ask, but what happened to King Faustus? Levi was unclear about how your father died."

"That's because he wanted to spare you the sordid details of his demise," he explains, clearing his throat as if that subject is just as painful to discuss as his mother's untimely death. "With my mother and I gone, and the north savagely stealing every western woman from their home to trade with the other kingdoms, my father just gave up. Gave up on Huwen and gave up on himself. Like you, he didn't expect me to survive my escape either. And when he heard no word from me, he threw himself off the tallest tower of the castle into the ocean. I think he believed it was the only way he could be reunited with his family since he knew how much my mother and I always loved the ocean. Ironic, really. My father had been a coward for most of his life when it came to water, never once stepping on board a ship for fear of drowning. And yet, his final act on this earth was to bravely face his largest fear head-on. For the longest time, I didn't know if I should weep or laugh at his single act of courage."

"Fuck, Attie. That is—"

"Intense? Tell me about it," he grumbles, running his fingers through his hair. "When that fucker, King Orville, lost his wife, he ensured that everyone shared his suffering. When my father lost the love of his life, he preferred death rather than spending a single day without her. Now tell me, Teo? If you lost *her*," he says, tilting his chin toward Kat, "what path would you choose? Because I have an inkling that it's different from mine."

A cold shiver runs down my spine as I stare deep into his light eyes and come to this realization—Atlas would burn the world asunder if he ever lost his queen.

Of that, I have no doubt.

I, on the other hand, have wished too many times for death in the past to not know the answer to his question.

Suddenly, his praising words about Levi being the better man out of the three of us rings truer than they ever had before. Even if Levi lost his beloved Kat, he would find a way to forge on, even if only for his people. He wouldn't go mad with grief or give in to his melancholy.

He would put his own needs to the side for the sake of his kingdom.

Even if his heart was broken and bleeding inside, he'd never show it.

For his sake, I hope it never comes to that.

"Enough fucking chitchat, Teo," Atlas utters abruptly. "It's been a long ass day, and I'm ready to call it a night."

Without further explanation, he pushes himself off the wall and walks over to the other side of the room where the girls are.

"Ladies, I must bid you all goodnight. It's been a pleasure, but it's time your queen went to bed."

While Kat blushes as she takes Atlas's hand to pull her up from the sofa, Brick lets out a large exhale of relief and rushes to his love.

"Thank the gods," he blurts out before rushing over to Inessa. "Come, my lady. It's time you went to bed, too."

He doesn't even wait for a reply as he hoists Inessa over his broad shoulder and runs out of the room before she has time to say a word in protest.

"Well, I guess that's that." Anya giggles before jumping out of her seat. "Cleo is probably going crazy without me too." She waves her goodbyes and skips out of the room.

Frozen on my spot, I watch Atlas and Kat head toward the door, stopping right under its threshold.

"Well," Atlas asks, the pair of lovers looking at me over their shoulders. "Are you just going to stand there all night, or are you coming?"

"He's coming, aren't you, Teo?" my kitten coos, holding her hand out for me to take.

Not having to be told a third time, I reach her hand in a few long strides and lace her fingers with mine. We walk out of the room and begin to head down a long corridor, my heart racing madly in my chest with each step we take.

"Did you have a nice talk with your friends, princess?" Atlas asks, looking completely at ease.

"I did, and I can confirm that Monad is officially off my list of suspects. Anya told me that on the way here, she prodded and probed him for information and concluded that he was as clueless as I was to everything happening in Aikyam," she states sullenly.

"I assumed as much. He wouldn't have risked leaving Tarnow to rescue you if he had been in cahoots with Adelid and your father," Atlas adds his two cents.

"Are you two seriously talking about politics right now?" I ask wide-eyed and amazed at how in charge of their feelings they are, whereas I'm completely losing my mind with what we are about to do.

"Have to get it out of the way before we reach Atlas's bedroom. Once those doors close behind us, then royal business is completely off the table." Kat winks at me.

"Well, let's pick up the pace, shall we?" I urge, pulling Kat by the hand and hurrying our steps.

"Looks like someone is in a rush," Atlas teases.

"Fuck off, Atlas. You've had her all to yourself for close to two months now. It's time you learned how to share." I laugh excitedly now that I'm finally going to hear my kitten purr.

"Oh, believe me, I'm ready." Atlas smirks. "And so is our needy queen, isn't that right, princess?"

When Kat's eyes go half-mast, her tongue peeking out to wet her parched lips, my cock instantly hardens.

Shit, but I missed how good she looks when she gets this way—all hungry and greedy for attention.

Images of undressing her with my teeth lead to more hurried steps.

"Where the fuck is your room, Atlas?" I grunt impatiently.

"It's upstairs," he replies, pointing to the large staircase a few meters away.

Aye, that's not going to work for me. Too damn far, and I've waited long enough as it is.

"What's over there?" I ask, pointing to two-pane glass doors at the end of the hall.

"That's the entrance to the greenhouse," Atlas explains, puzzled at what I'm getting at.

"You have a greenhouse and didn't tell me?" Kat interrupts, already eager to see the exotic flowers and plants holed up there.

"Forgive me, princess, but aside from staring at my bedroom ceiling, you didn't seem very interested in taking in the sights of my castle," he jokes, tapping his finger on the tip of her nose.

"It's perfect."

"Perfect for what?" she asks excitedly.

"For a little game of cat and mouse."

"Hmm. And who will be playing the mouse in this scenario?"

"Take a little guess?" I grin mischievously, giving her ass a nice hard slap for good measure. "Run, kitten. Run."

And without needing any more convincing, Kat takes off at record speed, leaving Atlas and me in her wake.

"Hmm. This should be fun." Atlas hums beside me as we reach the entrance of the greenhouse. "Please, guests first," he taunts, opening the door for me. "I would say beauty before young age, but Levi kind of took the fun out of that one."

I give him the finger and begin to whistle, so our girl knows that wherever she's hiding, it won't do her any good. Pity she won't have enough time to appreciate all the beautiful flowers here. Maybe I'll pluck one out for her and make her bite it in between her teeth while Atlas and I take turns devouring her pussy.

Atlas whistles and orders me to go left while he goes right.

"If you don't find her, we'll meet down the middle," I whisper, getting a consenting nod from him.

"Here, kitty. I have a treat for you," I taunt, cupping my hard-on.

"That's not how you play the game, Teo. You have to find me first," she teases back, her voice too far away for me to locate her.

My smile widens at her cockiness as I continue to scan the perimeter, looking for pale-blonde hair to give away her hiding spot. But five minutes into our little game, I start to kick myself for parting ways with Atlas. He must know this greenhouse like the back of his hand, while I haven't the faintest idea where the fuck I am.

"Humph!"

"Are you there, kitten?" I ask after hearing a muffled cry.

I start to head in one direction, only to stop when I hear the sound of a crashing pot.

"Kitten?" I call out again, and this time all I hear is a faint moaning sound—one I've heard many times before.

I follow the sounds, my smile stretching even further, knowing exactly what sight I'm about to find.

And as I turn a corner, my lust-filled hunger for her increases when I find her completely naked, on her knees, sucking Atlas's cock.

"Started without me, I see?"

"Oh, that's right. I forgot to yell that I found her." He winks, shoving his hands into her hair as she swallows him to the hilt.

Fuck.

"She looks good in your hands," I tell him as I begin to pull my shirt off, followed by my shoes and the rest of my clothes.

"Aye, that she does," he praises, staring down into her beautiful, entranced face.

I lean down just enough so she can see my face and whisper in her ear, "On your hands and knees now, kitten. It's time I got a little taste too."

Her heavy eyelids droop further as she obeys my command perfectly. Now on all fours, I take a step back and stare at her pretty pink pussy, just begging to be eaten.

I'm usually all for delayed gratification, but not tonight.

Tonight, I want to gorge on the beautiful feast laid before me.

I want to eat her out until she screams my name all over Atlas's cock. And after she's come, then the real fun begins.

Without missing a beat, I go to my haunches and spread her pussy lips apart.

"You're fucking soaked, kitten," I tease, running my fingers up and down her slit. "Is that all from sucking Atlas's big dick?"

She hums in delight, her slick heat beginning to run down her thighs.

"Fuck," Atlas grunts, squinting his eyes in pain. "This mouth is my undoing. Keep talking to her, Teo. My princess seems to like your dirty mouth."

"Oh, I know just how much she likes it dirty. Don't I, kitten?" I say before slapping her pussy.

"Hmph."

"Motherfucker." Both Atlas and Kat moan out loud.

"Now, now, kitten. You can't come yet. Not until I tell you to. Those are the rules," I reprimand, running my knuckles up and down her drenched pussy before giving it another slap.

"Fuck your rules, Teo. I'm about to burst as it is," Atlas says in pain, Kat obviously sucking the very life out of him.

Amateur.

Seeing as Atlas is too far gone to prolong my little game, I lean my head between her thighs and lick her from slit to crack.

"Oh, gods!" she wails, pulling Atlas out of her mouth long enough to look behind at me.

"You want more, kitten?"

She nods breathlessly.

"Then the next time I look at your face, I better see tears in your eyes from sucking your king off. Understood?"

Like a good little submissive kitten, she doesn't question my demand and takes Atlas back into the warm cavern of her mouth, knowing that my word to eat her pussy is as good as golden.

I start off slow. One lick first, followed by another, then another, until my mouth is completely latched onto her pussy. When her legs begin to tremble, unable to keep herself up, I slap her ass cheek hard to give her a moment of clarity and grant her a second wind. I spent enough time locked in a dark room with her to know what her body can take and what it can't. And we haven't even gotten close to crossing her limits.

Unfortunately for me, time and distance have played a cruel number on me, and all too soon, I'm the one who is close to the edge just by her taste on the tip of my tongue. I was teasing Atlas about being a lightweight, but somehow the tables have turned on me, since I'm unable to handle eating out her pussy without busting a nut.

Curse the gods.

Needing to come more than I need air in my lungs, my tongue begins to suck her clit while inserting two digits inside her. And as if on cue, Atlas grasps two fistfuls of her hair and begins to fuck her mouth with fervor while my fingers do the same to her pussy.

Kat's whole body begins to quiver, her orgasm hitting her hard just in time with Atlas's and mine. The woman hasn't so much as touched me, but it didn't deter her from making me come all over myself.

"Bad kitten," I whisper before slapping her red cherry lips with my cock. "No one told you that you could come."

Breathless and completely spent, she pops Atlas's dick out of her mouth, her gorgeous face now covered in tears, drool, and cum. I fall on my back and tap on my lap.

"Clean me up, Kat. And then, when it's nice and clean, I want you to hop on my dick."

On her hands and knees, my little kitten crawls over to me and begins to lap me up just like I told her to.

"You up for another round?"

"What do you think?" Atlas retorts, stroking his hard cock as he watches his princess lick me clean.

"Good girl," I say, brushing Kat's hair gently out of the way so I don't miss a single moment of this spectacular sight. "Such a good girl."

She purrs in contentment as she always does when I praise her.

"Now look at me, kitten," I order. Kat raises her head immediately, panting for the next set of instructions. "Remember that one afternoon that we walked in on Anya and Cleo by the pool when they were… how shall I say this… entertaining?"

She nods.

"Atlas and I are going to fuck you now like that. Remember, in these little games of ours, it may look like I'm the one in control when, in reality, you're the one who holds all the power. If you don't think you're ready for that yet, tell us now. There are plenty of other ways for us to have some fun."

When her loving gaze bounces from me onto Atlas, I already know what her answer will be.

"I want you both. I love you both. So much," she confesses with bated breath.

"Then you'll have us, kitten. Won't she, Atlas?"

"She already does," he admits, his tone so uncharacteristically soft that it takes me aback for a minute.

Like me, Atlas loves our Kat more than anything else in the world.

There is nothing he wouldn't do for her.

Nothing so outrageous that he would refuse.

He's all in, and by gods, so am I.

This time there's no need to waste precious time shelling out directions since Atlas proactively picks Kat up off the floor and straddles her on top of me before taking his spot behind her.

Her palms find purchase on my chest as Atlas brushes her hair to the side and begins peppering sweet kisses on her neck.

"Are you ready, my love?" I ask, feeling my heart about to explode inside my chest.

She leans down just low enough to press a kiss to my lips.

"I love you," she whispers before aiming the crown of my cock to her soaked center and dropping her ass to my stomach.

Oh, gods.

She slowly begins to bounce on me, her slick heat maddening all my nerve endings. And when she feels her walls nicely drenched, she turns her head over her shoulder and leans in to kiss an expectant Atlas.

"I love you, Attie," she whispers with the same loving tone she professed her love for me.

His usual stern expression is nowhere to be found, his face looking somehow younger and softer just with those three little words.

I then feel the head of his cock breach her core, and ever so slowly, he slides his girthy length inside of her too. As if in a trance of her making, we all begin to sway back and forth, in and out. I rise just a little to suck on one of her nipples while Atlas licks and bites down on the crook of her neck. We are fully connected now, not knowing where one of us begins and the other ends. It's almost like a beautiful piece of music. The melody is soft at first and starts increasing in tempo until it hits a crescendo, reaching its climatic note and giving meaning and purpose to it.

With a legion of 'I love yous,' we three come undone in unison, having experienced the most celestial dance known to the gods.

We're a mess of limp bones and sweaty flesh after that, holding each other so tightly as if fearing that something this good—something this pure—could somehow disappear.

No one should have access to this type of happiness.

And yet, here we are.

Having reached the pinnacle of the purest unconditional love we have ever experienced.

I must pass out along the way because when I wake up, Atlas is sitting across from me, twirling a marigold in his hands.

"Where is she? Where's Kat?" I ask, running my palm over the empty space beside me.

"Where do you think?" he retorts, taking in a large bout of air. "She will never be whole until Levi gets to experience the same thing we did tonight."

My head falls back to the floor, praying to the gods to give her the strength and fortitude to convince our stubborn eldest brother.

"Teo," Atlas calls out. "What did you mean earlier today when you said you had your peace with sharing Kat before you arrived here? She told me that, before she left Nas Laed, you weren't as inclined to share her heart with anyone. What changed your mind?"

"You did." I let out a sigh. "Or the evil version of you. The one I believed to be a threat to Katrina's life. It's true that I wanted her all to myself when she left me. But then, when I thought she might die in Huwen and that I might lose her forever, my resistance to sharing her love seemed not to matter as much. And after Levi and I made amends, it mattered even less. By the time I stepped foot into this castle, I had already made up my mind. If sharing her love was all it took for me to keep her, then there was no way I'd ever be able to deny her. I love Kat, Atlas. And I love my brothers. If we can be happy in this miserable fucking world, wouldn't you do everything in your power to hold onto it with all your might? To spend your life sustaining it just to watch it blossom and bloom into something few mortals will ever be privileged to experience? Aye, Attie. I made my peace a long time ago, and I don't regret it. Not for one second."

"Well, fuck me, you became a philosopher in your old age."

I throw Atlas my middle finger, his laughter soothing the anxiety in my soul.

One brother has already fallen under your spell, kitten.

I pray to the gods your magic is strong enough to bewitch the other.

I step into Levi's tent and pull the black cloak Inessa lent me off my head once I'm safely inside. My brows pull together, though, when I find the tent covered in darkness, with Levi nowhere to be found.

"Fuck," I hear him mumble, my heart instantly sighing in relief that he's in here somewhere. "Have you come here with more demands?" he slurs with scornful disdain.

"No, but I do want to talk with you, and I'd rather have this conversation face to face where I can see you and not under the veil of shadows. I might as well be talking to a ghost, it being so dark in here," I reply assertively.

Thankfully only a few seconds pass by before I hear the sound of a lighting match, successfully denouncing Levi's position and illuminating the bleak makeshift room. He lights an oil lamp on top of a table, picks up a full bottle of rum, and walks to the other side of the tent where his bed is. On the way, he kicks an empty bottle lying on the floor before falling down on the mattress.

"You're drunk," I state the obvious, slowly walking toward him.

"Aye, that I am."

"Drunk from rum, of all things," I add, taking a few more steps.

"Aye. Atlas gifted me a whole crate of the stuff. My little brother was always thoughtful like that," he retorts sarcastically before taking a huge gulp.

"He also offered you a guestroom back at the castle, and yet you accepted his rum while declining his hospitality. Why?"

Levi rises on the bed with his elbows and stares me dead in the eyes.

"Apologies, Your Highness, if I didn't want to sleep under the same roof where the love of my life was fucking my two dearest childhood friends. Because that's what you did, right? You fucked them both tonight the minute you got a chance to. Tell me I'm wrong." He scoffs when I don't give him a reply. "That's what I thought. I'd rather sleep in my tent than have to deal with listening in on that shit."

"Since you're drunk, I'm going to forgive such abrasive behavior."

"Forgive? Forgive?!" he blurts in outrage, his brows raising so far up on his forehead they almost touch his braids. "Are you really fucking going to stand there and talk about forgiveness?!"

"Are you insinuating that I'm the one to beg for forgiveness?" I counter, just as riled up as he is.

He jumps out of bed and throws the bottle across the room. He then marches toward me, and before I can step back, his hand is already at my throat.

"Is that why you're here? To beg?" he growls, his rum-filled breath smelling syrupy and bold, with an added hint of vanilla. "Is that why you barged into my tent this night? Because you've gotten a taste for begging? Were Teo and Atlas unable to curb that ache that you needed to come here and madden me with it?"

His fingers dig into my flesh as he pushes me backward until my ass hits the table.

"A queen does not beg," I state, just as angry as he is.

"No?" he taunts, kicking my thighs apart with his legs, his eyes scanning my face and landing on my lips.

"No."

"So tonight, when they had you—when their cocks filled every hole in your body—you didn't beg them for more? You didn't plead with them to fuck you harder? You didn't shout out to the gods for mercy, begging them to let you come? Because I know you, Kat. I know you better than my own fucking traitorous heart. You begged. And you fucking begged beautifully. And if I wanted you now, you'd beg for my cock, too."

I slap him.

I slap him so hard across his stubbled cheek that the satisfying sound of it urges me to do it again. And again and again, until I'm using both of my hands to slap his whole upper body. When I finally run out of steam, Levi's loathsome scowl hurts me far more than any slap he had to endure.

"You were my fucking heart, and you broke me. First, by falling in love with the man you knew to be my sworn enemy at the time, and then again with the man who kidnapped you against your will. You have cut me more deeply than any enemy I've ever encountered on a battlefield. There hasn't been a name invented yet to define your cruelty. But I will not fall prey to your charms again. Ask Teo and Atlas to fuck you, for I'll never lay a hand on you again."

And to prove his point, he releases his grip off my throat and turns his back to me.

Heartbroken and angry, I charge at him, but even drunk, Levi's reflexes are quicker than mine. He turns around just in time to grab me by the wrists and flings my arms behind my back, locking them in place with just one of his massive hands.

"What? What more do you want of me? What?!" he shouts in my face.

We're deadlocked in a stare, both of us panting with rage and more pain than we know what to do with it. And then, when my eyes land on his mouth, the same one that vowed to always be mine, I do the unexpected to silence him, the same way he had silenced me that night in the forest when the wolves tried to attack me all those months ago—I kiss him.

Just as I remembered them, Levi's lips are strong and warm, and before he knows how to fight me off, he falls victim to my kiss, responding to it with everything he has. With his tongue wrestling mine, he releases my wrists and hoists me up to his waist, my thighs hugging themselves around him as my heels dig into his back.

"Levi," I half-moan and half-sob at how good it feels to be in his arms.

How right it feels.

But Levi doesn't say a word, too preoccupied with grabbing the nape of my neck to keep me exactly where he wants to dominate my tongue with his while his other hand pulls at the strings of his pants. I quickly pull my cloak up to my waist to give him easier access, and then wrap my arms around his neck to keep me steady. And just as I feel the world start to tilt off its axis with just one kiss, I feel the head of his cock breach my center, and in one hard thrust, he's inside me.

"Oh, gods," I moan, my pussy drenched with need for him.

"Fuck this cunt. So fucking tight. Always so fucking tight," he curses after pulling his lips off mine, allowing himself to lick down my neck before biting my nipple through the fabric of my dress.

"Argh!" I shout, the little pinch of pain adding to the euphoria I feel with how ruthlessly he's fucking me.

"I can still smell them on you," he growls as he keeps to his torturous tempo.

Unhappy with having his way with me standing up, I tighten my hold on his shoulders as he walks us back to the table and plants my ass on top of it, almost kicking the oil lamp to the floor. I take my cloak off as Levi's strong hands grab hold of the neckline of my dress and rip it in two. My heart is stabbed with the memories of all the dresses he's ruined in the past, the urge to tell him how much I missed him, *missed us* , burning a hole in my throat.

His emerald gaze hungrily stares at my naked breasts before his lips latch on to one nipple while his fingers toy with its counterpart. I grab hold of the edge of the table for balance as my heels, at the bottom of his back, aid each powerful thrust.

I'm so close.

So close.

As if he has a direct line to my thoughts, Levi grabs my throat again, leaving his face just a few inches away from mine, and says, "Do you want to come, my queen? Do you want to come on my cock after so many others have been inside you?"

His crude, harsh words should insult me, but they just spur me on instead, making me pant with desire.

"Show me how lovely you beg," he taunts, his heady, lust-filled gaze betraying him.

He's as turned on by this as I am, and when I open my mouth to stick out my tongue, he doesn't hesitate and shoves his thumb inside my mouth. My eyes roll to the back of my head as I suck on his finger while he pounds my dripping wet pussy.

"Fuck. Is that what you like? Sucking cock while another fucks this pretty cunt of yours?"

I moan in ecstasy, feeling so close to jumping off a cliff that it's a miracle I'm still cognizant enough to hear his words of praise.

"That's it, my queen. Suck that cock. Show me how good you can swallow him down while I fuck your pussy."

Gods have mercy.

"Hmm. Maybe two cocks aren't enough for you," he moans, giving in to his wicked fantasy. "Do you need three, my queen? Three big cocks to make you come?"

"Oh, gods, yes!" I scream, feeling my pussy walls start to clench around his girth in a vise-like grip.

"Fuck this pussy. Strangling my dick with just the idea of having three cocks worshiping her. You want more, my queen? Beg me. Beg me to give you more."

My heavy eyelids force themselves to open so that I can look at my true love's face. He's ordering me to beg, and yet his eyes are the ones that seem to be pleading with me, begging me to take mercy on him.

I pull his thumb out of my mouth with a loud pop and breathlessly give him my answer, "Please, Levi, please."

"You want to come?" he asks in agony, so close to falling off the precipice himself.

"Yes."

"You want us all to fuck you?" he pants.

"Yes."

"Where do you want us?"

"Everywhere, Levi. I want you everywhere. Please."

"Fuck!" he grunts, pulling me off the table and back on my feet, just to turn me around and shove my face on the table.

"Remember it was you who asked for this," he threatens, giving my earlobe a hard bite, followed by a hard slap on my ass cheek.

"Hmph," I moan when he goes to his haunches and begins to lick my pussy clean with his tongue.

I throw my arms across the table and grab the opposite edge, needing something to keep me tethered to the ground.

"Oh, god… Oh… gods," I start to stammer when Levi replaces his tongue at my core to insert his fingers inside me.

He starts pounding away at my pussy as his tongue plays with the rim of my ass. The stimulation is just too much, making my vision go completely black as my body begins to convulse with the earth-shattering orgasm. Another hard slap on my ass rings out in the air, pulling me back to solid ground.

"I'm not done with you yet. Next time you come when I say you can come," he grunts, making me muffle the sound of a giggle with how he sounds so much like Teo right now.

But all laughter dies on the tip of my tongue when Levi wraps my braid around his wrist and pulls me back to his chest.

"You think this is funny? Ruining a man?"

I shake my head.

"No? Are you sure? Because it sure does look like you're enjoying yourself watching me lose my mind."

I rest my head on his chest and lean back to look at him.

"You're not lost, Levi. And even if you were, I'd always find you."

The hard edge of his gaze softens, and for a brief moment, I have my Levi back.

"Kiss me, Levi. Please," I beg before he has time to slip away. "For what is a heart if it can't be with the one it loves?"

Emerald-green meadows are set aflame in his eyes before he dips his head to mine and kisses me. My heart soars into the heavens as this kiss is unlike all the others he's given me tonight. This one tells me he still loves me and can't stop, no matter if his code of honor or pride says otherwise. This kiss is laced with hope, and it's enough to soothe my broken heart.

But the spell is soon broken when Levi pulls away, anger and fury back in his gaze.

"No, my queen. A heart can still beat even if its love is already dead to it. Let me show you."

And before I can say another word in protest, Levi shoves me back onto the table, his hand on the nape of my neck, forcing me still. His cock thrusts deep inside me, and at this angle, I feel every inch of him. When his fingers start to play with my clit, delicious shivers run up and down my body, as if each cell had been reawakened with want and desire.

"Isn't this what you wanted?" he starts to accuse, pulling his deft fingers away from my swollen clit.

"Levi," I begin to challenge, but my protest soon morphs into a loud moan of need as his thumb begins to play with the rim of my ass.

"Levi, what? Isn't this what you gave up our love for? To be fucked by every cock that crosses your path?"

I don't have time to be insulted since he shoves his fingers in my mouth and spits into the pink bud of my ass.

"Okay, my queen. Let me see at least once what you sacrificed our future for."

I bite down hard on his fingers when he pulls his cock out of my pussy, preferring to fuck me from behind. My eyes squint in ecstatic pain as white sparkling light blurs my vision. Even though the tone he just used was filled with malice, Levi moves ever so slowly inside me, giving me time and space to get accustomed to his size. I feel my juices run down my thighs with each small thrust, my pussy feeling bereft and empty without him.

I feel the exact moment when I no longer care what he thinks of me or that I've broken both our hearts beyond measure and that we will never get back to that sacred place we were in Arkøya. Something shifts inside of me, my mind going blank, leaving nothing but wanton need.

I begin to suck at his fingers unashamedly while Levi's thrusts become more confident in how much I can withstand. I whimper and moan as his tempo gains speed, his breathing turning just as erratic as mine.

"Fuck, Kat. But it's like you were built for this," he says under his breath, hooking two of his fingers inside my pussy to my heart's content.

Another loud wail leaves me as I swallow up his digits, spit and drool running down the corners of my mouth. Levi's punishing pounding escalates, creating a whole other myriad of sensations to run through me. My aching nipples graze over the rough wooden table, again and again, with each deep thrust. My body sings a heavenly melody of Levi's own creation. It's all too much, and yet not nearly enough.

Levi answers my unspoken prayers once more by taking his fingers out of my mouth and pulling me back against his hard chest just so he can kiss me. His tongue wages war on mine while his free hand grabs one of my breasts, his cock and fingers still inside me.

And like a natural disaster, I explode into his arms, my orgasm ripping me asunder and shattering me completely. My body is still convulsing when Levi grunts into my mouth, filling me with his own release. I swallow his moan whole and urge it to hide inside the crooked-edged pieces of my heart, needing this shared moment between us to live hidden away inside me, even after he's gone.

Our chests heave in unison as we stare at each other, hate and anger replaced with longing and sadness.

We've just had mind-blowing sex, and yet it feels like we're saying goodbye.

A single tear falls down my cheek, allowing Levi to catch it with his thumb and lick it dry.

"At least I can take some comfort in knowing your tears are mine, if not your heart."

Another silent tear falls for him on cue, followed by another one.

All the words I want to say to him burn inside me, creating hot, fresh tears to spring to life.

Instead of mocking my pain, Levi returns my sad gaze with one of his own, making my misery all that more agonizing.

"You won't be on a boat tomorrow, will you?" I ask with a sob, uncaring for being unable to keep my tears at bay.

"No, I won't," he admits, his eyes sparkling with unshed tears.

"Not even if I told you that I loved you. That I love you with all my heart and that there isn't a world where I'll ever be able to stop loving you?"

"I wish I could believe that," he whispers in pain.

"But you don't. Or you can't because I love them too."

He nods.

With tears still streaming down my face, I lean in and place a chaste kiss on his lips before I pull him out of me and grab my cloak.

Levi is lost to me.

My heart will never return to me again.

Not now.

Not ever.

He doesn't try to stop me when I start walking toward the small entrance of the tent, but when I reach the flap, he calls out my name.

"It's the same for me, you know? There isn't a world I'd ever be able to stop loving you. You will forever be my heart, Kat."

I swallow down my tears, my heart breaking into a million pieces.

"If that was true, then you'd fight to keep me," I reply with my back still turned to him. "You'd fight for us. Fight for our love even if it doesn't match the idealistic version you had of it. But instead, you've chosen to run away. I thought east-born kings were made of harder steel. I guess I was wrong."

And before I break our hearts any further, I walk away, knowing it will probably mean never seeing his glorious face again.

Chapter 38

~ Atlas ~

"Well, this is quite a crowd." Cristobal chuckles as he leans onto the railing beside me, eyeing the row of friends gazing nervously at the harbor. "I didn't realize that your new guests were so fond of Huwen. They all look so devastated that they are leaving."

"That's not the reason why we're all here waiting," I mumble, getting annoyed with my brother for every second he makes us wait.

"Waiting? Waiting for who?" he asks, intrigued, scanning the mob of men still boarding my ship, bringing with them the rest of the supplies needed for our voyage.

Instead of answering his curiosity, I turn my back to the harbor and cross my arms over my chest.

"What are you doing on my ship anyway, Cristobal? Don't you have your own ships to captain?"

"Pshh, my ships captain themselves. They don't need me to do that for them."

"You really are the worst pirate king I have ever met, you know that?"

But instead of getting insulted, he just laughs away, my disrespected comment rolling down his shoulders like it was nothing.

Maybe that's why I love the bastard so much.

Yes, he'll rob a person blind if you let him, but nothing ever gets him down for long.

Unlike a certain eastern king that is currently being a big pain in the ass.

"Argh," I grumble, swinging around again just to see if I can find Levi somewhere in the lingering crowd down at the pier.

"What's got you so upset, my young friend?"

"Who says I'm upset?"

"Don't bullshit a bullshitter, little cub. You won't win against the likes of me." He wiggles his dark brows.

"When the gods made you, they really went heavy on the cocky arrogance, didn't they?"

"Takes one to know one," he is quick to reply, followed by one of his boisterous laughs.

It's so loud that the sound even manages to vibrate along the rail, making Teo, Cleo, and Anya pull their attention off the dock and onto us.

"What's so funny? I'd like a little laugh right about now," Anya says with a sincere smile plastered on her lips.

"I bet you do, sweetheart. But alas, this is a private joke between me and the king," he says, using his velvety sexy voice.

Anya just shrugs and turns her attention back to the pier, Cleo's protective arm snaking around her waist as she follows suit.

"Now I understand why you decided to travel on my ship instead of your own." I shake my head at him.

"Can't blame a guy for wanting to spend the next ten days at sea looking at such pretty faces. And boy, are they pretty." He licks his lips, eyeing the two girls together.

"Hate to burst your bubble, but they are both taken," I tell him.

"Aye, young cub, I have eyes. I can see that they are a joint set. Doesn't mean they won't enjoy me playing with them for a bit."

I'm about to tease him that he'd have better luck getting laid on his own ship with one of his men than with one of the girls when, to my surprise, I catch Cleo winking at him, almost as if she heard his remark.

"Well, I'll be damned," I mutter, astonished, only to gain a chuckle from the other man at my side.

"That's my Cleo," Teo chimes in, leaning forward so he can catch Cristobal's eye too. "But don't be fooled, King Cristobal. She might let you play with her and her favorite plaything for a little bit, but make no mistake—if you so much as try to steal what's hers, she'll sooner cut your dick off than use it for her own pleasure."

Cristobal's face blanches, his hand going straight to his dick to make sure it's still there.

"Point taken and warning heard," he replies crestfallen, but when he catches Cleo whispering something in Anya's ear, followed by a flirtatious wave at him, his smile rapidly reappears on his face.

"But then again, a man has to die sometime, so he might as well be doing something that he loves. And right now, I'd love nothing more than to slide in the middle of such gorgeous creatures."

"I think your friend has little to no self-preservation instincts." Teo chuckles.

"Not when it comes to getting his dick wet, no," I smirk, but it quickly disappears from my lips when I see Inessa running up the ramp.

"Inessa! Over here!" Anya waves at her friend.

"Where's our queen? Where's Kat?" she asks Anya as she reaches us.

"She's resting in the captain's cabin. I don't think she had the stomach to wait for him on deck. Did Brick say anything to you?" Anya asks, concerned.

"No. Brick hasn't received any orders from the king except for the one he gave yesterday," she explains hesitantly. "He told them that they would ride back to Arkøya at the break of dawn, but so far, no one has seen him since. He's not in his tent and hasn't returned to the castle. He's nowhere to be found."

"Well, that doesn't sound very promising." Cleo scowls, perfectly vocalizing my own annoyance.

My aggravation increases further when I see Haldan's ships begin to sail, heading north, the other kings following his lead.

Fuck, Levi! Where the hell are you?

"So we *are* waiting on someone," Cristobal utters pensively beside me. "I hate to be the bearer of bad news, young lion, but it looks to me that your friend is not coming. Best cut your losses now and get your ship in gear, ready to sail. I know you believe me to be a bad captain, but I know enough to tell you that we are wasting precious daylight. Not to mention good weather. It can turn on us at any minute. I don't know about you, but I'm not looking forward to getting stuck in a storm just because we took our sweat-ass time to sail north."

"Just another few minutes, Cristo. Just give him a few more minutes."

Everyone leans over the rail, each one of us begging the gods to show Levi the way to us.

Some of us hold to that faith longer than others.

"He's not coming," Inessa says in sadness.

"He is. He has to," Anya retorts, biting on her nails.

"I don't know. The king of the east sure likes to hold on to a grudge," Cleo interjects.

"Have faith. Levi will do the right thing. He'll come," Teo adds in his defense. "Won't he?" he asks, looking at me for answers. Answers that I do not have.

"I don't know," I grumble, annoyed and pissed all at the same time. "Katrina did say that if he didn't come, she would release him from his vassal obligations. That means the east would be its own separate kingdom, not ruled by anyone but him. That's a lot for a man to turn his back on."

"We did," Teo quickly rebukes. "Kat made us the same offer, yet we chose her. And we would do it again in a heartbeat."

I squeeze his shoulder and release a drained exhale.

"Aye, but our wounds have found a way to mend where his have not. His cuts are still too raw, and I'm not sure our prideful brother will ever be able to heal them."

"No, I refuse to believe that," Teo retorts assertively. "And I refuse to let you lose faith in him too. This is the same brother who believed with all his heart that a frail, sickly boy could change his fate and follow his dreams of sailing across the sea. The same brother who found enough mercy in himself to forgive a wretch like me, even after all my father put him through. Levi has always been the best of us. You said so yourself. He's the king we strive to become one day. He'll come. He has to."

What Teo fails to say is that Kat will never fully bloom to her greatest potential without Levi. There will always be a missing piece in her heart that neither Teo nor I could ever fill. The same would happen if she lost one of us.

We four just fit.

Like a perfect four-sided diamond, we shine best when we get to lean on each other for love and support. Even when we were younger, we felt it. That connection. That need to always be around each other. It was always supposed to be us against the world.

If Levi doesn't come today, he's not only abandoning Kat, but Teo and me too.

Fuck, brother! Where are you?!

And as if the man himself has heard my desperate plea, I now see his troops marching into the harbor and boarding the various ships still docking there. Walking right at their center is their raven-haired king, along with his trusty sidekick trailing beside him.

The girls begin to shout and hug themselves in utter glee while both Teo and I let out a sigh of relief.

"Told you he'd come," Teo taunts, the worried lines of his forehead no longer visible.

"Aye, you did. But we're not out of the woods yet. Not unless we find a way to convince our stubborn brother that his place is at our side," I retort with a crooked smile.

"By the look on your face, I see you have a plan brewing."

"I always have a plan brewing," I taunt. "Tonight, after everyone has had their dinner, I want you to follow my lead. Can you do that?"

"If it keeps Levi from jumping ship—no pun intended—then I'm in."

"Good. That's all I need to hear."

"Are you going to include Kat in this little plan of ours?"

I shake my head, my smile widening on my lips.

"No. I think it will be more effective if we catch her by surprise."

"Whatever you say, Atlas," Teo replies, his full attention back on Levi as he begins to walk up the ramp.

Levi walks toward us with conviction, as if the gods themselves ordered him to be here.

"Have you come to join the good fight with us, brother?" Teo asks with hope in his voice.

Levi looks at Teo and then at me, only for someone else to pull his attention from us.

"Well, have you, Levi?" Kat asks, standing right at the center of the deck, her scrutinizing gaze fixed on his. "Have you decided to fight?"

"Yes."

The smile that crests Kat's lips beams brighter than the autumn sun above us, and I take it as an omen that this storm is just one of many that we will overcome.

Kat got him this far.

Now it's up to me and Teo to ensure he never leaves us again.

Chapter 39
Levi

"**S**top moping about, Levi. You've made the right decision," Brick states assuredly, giving me a pat on the back for a job well done.

"Have I?" I ask sullenly, eyeing the sun beginning to set on the blue horizon. "I just sacrificed Arkoya's only chance at ever becoming a sovereign kingdom in favor of helping the woman I'm in love with, who, in turn, is in love with my two best friends from childhood. By stepping on this boat, I agreed that the east will never be free from northern rule, just because I'm actually considering entering a polyamorous relationship with its infamous winter queen. In what way was my decision the right one for my people or me?"

Brick leans his back against the rail beside me and lets out an exhale.

"Just because it might look like a bad call on paper, doesn't mean it wasn't the right one."

"Are you saying that because you honestly believe it, or are you just telling me what you think I want to hear?"

"I'm telling you that sometimes you need to take a step back from your problems and analyze them from a different perspective. For example, let's imagine that you *did* take the queen up on her offer. If you had done that, then yes, for all intents and purposes, Arkøya would, in fact, be free, but at what cost, my king? The east's honorable reputation would be forever tainted, known only as the kingdom that refused to fight in the greatest battle Aikyam has ever faced. Look!" he orders passionately, pointing to the fleet of ships sailing north with us. "Never in all my years have I ever seen such an army. You know what I see when I look at all these kings fighting for a common cause? History in the making," Brick adds with a gleam of pride in his eyes. "We are soldiers, my king. We were born with swords in our hands long before we knew how to wield them. That is who we are. We fight, no matter the challenge. Not only will Arkøya understand the decision that you have made here today, but they will celebrate you for it, too. After Tarnow falls, every east-born babe will be lullabied to sleep with songs about how their virtuous king chose integrity and honor over a sovereign throne. Even if you believe that your decision was inconsiderately made, in the end, you followed your heart. Is there anything more noble than that?"

Though it was not his intention, the boulder on my chest feels ten pounds heavier. Not wanting him to see how his blind loyalty to me has affected me, I force a smile and plant my hand on his shoulder.

"You are a good general, Brick, but an even better friend," I say in earnest. "Now go and spend your time with your lady love, Inessa, instead of wasting it on me. For time is precious, dear friend, and in a little over a fortnight, who knows if either one of us will even be here to enjoy it. Go," I urge him.

"Are you sure?" he asks hesitantly.

"Yes. I'm quite sure." My forced smile widens.

"Alright, then I'll see you at dinner," he retorts with a sincere grin on his face.

The minute Brick turns his back to walk away, my fraudulent smile falls from my lips.

Because that's what I am—a fraud.

Even if Brick and all of Arkøya believe me to be a dignified and honorable king, I proved to myself today that I'm unworthy of their great esteem and loyalty. My decision to sail north was made with selfish and completely self-indulgent intentions. I've erased whatever opportunity my people had for freedom just because my heart wanted her too badly—longed for her too much.

Worst still, if given the chance, I'd make the same decision again.

That's how much Katrina has inserted herself into my heart and corrupted it from within.

She's changed me. Made me crave her love more than keeping my honorable vow to my own people.

I even left my home for her with the sole purpose of saving her.

Not once did I believe that the real danger awaiting me in Huwen was a broken heart.

I couldn't believe my eyes when I saw her.

Not only was Katrina safe and healthy, but she had given yet another piece of her heart to another king when, not a few months before, her heart belonged exclusively to me.

First Teo, now Atlas.

It was too much for me to take. Just too damn much.

If I had an ego before she came back into my life, then she has successfully chipped every bit of it with a fucking carving knife. Watching from afar how easy it was for her to give her heart, body, and soul away gutted me in ways I'll never fully be able to recover from. I've always been a proud man, but Katrina of Bratsk made sure to take that pride and step all over it with her heels, stabbing at it until there wasn't any more life in it.

But after last night… she's corrupted me in ways I never dreamed possible.

Gods.

Last night, I was a man gone mad.

When she found me in my tent, I was three sheets to the wind, drunk on Atlas's rum and my humiliation. When my eyes landed on her, I almost believed that my grief and sadness summoned the ghost of her, a mercy sent by the gods to ease the horrible ache in my chest.

But when I realized she wasn't a heaven-sent apparition but a woman made of flesh and bone, my melancholy gave way to fury. I wanted her to feel every inch of the indignity I had to swallow down watching her seated on Atlas's throne. I wanted her to experience firsthand the degradation I felt when rumors arrived from the south, all whispering that she had found her way into Teo's bed. I wanted to punish her for making me feel less than, for making me feel like my heart was not enough for her when her heart was all I ever needed.

Still hurting and desperate for her touch, I let her kiss me.

I let myself get lost in the sweet lie of her kiss, needing to feel something other than hate.

Needing to be hers again, even if it wasn't real. Even if only for a night.

I gave sway to the illusion, and to my utter shame, a more depraved fantasy grew wings.

If what she wanted was a harem to worship at her feet, then I was going to show her what fucking three kings would feel like. But instead of being humiliated by every filthy thing I said or did to her body, my Kat became alive in a way I had never seen before. Like a budding

406

royal blue rose, she bloomed right there in my arms with the fantasy that I was sharing her with them.

And that's when it hit me.

In my naivete, I always assumed it was a choice for her. That one day the winter queen woke up and ruthlessly decided one king would never fully satisfy her or her needs, and therefore, she would need a horde of them.

But it was *never* a choice for her.

No matter how hard it was for me to admit it, Kat could never choose between us.

Not because she didn't want to but because she lacked the capacity to. Even though her life would be so much simpler if she just chose one of us, Kat was incapable of it. Her heart would always be divided into three equal parts between Teo, Atlas, and me. Even when we were children, she never favored one over the other, needing to be close to all three of us.

That alone should have been the first sign.

The minute Kat sent out that decree declaring she would pick one king to marry, she set herself up for failure. No one could predict the events that would follow or that our hearts would end up being collateral damage to her best intentions of unifying Aikyam.

But here we are. At a crossroads.

I spent all night thinking about what she said before she left me last night.

Although the love she had to offer didn't fit the ideal fantasy I had in mind for us, it didn't make her love for me any less real.

So, while she was incapable of making a choice, I wasn't as fortunate.

Either I accept her as she is and live a full life filled with love and friendship with her and my brothers, or I could renounce my love for her, admitting that my male ego was just too frail and toxic to withstand sharing her with anyone else.

It was in my hands to decide my fate. It was never in hers.

So when she asked me to fight for her, what she really asked was for me to have faith in her love for me and that I needed to battle my own inner demons, for they were the ones keeping me from her.

Teo and Atlas were never my competition—my ego and pride were.

I'm my worst enemy.

And if I truly love her like I claim to—if my heart truly belongs to her—then I will find a way to fight for our love, no matter what it looks like.

That's the real reason why I rallied my men this morning and told them to board the ship. Not to overthrow a madman from his seat of power in Tarnow but as my first step towards redemption.

I have a long way to go, but if there is anyone worth fighting for, it's her.

My Kat.

My heart.

My forever.

"You should have seen him. The young lion didn't know what to do with himself." Cristobal laughs as he continues with his story about the first time Atlas visited the Melliné Isles.

At first, I didn't know what to think of Atlas's ostentatious new friend, but as dinner progressed, I started to see why Atlas is so fond of him. The man might not have any filter to speak of, but he is nothing if not entertaining.

"So, there they were. At least a dozen naked women bathing in the ocean together," Cristobal continues on with his tale. "Not just any nude women, but Mellinése goddesses. Each one more tempting than the other, all calling out his name, urging the young cub to join them. And what did Atlas do?" Cristobal asks to add a bit of suspense. "He doesn't so much as move from the beach, as if his feet have grown roots. The boy must have been sixteen, if he was a day, and yet he acted like he never saw a naked woman before."

"That's probably because he hadn't," Teo taunts with a chuckle of his own.

"Aye, I do believe you're right." Cristobal continues to laugh. "Because instead of rushing to strip the clothes off his body and join them, he politely declined their hospitable offer and said he had more pressing issues to attend to with their king Taurasi than bathe with them. My jaw fell to the ground right there and then, thinking the boy was mad. If the roles had been reversed, I wouldn't have thought twice."

"Not everyone is a slave to their dick, Cristo," Atlas teases, drinking his wine.

"Aye, but not everyone hates their dick as much as you did that day, either," Cristobal cackles. "Poor cub still had a massive bulge in his pants when he finally gained an audience with Taurasi. And it didn't let up the whole hour he ranted about revenge and justice for Huwen. To this day, I think Taurasi accepted to join forces with you more out of fear than loyalty for my beloved Lioness. He must have thought if this young cub gets hard with the thought of bloodshed, then best it not be mine." Cristobal finishes with an animated cackle, slapping his hand onto the table so hard the tableware begins to shake.

The whole table laughs with him, keeping to the unexpected celebratory mood.

"Having fun?" Teo asks beside me, low enough for no one to hear.

"Surprisingly so," I admit since I was a bit hesitant to be in the same room as Katrina and my brothers so soon.

Teo throws his arm around my shoulders and gives me a side hug.

"Glad to hear it, brother. Glad to hear it."

The unexpected show of affection only serves to wear down my resistance further. And when Atlas begins to laugh after some joke Cristobal makes, I'm suddenly pulled back to a time when our brotherly bond was the most important thing to me. A time when all I wanted to do was protect them and guide them into becoming the men I always envisioned they'd become.

And look at them now.

The young boy who only thought about himself, uncaring of anyone else's needs aside from his own, became a man who rules his beloved south with a kind heart and generous hand. Teo has proven himself to be a king worth his title. He may still have a mischievous twinkle in his amber eyes, but now there is humility in them, too.

And then there's Atlas.

He was just a sickly boy with an unattainable dream. No one thought he could survive his illness, much less succeed in captaining a fleet of ships. Seven years later, people shudder at the very mention of his name.

Two very different kings, complete polar opposites of each other, and yet, they fit perfectly.

We fit perfectly.

And it's all down to the queen sitting at the very end of the table, talking animatedly with her own friends.

As if sensing where my mind is, Atlas throws me a conspiring wink, and for the first time in months, the smile that crests my lips is genuine.

'Missed you too,' he mouths at me, his smile filling up a hollow part in my heart.

Curse the gods, but I missed him.

I've missed both of them.

And until this night, I hadn't realized what their absence had really done to me.

I was supposed to be their big brother, their champion, and instead, I almost lost faith and abandoned them when they needed me most.

When *she* needed me most.

I'm still wrapping my head around this new overwhelming realization when the girls at the end of the table begin to get out of their seats.

"It's pretty late," Anya says with a yawn. "Cleo and I are going back to our rooms."

"Is that an invitation?" Cristobal asks, wiggling his brows suggestively.

"Do you want it to be?" Cleo taunts with a smoldering look.

Cristobal's chair scrapes the wooden floor as he hurries to get up.

"Gentlemen, ladies, it's been a lovely dinner, but it looks like I'm needed elsewhere."

Everyone laughs except for Cleo, whose scrutinizing gaze is fixed on me.

"Will my king be safe in your hands, King Levi? Or will there be fresh bruises on his face in the morning?"

"The night is young, my lady. Who knows? Maybe your lord and king is into that kind of thing?" Atlas responds on my behalf, forcing Kat to spit out her wine.

"Attie!" she scolds and gives him a reprimanding shake of the head.

"I'll be fine, Cleo." Teo chuckles. "Go and enjoy your night. The three of you," he adds mischievously.

My shoulders slump as we watch both girls giggle and wave their goodbyes with a salivating Cristobal right at their heels.

"I think your right hand won't ever like me much after that day on the beach," I grumble.

"Don't take it personally, Levi. She likes to hold her grudges but will forgive you in time." Teo grins at me, the bruises on his face no longer as prominent as they were a few days ago.

"If it's any consolation, Cleo isn't a fan of people in general. It took her a while to warm up to me too," my heart says with a shy timbre to her voice.

It's the first few words we've spoken all night, and my chest swells with love just by the sound of her sweet voice. We just stare into each other's eyes as if there were this invisible pull between us, forcing us to stay tethered to one another. To my chagrin, she first breaks the connection when the handmaiden, still sitting at her side, pulls her chair back.

"Brick," Inessa calls out, and that's all she has to say for my general to leap out of his seat, the chair falling back to the floor as he races over to his lady love.

"Thank you for the lovely dinner, Your Highness," she bows to her queen while an impatient Brick waits behind her.

"Yes, yes. Fine evening and all that malarkey," he rushes over to Kat, already wrapping his hand around Inessa's waist to rush her out the door.

I'm still chuckling away with how my general makes no excuses for his behavior, letting everyone at this table know what he and his lady love are about to do when Atlas pulls his seat back and struts over to my heart's true desire to place his hands on her shoulder. My hackles rise when, at the same time, Teo leaves my side to head toward the cabin's door and locks it from the inside, placing the key inside his pocket.

Suddenly, all my good humor is wiped clean off my face.

"What is the meaning of this?" I ask, kicking my chair back, placing my palms on the table, and eyeing the traitors in my mist.

"This, dear brother, is a trap." Atlas grins sinisterly. "Whatever hangups you have, they end tonight."

"What are you doing?" Kat asks, craning her neck back to look at Atlas.

"I'm making sure you get your wish, princess. Trust me," he advises before leaning down to press a soft kiss on her lips.

The lump in my throat makes it hard to say another word as I watch their shared kiss morph from sweet to damn-near decadent. My heart pounds in my chest with each second that ticks by as their tongues swirl and dip, Kat's chest heaving for air.

When they finally break away from each other, Kat's lips are nice and swollen, my cock hardening when her half-mast eyes lock with mine.

Fuck.

No.

I'm not ready for this.

I'm not ready.

But neither of my brothers seem to care, intent on throwing me off into the deep end, forcing me to learn to swim on her shores.

Teo, now standing beside Atlas, pulls Kat's chin in his direction and captures her mouth in his. She melts into the kiss and purrs when he grabs her breast and squeezes it tight. By the time he pulls away, he's as worked up as she is, panting with the same need I'm currently being afflicted by.

I should run out of this room.

I should punch and kick and scream my way out.

But instead, all I manage to do is stay rooted to my spot, my eyes never leaving her.

"It's your turn now, brother," Atlas orders, with hope in his blue gaze.

But instead of walking toward them like every fiber of my being demands me to, I head toward the door like a fucking coward, only stopping when Kat calls out my name.

"Do you love me, Levi?" she asks with bated breath.

"Yes," I reply without missing a beat while still keeping my back to the three of them.

"Do you want me?"

Another yes.

"Then stay and fight for me."

I let out a breath and take in her words.

If I turn to them now, I'll seal my fate forever.

Choices.

That's what a life summons up to—a series of choices that a person makes, each one bringing them closer to an unknown destiny.

I made a choice when I boarded this ship earlier today, and if I turn around, I'll be making another—one that says that I'm ready to take a leap of faith and submerge myself in their waters.

So, I do the only thing I can in this circumstance.

I give into my heart and turn around.

Chapter 40

Katrina

When Levi turns around to face us, my heart swells with hope, thumping madly in my chest with each step he draws nearer.

Atlas gives my shoulder a light squeeze, reminding me of his presence and that he will do everything in his power for me to have all that I desire.

And at this minute, all I could ever ask the gods is for them to love me.

"Teo," Atlas says with a tilt of the head, and before I know what's happening, I'm being lifted by the waist off my chair and onto the table.

"Be a good little kitten and keep your eyes on Levi," Teo commands before going to his haunches and spreading my thighs apart.

Unable to string a sentence together, I just nod, Levi's piercing gaze inflaming a need in me that cannot be contained.

"Look at her, Levi. Look how anxious she is for us," Atlas coos, rubbing his tongue up and down the small sliver of skin behind my ear, causing goosebumps to rise on my sensitive flesh, as Teo leisurely raises my skirts up to my waist.

"Why deprive yourself of what you want when she's offering herself so beautifully to you? To us?" Atlas continues to cajole, stoking the flame I see in Levi's eyes.

My jaw slacks open as Teo begins to run his tongue up my inner thigh until his head is right there at my core. His breath alone causes me to grab the edge of the table, having to hold onto something for balance. And as if they had prepared their salacious foreplay ahead of time, Atlas sinks his teeth into my neck in unison with Teo's first lick.

I burst into flames, grabbing Atlas's hair to keep him in place at the crook of my neck while pulling on Teo's brown strands as he licks my slit clean. Not once do my eyes stray from Levi's, wanting to see his face as his brothers devour me.

Levi's nostrils flare in anguish, his hands balling into fists at his side as he takes another step until he's standing just behind Teo.

"Tell her what you want," Atlas groans as he grazes his teeth over my bare shoulder and lifts his head to bite into my earlobe, causing me to let out another wanton moan. "Tell her, Levi."

"I want you to come," Levi whispers with a pained growl.

Atlas chuckles into my ear, causing a shiver of delight to run through me.

"Be precise, big brother. How do you want her to come?"

Levi bites his inner cheek, still unable to say the words out loud, too stuck in his head to give into the fantasy Atlas is coaxing into existence.

"Tell her, Levi," he orders impatiently, covering the hand that has a fist full of Teo's hair and pushing it further in between my legs.

Teo's ministration with his tongue suddenly becomes more intense as he flicks my clit with urgency, his fingers digging into my thighs.

"Argh!" I wail out, rubbing my pussy on his face, craving that sweet friction Teo's offering to come undone.

"Tell her, Levi! I won't ask again," Atlas demands as he picks me up for a split second, only to plant me on his lap, his hard cock poking at the crook of my ass.

Teo doesn't miss a beat and continues to eat my pussy like a starved, crazed man, while Levi's resistance is starting to break before my very eyes.

"I want you to come on Teo's tongue," Levi blurts out, palming the bulge in his pants.

I sigh in relief as Atlas's rigid demeanor softens with Levi's order.

"You heard him, princess," Atlas whispers in my ear as he rubs his hard cock on my ass while keeping Teo's head exactly where it needs to be. "Come on Teo's tongue."

My heart stammers in my chest as I wrap my legs around Teo's shoulders, leaning back to give both my men enough room to torture me. I'm so close to coming undone, needing a flick of a match to consume me completely.

And as if Levi heard my silent prayer, he grabs hold of my throat and squeezes it tightly, forcing his digits into my mouth. I come in an instant, my loud wails of ecstasy bouncing off every wall in the room. Levi pulls his fingers out of my mouth and crashes his lips to mine.

Being consumed by a myriad of sensations, my body is still trying to catch up, but my tongue and lips know exactly how to respond to his passionate kiss.

"I want to see you do that again," Levi growls after breaking our urgent kiss.

"Oh, we will," Atlas taunts with a wicked grin, pushing me gently off his lap. "Take a seat, brother," he adds, kicking the chair beside us over to Levi.

Levi doesn't protest this time and does as his younger brother suggests.

"Teo, stay on the floor. You're going to like this next part." Atlas winks at him.

"Shouldn't I be the one ordering you all about?" I pant, still breathless from the orgasm Teo gave me and Levi's earth-shattering kiss.

"Princess, you won't even remember your own name in a couple of minutes," Atlas threatens, pulling me in and whispering in my ear our favorite mantra before capturing my mouth with his.

"My misery. My suffering. My blood."

I melt instantly in his arms and dive headfirst into his kiss, giving him free rein to do his worst. Once he ensures I'm left hot and bothered, he pulls away with a devilish look in his eyes. My heart rattles in my chest as I watch Atlas slowly drop to the floor, only to grab the hem of my gown and pull it over my head. Left in only my corset and white undergarment, my breath hitches when he pulls out a dagger from its sheath and positions it to my beating heart.

"Do you trust me?" he asks, his voice dropping an octave.

"With every bit of my soul," I reply.

The corner of his lips tug upward as he slices my corset and undergarment all in one go, leaving me completely bare to all of them.

Using the same tip of his dagger, he runs it down my throat, towards my heaving chest, only stopping when he's reached my breast to circle around my nipple with its sharp edge. My breathing comes out in spurts, danger mixed with lust, too heady of a sensation to bear.

"Fuck, kitten. I can smell you from here," Teo says, wide-eyed and hungry, lifting himself off the floor with his elbows just so he doesn't miss a thing.

Levi just growls, his eyes never leaving the dagger's tip as it travels down to my stomach and then south to my core.

"This is a very special dagger, princess. My mother gave it to me years ago, and I intend on using it to carve your fucking uncle's heart out," Atlas coos, as if death and fucking went hand in hand. He then flips it in his hand, grabbing hold of the blade's spine while its stainless-steel handle slides up and down my quivering slit. My legs begin to tremble at the cool feel of the handle starting to scrape against my swollen clit, still far too sensitive from the abuse Teo thrashed on it. And when Atlas begins to rub the hard edge into my opening, the foreign sensation is so overpowering that I have to hold onto his shoulders to keep myself from falling.

"I'm going to fuck you with this dagger in front of my brothers," Atlas forewarns, his heady gaze just as intoxicating as his words. "I want it slick with your cum, princess. So that when I dig it into that bastard's chest, it will be that much sweeter for me to enjoy."

Most women would run in the other direction after such a proposition. However, I stay exactly where I am, eager for Atlas to follow through on his threat.

True to his word, he gently pushes the handle inside me, his deft fingers already playing with my clit as he thrusts his beloved toy in and out of me. My gaze bounces off Levi's hungry expression and then over to Teo's sordid one, to finally circle back to Atlas's penetrating stare. They are as much invested in these deviant games as I am. The realization that I'm not alone in this feeling has me whimpering out, my juices coating the handle in no time.

"That's it. Look how beautiful you are fucking my dagger," Atlas smirks triumphantly, increasing the maddening tempo.

My nails dig into Atlas's shoulders, creating half-crest rips on his white shirt as he continues to fuck me. My eyes squint in misery as I chase after that euphoric feeling that doesn't seem to want to arrive. This is by far one of the most lurid things I have ever done, and yet it still feels like something is missing.

"It's not enough, is it, my heart?" Levi asks, his voice coming out hoarse and gravelly with want.

"It's never enough for our kitten. Isn't that right?" Teo chimes in, equally aroused.

I shake my head, needing a release more than I need air to breathe. I reach out for it, the blinding light right there on the horizon taunting me.

"Tell us what you need," Atlas pleads, falling victim to his own obscene little game.

"I need… I need…" I stutter, unable to form words, let alone a whole sentence.

"She needs us," Levi calls out, answering Atlas's question for me. "All of us. Together."

Atlas smiles, hearing the magic words he's been waiting for. He pulls his dagger out of me and makes a show of licking the handle, knowing full well that it would only madden me more.

"If that's what our queen wants, then that's what she'll have." He offers me a conspiring wink, licking his lips as if he could still taste me on them. "On your knees, princess."

I swallow hard, my eagerness to follow his instruction overwhelming all my senses. I do as he says while Teo positions himself on the floor in front of Levi. Not needing further direction, I crawl up Teo's body and straddle his waist, placing my palms on Levi's knees.

"Is this what you want, my heart?" Levi asks, urging to hear my consent.

"Yes," I whimper, every inch of my body begging to come.

"Then you shall have us," he whispers lovingly, his beautiful green eyes filled with such unconditional love that tears begin to form at the corner of my eyes.

I watch as he pulls his pants down, freeing his engorged member and stroking it in my face.

"Put me in your mouth, my heart," Levi commands, taking on a harsher tone, one that sends delicious shivers running up and down my spine.

I don't hesitate and lick the precum off the crown of his cock before wrapping my lips around him and sucking him as far as I can take him.

"Oh, you can do better than that, princess," Atlas scolds lightly, giving me a hard slap on the ass, making my juices run down my thighs.

Teo grabs hold of my waist and begins to dry hump my sensitive slit over his hard length. I try to focus on my task, but it becomes challenging when I feel Teo's cock slowly teasing my opening with the head of his cock.

Levi pulls me by the chin, forcing me to make eye contact with him as I keep sucking him off.

"Now, Teo," he says, still looking me dead in the eye.

I squint in an utter state of bliss when Teo thrusts deeply inside at the same time that Levi twists my hair around his wrists to force me down on his cock.

"Fuck, but she's strangling my cock," Teo groans as he continues to pound into my pussy, keeping to Levi's punishing tempo.

"That's it, princess," I hear Atlas praise from behind me.

And just when I think I'm about to go insane with this sweet torment, I feel a pinch at my backside, Atlas grabbing two handfuls of my ass cheeks and spreading them open for him.

"Tell me when she's close," he says in a ragged tone.

I'm not sure who he's talking to since he was right in his earlier assessment of me. I'm too out of it to make any orders of my own, completely at ease with letting them use and abuse my body for their own pleasure.

"Fuck. Fuck. Now, Atlas. Fucking now!" Levi growls like a wild beast, losing all decorum.

My eyes roll to the back of my head as Atlas lubricates his length with the juices dripping down my thighs, inserting himself inside me in one hard thrust. Tears stream down my eyes, drool and spit leaking from the corners of my mouth as I suck Levi to the hilt, gagging every time he hits the back of my throat. Teo's fingers pinch my nipples as he destroys my pussy with each pounding while Atlas fills me up from behind, slapping my ass with such force that I won't be able to sit down for a week.

This.

This.

This is how it was always meant to be between us.

Loving each other in the only way we know how.

My body, heart, and soul are finally united, ready to sing the melody they were always destined to learn. In a fraction of a second, I come undone, shattering into a million little pieces, knowing that they will glue me back together again with their love.

"Curse the gods," Teo grumbles, pounding into me two more times before I feel the warmth of his release coating my walls.

I'm still trying to regain the gift of sight when Atlas pulls me off Teo and plants me on Levi's lap, my king already ready for me.

"What's your name, princess?" Atlas whispers in my ear, and both his and Levi's cocks slide into me.

When I take too long to reply, Atlas grabs my hair and cranes my neck back as they begin to dance to the music my body is making for them.

"Who do you belong to, my queen?"

"You. I belong to you. All of you," I cry out, the tidal wave of another orgasm fast approaching on the horizon.

Levi grunts his approval before sucking one hard nipple into his mouth. Atlas crashes his lips on mine, keeping his hard pull on my hair, leaving my scalp on fire.

Complete and wrapped in a cocoon of love, I willingly throw myself at the mercy of the gods, coming on a loud cry—one that Atlas greedily swallows. Both my loves soon follow me off the cliff, Levi leaving his own teeth marks on the swell of my breast while Atlas gifts his for me to devour.

My head falls to the crook of Levi's neck, my body boneless and completely satisfied. I'm still in a world of my own making when I hear Levi ask where the captain's cabin is.

"Why?" my devilish blond king retorts.

"Because we're fucking doing this again."

With my eyes closed, I can't contain the smile playing on my lips as they gently carry me away, just to ravish me some more.

425

"Oh gods, just like that. Hmm," I moan, bouncing myself all over Levi's cock as he flicks my swollen clit while Teo watches us from the sidelines, stroking his own member in his hand.

Atlas had to step out after one of his crew demanded his attention up on deck. A challenging feat for him to do since the rest of us do not want to leave this room. We've spent the better part of the last ten days in the captain's quarters. The air in the room is heavy with the scent of our incessant lovemaking. We've eaten, bathed, and fucked in this room more times than I can count. We've also fallen more in love with each other inside these four walls, dreading the time that we have to leave them.

When Levi feels my pussy starting to clench around his hard length, he crooks a finger over to Teo to join us.

For a king who didn't want to share my heart with anyone else, he sure learned quickly how to share my body with others.

"Open your mouth, kitten," Teo orders, tapping the head of his cock on my lips.

"Fuck," Levi growls as he thrusts so deep inside me that I have no choice but to let my orgasm rip me to shreds. Levi fills me up with his release as Teo shoots his into my mouth, making me lick down every last drop.

"By the gods, that's the sexiest thing I've ever seen," Teo praises, running his knuckles down my cheeks.

Happy and satiated, I fall on Levi's chest and let out a sigh of utter contentment. No one should be this happy, and yet, here we all are, completely giddy with it. These last few days have felt like a dream, one that I never want to leave.

But just as the thought passes through my mind, Atlas barges into the room, looking like the avenging king I first met that day back in Huwen.

"What's wrong?" Levi asks, his whole body growing tense.

"Playtime is over, princess. Everyone, get dressed," Atlas demands, looking sternly at his brothers as he struts to a nearby window and pulls the curtains to the side.

"What? Why?" Teo begins to pout.

I rise to see what Atlas is pointing at through the window and come face to face with familiar, snow-filled mountaintops.

"Because I'm home."

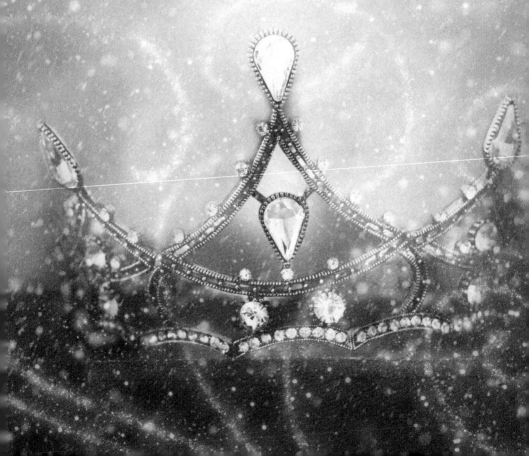

All Hail
The Winter Queen

Chapter 41
Katrina

Ten days by ship and another five on horseback is how long it takes for an army of a hundred thousand men to arrive just outside the gates of my beloved home. The manpower alone should be enough for my uncle to see that he isn't getting out of this one alive.

Every time I think of all the lies he fed me, it makes me sick to my stomach.

I honestly believed he was my closest ally. The one I could lean on for support. It took me leaving my home to fully comprehend how traitorous his heart was.

He wasn't an ally. He was my greatest enemy. A wolf in sheep's clothing.

And now that animal has my baby brother in his clutches.

My thoughts instantly run to Salome, as they always do when I think of Elijah.

How scared she must be that her only son is in such danger, wearing a crown that she never wanted to see placed on his head.

Unlike most women in court, Salome was one of the few who never aspired for such a regal life.

Salome never asked for this.

She never purposely flaunted herself in front of my father in the hopes she would gain favor with him. She was perfectly content living her life attending to my mother's rose garden when, unbeknownst to her, she caught his wandering eye.

With everything I've recently learned about the madness that had consumed my father in those days, I'm beginning to wonder if their affair was even consensual. At the time, no such thought ever crossed my mind, but now? Now I'm all but certain that it wasn't.

What was poor Salome to do? Deny her king and his advances?

A king driven mad by grief who needed any warm body to take the pain away?

No. Either out of loyalty or out of fear, Salome probably endured his attention with a smile, praying he would soon tire of her.

And my father sure did tire of her, abandoning her the minute her belly began to swell with his bastard inside her.

My poor dear Salome.

Not only was her reputation ruined for being the king's wanton mistress, but she also had to deal with my snide comments and dirty looks. Shame accosts me, remembering how I mistreated her, the mother of my baby brother—the same brother who pulled me out of my own grief and gave my life purpose again.

My sweet, loving Salome.

How frightened she must be right now, wanting to protect her son while still being loyal to me. Salome never wanted Elijah to be introduced to court life, much less be his own sister's usurper. All she ever wanted for him was a simple life. And all she ever wanted from me was to rise to the challenge of being the winter queen she always envisioned I'd become.

And here I am. The winter queen Tarnow needs—the one that will make sure that my duplicitous uncle pays for every last sin he's committed—starting with putting my brother and my surrogate mother in such a dire predicament.

"You're awfully quiet, Your Highness," Anya says, pulling me out of my pensive reverie.

"Aye. I was thinking about my brother and Salome," I admit sullenly.

"I'm sure they are fine. Adelid won't dare lay a finger on either one of them. He needs them too much." Anya smiles softly, always the one who wants to cheer me up whenever I'm down.

"I hope you're right. And I hope the prick at least had the decency to keep them locked away in a room with a window. I want my little brother to see me coming for him. I want Salome to not lose hope and to see that the winter queen is here to save them both," I reply, balling my hand into an almighty fist.

"I see that Teo's kitten finally grew some claws," Cleo teases, only to gain a dirty look from her lover. "What? I'm just trying to lighten the mood like you were."

"You really aren't a people person, babe." Anya shakes her head.

"I have my gifts." Cleo winks at her, making Anya blush profusely.

"Do you mind?" Inessa interjects sternly. "I've had enough of you two making googly eyes at each other. At some point, it becomes nauseating."

"This from a woman who goes all giddy any time her man even says her name." Anya giggles.

"I do no such thing," Inessa defends.

"Oh yes, you do," Cleo says, backing up her girlfriend's claim. "And that's not even the worst part. You forget we shared the room next to yours on the ship. It was a miracle we got any sleep at all. Tell her what she sounded like, Cherry."

"Oh, Brick! Yes, Brick. Just like that, Brick. A little to the right. Now to the left. Yes! Yes! Oh gods! YES! Brick! Brick! Brick!" Anya shouts, pounding on the roof of my carriage, pretending it's the sound of Inessa's head banging against a headboard.

"You two are the worst, you know that?" Inessa grumbles, turning her face to the side so no one sees her smile.

I can't help but join in on the laughter, and when Anya winks at me, I realize what she's done. Amongst all the teasing and animated banter, Anya succeeded in pulling me out of my wayward thoughts and giving me the small reprieve I needed.

'Thank you,' I mouth toward her, extending my hand for her to take.

"Any time," she mouths back, giving my hand a little squeeze.

Feeling less tense, I pull my curtain to the side and see my kings galloping together, having their own conversation. But while the girls and I try our best to keep our minds off the impending war, my kings look ready to march into battle.

I wish they had let me ride with them, but not one of them was keen on the idea.

'Adelid could have assassins spying right now, hiding amongst the trees, eager to pierce an arrow through your heart,' Levi had said when he saw me in my white riding gear. *'You and I both know how treacherous this forest is. You're riding in the carriage with your friends. End of story.'*

I would have argued with him any other time, but Levi has overcome plenty of challenges in the last fortnight. I didn't want to lay one more at his feet just because of my stubbornness.

So, since I can't ride alongside them, at least my eyes can drink their fill, admiring each one of my kings on horseback. Levi, in his traditional black clothes, leads the way, while right beside him, Teo smirks over some curse Atlas just said.

Oh, by the gods.

They really are majestic.

Twelve other kings and their troops ride behind us, all eager to follow in their command. I can't help but think how fortunate I am to have them in my corner instead of working against me.

The gods really have a quirky sense of humor. Not six months ago, I left my home thinking that all three of my kings were working together, with the sole purpose of dethroning me. Little did I know that the danger to my throne was closer to home than I could ever imagine.

Not wanting to sully my mood any more than it already is, I open the small carriage window just to take in the familiar scenery of my home and breathe in the winter air. I loved every moment I spent visiting the east, south, and west, but nothing beats the cold breeze of winter air nibbling at my cheeks. Especially when I see the cold air bite into my lovers' cheeks as if the northern wind is welcoming them home, too. I'm not sure how much time passes by as I ogle my men, but as the trees begin to subside, I know that we must be close, just a field of snow away from Tarnow Castle.

When all three men stop their horses abruptly from taking another step, forcing the train behind them to stop, the look of the blank expressions on their faces makes my hackles rise.

"What's wrong?" I ask.

"Stay in the carriage, princess," Atlas orders, pointing a menacing finger my way.

"What are you talking about? I am in the carriage."

Teo pokes his horse in the rear and rides over to me.

"Stay inside," Teo commands with a harsh tone that I've never once heard from him. "All of you. Do not leave this carriage."

"Teo? What is happening?" I demand, slapping his hands off the small window ledge to stop blocking my view.

"Nothing is happening, okay, Katrina? Just do as you're told and stay inside."

Teo using my full name tells me he's lying. I'm not even angry with him bossing me—his rightful queen—around. I'm angry that he's lying to me.

"Inessa, look out your window, please?" I order her.

"You will do no such thing! Inessa, don't!" he shouts, but it's too late; she's able to see what my men are actively trying to keep away from me.

"Oh, gods! No!" she screams, tears instantly falling down her cheeks.

I swallow dryly, knowing whatever Inessa just saw must be truly horrid since my sister never lets anyone see her cry, much less show fear.

Instead of asking for permission, I lean over to the carriage's other door and open it, sprinting as fast as I can out of the carriage without anyone stopping me. But as I do that, I'm confronted with the nightmare my uncle has bestowed upon my people.

A few yards from the castle walls are thousands upon thousands of wooden poles, buried deep into the snow to keep them tumbling over with the weight they carry. Their precious cargo—every northern man, woman, and child that ever showed an ounce of loyalty to me.

More than eighty thousand souls lived within Tarnow's walls, and standing before me, all badly maimed, beaten, and killed, are at least half of them.

No!

No!

No!

My coat flies off my shoulders as I run like the wind toward them, my tears blurring my vision, but not enough to keep me from seeing how savagely they all died. Women stripped naked, used, and abused with their throats slashed open. Men of every age gutted, their bowels hanging from their abdomens.

And the babes…

The innocent children…

Oh, gods!

Oh, gods!

Adelid didn't only kill my people. He *slaughtered* them.

I scream, cry, and curse the gods all in one breath for allowing this horror to happen.

I keep running through the wooden-pole cemetery, doing my best to look at each of their faces, begging them for forgiveness, needing them to know that I never meant anything like this to ever happen to them.

I was their queen.

I was supposed to protect them.

I was supposed to keep the peace.

How they must have felt abandoned by me as Adelid's animals surely tore them apart.

"I'm sorry! I'm so sorry!" I cry, wiping my tears away as I run over to yet another field of corpses in the snow.

"Kat!"

"Kat!"

"Katrina!"

I hear my name being called out in the distance, the agony in my kings' voices only adding to my misery.

While my people were dying, I was too busy falling in love to hear their cries.

"Curse you, gods! And your sick sense of irony! I curse you, stars!" I shout to the heavens, running away from the slew of hurried footsteps behind me.

My uncle must be laughing away at my pain, hearing my scream of pure misery for what he's done to my people. Their rotten flesh doesn't sicken my stomach as much as the idea of how much satisfaction my uncle took from butchering these people.

As if seeing his sick smile widen right before my very eyes, my bile rises up, forcing me to throw up all over my feet. With the sleeve of my dress, I wipe my tears, snot, and vomit away, obliged to keep going and continue watching each face that fell victim to his madness. The dead need to know that I cared for them. For every last person here. They need to know my heart bleeds for them. I will avenge them with fire and brimstone if I have to.

For this is no longer my home.

It's a burial ground.

"Katrina!"

I wipe my wet cheeks again and quickly pick up the pace before either Levi, Teo, or Atlas finds me and takes me back to where they deem me safe.

Nothing will ever feel safe to me now.

My uncle made sure of that.

And when familiar faces begin to surface in a straight line of poles, my sadness and anger morphs to unadulterated fear.

Hanging from one pole is the cook who used to sneak me cookies before bedtime when I was young, her intestines now around her throat.

On another is my governess, with her eyes gouged out from their sockets.

The pole next to hers is the young stable boy who helped care for Atlas's courier pigeons, his legs and arms all chopped off.

And then there is Kari and Ebbe, the handmaidens I left behind.

The things done to their bodies are utterly grotesque for me to look at for too long.

But it's the body hanging beside them that plummets me to my knees, ensuring that my tears will never stop from falling.

Salome.

My Salome.

Now hangs dead before me.

With one royal blue rose shoved in between her teeth.

Chapter 42
Katrina

I n the corner of the tent amongst the shadows, I hide my shame. I
stay out of sight from all the kings here present, not wanting any of
them to see how numb and hollow I've truly become.

Not that it would surprise them any.

They've already seen me at my worst.

Being dragged away, kicking and screaming, determined to stay on a
snowfield of desecrated corpses, unwilling to leave my dear, sweet
Salome hanging there like a piece of discarded meat.

No.

Don't go there, Kat.

Don't.

I discreetly wipe the tears that refuse to stop while holding in a self-deprecating chuckle.

Before I left my Tarnow, I never cried.

And now look at me.

I'll be forever known as the weeping monarch instead of the fierce winter queen Salome imagined me to be. I've let down everyone I love. Everyone who was under my rule, to care for and protect, is now dead. Their bodies left out on an open field for the vultures to pick at.

Stop, Kat!

Stop!

I slap my face hard, the loud smacking sound interrupting the serious conversation being held on the other side of the tent.

"Katrina?" Levi asks worriedly heading towards me.

"I'm quite alright. Please, don't let me interrupt you," I snap before he gets any closer.

His brows pull together, taken aback by my cold demeanor, but thankfully returns to the table.

Cold.

What a joke.

I used to have ice in my veins. Now all I have are these fucking tears.

I shake my head, needing to pull myself out of this hole I find myself in before I let it swallow me whole. So, instead of chastising myself any further, I try to occupy my mind by listening in on their battle strategies, knowing full well that none of them knows the enemy as well as I do.

"He's barricaded himself in the castle, the coward," Levi grumbles, slamming his fist onto the table where the map containing all the entrances to Tarnow Castle lies.

"What did you expect from him? A red carpet and a celebratory feast waiting for you?" Atlas snaps back, using that monotone voice that so evidently conveys his annoyance.

I stifle another humorless laugh at Atlas's peculiar choice of words since a celebratory feast was precisely what I walked in on when I arrived in Huwen.

"This is serious, Attie. Look here," Levi says, pointing at the map. "The gravesite surrounds the castle in a way that we won't be able to climb its walls. How are we to storm the castle if we're not even able to get close enough to do it?"

"So we wait the fucker out," Teo adds his thoughts on the matter. "It's been six months since his last shipment of food. I was going to send more but got a little sidetracked with Kat getting kidnapped and all."

"Aye, and I got the scars to prove that she's forgiven me for that little lapse in judgment. Now, can we please proceed and concentrate here?" Atlas retorts, scanning the map and trying to see if there is any way we can get inside.

"Agreed, young lion, but listen to what King Teo has to say. He might not be wrong in his assessment," Cristobal chimes in, his usual carefree demeanor nowhere to be found. "Besides, I hear too much rage in your voice. We need cool heads to come up with a peaceful resolution."

"I'm sorry. What did you just say?" Levi interjects as if he couldn't believe what he just heard. "Did you say *peaceful resolution?*"

"Aye, he did," King Taurasi chips in. "When the winter queen came to us for our help, she was adamant that she didn't want any bloodshed done on northern soil. We gave her our word."

"I think that vow no longer stands, Taurasi," King Halfdan interjects, glancing over his shoulder to throw a pitying glance my way. "After the genocide done to her people, the blood of all those responsible for it is exactly what she craves now. Am I wrong, my queen?"

Too many pairs of eyes look in my direction as they wait for any sign of life from me.

"No. You're not wrong," I reply through gritted teeth.

Halfdan smiles before turning his attention back to his peers.

"So blood it is. Now, how do we get inside this fucking castle?"

"Perhaps instead of trying to rack our brains for that answer, we can just sit back and wait for the fuckers inside to kill each other," Teo blurts out, throwing his hands in the air in utter frustration. "As I was saying before being so rudely interrupted," he continues, cocking his brow over to Atlas, "I say we wait it out and let those assholes starve. Their rations are bound to run out before ours do."

"That's a tall assumption to make. We have over one hundred men at our command, while they have close to forty thousand," Halfdan says, rubbing his chin in thought.

"Aye, but they have been feeding Tarnow for over six months on the shipment I sent them, one that was only supposed to last them a season," Teo affirms, completely convinced in his theory.

"You didn't send us one shipment. You sent us three," I whisper as I piece the puzzle together.

"What did you say, my heart?" Levi asks, his attention divided between me and his battle plan.

I take a step into the light and walk ever so slowly over to the table, as I try to step into my uncle's shoes, hoping it will enable me to think like him and see his game plan.

442

"Teo, when I asked you about the two missing shipments of food, were you being honest when you told me that you had, in fact, sent them?"

"I've never lied to you, princess. I wouldn't lie about something so inconsequential either," he says, sounding slightly hurt for not believing him the first time around.

I lace my fingers with his and give his hand a light squeeze.

"I believe you," I assure him, and then turn to the curious-looking faces surrounding the table. "Which means that my uncle has been garnering and storing food behind my back for this very purpose. Your plan to wait out the enemy until they run out of food is a good one, Teo. So good that it's the exact plan my uncle is banking on to use and win this war. Like Halfdan said—he has forty thousand souls to feed while we have a hundred thousand. We won't last more than five, six, months, tops, and that's if we started rationing this precise minute. Adelid and his men can probably last a full year without having to set foot outside the castle. While we freeze and starve, getting weaker by the day, they will endure just waiting to hear the loud sound of the retreating horn. He's very clever, I give him that," I sneer, furiously fisting my hands until I feel my nails sink into my palms.

"But that would mean Adelid knew we were coming, months before you even left Tarnow," Levi interjects, trying to understand my logic.

"Aye, my king. That's exactly what I'm inferring," I tell him, my voice starting to come out stronger. "Atlas, tell me, how did you know everything that happened between Levi, Teo, and I?"

"Because the young lion uses spies like the rest of us," Cristobal chimes in.

"That's right. He does. Just like you," I state, pointing at each king. "And you, and you, and you! Are we to believe that Adelid didn't have spies of his own? Teo, didn't you once tell me that you must appear obedient to the north for fear of retaliation?"

Teo nods, his eyes widening with every word that comes out of my mouth.

"And you, Attie, didn't you arrive on your western shores a year or so ago?"

"Give or take a month, yes." He nods, looking just as curious as everybody else.

"Answer me this, my king. That throne you love so dearly back in Huwen—the one made from bones and skulls—how did you come about such a thing?"

His light blue eyes turn deadly as if recalling exactly how he was able to adorn such a thing.

"I killed every last motherfucker Adelid had left to captain my ships, along with his patsies who tried to rule over Huwen while I was in exile. I killed all of them and then used their skulls to build my new throne."

Electricity buzzes through me as I confirm yet another one of my suspicions.

"I bet you did, my love, but in doing so, you also alerted my uncle of your stellar arrival. After what he had done to your mother, he knew you would come for him just as you had come for his men."

"Holy shit!" Cristobal blurts out, genuinely impressed with my conclusions.

"Wait, there's more," I announce, the tent going so silent that you can hear a pin drop.

"Levi, my heart, when you received word from Atlas and his arrival, what did you do?"

"I gathered up my men and marched north. I was to make camp at the border until Atlas was on his way. Together, we would sack Tarnow."

"Aye. Sack Tarnow," I repeat, the world around me beginning to make sense for the first time.

No more lies.

No more clever deceptions.

Only the truth.

"My uncle knew you were coming long before we did. He would end up being triumphant in his mission, while I, on the other hand, would have looked weak and clueless as to why armies were marching at my doorstep unprovoked. Tarnow would have had my head up on a spike long before my enemies could get a hold of me."

"Motherfucker!" Atlas shouts, his blue eyes a perfect storm of rage and fury.

But I don't have time to comfort anyone right now. Not when I see my mission so clearly.

"Cristobal, be a dear and bring Anya and Inessa to me, please? I'm going to need them both for the second part of my plan."

"Of course, my queen," he answers, immediately rushing out of the tent to do my bidding.

Feeling the weight of everyone's stare on me, I look down at the map and examine the fortress Adelid believes will keep him safe.

But nothing will do that.

Not even if he built wall upon wall. I'd still get my hands on him.

Somehow, someway.

"My kings, the reason why you are unable to see a way into the castle is because each man here is as honorable and god-fearing as they come. Unfortunately, our enemy isn't. If we want to vanquish him, then we will need to start thinking like he does and lower ourselves to his level." I take in a deep inhale before continuing on. "What I'm about to say may offend you, but it's the only way I see for your army to storm the castle and regain control of Tarnow. Here," I say, pointing to where the new forest of bodies is currently raised, "tell your men to cut down all these wooden beams. Tear them down and clear a large path on all flanks of the castle. Do it as fast as you can. I don't want to wait another day, gentlemen, for that monster still holds my baby brother hostage, and I fear what he might do to him now that I'm here."

"Once the paths have been cleared, I'll leave it to you to plan a battle strategy. Every king here is far more experienced on the battlefield than I am, so I won't insult you by pretending I know the first thing about military tactics. If Elijah wasn't somewhere inside that castle, my order would be for you to burn it all to the ground. But since we don't have that option, I'm counting on your expertise on that front."

Some of the kings look ready to tear the castle down, brick by brick, while others still look squeamish at the idea of desecrating the makeshift cemetery, but they have to overcome that and fast. Adelid is probably counting on the kings' superstition that the living should not interfere with the remains of the dead or be punished by the heavens itself, but what they fail to see is that the gods left this place a long time ago.

"My men will do as you say, my queen. They will make sure that those poles come down and that the dead aren't too badly disturbed."

"Nothing can disturb the dead, Halfdan. And even if there were, they no longer have voices to complain."

"Truer words have never been spoken. I fear, not the wrath of the gods, but the deeds of evil men. I will aid your cause in any way I can. As long as you keep to your word, I vow to keep mine," Halfdan is quick to say. "You will sit on your throne again, Queen Katrina. The north shall rise with their rightful queen ruling over it. On my life, I swear to it," he adds, placing his clenched fist over his chest.

The rest of the kings begin to utter the same mantra, clenching their fists over their hearts, the simple action sealing their vow.

But none are more important than Levi, Teo, and Atlas giving me their solemn vows.

"You will sit on your throne again, Queen Katrina. The north shall rise with their rightful queen ruling over it. On my life, I swear to it."

Chapter 43
Katrina

For the next two days, I watch from the sidelines as Halfdan's men clear the pathways needed for our army to climb my castle's walls. With a held breath, I watched as the soldiers chopped down every wooden mast in their way while protecting themselves from the fire arrows coming from above.

Levi had warned me that my uncle would try to delay the progress we were making. However, it was still hard to watch so many soldiers die following my orders, especially the ones who were just trying to carry back the bodies of the northern fallen in their arms.

But now the task is done, and all that is left is to storm the castle and bring the villain I call uncle to justice.

"It's a good plan, princess. A fucking good plan," Atlas praises, placing his chin on top of my head and his arms around my waist

"It better be." I bite into my cheek, my gaze never straying from the castle. "We only have one shot to save my brother. That's the only thing I can think about."

"I'd still feel better if one of us went with you," Levi says, standing beside me with his arms crossed at his chest as he stares straight ahead at the castle.

"I know, my heart. But like I told you a million times before, I'll be fine alone. I know my way around my own castle and, therefore, do not need a chaperone. Your armor alone would draw too much attention to us, and that would defeat the purpose of the whole thing."

The corners of Levi's lips dip into a frown, but he's smart enough not to push me to get his own way.

"Don't give Levi a hard time, kitten. He's just saying what we're all thinking. Not one of us likes the idea of you going alone."

"And who says our queen is going anywhere without us?" a familiar voice calls out, coaxing us to turn our undivided attention off the castle's high walls and onto the group of friends marching toward us with resolved conviction.

"Are you two wearing leathers?" I ask in utter astonishment, doubting my own eyes upon seeing Inessa and Anya all geared up.

"Aye, my queen." Anya grins widely. "If we are to be your bodyguards tonight, we might as well look the part."

"Wait? What?" Atlas blurts out, releasing his grip on me to step beside me, an stare at my friends.

"You heard her," Inessa states evenly with her head held high. "There is no way in hell we are just going to sit back and let our queen go in without us. Besides, Anya is the one who knows the secret passageway through the dungeons. Who better to guide our queen inside without raising suspicion than her?"

My heart swells two sizes, but so does the fear of losing them.

I step toward them and extend one hand for each of my sisters to take.

"I love you both with all my heart, but this mission will be dangerous. I can't ask you to put your lives in jeopardy for me."

"We know that, Kat. But this isn't up for debate. We're going with you," Anya replies steadfastly.

"There's nothing you can say that will change our minds, sister. He killed everyone we've ever known, too. Don't ask us to stand back and watch others do our fighting for us. We need to do something,. This is our home, too," Inessa adds, emotion coating her every word.

"Are you two okay with this?" I ask their respective partners, who have been uncharacteristically silent throughout this whole exchange.

"Am I thrilled that my Cherry is the only one who knows this secret passageway because she was hooking up with gods-know-who at the time? No, I'm not. Am I proud of her for standing up for her convictions and her queen? Damn straight I am." Cloe beams, looking lovingly at Anya.

"And you, Brick?" I turn my attention to the red-haired general. "Are you okay with Inessa accompanying me tonight?"

Brick swallows hard and squares his shoulders to look even bigger than he already is—a tactic I'm sure he does often to mask his fear from others.

"Inessa is an independent woman who knows her own mind, Your Highness. There isn't a man alive who could forbid her from anything she puts her mind to. And I will not disrespect our love by trying to force her to be someone she's not. I fell in love with the fearless woman that stands before you now, and I wouldn't have her any other way."

"Gods, but he is a poet," Anya whispers dreamingly.

"Hey," Inessa snaps her fingers right in Anya's face to take that dreamy look off her, "keep eyes on your own woman, sister. Brick is mine."

"Aren't we the possessive type?!" Anya claps in utter glee. "I can't wait for you two to start having a bunch of babies! It's going to be so much fun corrupting them and driving you mad!"

"Oh, for fuck's sake." Inessa rolls her eyes while Brick's cheeks turn even more red than the hair on top of his head or the beard on his chin.

I'm so overwhelmed with love for my sisters that I don't even hear another visitor's footsteps approaching.

"Your Highness," Monad bows, still looking like he's licking his wounds from the severe tongue-lashing I gave him back in Huwen. "May I be so bold to ask for an audience with you?"

"Say what you have to say, Monad. As you can see, neither one of us is in my throne room for such polite etiquettes," I retort with a bite to my voice.

"Your Highness is still disappointed in me, and for good reason. I let you down. I let all of Tarnow down. Not only was I not successful in bringing your brother to you, but I took loyal men who might have been able to stop the carnage our home faced in my absence. I will forever live with this shame," he states, his gaze lowered to the frozen ground beneath his feet, unable to look me in the eye. "Now, I'll never be able to turn the hands of time back to make different choices, but I can offer you my life in eternal service. If it would please you, Your Highness, I would very much like to escort you tonight in your mission. I may not be as young or strong as the kings standing beside you, but I swear my heart is pure, and I will protect you with my very life if need be."

I stare at my chief-in-arms and hear the truth in his words.

Monad, like my sisters and I, is suffering.

After witnessing how our beautiful winter home has been destroyed by the vileness of one man, it would be sacrilege for him not to stand up and fight against the oppressor who brought such ruin to it.

I take one step in his direction and call out his name.

"Monad, look at me," I order, with ice in my voice.

Ever so slowly, he raises his head to look me in the eye, the dark rings under his own eyes a testament to his guilt-ridden, sleepless nights.

"Tell your men to get their orders from King Halfdan tonight, for you will not be accompanying them but serving your queen."

Monad's eyes begin to sparkle with unshed tears, grateful for the mercy I'm bestowing on him.

"As you wish, my queen," he retorts, wiping at a stray tear that refused to be kept at bay.

I take a step back away from him to look at my friends and my beloved kings one more time.

"Now go. Rest and prepare, for we have a long night ahead of us," I tell them in earnest, inwardly reciting a silent prayer to the gods, begging to keep them safe and that I'm not sending every person I love to their deaths tonight.

"Keep your head down when you're out on the field. Don't say a word along the way. Once you get inside, don't forget to place a candle on the window. It will be our sign that you made it safely across and found your way into the dungeons. Once there, find Elijah and get the hell out of there. Is that understood?" Atlas instructs with a rigid expression on his face as he holds onto my shoulders.

He's so worried about me that I don't have the heart to tease him for relaying my thought-out plan back to me, word for word.

"You can do this, princess. I have every faith in you that you can save your brother and get back to us safely," he adds with certainty.

"I know."

"Still, you'll need protection."

"I thought Monad was my protection." I arch a brow.

"Monad is an old man who hasn't seen warfare in years. I'd feel much better if I knew you had something to protect yourself with. Here," he says, pulling his mother's dagger out of its sheath and placing it in my hands.

"I can't take this." I shake my head, the weight of it burning my palms.

"You can and you will. It will protect you just as it has protected me."

I swallow dryly and tuck it safely behind my back.

"Thank you," he whispers and then pulls me into his embrace, hugging me so tightly that the air leaves my lungs.

"You can do this, Kat. You can."

My chest tightens at how he keeps repeating those words, as if he had to say them out loud so they can come true. He pulls back just far enough to lift my chin up and press a chaste kiss on my lips. Then he steps to the side, letting Teo say his goodbyes.

"You stay safe, kitten. You hear me?" He smiles softly as he pulls me into his chest and cradles my head against it.

"Funny, I was going to tell you the same thing," I tease, taking in his scent.

"Don't worry about me. Not only do I have Atlas and Levi by my side, but Cleo too."

"Good." I let out a relieved sigh. "She won't let anything happen to you. I pity the man who tries to get in her way."

"Me too." He laughs while running his fingers through my hair.

When he doesn't break our embrace, I plant my palms over his chest and pull myself back.

"I'll be okay, Teo. I promise," I tell him, needing him to not worry about me.

"I know," he says, his amber eyes unable to hide his fear for my safety.

On the balls of my feet, I pull myself up and give a tender kiss on his lips, his gaze softening somewhat. Teo then stands to the side to join Atlas, giving Levi his turn to say goodbye.

My soldier king looks like the god of war himself, arms crossed over his broad chest as he stares at me.

"Are you just going to stand there, or are you going to say goodbye?" I ask him when he doesn't move an inch.

In two quick strides, he's on me with his hand on my throat and his bruising lips on mine. He kisses me as if it were our last, leaving me breathless and lightheaded. He then presses his temple against my forehead and breathes me in.

"Don't you dare fucking die on me."

"I wouldn't dream of it," I whisper to him.

Before I'm ready for it, Levi steps back and joins his brothers.

I give them all one final look, my heart full of love for them.

"I love you. Be safe," I tell them, and before they have time to say anything else, I cover my head with the hood of my cloak and walk over to my sisters and chief-of-arms, who are already waiting for me.

"Are you ready?" Inessa asks when I reach them.

"As ready as I'll ever be."

"Good. Well, let's do this. Follow me," Anya orders with a serious tone, covering her own red hair with her hood and racing onto the field of rotting corpses.

My heart drums in my chest as each one of us waits a few seconds before following her. The moonless sky is our friend tonight, enabling us to run through the snow field without anyone inside the castle being none the wiser. Anya stops every few seconds, pressing her back against a wooden mast, trying her very best to ignore the body hanging above it. We all follow her lead as we draw nearer to the castle's walls. Anya stops just a few feet away, with her back flush against a pole, and points to a hidden iron gate behind her.

I look over to Inessa and Monad to make sure they see the same thing I do, and once they give me a nod, I offer Anya one of my own. On cue, she breaks into a sprint and runs to the gate, opening it for us at record speed. With no time to lose, all three of us run toward her, stepping into a dark hallway as Anya closes the gate behind us.

"Easy-peasy." She giggles softly once we are all safe inside.

"We're not done yet," Inessa interjects, pulling the candle out of her cloak pocket.

"Give it to me," I order, scanning for a window just to find one a few feet away.

Anya flicks a match and lights it up before handing it to me. I place the burning candle on the windowsill and wait.

"Come on, come on, come on," I mumble, impatiently staring into the eerily silent field.

And then I hear it—the battle cry.

Suddenly, thousands upon thousands of brave soldiers run toward the field with their swords and shields raised up high, while others carry ten-foot-long ladders above their heads. My heart stops in my chest as my eyes land on my fearless kings, riding on horseback toward the castle with the sole intent of murdering every last soldier loyal to my uncle.

"Your Highness, we need to go. Now!" Monad urges beside me.

"Show us the way to the dungeons, Anya," I command, hoping my brother might be locked up in a cell somewhere.

"Follow me," Anya says, back to her serious form.

We do as she says, and I can't help wondering how many times my handmaiden must have come through these secret tunnels to know how to walk amongst them in complete darkness. Back then, Anya was always looking for love in the wrong places. It's ironic how she found her soulmate when she stepped into the light of the southern sun.

"This way," she says, turning a corner toward another iron gate.

Unfortunately for us, this one isn't open.

"Damn it," she curses.

"Is there another way in? Another route, perhaps?"

"Not to the dungeon," she laments.

"Then I guess it's a good thing I came along," Monad beams, looking proud of himself. "Ladies, if you would be so kind to step back, please?"

With my arms stretched out wide to protect my sisters, Monad pulls his sword out of his sheath, raising it up high before striking it down with all his might and breaking the lock in one mighty blow. He then swings the door open for us, his wide smile splitting his face in two.

"Your Highness." He bows.

"Good job, Monad," I tell him, his smile only widening further with the praise.

But then I hear it.

The sounds of battle.

Steel clashing with steel.

Cries for mercy and screams of pain.

They did it.

They're inside the castle.

Pride morphs quickly into panic.

"Okay, let's go," I order. "Adelid knows he's outnumbered and that death is coming for him. Let's not tempt a desperate man and find Elijah."

"This way," Anya whispers, urging us to follow down yet another tunnel, stopping at a door at the very end of it.

She turns the knob and lets out a sigh of relief when she's able to open it. The instant we step under its threshold, I know exactly where we are—my father's dungeon.

But if I thought I would only find my brother here, I was vastly mistaken.

The cells are filled to the brim with people, all looking like they have spent the better part of a month behind bars.

"Find me the keys to the cells. Now!" I order Inessa and Anya to split up and do exactly as I've commanded .

"My Queen!"

"You've come for us!"

"It's the winter queen!"

"She's here! We're saved!"

The prisoners begin to shout as Monad starts banging on the locks with his sword.

"Found them!" Inessa shouts back, rushing to the nearest cell to open its gates.

"Your Majesty! Your Majesty!" I hear a familiar voice call out.

"Otto? Otto, is that you?" I run toward the last cell.

"Yes, my queen. Come quick. I have the boy! I have the boy!"

"Inessa!!!" I hurriedly shout to my sister as I come face to face with Tarnow's treasurer.

"Otto! Where are you?!" I shout, scanning the large jail cell full of people.

"Give him room! Give him room!" the mob inside begins to shout, and suddenly, I see Otto walk toward me, my brother's limp body in his arms.

"Oh, by the gods! Is he hurt?! Inessa, come quick!" I shout, tears streaming from my face at the blank stare in my sweet baby brother's eyes. "What's wrong with him, Otto? What has happened to my brother?"

Otto looks worse for wear himself, but the way he cradles my brother's head onto his chest tells me that he did everything in his power to keep him alive.

"I'm here! I'm here!" Inessa yells, juggling the massive keychain in her hands. As she inserts one after the other, I hold onto the bars of the cell, staring at my baby brother's catatonic state.

"Otto, what happened to him?" I demand with a sob.

"He... made... the boy... watch," Otto stammers, his whole body shaking. "He made him watch!"

Salome.

My teeth grind so hard that my back molars threaten to break.

When I hear the familiar clink of a lock, I rush to pull Otto and my brother out of the cell.

"I'm here, Elijah! I'm here!" I tell him, kissing his sweet face.

But my baby brother just stares blankly at me, as if his mind had completely shut out the outside world.

"He's been like this since..." Otto begins to explain, the marks of his trauma marred on his face. "I didn't know what to do. I only knew I had to protect the boy," he adds, his voice strained with grief.

"Elijah? It's me," I whisper softly as I caress his cheeks.

But my brother doesn't so much as blink.

"Kat?" Anya calls out from behind me. "What do we do now?"

My grief and sadness give way to rage.

"You and Inessa take my people out of here and back to the camp. Otto, go with them and protect Elijah."

"Wait. What about you? Where are you going?" Inessa interrogates.

"Me and Monad have unfinished business inside the castle. Isn't that right, Monad?"

My chief-in-arms grows two sizes before me as he nods.

"I'm at your service, my queen."

"They're not going to like this," Inessa says, her brows pulled together in concern.

"They have their own fight to think about. Now go. Take my brother and my people to safety. Go!"

I kiss my brother's forehead and race to the stairs leading to the castle's upper levels with Monad right at my heel.

"Where do you think the bastard is?" Monad asks behind me.

"A king worth his salt would be fighting with his men to protect his castle."

"That piece of shit is no king," Monad retorts with vehemence in his tone.

"Agreed. Which means he's hiding somewhere. My guess is that he's probably in his room wondering how he might escape his death."

"Fat chance that will happen."

The smile that crests my lips must be as sinister as the one my Attie likes to wear when his mind is overrun by thoughts of vengeance and bloodshed.

When we finally reach ground level, we stop in our tracks and hear a loud sound of something banging against iron.

"Looks like your kings are knocking on the front door. Someone should really open it before they bring the whole castle down." He chuckles at his own joke.

"I don't remember you being this funny." I arch a brow and start racing down the hall toward the stairs that will lead me to Adelid's room on the second floor.

"War brings humor out of me. Some men cry, others rage. Me? I like to have fun with it." He shrugs as if it were a perfectly logical explanation as any other.

THE WINTER KISSED KINGS

I shake my head, rethinking my whole perception of him.

There was a time when his reminiscent talk of war aggravated my every nerve, but now I'm starting to understand that being a loyal soldier to the crown was his whole life's purpose. One that he took pride in. I thought him war-hungry when, in reality, all he wanted to do was be of service to me.

"You're a good man, Monad. I'm sorry that I was so harsh to you."

"No, my queen. You weren't harsh enough. I deserved every bit of your contempt. I failed you. I should have realized how important the boy was to you. Otto stayed behind because of him. I should have done the same."

My jaw slacks at the confirmation of my own suspicions. Monad told Otto of his plans to flee Tarnow and head west in the hopes that he could rescue me and bring me home. Monad was impatient to save his queen, while Otto knew I would gladly give up my salvation as long as my brother was kept safe.

The list of suspects that were in cahoots with my uncle has now been cut in half.

Not that it matters anymore.

He's the only head I want to see on a spike.

I'm about to run down a hall when Monad pulls me by my cloak and hides me behind one of my father's statues. He places his finger at the center of his lips, his silent way of telling me to stay quiet as a hoard of soldiers races down the corridor, all of them loyal to my pig of an uncle.

"All clear, Your Highness," Monad says after ensuring we can leave our hiding spot.

"You have come in handy, Monad. I'll give you that." I smile at him, knowing that my praise means more to him than any honor or land I could offer.

"Thank you, Your Highness." He beams as he keeps to my hurried step toward the stairs.

As we race up the steps, the sounds of battle continue on as my thoughts go out to my men, praying for their safety.

"This way, my queen," Monad urges breathlessly, the race up the stairs taking its toll on him.

My eyes fix on the end of the hall where Adelid's room is. However, when we finally reach it, we're met with bitter disappointment. My uncle's door is wide open, his belongings all spread out on top of his bed. I walk inside and find a treasure trove of diamonds and sapphires on his bed, each precious jewel bigger than the other. There are also two large chests filled with gold coins. This must have been the fortune he accumulated over the years with his slavery trade.

My nostrils flare in disgust as I throw one of his chests down to the floor.

"Curse the gods! Where the hell is he?!"

But just as I ask the question aloud, I hear a resounding thud of a door closing behind me, forcing me to turn around and face the villain himself with a dagger on Monad's neck.

"Now, now, niece. Where are your manners? You know how much I hate uninvited guests barging into my room while conducting business." He grins maliciously before slicing Monad's throat open.

Monad's eyes grow wide, his life flashing before his eyes as my uncle throws him to the ground like discarded trash.

I bite my inner cheek to keep my horror in check and take a step back away from the villain in the room.

"Ah, niece, you have me in quite a predicament," he coos, walking closer to me. "I thought for sure when I received that letter from the rebel king that he'd kill you for me. But alas, I see he's still the same weakling he's always been."

"Don't you fucking dare talk about Atlas that way! You're not even half the man he is."

My uncle's silver eyes turn deadly as he pierces me with his gaze.

"Watch your tongue, niece, before I cut it out of you."

I fist my hands behind my back as I take another step away from him.

"Still, the gods must be in my favor if they sent you directly to me. You'll be my shield out of this hell."

"You'll die here tonight, uncle. I swear you will."

"Is that a fact?" He has the audacity to laugh. "No, I don't think I will die. See, you've made a lot of friends on your voyages through Aikyam. Friendships that can prove useful to me in this time of need. I doubt it very much that the kings you proposed marriage to will deny me a thing as long as I promise not to kill you. Although I must say, I'm a bit disappointed in your recent behavior. Bedding all three kings? Really, niece? You've acted more like a paid whore than a queen." He sneers. "My own fault, perhaps. If I let my sister live a little longer, maybe she would have been able to teach you how to keep your legs shut before marriage."

My world starts spinning, the ground beneath my feet feeling like it's going to tilt at any minute.

"Oh, you didn't know," he taunts, taking another step in my direction. "Really, child, how naive can you be?"

"You… you… killed… my mother?"

"Aye, I did," he affirms proudly, as if he should be rewarded for such an accomplishment.

"She was your sister!" I yell in outrage. "Your own flesh and blood!"

"She was a meddlesome inconvenience at best." He waves me off. "Always whispering in Orville's ear how I was a bad influence on him.

Pfft. What about her, huh? If I was such a bad influence on her husband, what the hell was she? Alisa had one job. One fucking job to do—bear a son. And instead, all she was able to pop out was a spoiled princess who lived in her head and knew nothing of the world. I did your father a favor when I gave her the hemlock tea to drink. Before she died, he was a pathetic king, always craving attention. Always throwing lavish birthday celebrations and treating his vassals as peers when they should have been kissing the ground he stepped on. But the minute she left her mortal coil, Orville became the king he was destined to become. I did that. Me!" he shouts, pointing his finger to his chest.

"You made my father insane! He went mad after my mother died. You call that being a king?!" I shout back, equally enraged.

"I admit, he did get carried away a little bit, but then again, so did I." He smiles as if he were fond of all the memories of that time.

"Oh, by the gods! You're just as maniacal as he was! No! You're more! You killed Rhea! You killed Atlas's mother and did nothing to prevent the murders of King Krystiyan and Queen Daryna of Thezmaer! You did all of that with no excuse except for your own sense of entitlement and greed. Do you deny it?!" I spit out with such hatred that it physically pollutes my bloodstream.

"I deny nothing. Why would I deny it when I rid the world of Tarnow's enemies?"

"They were never our enemies. They were our allies. But, of course, to a man like you, I'm sure it must be so difficult for you to make the distinction."

"They would have turned on Orville given the chance. Not that it mattered in the long run. Your father was his own worst enemy. He had everything at his fingertips, all the prestige and power he could ever want, and still, he insisted that *you* be his only heir. You, a woman who wouldn't know the first thing about the sacrifices it took to rule a kingdom, much less four of them."

Suddenly, the earth tilts on its axis again, flinging me every which way with his admission, so much so that I have to grab hold of his bedpost to keep me from falling to my knees.

A faint memory comes to the forefront of my mind of me walking into my father's bedchambers after he was pronounced dead by the castle's physicians. Neither one of them could tell me how he passed away, most likely from a stroke or a heart attack, given his age and unhealthy diet. I remember how ironic it was that there was a teacup and saucer on his bedside table instead of a bottle of his favorite cherry wine.

Hemlock tea.

That's what Adelid used to kill my mother.

And that's what he used to kill my father.

"Is that why you killed him? Killed my father? Because he wouldn't name you heir in favor of his own daughter?" I ask, my tone so calm it almost makes me cringe at the sound of my own voice.

"Well, well, well. Look at you, adding one plus one together. I must admit, I'm impressed." He throws his head back in a cackle. "Mind you, I was very fond of your father. I always felt that, with the right encouragement, he could have been a god amongst men. But alas, he didn't take my advice when I suggested he remarry. Another queen on the throne, a much younger one at that, could mean more children. Male heirs that would do the title justice. Not the bastards he decided to fill Tarnow's halls with. For years, I kept insisting that he change his mind and find himself a young bride. Until one day, he did broach the subject of marriage with me, just not his. Instead, he started to make plans for *your* betrothal, ordering me to send letters to every eligible king willing to marry you. I couldn't believe what I was hearing. After all I had done for him, he preferred to place a complete stranger on the throne rather than me—his right hand. If I was going to all this trouble to stop a woman from taking the throne, I sure as hell wasn't going to give it to a foreigner who knew nothing of our ways."

I stare at the man in front of me with brand-new eyes.

All his scheming ways, all the lies he told, the deceit, and the blood he spilled still got him nothing in the end.

Nothing except what's coming to him.

"What now, uncle? What are you going to do with me?" I ask, my mind already made up.

"Now, you and I are going to take a walk. You're going to be my way out of this chaotic mess," he sneers.

"Fair enough. And will you be taking your precious jewels and gold, or will you live the remainder of your days hiding away somewhere completely destitute?"

Like the greedy pig of a man that he is, his gaze moves away from me and onto the bed where his treasure lies.

"I'm too accustomed to court life to live as a commoner. Good on you, niece, for reminding me of my worth." He winks before taking a step toward the bed but then stops to throw me a glower. "Don't even think of running away, niece. I'm not averse to gutting you like a pig."

"Funny. I was thinking the same thing. But *alas*, you're the one with the dagger in your hands, while I have no such weapon in mine," I tell him, using his new favorite word. "But then again, why would a woman need such a thing?"

"Aye, why would she?" he cackles, racing to his fortune and hurriedly filling his pockets.

I bide my time until he reaches the conclusion any greedy man in his situation would—time is of the essence, and he can hoard a lot more gold if both his hands are free. The instant his greed overpowers his sense of self-preservation, I unsheathe the dagger behind my back and fling myself at him, slashing him from ear to ear. I then pull the blade out as he falls to the floor, his eyes widening in both shock and confusion when I straddle him and begin stabbing at his chest. Blood spurts out of him and onto my face, neck, and chest, tainting my white gear with his crimson fluid .

Rage consumes me with every slice of the knife into his flesh, every cut deeper than the next. My blinding fury comes at me in full force, remembering all the lives he took away from me. How he managed to destroy everything and everyone I love for his own gain.

Sitting on top of his unresponsive body, I plunge my hand inside his fully exposed chest, pull out his non-beating heart, and bite a chunk of it, spitting it out onto the floor. I'm still in a crazed daze when the bedroom door opens in front of me, revealing Levi, Teo, and Atlas, standing under its threshold, ready to take the monster down.

Bloodied and mad with fury, I throw my uncle's cold heart in the air, Atlas catching it in his hands with ease.

"Give the rest to Halfdan. I already took my pound of flesh."

Chapter 44
Katrina

Three months later

"They're pretty, aren't they, Elijah?" I coo softly, running my fingers through his hair as he stares at the blue roses. "They were my mother's and your mother's favorite flower. Both of them would spend hours just admiring them," I add, trying to coax any reaction I can from him. "Your mother used to let me tend to the garden too. She didn't let anyone else do that, but she let me help her any time I asked. I think it's because she knew how much I missed my own mother, like I know you're missing yours. And one thing I know for sure is that she misses you too, wherever she is. She loved you so much. So very much. Never forget that, sweet boy."

I stare into his eyes, waiting for a flicker of life to shine back in them. I frown when his empty stare moves past his mother's beloved roses and onto the other orphans on the other side of the garden, who are currently helping Teo with his own gardening experiment.

I let out a sigh and stand up straight, offering him my hand to take.

When Elijah laces his hand in mine, my heart fills with hope.

A couple of months ago, he wouldn't have done that on his own. In fact, for that first month, after I found him in the dungeon with Otto, Elijah didn't have enough strength to do anything on his own. He couldn't walk, eat on his own, or follow the simplest of instructions. Now, he's almost self-sufficient. Though he hasn't spoken a word to me yet, I know that one of these days he'll come back to me.

"Okay, sweet boy. You want to play with the other children and help Teo plant some vegetables?"

Again, he doesn't reply, but he does tighten his grip on my hand and leads me to where his friends are.

Well, not friends, plural, but more like one friend, singular.

The minute Zara sees the two of us coming, she drops her little shovel and races toward us.

"Elijah!" she screams with happiness before giving him a big hug.

That's another thing that I've seen improvement on. He's now also able to allow physical touch. At first, he only let Otto and me take care of him, screaming at the top of his lungs whenever anyone else tried. But slowly, he got accustomed to the other people in my life who would end up being just as important in his life, too. Most importantly, the kings I've vowed to share my life with. Elijah now knows that he can seek refuge with either Levi, Teo, or Atlas. However, the person he's fondest of is the one staring cheerfully into his eyes right now.

"Elijah, do you want to help me plant turnips? I don't like how they taste very much, but Teo says that after we plant them, we can start planting carrots. Those are my absolute favorite. Do you like carrots? Of course you do. Who doesn't like carrots?" She laughs, bouncing on the balls of her feet.

Thank the gods for Teo's sister, Zara.

Elijah might not say a word, but she says more than enough for both of them.

I must admit, I was a bit wary when Teo told me he had sent word to his people in Nas Lead to bring his baby sister here with her governess, but she's been a true blessing in Elijah's life.

"Zara, are you talking Kat's and Elijah's ears off again?" Teo jokes, walking over to us while cleaning the dirt from his hands with an old rag.

"No, I'm just telling Elijah about all the vegetables we're planting today," she answers, turning her attention over to Elijah again. "Did you know that even in the snow, you can grow all kinds of food to eat? Like kale or brussels sprouts. Ooh, and beets and cabbages! You can even grow spinach! Isn't that amazing, Elijah?"

It's no wonder my baby brother likes to be around her so much.

Zara's enthusiasm and zest for life are so contagious that no one could be near her and not smile.

"Kat, can Elijah help me with planting the turnips? I promise that I won't let him out of my sight. Can he, Kat? Please?" she begs, batting her eyes at me so innocently.

Teo is in big trouble.

When Zara grows up, she's going to be a heartbreaker.

"Pretty, pretty please? Can he? Can he?" she begins to jump impatiently.

"Well, we'll just have to ask him, now won't we?" I go to my haunches and smile. "Do you want to play with Zara for a bit?"

He stares at me for a moment, then lets go of my hand and grabs hold of Zara's instead.

"Guess that's a yes," Teo chuckles.

Zara doesn't miss a beat and continues to talk animatedly with Elijah as they both join the other orphans who are busy planting their vegetables.

"He looks like he's having a good day," Teo says beside me, eyeing his sister and my baby brother together.

"Aye. He even slept a full night. No night terrors to speak of."

"That's good. Maybe now you'll be able to sleep a full night in our bed." He smirks.

"And when have I ever *slept* a full night with you three always on me?" I tease, wrapping my arms around his neck.

"On you. Behind you. Beneath you. Oh, kitten, there are so many positions we could start listing here, but that would make me want to sneak off into a dark corner somewhere and fuck your brains out. As you can see, I have a garden full of children to attend to," he informs with a mischievous grin.

"You're very dutiful, my king," I taunt, leaning my body closer to his.

"Kitten, play fair now and put away those claws of yours."

"Kiss me, and you won't hear a peep out of me."

His amber eyes smolder as he leans in and kisses me. His warm lips mold themselves to mine as I run my fingers through his hair, pulling at the strands to deepen the kiss. He groans into my mouth as his tongue wrestles with mine for dominance, his hard body pressed against mine. But then I feel another pair of hands at my waist, pulling my butt back to rub against another hard body. When I feel the grazing of teeth on the nape of my neck, I moan into Teo's mouth, giving myself up to the spectacular sensation of being pinned between him and Atlas.

"That's enough," Teo grunts after stopping the kiss.

472

"Oh, but I was only just getting started," Atlas pouts, wrapping his arms around me and placing his chin on my shoulder.

"Aye, I know exactly what you want, but as you can see, I got shit to do," Teo grumbles as he lowers his eyes to the bulge in his pants. "Gods damn it, Atlas. Now I've got a fucking hard-on. What if the kids see?" he points to the children playing around the garden.

"Tell them that you have three legs instead of two. I'm sure they'll buy that."

"You suck, Attie," he half-grumbles, half-laughs. "Now, take our woman out of here before I change my mind."

"Are you sure you don't want to take a little break with us?" Atlas taunts, licking my neck and palming one of my breasts in his hand.

"Motherfucker!" Teo grumbles, annoyed, throwing his arms in the air in desperation before turning his back on us to join the rest of the children.

"I think you got him mad," I giggle, rubbing my ass on his hard mast.

"Hmm. We'll make it up to him tonight," Atlas coos after biting on my earlobe. "Now, how about we go for a little walk. Just the two of us?"

He swings me around and pulls me into his chest,

"Actually, a walk would be nice right about now. There are some things I wanted to discuss with you."

The gleam in Atlas's blue eyes instantly dims.

"Princess, when I said let's go for a walk, what I really meant to say was let's find a room where I can bend you down on a table and fuck that pretty pink pussy of yours."

"Gods. Is that all you men think about?" I snap, trying to pull out of his embrace.

"Tsk, tsk. Such a pretty little spoiled princess, pretending we're the only ones with sex on the brain when she can't keep her hands off us either."

I bite the corner of my lips and smile because he's got me there.

"But if it's a walk and not a fuck you fancy, who am I to judge?" he teases, releasing me from his grip and giving the crook of his arm to hold on to. "So what's on your mind, princess? To my chagrin, we've already established that it's not sucking my cock."

"Attie!"

I slap his chest and laugh.

"Okay. Okay. I'm just teasing." He laughs, pulling me closer to his side.

"Well, I've been thinking, how long do you think it will be until Tarnow is rebuilt and self-sufficient?" I ask as we begin to walk through the corridors.

"Hmm. A year, maybe. Two at the most."

"That long?"

"Unfortunately, a lot of damage was done to the castle during the siege. Not to mention the emotional toll on the survivors. These things take time, princess."

"I know you're right, I just—"

"Kat! Get out of the way!"

"Move, Teo! Move!"

We hear Anya and Cleo shout from behind us.

"What the he—"

But before I'm able to finish my sentence, Atlas pulls me to stand behind him, dagger already in his hand.

My jaw drops to the floor when I see Anya and Cleo wearing men's clothes, running away and laughing like banshees along with a happy-go-lucky Cristobal running after them.

Atlas puts two fingers in his mouth and whistles. "Nice rack, Cristo! Didn't think you had it in you," he teases as Cristobal passes by us in a woman's dress, corset and all.

Both of us burst out laughing at the sight of Cristobal running after his girls, looking absolutely giddy in his chase.

"You think they know they're in love yet?" I ask, laughing.

"Doubt it. Cristo isn't the sharpest tool in the shed when it comes to women."

"Oh, I wouldn't say that. He sure has found a way to be a permanent fixture in Anya's and Cleo's relationship. I was certain that no one could get in between them."

"Technically, that was Cristobal's first objective. To physically get in between them," he teases.

"You know what I mean. I think he has real feelings for the girls. I don't want to speculate since Anya hasn't outright said anything to me yet, but I believe both Anya and Cleo genuinely care for him too."

"Nothing surprises me anymore when it comes to those three." Atlas laughs as he puts away the dagger I used to carve my uncle's heart out.

My hand instinctively goes to my throat as if I can still taste his hot blood sliding down it.

I was completely deranged that night. The whole thing is a hazy blur, except for some parts that my memory refuses to forget. I started that night feeling numb, still trying to wrap my mind around never being able to tell Salome how much she saved me, how much I loved her. And then, when I saw my baby brother in that catatonic state, something snapped inside of me, and all I wanted was to see Adelid's heart pumping in my hand.

That night, I was what everyone accused me of being—my father's daughter. But while he no longer had my mother to tether him and keep him from falling off the cliff of madness, I had my family. I had Elijah. I had my sisters and their partners. But most importantly, I had my kings.

They were my saving grace.

"Hey, princess? Where did you go just now?" Atlas asks, concern tainting every word.

"Sorry. I'm here. I'm here. Let's just walk, okay?"

He nods and offers me his arm again. I snake my arm around it and lean into his side, my head resting on his forearm.

Sensing that I need some space to process my thoughts, we walk in silence all through the ground floor, watching everyone hard at work to restore Tarnow to its previous glory.

"Levi should be outside building the memorial. Do you want to go and have a look at how far he's coming along?" Atlas asks, still worried about my well-being.

I wish that I could say that I'm fine. That I'm completely over everything that's happened to my home. But that would be a lie. Like Elijah, I'm still trying to fight my own demons and trauma. It's going to take some time for us to finally feel like someone isn't going to steal the rug from under our feet.

"Princess?" he repeats, concerned.

"Oh, right, the memorial. Yes, I'd love to see it." I force a smile.

But instead of heading outside, Atlas picks up my chin and frowns.

"You know you don't have to do that with me. We don't hide ourselves from each other or keep secrets. My misery. My suffering. My blood. Remember? Do your worst, princess. I can take whatever you throw my way."

"I love you. You know that, don't you?" I smile and mean it.

"Of course you do. What's not to love?" he teases.

"Most men would kiss their woman when they confess their love for them," I retort back with a grin.

"Aye, but I am not most men. Not one of us is. We're kings in love with the most extraordinary winter queen the gods could have ever created. And fuck, do we know how incredibly blessed we are to have you."

"You almost sound like one of Brick's sonnets," I say, my soul in tatters after such a declaration of love.

"The red-haired behemoth has nothing on me, princess. You want sonnets? I'll give you all the sonnets you want. My tongue will make your pussy sing every note and hit a high-pitched key until you know the chorus by heart."

"And there he is. That's my Attie." I laugh, feeling much lighter than before.

And by the sparkle in his eyes, that was his exact intention.

Instead of asking for a kiss, I grab him and crash my lips onto his. Every limb in my body relaxes as he devours my mouth, giving me exactly what I need, when I need it.

People pass us by in the hall without so much as a word, already accustomed to this type of thing from me and my kings.

Atlas is the first one to pull away, his heady gaze telling me that it was either stopping our kiss or fucking me right here in front of the servants.

"Come on, princess. Let's get some air. Gods know I need it."

He grabs my hand and leads me down the hall and into the courtyard. Carpenters and builders are fast at work trying to get all the resources ready for Levi and his men to complete the memorial, which will circle our castle.

The thought of those brave souls forgotten through the years didn't sit right by me. So Levi came up with the idea for a memorial made out of glass, steel, sand, and iron, which are found in our four kingdoms, as a way to pay homage to all the lives lost.

As Atlas and I walk onto the field, we see him hard at work, trying to make his vision a reality just because he knows it will lighten my heart.

"Does he really have to work with no shirt on?" Atlas taunts beside me. "Show-off."

My eyes greedily drink up all of Levi's hard abs and tanned skin, licking my lips with how sexy he looks right now. He wipes the beads of sweat off his brow with his sculptured forearm and raises a large mallet with his hand, only to bash it onto a large boulder and split it wide open.

"You are drooling, princess," Atlas mocks, cleaning the drool at the corner of my mouth with his thumb. "What was that you said earlier? Something about only us men having sex on the brain?" he taunts, with a roll of the eye, slapping my ass for good measure. "Go ahead. I need a cold bath anyway." He laughs, turning around to head back inside.

Without a second thought, I break into a run toward my heart.

"Levi!" I yell.

The minute he sees me, he lets go of the mallet and opens his arms for me. I jump into his embrace, my legs wrapping around his waist as he flings me around.

"There's my heart. I've missed you," he says, peppering me with kisses.

"You just saw me at breakfast," I giggle and then moan when he begins to nibble at my neck.

"Aye. Still missed you, though."

My heart jackhammers in my chest as I cup his stubbled cheeks and kiss him. We're all teeth, tongue, and lips as we give into the kiss, indifferent to the onlookers. But just like Atlas, Levi breaks our kiss before he doesn't have the will to stop.

"Did you come to see how the memorial is going?" he asks, rubbing his nose against mine.

"I did. It looks perfect," I tell him, never wavering from his beautiful face.

"Aye. It is perfect," he says matter-of-factly, his eyes also never leaving mine.

"So perfect that I was thinking maybe it's time Tarnow had a small intimate celebration to commemorate it."

"Oh?" He arches his dark brows.

"Hmm," I hum, running my fingers over his braids. "Atlas said that the full reconstruction of Tarnow castle would take close to one or two years."

"At best," Levi agrees.

"Which means we will have to postpone our plans of living a season in each kingdom," I add.

"Aye. Right now, the north needs us more than the east, south, and west combined. So yes, our plans do have to be postponed. But just for a little while. Two years will pass in a blink of an eye. Trust me," he tries to console.

"I know. But that doesn't mean we have to postpone all our plans. There is one in particular that we can do now."

"Are you saying…" The words fail him, his green eyes shining with unshed tears.

"Yes, my heart. I'm saying that Tarnow is owed a wedding. And it's time we give it one."

"**I**'m telling you, it's a proven fact that everybody cries at weddings," Cristobal says to Cleo, who is currently focused on fastening some type of colorful ribbon around Teo's neck.

Looks more like a noose to me, but then again, what do I know about clothes?

I'm perfectly content in spending my days in my leathers and white shirts, as Levi is happy to wear nothing but his favorite color—black. The only decoration I need is my beautiful bride in my arms. Everything else is frivolous nonsense.

"That can't be true. If you said everyone cries at funerals, maybe I'd believe you. But weddings? What's there to cry about? It's not like it's a forced marriage. They willingly want to get married, so I see no reason to cry about it. Maybe in ten years or so when they are bored out of their minds. Or, gods forbid, they have babies. Then they have good reason to cry their fill. Not today, Cristo."

"You don't believe in love, so the rules don't apply to you," Cristobal rebukes with a teasing grin.

"Who says?" she balks, stopping with whatever she was doing to poor Teo's neck.

"I say. For one, if you love someone, you let them know," he pouts, crossing his arms over his chest.

"I do let them know, you big oaf! I love Cherry with all my heart and tell her as much every day."

"Anya is different. You'd have to be heartless not to fall in love with Anya. Even I can't help telling her every day how she's bewitched me, body and soul. You, on the other hand—"

"What exactly does that mean?" Cleo begins to shout.

"You know what it means?" Teo interrupts them. "It means that Levi, Atlas, and I picked some crappy groomsmen. That's what it means," he reprimands, taking the large ribbon out of Cleo's hand and strutting over to the mirror to put it on himself.

"Hey, what did I do?" Brick blurts out, taken aback for somehow getting caught in the middle of their fight.

"You were supposed to keep these two lovebirds apart long enough for us to get ready for our wedding. That's what you did, Brick. Or, in your case, didn't do," Levi explains while fixing his hair, making sure all his braids are nice and tidy on his head.

"I tried, Levi. Believe me, I tried. How was I to know that without Anya, these two are impossible to be around with?"

"Hey!" Cristobal and Cleo shout in unison.

"I'll have you know that Cristo is well-versed in many languages and cultures and a complete delight to talk to," Cleo defends passionately.

"And Cleo is one of the most remarkably beautiful and confident women I have ever had the pleasure to spend time with," Cristobal rebukes with a scowl. "You should be so lucky."

"Great. So now that that's settled, can you two please kiss and make up so we can at least have one moment's peace? This is our wedding, you know? It's kind of a big deal," I scold with a teasing grin.

"Come, my lady. It's clear our colorful and complex personalities are wasted here on this lot," Cristo says, offering his arm to Cleo. She hooks her arm to his and begins to strut toward the door.

"See you all inside. Don't be late. Only the bride gets to be late," she says, pointing a menacing finger at us.

"I probably should check up on Inessa too, just to see if she needs anything," Brick says before following them out and making his own great escape.

"Remind me again why we are friends with those people?" I ask with a smirk.

"Because we love the damn idiots." Levi chuckles while Teo is having a minor meltdown on the other side of the room. I go over to him as he fiddles away at the piece of fabric, trying and failing to tie it around his neck.

"You know what? I give up," Teo blurts out, throwing the ribbon to the floor.

"About time." I laugh, standing behind him and locking eyes with him in the mirror. "You don't need all those fancy accessories. You're pretty enough," I mock, slapping his smooth-shaven cheek to drive the point home. "Also, remind me to congratulate Ulrich on the bang-up job he did to your nose. You can't even tell it was broken before."

"Aye. He really knows his stuff." Teo smiles widely as he vainly looks at himself in the mirror to admire the job Ulrich did on his nose. "Now I can officially say I'm the beauty in this trio."

I can't help but laugh at the remark.

"Is that right? Then what am I? What is Levi? Chopped liver?"

"No," Teo retorts with a shrug, never straying his gaze from his reflection in the mirror. "You're the brains, and Levi is the brawn."

"Come again?" Levi stops what he's doing to look at Teo. "I'm the brawn? Why not the brains?"

"Were you the one who got an army of one hundred thousand men to sail to your kingdom?" Teo arches a brow while Levi frowns. "I didn't think so. Atlas is definitely the brains in this trio."

"You know what? You're both wrong. Our woman is the one with all the beauty, the brains, and the brawn. She's the woman whose beauty lights up any room she walks in and outshines us all. It was Kat who was able to decipher her fucking uncle's plan to take Tarnow, and it was her inner strength that served as inspiration for those one hundred thousand souls to bravely fight for her and pledge their allegiance. But most importantly, she's the reason why we found each other again. We wouldn't be shit without her," I announce with utter conviction, my brothers instantly nodding in agreement.

"And we're about to marry her? Can you believe it? I thought for sure this day would never come," Teo chimes, equally emotional.

"It almost didn't. The gods sure made it hard for us, but not even they could keep us apart," Levi adds, his gravel voice dropping an octave.

"Like I always say, fuck the gods. We make our own fate."

We stare at each other with such love and brotherly affection that tears begin to well up in our eyes.

"No!" I point to each one of them. "We will not cry and prove Cristobal right, or we'll never hear the end of it."

We're still trying to pull ourselves together when someone knocks on the door.

"Now what?" I grunt, walking over to the door to see who it is.

But to my utter shock, it's the last person I expected to see.

"Halfdan?"

"Atlas." He smiles, the tired and angry wrinkles I'd been accustomed to seeing on his face no longer there.

"You came," I whisper, still shocked to see him here.

"Of course, I came. I wouldn't miss your wedding." He smiles sincerely.

I'm taken aback, not only by his presence but also by how different he looks. Almost like the weight of the past seven years was lifted off his shoulders.

When he starts eyeing me curiously, I realize that I'm just standing under the threshold of a door, gawking at him.

"Thank… you… Halfdan," I begin to stammer, having to clear my throat to gain some composure back. "I know it will mean the world to Katrina that you're here. She'll be so happy to see you."

And then the oddest thing happens.

He places his hand on my shoulder and gives it a comforting squeeze.

"You're my kin, lion. There is no place I would rather be than right here with you. Rhea would be so proud to see the extraordinary man that you've become. I most certainly am."

Emotion burns a hole in my throat, and I am unable to push one word out of my mouth. And when he pulls me into a hug, the smell of the sea still in his hair, it almost feels like my parents are with me at this moment, celebrating my joys and all my accomplishments.

After a long embrace, Halfdan steps back with his smile intact on his face.

"Also, your friend Inessa asked me to warn you that the queen is ready to come out. Best you and your friends hurry to the altar. Although, it's a mighty good sign when the bride is as eager as her grooms to get married." He then pats me on the back and goes his merry way.

I walk back into our shared room and wipe my eyes before my brothers see me in a chaotic mess.

"Our queen is ready for us. Let's move."

Without needing any more words of encouragement, Teo and Levi rush to the door and walk beside me as we make our way to the great hall, where everyone is impatiently waiting for us. We hurriedly walk down the aisle toward the altar where the minister officiating our wedding awaits. Brick, Cleo, and Cristobal are now the epitome of well-behaved groomsmen, all standing tall behind us as we take our respective places—Levi first to the right side of the minister, then Teo in the middle, and at the very end, me.

Someone must have been on the lookout for our arrival because the minute we are in our places, the wedding march begins. Without further ado, Anya steps into the great hall and proceeds to walk down the aisle, wearing an ice-blue gown with sparkling diamonds in her hair. She is all smiles as she takes her place on Katrina's side of the altar. At the same time, Inessa makes her grand appearance.

My heart squeezes in my chest to see how my princess's handmaidens have been ordered not to waste any time walking down the aisle, a telltale sign that my princess is just as anxious to solidify our bond as we are.

After Inessa has found her place behind Anya, it's little Zara's turn to shine as the flower girl. Teo's sister throws petals in the air and skips down the aisle as if she, too, were well instructed not to procrastinate.

"This is it," Levi whispers hoarsely beside us, his emotions already getting the better of him.

"It's finally happening," Teo adds, just as overcome, lacing his hand in mine and Levi's.

But I have no words for my brothers since every letter in the alphabet evaporates from my memory the minute Katrina of Bratsk steps foot into the great hall.

Gods be good.

Kat looks like she was sent by the heavens themselves.

Wearing a white sleeveless gown with a simple flowered sash around her waist of green hydrangeas, golden sunflowers, orange marigolds, and her beloved blue roses, paired with familiar heart-shaped necklace resting just above the swell of her breasts, Kat walks toward us while holding onto her brother's hand since he was the only one who merited the honor of giving her away.

My heart is at my throat as I watch her approach us with such unconditional love in her eyes that it takes everything for me not to start weeping.

As she comes to the last step, she goes to her haunches and tells Elijah how much she loves him and how grateful she is for him to be the one giving her away.

But just as Kat starts to stand up straight, Elijah pulls at her hand and whispers something in her ear. Tears stream down her cheeks as she hugs him to her and then lets him sit beside Zara on the first row of chairs.

"What did he say?" Anya whispers to the love of my life.

Kat looks at all the people she loves standing at the altar, her happy tears free falling now.

"He said that he loved me, and that I looked like an angel."

Curse the gods.

Cristobal was right.

Everyone does cry at weddings because there isn't one pair of dry eyes on this altar.

Not me.

Not Teo.

Not Levi.

And especially not our friends.

As my princess walks over to us with happy tears in her eyes, asking us to take her hand in holy matrimony, Cleo's skeptical words about marriage from earlier come back to the forefront of my mind.

I will never get tired of my princess, not in ten years, not in a million.

And if the gods grace us with children, then I will cherish and love each and every one of them.

But if babies aren't in the cards for us, then so be it.

Because we already have the most precious gift of all.

We have each other.

And that's all we ever wanted and all we could ever hope for.

My misery. My suffering. My blood.

We've survived the worst our past threw at us.

Now it's time we enjoy the best that our glorious future has to offer.

Together.

Always.

The End

THANK YOU SO MUCH FOR READING
THE WINTER KISSED KINGS

If you enjoyed this book, please consider leaving an honest, spoiler-free review.

It may only take you a minute to write, but reviews are how books get noticed by other readers.

By writing a small review, you are opening the door for my love stories to be enjoyed by so many others.

I'd also love it if you would check out my website at https://www.ivyfoxauthor.com/ and I invite you to join my Facebook Reader's Group at https://www.facebook.com/groups/188438678547691/

Much love,

Ivy

xoxo

Ivy Fox Novels

Reverse Harem / Why Choose Romance

The Winter Queen Duet
A Royal Enemies-to-Lovers Romance (Completed Series)

The Privileged of Pembroke High
A High School Bully Romance (Completed Series)

Rotten Love Duet
A Mafia Romance (Completed Series)

Bad Influence Series
A Forced Proximity Romance (Interconnected Standalone Series)

Contemporary Romance / New Adult

The Society
Secret Society Romance (Completed Series)

The King - After Hours Series
Office Romance

Cowrites And Collaborations

Binding Rose - Mafia Wars Series
Mafia Reverse Harem Romance (Completed Series)

Co-Write with C.R. Jane
Breathe Me Duet
Second Chance Romance (Completed Series)

The Love & Hate Duet
Stepbrother Bully Romance

Co-Write with K.A. Knight
Deadly Love
Stalker Dark Romance (Completed Series)

ABOUT THE AUTHOR

Ivy Fox is a USA Today bestselling author of angst-filled, contemporary romances, some of them with an unconventional #whychoose twist.

Ivy lives a blessed life, surrounded by her two most important men—her husband and son, but she also doesn't mind living with the fictional characters in her head that can't seem to shut up until she writes their story.

Books and romance are her passion.

A strong believer in happy endings and that love will always prevail in the end, both in life and in fiction.

Printed in Great Britain
by Amazon

39416139R00274